Falling From the Sky

PETE & NICKY —

Falling From the Sky

An Anthology

Edited by Craig Quackenbush

Cover art by Chris Roberts

Another Sky Press
Portland, Oregon

BECAUSE I'M SURE YOU HAVE
NOTHING ELSE TO READ... GRIN!

I ENJOYED YOUR STORIES — HOPE
YOU ENJOY MINE ... PGS 65 & 269.

Printed in the United States of America
ISBN 0-9776051-2-4
First Edition, April 2007

Contact information for authors can be found at
http://www.anothersky.org/in-print/falling-from-the-sky-anthology/

Contact Craig Quackenbush at craig@anothersky.org

Cover artwork copyright 2007 Chris Roberts
Contact Chris Roberts at deadclownart.com

Design and layout by Kristopher Young
Contact Kristopher at kristopher@anothersky.org

Another Sky Press logo by Steven Spikoski
Contact Steven at stevenspikoski.com

Another Sky Press logo variant (back cover) by Ryan Scott
Contact Ryan at ryanscottdesigns.com

GF Halda Normal font by Lorenz Goldnagl
Used with Permission
Contact Lorenz at http://www.goldnagl.at

Falling From the Sky brought to you by
Another Sky Press
P.O. Box 14241
Portland, Oregon 97293
anothersky.org

Dear Reader,

Another Sky Press is a non-traditional publishing company located in Portland, Oregon. We operate under a progressive publishing and distribution paradigm that aims to directly benefit both audience and author.

The entire text of this novel is available for free online with a contribution requested but not required. We believe you, the reader, should be able to decide the value of art.

You may also purchase a trade paperback of this novel directly from our website at a sliding scale price that you set: the fixed third-party printing and shipping costs plus an optional contribution. This allows you to decide how much the authors and publishing team earn by contributing at a level that is comfortable to you both ethically and financially. Removing middlemen such as bookstores and distributors (which can account for over half the cover price) allows us to ensure that significantly more money actually goes to the authors per book sale.

If you came across your copy of this book via a library, used book store or friend please consider contributing directly to the authors at our website. This promotes passing along a book when you're finished with it (thus saving trees) while still allowing each reader to compensate the author if they choose.

100% of the profits from this book are distributed as royalties to the authors and individuals directly involved in making it happen.

Embrace the future. Support that which you love.

Thank you,
Another Sky Press
www.anothersky.org

psst! pass it on.

Falling Upwards

It was the last story.

I was deep into one long weekend in March—on the couch with music in the background and blanket draped over my shoulders. I stretched. Leaned back. The editing for *Falling From the Sky* was done. It didn't—it doesn't—seem real. Over the course of several months, a great deal of time and effort went into this anthology. These stories, and this anthology, have become a part of me.

I first discovered Another Sky Press back in the Spring of 2006. The concepts behind the press instantly struck a chord—it was a new kind of publishing paradigm and I wanted in. I offered my services as an editor and suggested a short story anthology. It would give us the opportunity to showcase an ensemble of writers, each with their own voice. In a burst of inspiration, the title came to me—*Falling From the Sky*. It summed up everything I wanted this anthology to be—a collection of prose from beyond the mainstream, tumbling into the Press and onto the printed page.

The stories filtered in from across the globe, the hearts and minds of dozens of people combining into something wonderfully diverse and imaginative, worlds within worlds. In these pages you will find an eclectic assortment of short stories. You will find from-the-street realism and gritty surrealism. There are tales of heartbreak and loss, levity and whimsy, and the search for higher meaning.

These authors and their stories fell directly into our lives here at Another Sky. And your occasionally humble editor couldn't be more grateful.

—Craig Quackenbush, Editor

Contents

Reflected

John Hines Jr.

FROM WHAT I CAN SEE of the level meter, I am being recorded. That's the best I can hope for at this point, so I won't worry about it. It's not like I'm going to say anything profound which needs to be entered into the historical record for the twenty-first century. I probably won't even say anything worth repeating.

Alas.

I figure I've got about twenty minutes before things get so bad I won't be able to continue. Not to worry, I've already taken care of the important things. Now I'm just waiting.

To my family and friends, I love you. I know it's probably too little, too late, but it is what it is. I could spend the next few minutes talking about the past and how much fun I had with each of you, but I'm not going to. I'd rather spend the time trying to explain how I got to this point and why I did what I did. Maybe something good can come out of this mess.

I wasn't in the dorm when Michael Scoggins first concocted morphete. I wasn't even in the state. By the time I got back from the Thanksgiving holiday, word of the new drug had spread to the entire campus: staff, faculty, and all. That was, what, two months ago? Yeah, that's right. Seems longer. Anyway, I wasn't here that night. But my roommate had scored. Not a stash of the stuff, but the recipe itself. It was easy to make and Todd was on his second batch when I showed up.

I didn't know what he was doing. There were boxes of medicines, vitamins, cleaning products, and pool chemicals spread all around the room. The table was clear, except for two glass bowls, and a box of coffee filters. Todd was stirring some disgusting-looking stuff in one of the bowls. I remember the way he smiled at me when I walked into the room. Perfectly content. Just a hint of amusement. All of my frustration with the mess melted in his smile.

"What is it?" I asked. "What's going on?"

"Expansion of the mind," Todd said. "Better living through chemistry."

Todd finished the batch and poured it through the coffee filters. He began hanging the filters up to dry. I helped him with this, seizing the opportunity to probe for more information about the nature of his experiment. He said he couldn't explain it, but that I had to try it.

Todd held a small bowl of purple powder out to me. "Take just a pinch and sprinkle it on your tongue. Just a touch."

Now, I'd tried a couple of mind-altering substances before this. Ecstasy, pot, and everybody's friend, Mr. Beer. So, I wasn't exactly reluctant, but something in that smile made me think of an old *Twilight Zone* episode. I should have known. I put my fingers into the powder and pinched a little. The grains were large, like sand or sugar. Crystalline. I tilted my head back and let it fall onto my tongue.

Nothing happened. I looked at Todd. "What?" I asked.

"You'll see." He laughed as if this was the funniest joke in the world. Looking back, I guess it was pretty funny.

I still didn't feel anything. It tasted kind of like I would expect powdered pickles to taste. Not bad, but not something I'd eat just for the flavor. I waited, but still nothing happened. "How long do I have to wait?"

"Any minute now," Todd said. That same knowing smile was on his face.

I got busy cleaning up the room. I cleared a pile of empty boxes and was reaching for a box of children's cough drops when it happened. I was looking at the familiar package and then I was seeing something else entirely.

"Now?"

I nodded. I looked at the box. I could see it. All of it. Every single detail. The crisp detail of the logo, the depressions in the cardboard where the expiration date had been stamped. The bulge in the end of the box where the flap had been glued shut. I could see beyond that, too. There were hills and valleys in the paper surface of the box, tiny imperfections in the plane which weren't normally visible. A vast landscape which had never been fully explored.

I forced my eyes to refocus on the box as a whole. It appeared different than it had before. Now the pristine white surface was cut and sliced by lines and arcs of color. I don't know how long it

2

took me to realize what I was seeing. The patterns were reflections of the things in the room: the table's surface, the bottles and jars on the counter, even my own face, all reflected mish-mash on the rough and uneven surface of this simple white box.

I must have stared at the box for a long time. "Ray?" Todd whispered. "You okay?"

"Yeah," I said. I think I said. I may have screamed it. My ears hurt from the sound. It was as if my voice had been amplified through the world's loudest PA. I flinched and closed my eyes. I heard a loud, wet squishing sound. It was disgusting. I opened my eyes to see what Todd had done. I heard it again.

The sound was the blinking of my eyes.

"Don't worry," Todd whispered. "This stage passes quickly."

Every stimulus for all of my senses was suddenly raised to an intensity I'd never considered. Sounds I'd never heard before were suddenly clear: a buzzing from the light bulbs, the hum of the cell phone in my pocket, the rumble of a thousand footsteps in the hallways, all layered together and served to my unprepared ears.

And the sights! I could see details that should have been visible only under a strong magnifying glass. I could feel little pinpricks from the imperfections in the fabric of my clothes. I could feel individual bands of elastic in the waistband of my underwear. And the smells. Oh god, the smells were awful. My cologne was overpowering, and beneath that, I could smell my own body, and beneath that, I could smell the inside of my own nose.

I fell onto the couch and gripped my head. I shut my eyes, covered my ears and tried not to breathe. The sensory overload was too much. I moved as little as possible. But nothing I did could assuage my taste buds.

I could taste bits of the cheese pizza I'd had for dinner. I could taste the fries I'd had with lunch. Behind that, I could taste the toothpaste from that morning and behind that there was the sulfur from the bacteria growing in my mouth. I became nauseated.

And just as it had come, the sensation was gone. Suddenly I was back to normal. Normal? Not quite. But close. "What happened? What the hell?"

"Sensory upgrade," Todd said. "That's what people are calling it. You feel normal, right?"

I breathed in through my nose and looked around. I nodded. "Yeah, I seem to be."

"You're not, though. Look out the window. What do you see?"

"Nothing." It was true. There was nothing to see. It was dark out, and we live at the end of the street.

"Keep looking. Try looking at the edges of the glass."

I did. There was nothing there. Then there was. Little bands of color. It was beautiful. Trapped at the edge of the glass, near the bottom and the right-hand edge, was a razor-thin band of color. All the colors. Not a rainbow, not separate color sections. Just color, leaking out of the glass, coming through all at once.

"What is it?" I asked.

"Reflected light from down the street. It's faint, but you can see it, right? It's coming from the porch lights and headlights from blocks away. It's reflecting from windows, car doors, broken bottles, all kinds of stuff." He smiled that smile again.

"How do you feel?"

"Scared," I said. "How long does this last?"

"A few hours. What do you feel besides scared?"

I thought about it. "I feel good. Like my breathing is a little deeper. I feel powerful." It was a good feeling. "I feel invincible."

"Just don't forget that you're not," Todd said.

"How much have you taken?"

"Not much. I gave away most of my first batch. This is my second. When the crystals dry, I'll take some more."

"This is great." The longer I waited, the better I felt. I held my hand up and concentrated on it. I could see the skin stretching with each beat of my heart. I could hear the tendons and ligaments extend as I made a fist. "I feel connected to everything."

"That, my friend, is the best description of the feeling I've heard yet," Todd said. "We should write it down."

"I want some more."

That was how my first experience with morphete went. After that, I kept taking the stuff. It got better every time and each time it ended, I was left with slightly keener senses. I couldn't stop. I was addicted to the colors, the sounds, the smells.

Even things which normally smelled bad took on a new life. The smell from a garbage can isn't a single smell. It is a symphony of odors, reflecting the transient contents, odors as discarded snapshots of our lives.

And ice cubes. Ice cubes have a smell. Not just the minerals in the water, but ice itself has a distinct smell. It's different than water. Water smells ancient, while ice smells organized. Not words normally used for odors, true, but they are the only ones that fit.

After a week, I realized I had to take increasingly frequent doses of morphete to put me in the intense zone. But, I also noticed that even after a long period without it, I remained able to sense things well beyond my normal senses. And the feeling! I felt great. The feeling of invincibility faded, but the feeling of connectedness stayed strong. It is a powerful feeling.

Todd has stopped taking morphete but he still hears and sees and smells things as if he were taking it daily. He still has that connected feeling. He retains the benefits of the stuff, but doesn't have to take it. I hate him.

I'm running out of time here, but I still have more to tell. I guess I'll skip ahead to the first sign of trouble. It was my own fault. I took a large dose. I wasn't the first person to do so. Carry Fulbright has that honor. He took a double dose. He said it was the best ride of his life, but that he didn't want to do it again because he saw things he couldn't comprehend. We sat around and listened to his story, nodding and telling him we understood. But when he left, we made fun of him and called him a pussy. And that's when I took the large dose.

I meant to take a double dose, to match what Carry had done. I grabbed the first pinch and dropped it on my tongue. I put the second one in as well. I put in a third. With each hit, the light caught the purple of the crystals, sending sprays of violet light deep into my head. I kept seeing the crystals falling, tumbling, shining, reflecting and refracting. I would have watched them forever, but Todd knocked my hand away at some point. How many doses? I don't know. Todd says at least six. To me, it seemed an endless cascade of crystals falling onto my waiting tongue. And I swallowed them greedily. I remember that much.

After the big dose, things became difficult to understand. Sounds didn't make sense anymore. Everything came through as little pops and clicks, peaks and troughs, as if I was hearing the individual compression waves that made up the sound. I couldn't associate one wave with the next, so aural processing was out of the question.

The only thing I could taste was my own saliva. The only smell getting to my nose was the blood in the capillaries inside my nasal passages. I smelled the blood through my own tissue.

My sense of touch was equally off. I could feel the points where my nerve endings erupted from my skin and the air that rubbed against them. That sensation was overpowering all others.

Sight was the only thing left to me. I could see everything. The bands of color at the edge of the windows? That was nothing. I could see images of the individual reflected objects coming around the edge of the glass. I could see around corners. The side-images were confusing, like watching a scrambled cable television channel. I'd catch bits of something I could recognize, but nothing whole.

Looking directly at an object was mentally painful. Each surface was no longer solid, but only a strung-together arrangement of imperfections and accidents. Nothing was true, nothing straight, nothing flat. I could see the whole of a car, but at the same time, I could see mountains and valleys in the paint, huge impurities in the glass of the window, and gaping holes in the tiny edges of the trim. Everything seemed to be held together by a promise. I kept expecting things to fall apart.

I stayed awake for three days. Closing my eyes didn't shut off the flow of information to my mind. I could see the veins in my eyelids and watched the individual blood cells float across my field of vision, bumping into each other gracefully in the eddies, running headlong in the currents in the tight vessels. And, behind the blood, I could see the shapes and outlines of the room around me. Sleep was unattainable.

If it had lasted much longer, I think I might have cracked. I was probably close to it when it ended. Once it started to let off, it went pretty quickly. I realized I could hear things again and that I could feel my clothes and the towels I had wrapped around my head. After three days of living in a darkened closet, I unwrapped my eyes. Everything seemed normal. And by normal, I mean pre-morphete normal. Flat. Dead. Three-dimensional. Colorless. Lifeless.

It was like I'd burned out my senses. After a couple of days, I convinced Todd to let me have a little morphete. I was getting depressed by the ordinariness of my sight and hearing. I took it, but it didn't do anything. No effect whatsoever. I took a second dose, which also did nothing. I tried to take a third, but Todd wouldn't let me. He didn't want me drooling in the closet for another three days. I don't blame him for that.

The real problems began a few weeks later. I noticed that I had to turn the TV up a past a normal level to hear it clearly. Light bulbs seemed dimmer. Food was bland; I ate whole jalapeño peppers, but tasted nothing. I couldn't masturbate because I could barely feel the presence of my hand on my cock. Within a couple of days, I couldn't hear much at all. I could only see in brightly lit rooms.

Taste, smell, and touch completely abandoned me. I panicked. I broke into Todd's room and took all of his morphete. I regained a little vision for a single day, but that was all. I was terrified.

I am terrified.

The worst part isn't the loss of any particular sense, but rather the loss of all of them at once. That, and the fact that I lost the feeling of connectedness and power. I do not feel connected to anything anymore. I feel isolated, cut off. Powerless. I can't face a life like that. Not after having seen what it could be. Could have been, if I hadn't gotten greedy and tried to take it all. The wax in my wings has melted and I have fallen to the earth. Overly dramatic? Probably. Care? No.

I took the pills. They've taken longer to work than I imagined, but I made sure it was enough to do the job. I can feel them working now. Slowing things down. I'm sure you've noticed my slowing, slurred speech. Breathing is a little more difficult. That's a good sign. I'm lying down now. Sitting up was too much work. I'm feeling better about things. I can't form thoughts much now. I'm going to take a nap soon.

Just rest my eyes.

I'm Dreaming Of A White Christmas

Tony O'Neill

I was living in a shack in Ghost Town, Venice, CA at the time. How I got there is a long story. I often wondered about it myself. I'd wake from an uneasy sleep and look around the place; the collapsing little fold out bed, the discarded needles, the piles of my papers covering every available surface and I'd think, "What the fuck happened?"

I was living with Susan, poor crazy Susan. She was ten years older than me, clinging to her sanity with slipping fingers. Every day she dosed herself with Xanax, heroin, cocaine, a pile of anti-anxiety tablets, panic-attack tablets, anti-depressants and sucked down a pack of Marlboro lights, but it didn't help: she just got worse and worse and worse. She was stinking up the place with the stench of the living dead and I started to look upon her with a kind of awful wonderment... usually when people change it is in tiny, unnoticeable steps. It's after you get some time away from them and then see them again that you realize just how brutally life has treated them. With Susan I felt that kind of shock recognition every morning when I looked at that death mask face as she nervously probed for a vein, a shaking cigarette dangling from her lips. This woman had once been the CFO of a profitable company. Now she was no use to anyone, except the drunken Johns who didn't care what she looked like, and maybe the worms.

We had gotten married in a moment of drug-fueled madness. An old Dominican lady did the ceremony out of her house in East L.A. She dragged one of her daughters downstairs to act as a witness. After my divorce from Nadine I had a whole host of I.N.S. troubles, and although I missed London, returning there was out of the question. It wasn't that I wanted to be in Los Angeles anymore—just that my habit was such that I could not travel too far away from my sources of heroin without being completely incapacitated by dope sickness.

The marriage was hastily arranged. Up until that point, Susan was just some crazy girl I was getting high with. She still had a job then, and was lucid enough to ensure that the flow of money and drugs remained uninterrupted. So we decided to get married to keep me in the country. The marriage was as sad a spectacle as one could imagine. We stopped at the needle exchange in East Hollywood first to pick up a box of two hundred insulin needles for the week. Susan was wearing a white dress, and I was in a crumpled red sharkskin suit.

"Wow," Todd, the dreadlocked ex-junkie who worked there on Tuesdays grimaced, "you two getting married or something?"

"Yup" we replied, dropping off the shopping bag full of used needles and picking up the box of fresh ones. "We're on our way there now."

As bizarre as this was it didn't merit any kind of response. Needle exchanges are like porno bookstores or public bathrooms. Nobody wants to talk or even make eye contact if they can possibly avoid it.

The whole getting married so I could stay in the country business didn't work out. We were too high, and—as our habits increased and Susan's ability to hold down a job decreased—too broke to file any of the necessary paperwork. Instead, I ended up married to this crazy junkie for no good reason, and somehow over time I started feeling a terrible sense of responsibility towards her.

The first reason I stayed was pity. She'd had a horrible time of it before I came along. Her grandfather had plied her with booze and raped her when she was a teenager. The way Susan related the story, when she returned home sobbing and hysterical, Mommy didn't seemed too bothered about the whole thing.

"Well, I did warn you about this" she told her. "You know he's into that kind of shit. I told you what he did to me when I was your age."

"What?" Susan sobbed. "Told me WHAT? YOU DIDN'T TELL ME ANYTHING!"

"Oh," her mother replied with a faraway look in her eyes, "maybe it was your sister I talked to. Anyway... you'll get over it. I did."

After that trauma there was a host of others. Rapes. Beatings. It all sounded too outrageous, too Gothic, to be made up. Who makes that kind of shit up? At the time, I was shocked and began to feel very protective towards her. Only later did I realize that, among female junkies, Susan was no exception. All of the females I have come into contact with on the scene had similar stories.

Rape. Child abuse. Incest. Female addicts predominantly are a certain type, and that type—unfortunately—is the used and the abused.

Also, my perception of myself started to change. I faced it every morning in the filthy mirror: I was an intravenous heroin user, out of necessity a thief and a scam artist. My looks were shot to hell, my arms were open sores, and my teeth were falling out of my head. I was turning into some horrible mirror image of Susan. I felt as if I had taken so many steps into a maze that I could no longer retrace them and find my way back to the start. I had no option but to keep going and pray that I chanced upon a chink of sunlight. I was lost, lost, lost and could only find sustenance in drugs and our encroaching despair.

It was Christmas Eve. We had twenty dollars left. We had started up on crack early that evening, and now the money was gone, and we were in trouble. Twenty dollars worth of crack is nothing once you've taken your first hit. It won't even sustain you. It will maybe avert the crash for ten minutes. Try and split a twenty dollar rock in two and you may as well light the bill itself and try to get high off the fumes. It was 11 p.m. Susan was on my last fucking nerve, begging and wheedling and pushing me to go out and score more crack.

"I'm not going out there," I told her. "That's it. At least we have twenty bucks for tomorrow. The place is crawling with pigs. Everyone is drunk and high and crazy. Anyway, it's Christmas Eve for chrissakes. All of the dealers are gonna be back home. The only people out there are gonna be scam artists looking to rip off stupid white kids out trying to score."

She was cleaning out the pipe, trying to find a grain of residue that she had missed on the previous five rounds of cleaning the pipe. The pipe was clean as it could be. It was gleaming. I knew it was futile. She knew it was futile. But she persisted, heating up the stem and, using a piece of wire to drag the Brillo through the glass repeatedly, tried to pick up some melted cocaine.

"Then I'll go."

"You're not going."

"I'm gonna go. I'm a girl. They'll cut me a break."

"They'll cut your fucking throat after they're done gang-banging you. Now don't be so fucking stupid. We're gonna need smack tomorrow. We ain't spending our last twenty bucks on a rock. It's over. Take some pills and go to sleep."

She continued to clean the pipe, held it up to her lips for a futile attempt at smoking the residue, cursed, got back to work.

"You are a motherfucker," she told me matter-of-factly.

"And you're a fucking crack head. You're out of your fucking mind. Now give it up."

She carried on scraping the pipe and tried to take another hit. Of course there was nothing. She started to cry, big heaving sobs like hot needles inserted into my nerve endings. Then she picked up one of my books, one of the big ones. Celine maybe, or a dictionary or a medical book. I don't remember. She held it in both of her hands, gripping it tightly until her knuckles turned white, before she started to smash herself in the face with it, her sobs becoming more and more frenzied and grating. After the fourth or fifth thump I yelled at her to knock it off. I grabbed my keys.

"I'm going, you stupid cunt," I hissed. "I won't be long."

The streets of Ghost Town were alive with junkies, dealers, and all kinds of human flotsam. Most of them were rip-off artists. On more than one occasion I had been sold soap or some other unpleasant tasting shit instead of the crack I wanted. I retraced the steps I had taken earlier, hoping to find the last guy I had bought off of. I turned the corner and tried to locate the kid's spot. I coughed to draw attention to myself. The bastard popped up, right on cue: "Psst!"

We did the deal and I split back for our place. Sirens provided constant background noise, as well as the throbbing of helicopters circling overhead. It was like living in some grotesque, drugged-out *Blade Runner* hell. I was thinking this as I stepped off the curb and into the path of a LAPD patrol car, lights blazing, sirens roaring, and speeding towards me.

I had no time to react. I was momentarily bathed in light. My feet left the ground and my whole being shook... I flipped back weightless and graceful, a moment that seemed to stretch to infinity.

Crunch!

I couldn't even process the information until after I had bounced off the car's hood and back onto the tarmac with a yell of surprise. I looked up and saw two cops looking down on me, like angels of doom.

"You okay?" one of the cops asked.

"Yeah." I said, getting to my feet gingerly.

The other cop radioed in to the station as I felt warm blood trickling down my left leg.

"You just stepped out," the cop nearest me—a virtual man mountain with a buzz-cut—explained. "We couldn't stop. We were in pursuit. Didn't you hear the sirens?"

Well, of course I heard the sirens, but I'd heard them so often, all night, that I had begun to block them out like all the other city noise. I was concentrating more on getting me—and the crack—back indoors.

Oh, Jesus. The crack! My stomach began to churn and fear welled up inside of me. I talked fast.

"You know, I wasn't concentrating on what I was doing. Preoccupied. Completely my fault, I'm really sorry."

"What are you doing out here? This isn't a good neighborhood."

"I live right down there. I'm on my way home."

"Well, we're gonna radio for an ambulance to have you checked out—"

"No need!" I insisted. "I'm fine. Listen, my wife is at home— she's gonna freak out if I'm not back in twenty minutes... You know how it is in this neighborhood. I'd rather just go home and forget about it."

The cops eyed me for a while. It was quite obvious to them that I was half out of my mind on drugs. It was also obvious that I could create a bunch of paperwork for them if I went to the hospital because they hit me while I crossed the road. They didn't want the paperwork and I didn't want to have my pockets turned out.

"Well," said the cop with the buzz-cut, "if you're sure you're all right... "

"Positive," I beamed. "Never better! Happy Christmas officers!"

"Yeah, you too," they growled, getting back into their car.

I limped back into the guesthouse. I sat down and rolled up my pant leg, exposing a large ugly gash running up my shin.

"Jesus!" Susan came over to look. "What happened?"

"I got knocked over by a cop car. They let me go. I told you it's a fucking mess out there tonight. I should have never gone. Fuck!"

I went to the bathroom and peeled off my bloody jeans, tried to wash the dirt out of the wound as best I could. Susan popped her head in the door after a few minutes.

"You could have been busted," she said, quietly.

"I know. Or killed. Imagine that. Killed on Christmas Eve by a speeding cop car. Jesus!"

Susan smiled a little. "Pretty funny, huh?"

I just glowered at her.

"No." I told her eventually. "Not really."

"Did you get the rock?"

I sighed and nodded towards the bloody jeans. She retrieved it and scuttled out of the room.

I got cleaned up and found her playing with the pipe, exhaling white smoke. I limped over. "Where's mine?" She handed me the pipe. I held the lighter up and took a long drag. Nothing. Not even a glimmer of something.

"Where's the rest?" I asked her. "You killed this one."

"That's it."

"That's it?"

"Yeah… it was a small rock. That's it."

"Well, thanks. That's fucking great. Thank you so fucking much."

"Don't yell at me!" she said, before adding quietly, "It is Christmas, you know."

I looked at the clock. Ten after midnight. Well, she was right about something. It was Christmas. I looked out the window but could see nothing but vast, endless black. Somewhere out there was the moon and the stars and the Pacific Ocean, but from where I was looking I could have been a thousand feet underground. I could hear her, somewhere behind me, starting to nervously clean out the pipe again. It would be less that an hour before she started up again, maybe two before she started bashing herself in the face with my books and sobbing. But for now, for a moment, there was peace on earth.

Night Time Is the Right Time

Mallory Small

IT DIDN'T SEEM ANY DIFFERENT THAN USUAL.

Before I get started, let me hip you to something. I worked in a ratty residential hotel in San Francisco's "infamous" Tenderloin district, so "the usual" more often than not added up to all kinds of shit, especially as I worked more or less by myself from midnight to eight in the morning.

This particular night, cool in early fall, was no different. By ten after twelve, I'd already called an ambulance because someone I could name, but won't, snorted too much drain cleaner. She screamed and writhed in anguish as they pulled her out of the elevator on the gurney. Her "boyfriend" babbled incoherently, perhaps offering tips on medicine interaction, perhaps just babbling on and on about moon landing conspiracy theories, or whatever it is tweakers like to babble about.

Next, around one-thirty, the shift changed at the massage parlor on the corner. Which one? Does it matter? I mean, honestly, one massage parlor is just like the next. I guess. This particular one was "Winds of Paradise" on Jones Street. They had some sort of deal with my boss and some of the ladies stayed with us. My boss had all sorts of weird deals with a menagerie of unsavory people. Two of the ladies, May and Lin, were cousins. That was according to Lin, whom I had engaged in furtive conversation as she waited for a taxi during a spring rainstorm. May was kind of aloof—the un-hip would call it stuck up or bitchy. The deal was, her Engrish was terrible and she felt self-conscious about it.

One day as she was paying her operator day-assisted (plus forty-five percent) phone bill, I told her it was all right. She didn't have to say anything. She actually smiled. With the way it crept forth and flared into radiance I could tell she didn't smile that often. I felt a special kinship with these two. I felt we were all exploited in some way or another and that, more specifically, that's how it went in the 'Loin.

From time to time I still remember that uncertain smile. Anyway, the swing shift that included May and Lin was coming off and the night shift, a generally haggard looking bunch, was coming on. May waved, exhausted. She dragged her feet as she mounted the stairs up to the second floor

Lin had what looked like a black eye. Somebody pasted her one and she'd applied makeup that wasn't quite the proper shade to cover it up, which only made it more obvious. That kind of riled me. I had her wait while I fetched two instant ice packs from the First Aid locker. I demonstrated how to get them from what looked like a plastic bag with sandy shit rattling around inside to actual cold relief by squeezing the top and letting the chemicals in the two ingredients commingle. She touched the ice pack, now cold, and withdrew her hand, startled.

"Better living through chemistry."

Lin missed it.

Sometimes I talked too fast or mumbled, and it took a minute, so I made hand motions like I was slapping my face for forgetting something. She took the ice pack and, wincing, put it over her eye. I would have given anything to show my disapproval to whoever had given her that black eye. Then again, it was going to get heavy enough, and soon.

Half an hour later or so Sunshine and Moonbeam, as Chuck Argast, one of my colleagues, and I called them, came in off the street. They smelled of patchouli, stale pot smoke, and (as Chuck put it) "humanity". I wondered if they ever took a dammed shower, or if they just put on another coat of patchouli when the smell of their own asses got to be too much. I had to stand well away as Moonbeam (the male hippy) paid their bill mostly in crumpled tens and twenties that had been in circulation for a while.

"Had a good day did we?"

"Oh yeah man, Haight street was crawling with heads."

When he said "heads," he didn't have to say potheads, I knew. That's how S&M were going to buy their house in Mendocino— by slinging dubsacks and haighths. A haighth is what is foisted on dumb white boys from the 'burbs who looked for an eighth of an ounce of weed. Dubsacks went by all kinds of names. That was twenty dollars worth of weed (or thereabouts). I called them dubsacks, because that's what Snoop Dogg called them, and if anyone knows the proper terminology, it'd be Snoop, right? These two throwbacks to a gentler time were actually ruthless drug peddlers corrupting the minds of America's youth. Curse them, dammed filthy hippies. They flipped me a little taste tester, which as it turned, would come in handy later.

They picked up another week. As guests went, we generally didn't have too many problems with them. I did have to explain the proper use of hotel linens under doors to keep the third floor from smelling like an opium den. Sunshine, the more pragmatic of the two, saw the advantage, as she herself had witnessed two or three of San Francisco's finest drag a "perp" out the front door, not even slowing down as he cracked his head solidly on the steel of the door frame.

As soon as she'd related what she'd seen in semi-maternal tones to Moonbeam, he began to see the wisdom as well.

Since that time we'd had no further difficulties and the third floor smelled more or less as it did before they'd come along, that is, just like piss and mothballs.

By now it was coming up on two. Throughout life some people may attempt to pound into heads of others the idea that midnight is the witching hour. Those that would do so are wrong. Midnight is a whole two hours before the fun really begins, at least on Jones Street. I don't know, or particularly give a good goddamn, how they do it in your neck of the woods. If it's that much different, write a story about it.

The bar across the road was closing up for the night and some beat up old drunks yelled out their good-byes to one another. There were art students who tried hard not to be bored stiff by the whole thing. They stood around in a knot clustered around one of their number who showed off his new bicycle.

Then there was Arnulfo Gravas. Those who have never been to Mexico and listened to Radio Zapata would have just thought him a really eager fellow who seemed to know a lot about soccer. Hector Reyes, one of my nighttime comrades-in-arms, knew better.

Hector was one of millions who would stay up late, tuning in and getting all of their "futbol Mexicana" and quietly idolizing Senor Gravas—and sometimes not so quietly. I returned from a night on the town, cheap wine pickling my insides and making my breath a marvel to behold. Srs. Gravas y Reyes were in the middle of a semi-heated discussion. From what I gathered (my command of Spanish being no better than my command of, say, Mandarin), it concerned two teams from the hinterlands, Durango and Zacatecas. Sr. Gravas was really enthused about Durango's chances. Sr. Reyes didn't see it that way, for he was, as near as I could tell, a lifelong Zacatecas supporter.

"Go Niners." I punched my fist in the air for emphasis.

They ignored me and kept right on going, back and forth. I knew they'd probably be at it all night, or until one or both of them fell asleep. I bid them goodnight and dragged my bitch ass off to bed. Tonight our man Arnulfo was in rare form; I hadn't seen him swaying back and forth in the wind like that since the night months before when he'd staggered in off the street sans wallet—thanks to an enterprising hooker—and tried to book a room with a company card he no longer possessed. In time, after many, many phone calls, we got that mess sorted out. Since by then I'd even grown to like Sr. Gravas in a weird way, I still didn't know what he was saying half the time. But through pidgin Spanglish and hand signals we communicated quite effectively, I thought.

"Buenas amigo!" He called out to me.

"Sr. Gravas como estas?" That, of course, was about the extent of my Spanish, a fact he ignored as he piled into the fake Italian sofa of chrome and foam.

He immediately launched into a tirade. From what I gathered, Radio Zapata wanted some hard news, not this boring human-interest stuff. But then he could have just as easily been discussing Chinese Tea futures for all I know. He blathered on for some time, and eventually his voice grew fainter, ever fainter, until at last he nodded off. Of course this was nothing out of the ordinary. He'd do this once or twice a week. For the first week or so I'd get annoyed and wake him so he could go upstairs and finish sleeping it off there. Nowadays I would just let him snooze. He wasn't hurting anybody and no one else seemed to really give a damn, so what the hell.

Now it was edging closer to three.

From the streets, ragged from the journey, came a lady called Magda. Her eyes were blank, her posture withered. She couldn't have been more than thirty, but there was something about her life that was killing her.

It could have been booze or pills or mixtures of the two, or maybe she had a man somewhere that wore her down like this. Whatever it was, it was depressing to watch sometimes. You could tell just looking at her that somewhere in the vast wheat fields near Kiev, some blink-and-you-missed-it village was missing the queen of its annual wheat and vodka parade.

You could almost hear her telling old girlfriends about the move to America, the bright shiny beacon. Somewhere along the line she found out the hard truth. She asked for towels and waited patiently in silence as I went and snatched them from a nearby linen closet.

She thanked me in a hollow voice and nearly jumped out of her skin as Sr. Gravas snorted in his sleep. She hadn't seen him sprawled out there, I guess. I'm also assuming that drunks passed out in hotel lobbies are an everyday thing in Russia, for once she regained her composure she didn't say anything. She waved from inside the rickety cage elevator circa 1919. But it seemed that if she wasn't exhausted, then she was at least unenthusiastic, and not into this scene anymore.

That was the drag of it all. There seemed to be a lot of people who stayed where I worked, who for one reason or another had ended up here in the 'Loin and who shrugged their shoulders and went about their business, trying to muddle through somehow or another.

Then there were the guys like me who looked for the sex and danger because somebody else got picked for the next Bond film. Guys who maybe thought, yes, it was grotty, and you ended up privy to all kinds of unwholesome shit, but that it was here or the Marina, and who had time for that shit. This is what I started tripping on.

It was late and my paperwork was handled to a certain extent, and I started to daydream, funny as that sounds, daydreaming at three a.m. in the 'Loin. Shit, I was dreaming of the day my ship would come in and I would bounce up out of this bitch. My dreams of pretty girls lighting Cuban cigars for me with five-dollar bills in the back of my Maserati, turned back into ugly reality in short order as the phone rang.

On the phone it was Aldolphus Niedermeyer, late of Kansas City. When I say late I mean some time after Kansas decided it was going to be a non-slave state, before the war of Northern Aggression, as Larry Defoyle, another of my erstwhile colleagues, liked to call it.

Anyhow, Mr. Niedermeyer, was a light sleeper, as he liked to tell me over and over and over. He also stayed in a room on the top floor, unfortunately for me, right next to the hatch that led to the roof that people used to fix the T.V. antennae or make subtle adjustments to the already fine-tuned elevator via the elevator shack. Mostly fools just went up there to get high, and I don't mean off the ground, yeah?

Anyway, whenever anyone went up there for any reason, Mr. Niedermeyer would call and complain. It didn't matter the time— it could be high noon or dead of night. He was always trying to sleep and there was always someone interfering. Tonight was no different. I bet I knew who it was, too, as I rode up in the lift that threatened to conk out any minute, leaving me stuck in between floors by myself in the dark until maybe, one day, someone noticed the smell of my now rotted corpse and called the repairman.

Wheezing in metallic protest I made it all the way to eighteen, the topmost floor. Given the right set of circumstances, you could conceivably gaze from a window out across the other scabbed-over buildings to the actual city beyond this burnt out piss-stained sector.

Down the hall I went, my feet scuffing on the battered carpet and up the last flight of mildew stairs and into the cool night air. Shit, it wasn't who I thought. I half-expected to see Sunshine and Moonbeam up there giving thanks and praises to the Most High, but since I'd caught them with their pants down, literally, once upon a time (too much for even a hard-boiled writer such as myself to describe—the thought of the smell of those two getting it on makes my stomach turn, even now), maybe they didn't come up here anymore.

I was thrown for a loop. I found it to be this lady named Jean who espoused, among other things, a strict Vegan diet and yoga, neither really my thing. Other than that she seemed all right. I explained briefly the situation and pointed out where she could walk around, as long as she wasn't jumping up and down. She thanked me, and as I turned away to avoid conversation about her 600 year-old Yogi, and the benefits of wheat grass juice, she asked me to offer her apologies to Mr. Niedermeyer. I said I would. It was a lie, of course. I tried to spend as little time conversing with Aldolphus as possible.

Back in the lift, back down to the lobby, goodnight moon.

On the ground floor I hauled open the doors to see Arnulfo still dreaming of Zacateca fight songs, but standing at the desk was a quiet-looking gentleman. With a soft voice that almost had a hint of Polish, he asked if we had any rooms. I didn't think anything of his appearance or demeanor. He didn't have any luggage with him, but that wasn't too strange since lots of people checked in with no luggage. This guy wasn't looking for a place to shoot up or a booty call, though. There was something I couldn't necessarily place. I told him I'd have a look and I turned away to go in through the doorway to the desk and office.

I caught a dull gleam out of the corner of my eye. As I reached for the doorknob he pressed what I quickly realized was a pistol to the back of my head.

"No funny business."

"No hassle." I put my hands up. He reached around and grabbed the key ring.

He stuck the key ring in my face. "Which key? Point to it."

By now I was ready to shit my pants. I pointed to a bronze key that had turned green over time.

He shoved it at me, clearly put off by my lack of haste.

"Okay, open it." I guess he meant the door but he wasn't being all that specific.

"Take it easy, don't shoot." My hands shook a little but I got the door open. By the counter just behind the door we kept a Louisville slugger for just this kind of shit. I couldn't reach it and he kicked it out of the way anyway, it clattered down the cellar steps. Any hopes of bludgeoning him with it rolled to a stop on the landing below.

Keeping me covered with the piece, he moved to the register. He jabbed the "no sale" button like an old pro. Perhaps before he'd turned to a life of crime he, too, had worked in a fleabag hotel, off the interstate perhaps.

I don't know what he was expecting—it's not like people paid a lot to stay with us. Hell, some of them even paid with one kind of credit card or another. It all added up to about two hundred and change.

"*That's it?*"

I nodded gravely and swallowed the lump in my throat.

"Okay, fine, where's the safe?"

I shook my head in the negative.

"What do you mean no? Don't tell me no!" He gestured nervously with the gun.

"I don't mean, no you can't have it," I said as cool as I could manage. "I mean no, I don't have the key, to put it plainly." Considering the circumstances, I must add that maybe he hadn't been at this armed robbery deal for long, but he was staying pretty cool. This potential Dillinger actually thought about what he was going to do next instead of freaking out. It must be the Pesto pizza.

"Okay, I'll take what's there—and your wallet."

I'd expected him to ask me to give up my shit. I did, but what I hadn't counted on was my reaction. I could care less about the till. One of my colleagues regularly "borrowed" from it. I won't say who...

And it was my boss' money. My boss—the one exploiting me and putting me in fucked-up situations such as the one I was now in, fuck it. Take it, come back and rob us again tomorrow. We'll split it.

The way he just threw my wallet in like he was ordering some fries to go with his double bacon cheeseburger made something snap. I can fight, and I have. Barroom brawling wasn't my style, but it wasn't entirely unheard of, either. However you chose to look at it, I was more lover than fighter. Looking at the security tape (and we have since we copied it and are looking for ways to market it somehow), you wouldn't get that impression.

After something gave, I yelled and charged at my would-be assailant. I smashed his head into the back of the counter. As he stumbled backwards, falling over a suitcase, the gun went flying. I scrambled to retrieve it and saw that it was a puny little pimp gun, meant as a boot-stash, and no good against, say, an elephant.

"You were going to shoot me with this?" I shouted at him as he rolled into more or less a standing position. I pointed the two-bit pearl-handled purse gun in his direction.

Something in the way I looked perhaps indicated the mayhem on back-order, so like a cannonball he went headfirst towards the doorway. He'd stepped on a stray quarters roll and it was fucking up his footing. He made a desperate bid for escape. He was about two arms breadths away when I remembered the gun. Not thinking of the consequences for once, just furious, I shot at the fleeing soon-to-be ex-robber, but missed.

The tiny bullet, after the report like a firecracker and the puff of smoke reminiscent of lit books of matches, made a nearly unobtrusive little gouge in the door frame. That didn't stop our guy. He bolted into the night.

I stood looking after him, warm gun in hand, trying somehow to get my heart to stop beating so fast. Arnulfo roused himself and groggily asked me for a glass of water.

Who was I to say no? I am, after all, but a humble hotelier.

A Regular Passage to the New Fiction

A Re-mix (Barb's story)

Scott Wayne Indiana

BLUE BLOOD AND OLD MONEY. Easy to spot.

Those first words of his new story were in the back of his mind for ten days or so before he actually got to the business of writing them down. (There was an interjected story that had been rejected for other publications about a monk that never existed.)

But after he wrote them he remembered that the words, "blue blood" weren't actually supposed to be there. They were new words in the old money first sentence.

Old money waiting. Rotting. Slowly moving.

"People who read stories like this one, in magazines like this one, don't want to wait for the hook. They want to know quickly if it's a story that they actually want to read. Sink it in early. The hook."

That thought lingered in his mind as he began the second sentence. But before he could type any more words, his cell phone rang.

"Mm-hmmmm." That was his way of saying hello.

"Are we god?"

The person on the phone actually asked, "Are we good?"

But the writer...

"More coffee please." (While editing, he reached for a beer. She reached for the beer.)

Jackson issued his warrants on the waitress and they made way for the restroom, as usual.

"What's it going to be?"

"These are some serious charges, Barb."

"I know."

They always talked about Barb's problems in the rest room.

There was an issue with their passports. The writer wasn't sure what kinds of issues there could be with passports at various checkpoints in the country they were in, which the writer had not yet decided upon, but there were issues nonetheless. No one was going anywhere until the issues were cleared up.

"Are we god?" Barb flushed the toilet.

"So, Jackson, what do you want from me? The regular payment?"

"I think I'm going to have to take you in this time."

"I can't let you do that Jackson. My kids are at home, and they need me. You know that."

"Barb."

At the checkpoint on the border all the crowds stirred half asleep in the middle of the night. The bus was full, and the driver was waiting.

"What are your intentions?"

"Sight seeing. Traveling around."

"Drugs?"

"Maybe some drugs, yes." He spoke plainly, like a monument.

"We can't let you into our country if you are admitting that you are going to seek drugs."

"You only allow dishonest people in then?"

Barb returned to her shift. Six hours to go. She refilled coffee cups and then quickly wrote several notes in a little book that she kept under the counter. The taste of mouthwash was fresh in her mouth.

"Pakistan. Passport trouble. God. Old money. Slow moving. Felt hats. Blue blood. Issues... "

Jackson sped away, but two blocks later screeched to a halt like a cartoon car, and he pulled over.

"Janet, get in the car."

She got in.

"What in the hell are you doing out here?"

"Are you going to arrest me again, Jackson?"

She had a new tattoo. A rose on her shoulder. So new it was still raised and red. Janet was no ordinary woman of the night. (Well, actually she was, but Jackson liked to think she was special. Different. She wasn't.)

"No. But you know this is breaking your parole. You're going to get arrested tonight if you don't go home right now."

"I needs money."

The writer laughed.

"I needs money. I needs money. I needs." He said it aloud. "Who writes that in a story?"

Do I write myself in as Barb? Is Barb writing this?

Is whoever reading this still waiting for the hook that was supposed to come early? Was there already a hook? Was it the line when Barb wrote notes about some of the words in this story? Was that the hook? Or was it the accidental use of the words "blue blood?" or the intentional use of "old money?"

Jackson drove off. He knew he'd have another run-in with Janet again later that night. (He hoped.)

"Man," he said aloud in his car, "this place is fucked up." He knew that he was a character in a story, a dirty undercover cop, and there was nothing he could do about it. (He knew that he was unable to pray, but he wanted to. There was a time when he'd met a monk who never existed, not even as a character in a story. "Such monks are the holiest of all monks," he remembered thinking as the monk wandered away in darkness.)

(In referring to, "this place," Jackson was talking about Pakistan. That's where he was. He was a plain-clothes cop in Pakistan. The people in his neighborhood were named Barb and Janet. They were Americans too. It was a small neighborhood where expatriot Americans lived. Most of them heard of this new locale back in Pittsburgh, where Danny Madden had set up an information table every day for three weeks outside the Greyhound station.)

"Bullshit," Barb yelled, "this is not the story."

"Barb?"

"Shit, do you want more coffee?"

"Barb? You don't like it?"

"You fucked it all up. Pakistan? What?"

"But you wrote Pakistan, not me."

"That was for the passport thread not every character. Not us! Jesus, we're not in fucking Pakistan."

Jackson pulled back into thick traffic, Janet in his mirrors. Middle of the night. Onto the interstate, he sped into the fast lane. The left lane. It wasn't long before he was out of the city and in the desert. At least once a week, Jackson needed a midnight reprieve from Vegas.

The porch light was on, which meant it wasn't too late.

Doorbell. Partially open. Chain lock.

"Jackson, come in."

"Not too late?"

"Light's on, right?"

"Right. How's the research coming?"

"Slowly. Pulling cash out of the old money fucks reminds me of Pakistani militants. But I need funding if I'm going to get the fake passports. Fucking blue bloods."

"Can I help?" Jackson exposed his gun and smiled. It was the cheesiest gesture in the whole story, but it made the writer laugh, so it remained, for now. (He thought of writing, "Do you needs help?")

"Right. You're going to march right up to Danny Madden and shoot him. Right."

"Let me know what you need."

"I need ten fucking thousand fucking dollars. That's fucking what I fucking fucking need."

She popped the cap on a bottle of pills and swallowed three or four, all in one gesture.

"Well fuck."

"Like I said, we can't let you into the country if you are going to take advantage of the poor people who resort to the sale of illegal narcotics for a living. It's people like you and your partner over there who continue our cycle of violence and crime in this country."

"So, how about if I promise to not seek any drugs then?"

"Do I have your word?"

"Yes."

"You may pass."

The guard waved to the driver who flashed his lights in return.

The travelers hopped aboard with tired smiles. Most of the people on the bus were asleep already, but a teenage kid whispered to them as they passed.

"Hashish?"

They made the exchange before the bus went into motion.

"It's Barb, you dumb fuck, your personal assistant. Are you high again?"

Silence.

"Jackson, wake the fuck up you cracked out mother—"

"What?"

"Are you coming to pick my ass up or do I need to blow the next goddamned truck driver to get a ride home?"

"Jesus, Barb, a cab is ten bucks."

"We were supposed to talk about the story."

"Okay, okay. I'll be right there."

"I hope you didn't fuck up the whole Pakistan thing again."

"I might have, I'm not sure. I'll be there in a few minutes. We can talk."

The third time he was mentioned in this story, Danny Madden had a new bullet in his head. That should read, a new bullet hole. New Jersey nights. Detroit nights. Vegas nights. Blood red violent cities.

The concept of a thug getting nailed.

The wonderment of how and why.

The passage of time.

The passage.

Barb wanted him buried already. She had her reasons. She wanted the bus to crash in the mountain pass. She wanted to yell more at Jackson. She wanted Janet to return.

"I used to be old money, you know."

"No one ever used to be old money, Janet."

She paused, blew cigarette smoke out of the window. An entire passage takes place where the reader develops a sense of closeness to Janet. There's compassion for her back story. There's new understanding about how she used to be old money, but she gambled with all her arrangements one too many times.

"One too many times," she whispered.

"Barb wants you back in."

"That's why I'm here?"

"And she killed Danny without giving him a line."

"Wow. What about you Jackson? How did you weave your ass into Barb's good graces? You're practically running the fucking show, making her wait, thinking of things that never existed, that you never knew, that you don't remember."

"Please don't say that out loud."

To Waltz

Kristina Jung

THE WORLD, IT'S ABOUT TO FALL off of its axis. I heard the other day, "Things will get better." Who were you talking to? Hegel? You're such a smart-ass. The only words you've learned how to say in the past two years are, "Thesis," "Antithesis," and "Synthesis." Let me tell you something, boy, I don't give a fuck about antitheses. If I were lonely, I would have told you. You could have held my hand? You could have touched my breast? You could have climbed in bed with me after I passed out on Manhattans? No. If I were to try and remember death, I'd forget. If it were love I was looking for, I would have found it. These days, you're laughing without feeling. And, dear, I'm laughing with it. What day was it, when you fell into apathy? What time was it, when you decided that unhappiness would suck you dry? Who cares? It doesn't matter, the hour, really. The road, it stretches out, longgg. In front of us. Behind us. To the sides of us. Above us. Below us. After us. Before us. Look. Listen. Touch the ground. Feel the land between your hands. Between your fingers. It's gritty. It's wet. It's dry. It's… Refresh. From dust to dust. Nod. Look back. Look forward. Run. Run! "Run, comrades, the old world is behind you!" Wait. "Wait." "Waaaiiittt!" Why are you running away? Where are you going? Didn't your mother tell you, the truth, my dear, there is no telos. Eschatology is myth. You were waiting for Godot. And when he didn't come, you went chasing after him, not knowing where to find him. Darling, darling, he doesn't exist. Godot doesn't exist! Listen, listen. I must be going. It's Toronto. It's busy. I need a Manhattan. It's the beating of my heart that I'm trying to distract, that's all. That's all. That's all? But, listen, darling. I've got a fairytale for you. Stop by tonight. I've got green tea and a fairytale…

PART I

Swing, swing. Hips. Swing, swing. I saw your shadow in the alleyway. Last night. Peeked through the pub windows. Saw you. DJ. You were shake, shake, shaking. Just a little. Your head. Nod, nod, nodding. No smile. You're still not smiling. Your shadow tells it all. Tall, skinny. You never smoked crack. I swear, I saw you smoking crack. Provided by Mister Jung, himself. Forget backyard pool parties. Forget backyard barbecues. Backyard wrestling. Backyard fights. Backyard kissing. My stomach is turning. Turn, turn, turning. Left, right. Left, right. My bed is empty. My love space is empty. I fought tears, for one hundred nights. Swing, swing. Right fist. Swing, swing. Miss. Miss. Hit. Miss. Thought I was dying. I thought wrong. We traveled from Germany. Detroit. Los Angeles. Toronto. London. Paris. Where have we been? Where have I gone? Where were you the night the lights went out? Crickets sang to mother. Vodka swept away grandmother. Your glory days were never behind you. Never look back. Hold on, but never look back. Look, look, look. Looking. See, see, see. Seeing. Listen, listen, listen. The fireflies are flying. The darkness between them is speaking. Listen. It's stealing our hearts. Warm. Freeze. Stuff them in a thousand tiny jars. Mantle pieces. For your suburban friends to stare through. Stare, stare, stare. Silently. Swing, swing. Hips. Swing, swing. I wish we were madly in love. Fall. I wish we were madly making love. Swing, swing. Hips. Swing...

PART II

Click. Click. Click. Yawn. Click. Click. Click. "Is this it?" "No." Click. Click. Click. Yawn. Click. Click. Click. "Is this it?" "No." Click. Click. Click. "Promise?" "Promise." Click. Click. Click. Smile. Stop. Smile. Click. Click. Click. Stop. Stand? Stand. Run? Run. Thank you, for the ride. You drove from Portage, Michigan to Toronto, Ontario. Onward. Toward Hartford, Connecticut. And, finally, we ended up in the town where my grandfather died. Ocean City, New Jersey. Click. Click. Click. Your feet. My feet. Your feet. Your feet. Your feet. Ocean. Sand. Saltwater taffy. Click. Click. Click. Smile. Click. Click. Click. It's raining, again. It rained all weekend. Rain's in the forecast. Fog. Where did you come from? Dear, oh dear, where in the world have you come from? "Detroit." Oh, darling, Detroit. My father listened to jazz there. "Eight mile and Livernois?" My mother cried there. "Everything?" My sister was raised there. Fled South. "South?" Click. Click. Click. Nervous feet. Click. Click. Click. A nervous heart is faking me. Click. Click. Click. Don't touch my hand, unless you mean it. Click. Click. Click. Yawn. "Yawn?" Laugh. Click. Laugh. Laugh. Laugh...

PART III

Bump. Bump. Bump. One decade. Bump. Bump. Bump. And, I find myself on an aeroplane. Flying home, for the first time in years. Or, should I say, the place once referred to as "home" by my long forgotten neighbours. Bump. Bump. Bump. Before my parents divorced they resided in Detroit in the early 80's, but their home was always in small-town Indiana. A small-town that still smells of an old Whiskey factory and a rotting levy. So, here I am, I'm flying "home." Drone. Drone. Drone. To a place where I remember running away from the ill-maintained cemetery across from the Grosse Pointe United Methodist Church. A place where I learned to ballroom dance, properly. A place where inheritance money bought me sailboats. Shake. Shake. Shake. But, now, the world has got me by her hand. Shake. Shake. Shake. She's draped me in her palm. Shake. Shake. Shake. I've spent the last leg of my youth stumbling through Paris' streets, drinking in London's pubs, singing on Toronto's steps. I've studied under famous men, only to see their dicks pulled out in the circles of higher and higher academia. I've cradled orphans in my arms. I've learned that orphans laugh more than lovers. I've held young lovers in my arms. I've learned that lovers cry more than orphans. I've kissed one thousand cheeks. Left. Right. Kiss. Kiss. Kiss. I've learned that some kissers will kiss you in the midnight hour, and leave you during sunrise—don't sweat it. Smile. Smile. Smile. I've learned, though, that most kissers, the real ones, never stop kissing—or holding hands. Yes. Yes. Yes. Some kisses are stained in blood. Others are sealed with it. Kiss. Kiss. Kiss. Shake. Shake. Shake. Kiss. Kiss. Kiss. I've left friends behind—to foreign lands. Aeroplane food is stale. Kind of like Detroit's coffee. Sip. Sip. Sip. But, still, we've yet to experience anything sweeter... Now. Now. Now. (Now we're dancing, Mister McCabe). "Now we're dancing?"...

Camera Shy

Henry Baum

"I'm so glad I met you."

She looked beautiful. She looked like a princess in a white low cut gown, but not too low cut, and her hair up, a couple strands falling on the shoulders.

The entire audience seemed to gasp when she came out, as if this was the most magnificent she would ever look, or anyone could look. She seemed to know it too. A brilliant kind of light in her eyes, in her whole gown, like she was happy.

She was accepting an award. She had won best actress. She was saying, "I love you," to her new husband. Did she have any idea what it was like for me, for anyone who wasn't in that room, on top of the world, for anyone who wasn't happy? I doubt it.

I went to high school with her. We were chemistry lab partners. She was beautiful then, always a princess. Diplomatic, too. Popular, but nice to me. Sort of condescending, but in such a way that I was grateful for it.

We were sort of friends, at least in chemistry class. We did a report together. I don't remember what it was about, but we had to get in front of class. Halfway through, my hands were shaking so much I couldn't hold the index cards with my notes. People in class were mimicking my shaking hands. I looked over at Robin who gave me a pitying look, a warm, motherly kind of look. "Well," she said. And then she gave the entire report herself. She was confident even then. We were given a C because of me. It was one of the worst moments in high school and the one that's stuck with me the most. Those kids mocking my shaking hands.

"I'm so glad I met you."

She was talking about her husband, Tim Griffith. They didn't show him, but everyone knew who she was talking about. She looked the most happy a person could be. I've seen all her movies.

Two years later I ran into her at the supermarket where I work. I'm a manager, but it's still only a supermarket, so I was a little embarrassed to see her.

Sandra, a checkout woman who was fat and unattractive and made herself look worse with a strange mullet-type hairstyle, short on the top, longer on the sides, told me. Sandra always wore the color light-blue which wasn't good on her. She looked like she dressed the exact opposite of what would make her look fine, like she was hurting herself but didn't know it. She was dog-like. It's standard to call an ugly woman a dog, but she actually resembled a dog. Like she had been a dog in a former life.

Sandra came up to me. I was in my office, tucked back from the market. It smelled like a refrigerator. Same lighting as the market. Bright so you could see the products.

Sandra filled up the doorway, left to right, not up and down.

"Did you see who's here?"

"No, I've been back here," I said.

"I know, but Robin Culver's here."

"Really?"

Celebrities weren't that out of the question. Our supermarket was in New York City. But I knew Robin. "I know Robin."

"You do not. How?"

"We went to high school together. We weren't friends really, but I knew her."

Sandra's eyes widened. "Are you going to say anything to her? You should go up and say hello."

"I don't know, Sandra. She doesn't care about me. She—"

"C'mon, right now. This will be fun. Go out and say hello to your friend from high school."

Sandra stepped up to the desk and lifted me up by the elbow. I have to admit, I was kind of pleased. It felt a little bit like being famous. Fame by association. It would give everyone something to talk about. Which was nerve-wracking in a way—I didn't like people talking about me. That's why I liked the office tucked in the back of the market. But somehow, because Robin was famous, it made it okay, as if criticism didn't hurt.

When I left the office, I could see people smile, whisper to each other, look in Robin's direction. It was the kind of music that greeted her wherever she went.

I stood at the registers. Sandra was back at her station. I heard her say, "Sally knows Robin Culver."

"She does?"

"She's going to talk to her."

I was nervous that something was expected of me. Like it was that chemistry report all over again. But I thought, *I'm fifteen years older now. Things like this shouldn't matter anymore. I'm not the same person I was.*

So I walked the aisles and found Robin with the juices. She was looking at the shelves and it was like I was in the wild and suddenly came across some rare animal. She looked great. She was wearing sunglasses as if to be inconspicuous. But she didn't really need to because they didn't disguise anything. But they made her look sort of aloof.

I think she had just gotten done exercising. She was wearing tight black bicycle-type pants. I don't know how a person could be that thin. Not *too* thin, perfectly thin. It was like having money and being successful had transformed her body, made her not completely human.

She was cradling a basket in one arm. There were only three items in the basket. *She could afford to put anything in that basket*, I thought. She could afford the entire store.

I walked up to her and I said, "Hi, Robin."

"Hi," she said, and looked back at the shelves. She had a sports drink, a jar of artichoke hearts, and some pita bread, that was it.

"It's me. Sally Cooper."

She looked up at me and raised her glasses above her eyes.

"Sally Cooper!" she said cheerily. "It's so great to see you."

There was nothing in her voice. It was high-pitched and friendly-sounding, but empty.

"From high school," I added.

She studied me and her smile turned to a frown.

"Do you remember?" I asked, smaller.

"I'm sorry," she said, not smiling at all. "A lot of people say they went to high school with me. It was a long time ago."

"We did a chemistry report together."

"Like I said, I don't remember," she said curtly. "It was good to see you though."

With that she walked down the aisle away from me. She bought her things and was gone.

I was left alone in the juice aisle. I straightened what she had been touching. She hadn't messed it up, but it was something to do. I felt like crying. In fact, I did a little bit. I felt like all the products were watching me.

I guess I was unrecognizable. I was never very pretty. This isn't like a movie where I blossomed into some kind of princess. I stayed fairly plain. Attractive to someone out there, probably, but not to most people. My hips were wide. There's a heaviness beneath my chin. I could probably get rid of it with exercise, but exercising that much feels foreign to me, like looking at myself in the mirror for too long. I avoid mirrors. The point is, I didn't blossom, but I did look different. I had aged. Already gray. Like I had aged twenty years and Robin Culver had only aged a couple. Seeing me in the fluorescent light of the supermarket probably wasn't so flattering. It looked good on her, but I probably looked like someone she didn't want to recognize.

A few months later something happened. Her husband, Tim Griffith, was shot by a deranged celebrity stalker named Raymond Tompkins. He wanted to make an example of Tim Griffith, who he thought represented superficiality. That's what it said in his letter which was found in his apartment later on. Robin Culver's life was turned upside down. They were at a premiere and she watched her husband get shot. I work at a supermarket so I'm surrounded by the tabloids. This story was written about in some form for many weeks.

I thought about writing Ray. I don't know why exactly. He was misguided, but also I didn't like how everybody in the supermarket, how everybody everywhere, was talking about the shooting. Like it was as great a tragedy as the JFK assassination. I mean, please, I don't advocate anyone getting shot, but Tim Griffith was just an actor. "I feel so bad for them," they said. As if it was worse than something happening to their own family. These people that made $8.00 an hour were distraught because some millionaires had some trouble.

So I wrote to Raymond Tompkins in prison. I said that I didn't condone what he had done but that I understood where he was coming from. Celebrities do get too much credit. They don't understand what it's like for regular people, even if they play them in the movies.

It didn't take too long, and I got a letter back. The letter came in an envelope stamped with the name of the prison. Funny, it was like getting a letter from a celebrity. How often do I get a letter from someone in the news, from anyone for that matter? I was nervous opening it. In fact, I didn't open it for a few minutes. I just stared at the envelope. I was sort of pleased with it and I didn't want to ruin that feeling by reading what he wrote to me. I didn't know the man. He was crazy, they said. Maybe he hated what I wrote to him. My heart couldn't take that. It was like I wrote a story and sent it to a publisher and I was waiting for acceptance or rejection. Of course, I was curious, so I opened the letter. Inside there were four pieces of notebook paper, cut neatly along the perforated edge, handwritten. His writing was easy enough to read.

Dear Sally, it started.

It was so great to hear from you. I get some hate mail, some love letters. Yours was one of the only ones that was in between. You addressed me like a person, not some kind of freak. So I liked it. What is it you do out there in the real world?

Life is boring here. I won't bore you with the details. They say they put you into prison so you'll think about what you've done. Really, I think they put you in here to bore you to death. So you'll never want to come back to a place this dull again.

About what you wrote. Yeah, I've kind of come down from where I was. I was obsessed or possessed or both. Sometimes I feel bad about injuring a person. Maybe that's a cop-out. I'm glad he's not dead. I was more interested in making an example of an idea. I think I've done that much. I could have gone and shot the Hollywood sign, but that wouldn't have done any good. Maybe I should have set it on fire.

I'm glad you haven't gotten sucked into the news about this. It's all propaganda. Some guys here are afraid of me because of it. They don't know what the hell to make of me. Some guys are assholes. Like they're protectors of movie stars. The news is of course slanted entirely against me. What they don't know is that I've gotten in contact with people like you, good people. So how could it be entirely wrong?

I hope you'll stay in touch.

Ray Tompkins

I read that first letter four times through, right away. It was exciting, really one of the most exciting things I'd ever done. It was safe, too, because he was stuck in prison so he could never come after me. I was a little afraid. I never wrote that to him, but it was on my mind, at least at first. I wrote back:

I hope you're safe. The other inmates must feel weird that you tried to kill somebody who kind of belongs to everybody. I've heard they try to kill child molesters in prison. Please take care of yourself.

You asked, so here goes: I work in a supermarket. A pretty dull job when you boil it down. I won't call it as bad as prison but I just go to work in a small, fluorescent-lit office, come home and sit in my apartment. Sometimes I read or watch TV. Then I go back again.

I felt bad about that letter. The part about TV. He hated TV and celebrities and all that, so he might judge me for it. But he didn't say anything. He just wrote back that he liked my letter. And some stuff about what he was going through in the months before the attempted murder.

I would check the mailbox every day. When I got a letter, I'd write back as quickly as possible just so I could receive another letter. It was the brightest part of my life. I sailed through the workday. When I went to the supermarket, I'd feel as though I were in love. Like I had this beautiful private world that no one knew about. I was happy.

In one letter, he asked for pictures. I had been expecting it, but it still threw me. Why shouldn't he want to know what I looked like? He was a lonely man in prison. And he might be picturing someone else. The magic could come out of it. Still though, it seemed unfair that I should see so many pictures of him—pictures from the trial, pictures from his childhood, pictures with his parents—and he shouldn't see a picture of me. I'll be honest too, I liked the idea of my picture keeping him company.

I took photos with a digital camera in my bathroom. I put up this nice tapestry I have—an Indian print—for a background, put on more make-up than I usually do, eyeliner, blush, and took a batch of pictures. Four came out right. I always blink for flashes. It's a weakness or a compulsion. There aren't many good pictures of me because I am always blinking for the flash. I think part of me just doesn't want my picture taken.

He wrote back:

I loved the pictures So many people look like they're trying to look like somebody else. You look like exactly who you are. I don't know, timeless maybe. I think it's beautiful. I've taped up a picture in my cell.

What he didn't tell me was that other inmates were making fun of him for having a picture of a woman who didn't look like a model. He didn't write that, but it's what I imagined.

One morning at the supermarket, I made a mistake. There was another manager at the market, John, who was higher up in the ranks and came in occasionally. He was nice enough. He sort of reminded me of myself, but a man. Not womanly, but he was overweight and balding. He looked like he might have been decently attractive for a couple of years in his twenties but it faded quickly. He even asked me out once, but I said no because we worked so closely together. And he wasn't good enough. I don't know what it was about him. Too eager, maybe.

I told him I had been corresponding with Ray Tompkins. I was just eager to tell someone about it. It was such a special part of my life. At first, it was nice to have this kind of secret, but then I felt like telling someone.

"You know Ray Tompkins?" I said. We were in the fluorescent office, the two of us, which made the room a whole lot smaller. John was always self-conscious around me, always acting like we were touching.

"Who? Does he work here?" John asked.

"No, Ray Tompkins. The man who shot Tim Griffith at that movie premiere. Around a year ago."

"Oh yeah, him. Nutcase. What about him?"

"We've been sending letters back and forth. He's actually a pretty decent guy."

"I bet," John said derisively. "Why'd you want to do something like that?"

"I thought he seemed interesting."

"He's a murderer."

"He's not a murderer. Tim Griffith is fine now."

John gave me a look and I realized this was a mistake. I forgot that I would have to defend myself.

John was a senior manager at the market, the liaison between corporate headquarters and all the markets in the region. It was a stupid mistake to tell him about it. Really stupid.

That night I wrote to Ray about how I told my boss, but it would be a while before I got a response. In the meantime, John recommended that I go into psychological counseling. The corporation had their own counselor.

"It's weird," John said.

"You don't understand. He's a good person. He just went through a bad phase."

"He's a lunatic and a criminal and it doesn't look very good for someone who works for this corporation in any capacity to be involved with him. You need to stop this correspondence."

"And what if I don't?"

I felt like I was in high school again, asking daddy for a later curfew for one night, which didn't happen very often, and being turned down. I felt weepy and small.

"If you don't," John said, "then I think we will have to look into terminating your employment with us."

Fuck him, I thought. And that's what I said, "Fuck you."

He looked shocked, a quick intake of breath, like I'd just slapped him.

"Sally, don't do this."

"No, if I can't have some kind of extracurricular life, I don't want to work at this market anymore. It's like a prison."

"Okay." He looked regretful then, like he didn't really want to fire me, but he had to. He was a nice enough person. A robot, but a nice person. "We'll have to let you go."

"Okay." I turned and walked out of the office quickly, as if to keep myself from having second thoughts, even though this was out of my control. I walked up to the registers kind of triumphantly. "I got fired." I felt teary and sort of high, like a western standoff where I might die, confident and fearful at once.

I walked away before I could get a response. I wanted to be left with the image of their shocked, pitying looks, and my triumphant gait, probably more upright than I had been in years. Then I walked out of the supermarket, as if for the first time in my life.

Sally, Ray wrote, *I'm sorry that you lost your job. But fuck them. Now we can be together.*

Pillowcase

Sherry Bryan

Fay SET HER ALARM EARLY every Saturday so that she could beat her neighbors to the washing machines. With only two washers and dryers to accommodate the entire building, the tenants became pack animals armed with All Temper Cheer and Bounce. All of the politeness they had exchanged by the mailboxes or on the front stoop dissipated in desperation for clean clothes. Most weekends Fay would find the familiar laundry basket of her seventy-year-old neighbor Helena staked out on the machines, preparing for multiple loads. Fay bitterly thought Helena could just do her laundry during the week when the rest of the building was at work. But, with a smiling face and resignation she would politely concede the machine to the alpha of the pack and retreat back upstairs.

This weekend, however, when Fay grabbed her hamper and jogged down the stairs, quarters jingling in her pocket, the building was still—everyone was sleeping. She opened the door to discovery the laundry room was empty—it was hers. Fay could wash, spin, and tumble dry in peace. Smiling in triumph, she tossed in her clothes, towels, sheets and favorite detergent. Laundry was such a small act that gave her such a tangible sense of satisfaction. She went back upstairs to a pot of brewing coffee that filled the apartment with a comforting scent.

She turned on her cell phone to check her messages. As expected, he had called.

Hi baby, isss me. It's... about 2 a.m. Jus' finished up my last game of pool. And—HEY! Manny—whas' up, man? Yeah. Anyway. Fuck, I'm buzzed, baby. Wish I could come over. Mmm. Miss you. You're probably asleep. Oh well, jus' wanted to say hi, and I was thinking of you. If you get this, give me a call. I can be over in like ten minutes or something. You know... Manny, you dick! No, this one's on me! I'm a have one more and—

Click.

She was irritated at his slurred words and Jim Beam-fueled affection. On another man, she might have found this charming, or even saved the message. But on him, this was unattractive. She just didn't want a night of sloppy, drunken kisses. Well, not with him.

They had been dating for a month, and she had tried. But... . *I'm going to have to break up with him. Damn.*

She looked out the window at the morning sky. God, it was gorgeous. She had the whole day ahead of her.

An hour later she was folding her clean, warm laundry on the couch. Her building was beginning to wake up, through the walls she heard her neighbor moving around and the scratchy sounds that came from his clock radio.

She picked up her softest, oldest pillowcase with great affection. It was the color of lavender, and so soft. It was almost threadbare; she'd had it for years. No matter what sheets she bought, she always kept this pillowcase, and put her favorite pillow in it so every night she could lie her head down on the softest pillowcase in the world. She pressed it to her face and breathed in the scent of her dryer sheets.

She looked for the familiar gray smudge that had marred the fabric for several months. It was traces of mascara. Her pillowcase was stained on a warm summer night that had followed a bad day, the kind of bad day that one could remember in excruciating detail for years. On that day Fay had managed to hold the weight of her tears until she was safely home and completely alone. Her head felt so full, so heavy, she had to lie down—a tempest churning under her skin. She was not one for self-pity, but that night she was beyond her own discipline.

She had curled up on her bed and cried. It was a hard cry; gasping, candid sobs, sniffles, and fat tears that rained from her eyes. She cried until her eyes stung and there was nothing left. Finally, out of exhaustion, she drifted off to a dreamless sleep, determined that was that. Tomorrow would be different. Tomorrow she would begin letting go of him.

A perfect storm of mistakes, misjudgments, and misguided hope had been a long time coming and hit with F5 fury.

Fay never saw him coming. She never expected him.

With her laundry scattered over her, she began to recall all of it. Her spell was broken by the sound of her neighbor's radio. She heard Louis Armstrong sing of "dark sacred nights." She liked that. She'd like a dark, sacred night.

Fay had a propensity for guilt and great embarrassment, and sometimes she would lie in bed on a dark and not-so-sacred night and think about the larger missteps she had made, the ones that caused the most damage. She wanted to repent. But redemption is slippery, and hers were not nimble fingers.

The first time she saw him Fay had the slight sensation of being punched in the stomach. And looking at him, she saw something utterly lovely and completely unique to her. It wasn't a physical or sexual response, well not at first. It was just a tremendous *something* that she saw, that she believed that only she could see. She could feel it, the rare beauty that lived in him. She saw him in a way that made her senses sharpen and made her completely understand fragments of lines by Theodore Roethke or e e cummings that she had read long ago.

That was months ago, before everything went to hell and she ruined her pillowcase. It was with impossible sadness that she realized that she wouldn't inspire any such poetry in him. He didn't see *her* and never would. So she let go of all her daydreams, her hopes, her very secret and embarrassing wishes that humid night, and cried away the expectation of him.

As Fay fingered the gray stain, she realized that it had become her badge, her souvenir. It was an unsought education: that purity of intent and desire is not necessarily enough; that wanting with a true heart, mind, and libido insured nothing. It reminded her that sometimes the truth is ugly and hard, and no place for e e cummings—or her heart. But above all, it reminded her that for a brief time, she felt dizzy and taken by love—raw, unruly, unreciprocated love. Despite the outcome, Fay felt fortunate to have had even a few months consumed by such powerful feelings. She had been so high that everything felt vibrant and new, and that was a gift.

Fay went to her bedroom and tenderly put her pillow in the pillowcase. She stretched out on the bed, her hand tracing the mascara stain. This was the only piece of him she could have. But, she felt only comfort as the closed her eyes. The small piece of him that held her head as she slept was as precious and sacred as a prayer.

Red

Janis Butler Holm

I SEE TWO PEOPLE having coffee. I see her full red lips leaving dark stains on the cup. I see his hand shaking with desire, the coffee spilling just a bit, unnoticed. I see them rising, moving quickly out the door and toward the shaded park. I see them kneeling in the grass. I see their insistent blood, heating, drumming, leaping. I see them clutching and falling. I see the grass receive their bodies. I see them panting and pushing, with mouths like those of ravening birds. I see them bumping and biting. I see them moaning. I see them crying out in wordless phrases. I see them seizing, convulsing, their bodies meaning everything and nothing. I see their limbs relaxing, then lying still. I see him clearly. I see the coffee, the grass stain, the lipstick on his shirt. I see his blood.

Family Dinner

Daniel Scott Buck

"IS THAT A REAL BABY?"

The question had been nagging at me since I got there.

Everyone went dead silent.

We ate quietly, with the exception of a few compliments to my mother's cooking. Someone would ask to pass the salt. Someone would ask to pass the pepper. The baby sat in a highchair, staring disinterestedly at some mashed potatoes. Not moving, as far as I could tell.

"She's sleeping again," my sister whispered.

The baby's eyes were wide-open, glistening like glass. I looked at my mother; she could feel my eyes slit her apart like scalpels; she refused to look at me as they cut her. I wanted to pound my fist on the table and demand some answers, but I didn't want to upset my sister. She looked like she was on medication. Her body movements were slow and measured with difficulty; a startle could send her into a seizure or shut her down forever. I was her big brother. And if there was anyone I felt anything for at this table, it was her. Even if I had never seen her before.

I would have to save all of my questions for later; and that meant, I reflected morosely, I would have to see my mother again. I would have to sit down with her and have a talk. We would have to work out this family problem.

I tried to change the subject, then.

"Where's Jerry?"

My mother looked at me like she didn't understand. My sister didn't hear me. And my brother mumbled. He was very thin and wore baggy clothes to cover up the flesh that was missing from his body. His hair had fallen out in patches. His face was pallid, and fierce blue eyes, set in the jaundice clay of his eyelids, occasionally looked at me with a violent intensity. Perhaps he was simply taking note of my decay. That beyond the glory days of my youth, I had become a strung-out, chain-smoking, withering alcoholic.

My mother finished her plate. The rest of us had hardly managed more than a few bites. She excused herself from the table and went to the kitchen, and returned to the dining room table with her dish piled high with seconds. She forked several green beans, dipped them in gravy, and put them in her mouth.

"Do you have a girlfriend?" my mother asked.

"Yes," I said, a little too sure of myself, "her name is... Sandra."

"Sandra!" my mother repeated. "You should have told me. We could have invited her to dinner."

"Sandra has other obligations this evening," I wiped my mouth with a napkin. "In fact, she has a very busy schedule. She is a legal assistant in my office and serves on several boards related to public service." I wanted to stop myself at this point, but I couldn't after seeing my brother snarl. "She does a lot of volunteer work for charitable organizations. This evening, she is mentoring some disabled kid. Poor thing has Dyslexia, one arm, one leg." I checked my brother's temperature—he was red hot. "Sandra was accepted to law school—she's going to be a lawyer. She's already read the textbooks for the first semester. Very studious, very intelligent, and I must say, the most compassionate and nurturing woman I've ever seen." I gave my mother a look to suggest that I might be speaking a foreign language. "I look forward to introducing you. But, like I said, she's busy. We spend as much time together as we can while at work, sometimes a few minutes in the bathroom is all we can manage. But we see each other every night; she usually comes over and stays at my place. It is what I have to look forward to, the private moments we share before falling asleep." And then I added, as if seized by a dream, "We call them our little Moonlight Sonatas!"

My brother looked at me with incredulity; either he was spinning with disbelief, or thoroughly repulsed by the possibility I could get married and have offspring.

Sandra was more than likely getting fisted at a swinger's club—while barely legal girls suckled on her pierced nipples.

She didn't have a job, as far as I knew. I had just met her the night before. How well can you know someone after twenty-four hours and an eight-ball?

I leaned back in my chair, calm and confident, a man of certainty, as if transported back in time to the embrace of the previous night. I opened my eyes, almost weepy.

That's when I said:

"I'm thinking about asking her to marry me. She would make a good wife, a good mother. She's an excellent cook, and she likes to iron my shirts. It's a fetish."

My brother took a sip of his water; apparently, the sound of my voice dehydrated him. And, as was evident by the way he let his fork tumble from his fingers, dinner was over: He could not stomach another bite of his food, nor another word about Sandra.

I recoiled for a moment. Why did I say that part about ironing my shirts? The shirt I was wearing looked like it had been pulled from the bottom of a laundry basket. It smelled like it.

My mother clapped her hands like an imbecile.

"I'm going to have another grandchild!" she said.

She was hopping in her chair, all two-hundred pounds of her body moving as energetically as a teenager, slapping the table with the palms of her hands.

"I'm going to have another grandchild!" she repeated to no end.

My brother wanted to end the evening with a ceremony: The Friendship Circle.

He asked everyone to sit on the floor, but my mother's knees were bad, she said, and plopped herself onto a recliner. I flung myself onto the couch in a manner that let on that my mind and body were elsewhere, that this was an opportune time for a nap. My sister sat on the floor with the baby in her arms.

The baby, with its frightened China Doll's eyes, looked upon this damning spectacle with an eerie silence.

My brother lit four candles and placed them, so he said, "according to the four winds."

He cast a vicious glare at me after I lifted a foot and farted. I licked my index finger and held it in the air, pretending to understand the weather.

My brother then asked my mother to pick an object of some importance that we could all pass around; we were to take turns holding a bag of dice in a red velvety bag that was tied at the top with a gold string. There was a small yellow cross threaded into the fabric.

My brother asked her to go first. Apparently, we were supposed to say something pleasant about our lives and, if I heard him correctly, the future. So the evening was becoming impossible.

My mother held the bag of dice in her hand.

"I am so happy," she was being serious, "to be with my beautiful family." She took turns looking each of us in the face with a dopey expression of love and gratitude. "I know I've made a lot of mistakes," she continued more soberly, "but I feel like this is a new beginning. What I want, more than anything, God help me, is for everything to be good for us. I know I can't change the past, but if you'll let me, I can make things different. God knows I try. God knows I'd do anything to keep all of you in my life. God knows I'd do anything for all of you."

She was crying. And I was looking across the room through a heavy brainstorm, wondering: Who is this woman? She was making me nervous.

My sister reached out and put her hand on my mother's hand and spoke thus: "We all love you mama. Please don't cry. We are all together now."

My mother handed her the dice, then blew her nose.

"I don't have anything to say. I don't know what to say."

My sister handed the dice to me. The bag was warm and damp. I squeezed the dice through the velvet; there were about six or seven of them. I stared down at the yellow threaded cross and gently pinched at the fringe where it was frayed, pulling off little fibers of yellowish-brown cotton.

Brevity was not going to be a problem, it was the delivery I was worried about, somehow saying something short and sweet and having it sound as if I meant it.

"I want to say," I paused to look up from the bag of dice, "I want to say that I am thankful for this night." I stopped and thought about the challenges of fashioning Sandra into something that didn't look criminal. "The truth is, had I encountered any of you on the street, had I walked by you and stared long and hard into your faces, I wouldn't have recognized you. And that kind of scares the fuck out of me. You know what I'm saying?"

My sister was stroking the plastic face swathed in the blanket; her eyes spun in my direction, then stopped before rolling out of their sockets. My mother heaved herself out of the recliner and rushed to the bathroom in a fit of tears, and returned a moment later without her dentures. She was holding a tissue.

My brother was clearly agitated; not only had the congruity of the ceremony been disrupted, but now we all had to adjust to the novelty of seeing our mother without her teeth, which had the grotesque effect of making her look like she was missing half of her face.

Nonetheless, my brother waited triumphantly for everyone to become settled.

"First and foremost," my brother began, "I am thankful for Oxtail and Roadmaker... " He went on to mention some other Pagans with whom he was on a self-styled name basis, then blew out the candles. I regained consciousness after a waft of smoke settled in my nostrils.

I got up to leave, explaining that I couldn't stay longer because Sandra was expecting me. As I walked out, I shouted, "With a real dinner!" and slammed the door. That's when I saw the apartment numbers staring back at me. I looked at the back of my hand, where I had scrawled the address with a pen earlier in the day, and glanced at the door again. They didn't match. But it didn't matter. I'd be back.

Slipping Away

Lindsay Bull

THE AIR IN THE PLAZA was heavy with moisture and I squinted through the vapor at a slender woman in a red dress, staggering down a steep flight of concrete stairs. She had a bundle tucked under one arm, the other arm splayed out to maintain equilibrium, and a cigarette balanced between her fingers. She was a spinning mobile: a bizarre, human version of the brightly-colored toy that used to hang above my sister's crib. I watched, hypnotized by the delicate limbs affixed to red slips of fabric and shiny bits of hair.

The woman distracted me.

I was supposed to meet someone in the plaza, although I couldn't remember who. I checked my watch: quarter after ten. *How long had I been waiting?*

Sometimes, I slip away from myself. That's when I feel my blood pump backwards, pulling my fingers into blue-veined fists, pulling my toes into cat claws. It's always the same feeling. The only thing I can do is wait it out.

The woman in the red dress descended, stumbling a little more with each step. The white of her firm arms reflected the light from the street lamps and there was a charming innocence in the way she moved. I might have given her my number, if I had been the type. I imagined her white arms wrapped around my neck, her little toy fingers snaking through my hair.

It didn't matter. I couldn't have helped her. I couldn't have done anything, really. I stood on the sidewalk and braced myself against a brick wall. That's where I watched it all happen.

Slim ankles buckling, her high heels scraped against the pavement and she gripped the railing with a sharp scream. The bundle she had been carrying fell, hitting the corner of the step in front of her and then bouncing down, down, down.

The woman's scream escalated into hysterical wails. She raced down the stairs, shaking her empty hands. I could hear her shouting: Callie. Callie. Callie.

I stared at the bundle at the foot of the steps. It had been wrapped in a brown blanket, but the fabric had unfurled during the fall. I squinted, trying to make sense of the tiny contorted shape, the fleshy color, the dark liquid puddle.

I closed my eyes and felt the familiar stranglehold of panic, the image of my baby sister before me. A brown tangle of curls framed her blue-gray eyes. She had a high-pitched, startling laugh. I used to push her on the swing in our backyard and she would laugh with such abandon that my mother would make us go back inside so we wouldn't alarm the neighbors.

It was happening again

I was a few steps behind Callie when I saw her stumble, her ballerina hands grasping at the air. She rolled down a series of concrete steps before slamming into an empty bike rack. I ran to the base of the steps and grasped her by the shoulders. Callie's eyes were open, her nose and ears were dripping with blood. I don't remember how long I held onto her. My hands can still feel the weight of her bones and blood.

I was pulled away from Callie just as the sun was setting. I remember flashing lights and the buzz of human voices. Then, my mother full of rage: "There's nothing we can do. She's gone. Oh my God. She's really gone."

"I want to see Callie," I told her.

"You can't. You saw what happened. She's gone." My mother trembled. She looked me in the eye and with one swift movement, slapped my face. I felt her wedding ring slam against my nose.

"Why didn't you tell someone? Why didn't you do something?"

"I was scared," I said.

My mother's response was my sister's name, repeated over and over while she hugged her knees and rocked back and forth in the hospital waiting room.

Callie. Callie. Callie.

I didn't see Callie again until I went to church with my grandmother and we laid flowers next to Callie's lifeless body. Callie was two when it happened. I was ten. I was old enough to hold Callie's hand while we walked to our babysitter's house. I was old enough to know how to walk down stairs.

There was nothing I could have done. I couldn't have saved her. I couldn't have done anything, really. But I was back there again: ten years old, grasping for Callie's hand, holding her bloodied head, waiting for her to wake up. I kept seeing her fall, her body in a crumpled heap of limbs and baby fat on the concrete.

Willing the images to disappear, I tightened my purple fists. I took shallow breaths, hopeful that the woman in the red dress wouldn't hear me. She was on all fours at the base of the stairs, crying, gathering the folds of the blanket. She picked up the bundle from the thick ooze beneath it. That's when she saw me standing in the shadows. I froze.

She retrieved her smoldering cigarette from the concrete and walked towards me, carrying the dripping bundle. My skin tingled and burned with the urge to escape. I clenched my jaw hard and my lungs seized. Her image was hazy, but I saw a slow smile creep across her face.

"Jake, are you okay?" she said.

I blinked, waiting for air.

"Jake? Seriously, you're scaring me. Didn't you see me take that fall? You could have helped me out a little, you know."

"I was scared." I said.

"What?"

We stared at each other. I knew her. It was Karen. I was supposed to meet her in the plaza. We were going to a nearby bar to celebrate her birthday.

"Sorry, Karen. I'm sorry. I'm fine."

"Well, I brought us some whiskey, but I dropped it during my crash landing back there." She took a long drag of her cigarette. "God, I hate paying full price at these places."

She was holding the bundle: large shards of glass from a whiskey bottle and soaking wet pieces of a brown paper bag.

"We can either suck on the paper," she said, "or you can buy me a drink."

"I'll meet you in there. I just need a second."

"You're okay, right?"

I nodded and forced a smile. Seemingly satisfied, she turned on a heel and sauntered across the plaza toward the bar. The word "Linda's" flickered in red neon and the smoke from Karen's cigarette snaked a murky red trail behind her. The irregular clicks of her high heels echoed in my ears.

I stood there until my fingers relaxed and my breathing steadied. Then I followed the trail of smoke into Linda's and ordered two martinis. I drank until I had fallen away from the neon lights, from Karen, from the laughter and loud music. I kept falling further away, until I was falling down those stairs with Callie again.

The only thing I could do was wait it out.

Stirred By A Passion

Greg Gerding

I WAS STIRRED BY A PASSION this evening and my numb mind doesn't know what to make of it.

I surrendered to an evening of leisure after a twelve-hour workday—a day that went well. "Well" meaning fast and without incident. I never got stressed. I was never lifted out of my seat and forced to move outdoors. In fact, I never once saw the sun or anything outside.

I went home looking forward to a pizza, a few beers, and a few phone calls and nothing else. But I was stirred by a passion this evening that I had not been prepared for. I called my lover at 11:00 p.m. and found out that she was drunk, and that she wasn't alone.

After I figured that out, she says to me through the phone, "I'll call you later." Five seconds later, I'm pounding the back of the sofa with my fist and throwing my shoes back and forth across the room and pacing. I call again and again and again and she's not picking up the phone. Even the answering machine stops answering and the phone just rings. I begin to lose my mind.

I jump in my car and do ninety all the way from my house to her apartment. On the radio—as if on cue—violent heavy metal music rages. And there is nothing on my mind but an excuse for a cop and a homicide or two.

I turn a half-hour drive into fifteen minutes and, once I arrive, call somebody else in the building and make up a story that admits me through the front door. I race up four flights of stairs and stand before Apartment 419 and begin pounding on the door.

"Oh shit," I hear her say. "I can't believe it." This is followed by a commotion of shuffling.

"Open this fucking door!"

And shuffling—and shuffling—and, "Oh shit"—and mumbling. Mumble, mumble.

I just keep pounding.

She eventually steps through the door, out of the darkness and into the light of the hallway.

And me, "What the fuck are you doing?"

"I'm drunk."

"Yeah? No shit!"

She's there with a lit cigarette in her hand and shrugging at me saying, "What? What?"

I smack the cigarette out of her hand and the force of the blow knocks the cherry from the stem. The cigarette sits there, one half.

She tries talking me down. "I want a ring. I want to marry you. I love you so much. Don't you love me?"

I say, "Well, I'm here aren't I?" And to me that seems enough.

She eventually gets me to leave when she assures me that there is nothing going on and he is not staying the night.

I pick up the half-cigarette and move down the hall with it between my lips, unlit. I pause between the second and third floor to take a piss in the stairwell corner.

I return to my car and begin to drive away, but thoughts continue nagging me, and I hear my best friend in my head who's pissed at me for not storming in and kicking that guy's ass.

I do a quick U-turn and speed back and try to phone her first, but it just rings and rings and rings. And my mind thinks and thinks and thinks the worst, of course.

I call another sucker to buzz me in and go back to pounding Apartment 419's door. I hear movement between the living room and bedroom and then she busts through the door saying, "Fuck! What? I just want to sleep!"

And me, "I thought he was leaving? What the fuck is he still doing here?"

She tries to assure me that nothing is going on, that she loves me—that she wants to marry me. I just want to kick this guy's ass because my best friend is screaming at me in my mind. I tell her I can't leave.

She says, "I love you. I know we have a future. This means nothing. Don't you love me?"

"Well, I'm here again, aren't I?" And it still seems enough, but it's not.

She wants me to be her husband.

I say, "Why?" But then I say, "I want you to be my wife," and "I love you too."

She says, "This means nothing," nodding back behind her. I wonder why she is whispering this fact to me.

"Okay," I say.

Now, I guess I'm engaged, but I don't know.

I wish I had more guidance. I wish I were more violent. I wish I were more drunk. I wish I were more simple. And I wish I were more sure, but I don't know.

I guess I'm in love, because I was stirred by a passion that moved me to action, but I just don't know if she's the one. Or maybe there isn't a one, just a two that exists. I wish I knew what love is so I could identify it and squeeze it tight.

I move down the hall once again. I am assured that the guy is sleeping on the couch. I never saw him, but he is either a limp-dick wuss or a big fucking linebacker or maybe he doesn't even exist at all.

And maybe none of this happened.

And maybe I really am in love.

And maybe I really am engaged right this very minute.

World With A View

Joe Shipley

I HAD GROWN UP in the suburbs of Atlanta. The sky was a deep, orange-black that was oddly bright on overcast nights, when the clouds became a reflector for the light of the city. I remember counting maybe three or four stars on clear nights, maybe a couple more if you spent a couple hours outside just watching. I was an indoor person, despite having a lot of friends obsessed with the night sky. My particular skill was invention, and it was their inspiration that brought about one of the first things I actually blueprinted out. It was an improved streetlight that resulted in eighty-percent less upward light pollution. It was somewhat successful, not being any more expensive than the normal lights, but light pollution isn't on many people's minds these days. I wondered if a city's collective subconscious somehow enjoyed blinding itself to the Heavens. It certainly makes you feel more important.

I was a long way from the city now. Julie had dragged me out on this boat she had conned me into renting, though it did have a comfortable interior and an impressive electronics array. We were headed towards a dark sky and a tiny island some hundred miles north of the North Carolina outer banks. She says that it's too cold for the humidity to be bad. That, I certainly believe. She's hoping for a pristine sky, dark and clear, with as little ambient light as possible—the far side of the moon, away from the sun. But we're getting close to the zenith and the sky is still completely overcast, filled with dark clouds.

She is still smiling. It is both aggravating and adorable. She seems to know her way around boats—some part of her past she's never told me about. She lowers the anchor, turns off all the boat lights, and I begrudgingly hop out. I bring our lantern, complaining that we won't be able to find the boat in the dark but she shushes me. She trudges up a hill to the top, laying out a picnic blanket on the sand, then tightening her parka as the chill wind bites at us. She pulls her toboggan down a little, too, and tucks her hands into her coat.

I sit down, place the lantern between us and glance up at the clouds before looking at her. The lantern's red-tinted light defines her profile, her smooth skin highlighted and eyes twinkling like they contained a galaxy of stars of their own. I know they do, though I doubt I'll ever see them as closely as I'd like. I shrug, sigh, and look away towards the coast, our light disappearing after a few feet, giving the bizarre impression of being on a little floating island of red in the middle of an infinite blackness. I can hear the waves lap against the beach.

"I have to be at work tomorrow, you know." I act irritated at this whole endeavor.

She looks at me, face wrapped into that quizzical, sarcastic expression I know so well. "Tomorrow is Saturday, Matt."

I throw up my hands. "I know. But NIH grants don't care about weekends."

She tilts her head and shoulders up, shifts her weight to her elbows, the rest of her features coming into focus in the lantern light. "They will wait a few hours for you to catch some sleep and go into work Saturday night, right? You have a key. I swear, you are the only friend of mine who has a real job." She somehow says that like it's an insult.

We are quiet for a few minutes. She reaches into her parka and pulls out a little steel flask, taking a couple quick gulps of something obviously spirited. She doesn't grimace. I roll my eyes and she laughs. She takes another couple sips, places it on the ground between us, and starts talking.

"You really have no sense of perspective, Matt. I know you don't know this, but I am... deeply religious." I almost laugh out loud. I didn't realize she brought me out here to preach to me. She keeps on going.

"It's not what you expect. I don't believe in Allah or Jesus or any patriarchal father figures punishing us for saying fuck or thinking dirty thoughts... though I guess it is possible. I just think about the math of it all."

I blink. "The math of religion?" The sky is still overcast. I am cold, not quite intrigued yet by her babbling, and wonder when she is going to give up and let us go back to shore.

"Sure. The way I see it, a person is run by math—chemical processes in our brain, sure, but math all the same. You could do the work with pen and paper and end up with the same results." She takes another swig.

I glance at her again. That haughty superiority somehow makes her more attractive. She puts the lantern above our heads and scoots over a bit, probably feeling a little cold, too. She presses against my side. I can't help but think this is the closest we've ever been to each other. She keeps her arms crossed, leans back, and stares at the empty sky. I get bored of waiting for her to continue. "How is that a religious belief?"

She chuckles, finally cued. "We're slowly cracking the secrets of how the brain works. And when we do, it would be theoretically possible to simulate a human mind. Which means we may be no more than constructs or simulations ourselves."

I shake my head. "I don't think it really works like that. I mean, we're here, why would... " She cuts me off.

"You are just a random selection within a large number of humans. And if you could be simulated, then we all could be. And the world that could simulate us might be simulated itself. Thus it goes on for infinity in both directions, everything a simulation."

Her tone is laced with mysticism. It's pretty aggravating. I hate metaphysical discussions. Her voice has always had a kind of high-pitched quality I never totally liked. She continues, "You see, even if we're in the 'base' universe, before we simulate or are simulated by any others, how likely were you to come into existence?" She takes another drink. Despite experience, her size makes her a lightweight and I suspect it's starting to affect her. Her argument is definitely starting to falter. I'd already be gone, more so than her—which is why I don't drink. She sighs. "The chance of a hundred billion in a hundred billion to the billionth power is very, very low."

We sit in silence again for a few minutes. I can sort of see what she's trying to get at, but it seems useless, silly. Our lives are still the same out here, regardless. It's just not practical knowledge. I turn my head and look her in the eyes. She maintains the stare for an eternity. Then a smile creeps across her face, spreading into a wide, beautiful grin. She winks, touches my cheek and points upwards.

The clouds had rapidly thinned out and she turned the lantern off. The universe shined down on us. The clarity was so amazing, I could almost feel the scale of it, our dark eyes viewing more stars than we have thoughts. I felt her grab my hand. She pressed her head against my shoulder, sighed. Then she laughed and whispered playfully, "You're an idiot, Matt," before hugging me. I didn't know what to think. The universe had been hidden so long from me, the universe that the city had tried but failed to outshine.

Plastic Meow

Chris Roberts

AWAKE

MAYBE IT WAS THE WALLPAPER.
once bright. now faded colors. happy frozen animals circle my room. what an organised parade. alphabetical zoo. marching marching marching to dim tin pan music. organ grinder music. tiny monkey tiny hat. dime? quarter? clink. anteaters, beavers, cats, deer... walruses, xanthippes, yaks, zebras. xanthippes are real. look it up in an encyclopedia. not like unicorns. at least not here or now. 26 smiling staring still. glued to wall forever. not moving. well... moving slightly. swaying in this near sleep. this long only-blinking. really. sharp blurry sharp blurry. twitch. eyes wide open. not where they were before. eyes dizzy. eyes failing. time for sleep. brief glowing image. animal parade. back of... heavy... dark... lids...

NEARLY ASLEEP

maybe it was mother. maybe it was father. mother's smile. father's nose i suppose. bad habits. doubt? could never tell with father. things they taught me. contradictions. ping pong patter mind fuck. pulled & twisted toaster coils. brain to point of snapping. mood swing. trust. never put sharp objects into your mouth. never. damage gums teeth. future as teeth model? lead in a fleeting movie of the week? starring who again? nice teeth whoever however. good parenting. off to the dentist? fuck. i hated the dentist. hate him still. always him. odd robot chair. deceptively comfortable. *clean teeth are happy teeth* and *3 times a day* posters on the ceiling of all places. should say *squirm sweat panic bleed spit.* mechanical chair. no shackles? hours in the waiting room for this? magazines you've never heard of before. mother doesn't subscribe. father? certainly not. no jugs in these mags. enter perfect clean dentist. hair just. coat just. teeth just. of course. white native. small efficient spear. counting teeth. poking prodding tender gums... one, two, good, three, four, nice... poke poke poke. tiny weapon breaking ground. tender mouth.

tiny spots of blood you suspect. acupuncture jackhammer. tears gathering. tight fish net. more toys from tray. all sharp. every toy feels the same. seems to do exactly the same damn thing. missed a nerve. final nerve. pins & needles. deep. after rack hot coals chinese water torture. blood saliva spit. *that wasn't so bad was it? really?* must not recall *his* childhood dentist. hopefully i won't either. do recall mother's warning, father's warning. as mouth throbbed & ached, began to learn the importance of doubt.

maybe it was father/pastor/minister/reverend. my family attended. i accompanied voluntarily by force &or bribe. or else. ice cream. whatever. not my church their church. instantly recognised things that others didn't. or didn't see? lost blind robotic sheep. nice clothes. looking for god in words books songs hymns robes stained glass. take & eat. stale dead bread. take & drink the grape juice of christ? um. false luster of the collection plate. god doesn't need $. people need $. details. our father/pastor/minister/reverend had a personal relationship with christ. barbecues & such i reckon. poker on thursdays? i wouldn't play poker with jesus. walk on water, check. water to wine, check. back from the dead, check. poker... please. fold. apparently important to accept this stranger into our hearts minds lives. barbecues. poker night. eternal salvation.

never talk to strangers. even strangers that don't look like strangers. normal people can be strangers too. wise mother words. over & over. strangers are bad. got it. broken parrot. squawk. how about thin scraggly scantily-clad bloodied thorny fellows, mother? mother never answered because i never asked. morbid not stupid. doubt. continued to fester. prometheus scab. pick edge flick eat. same bat time. same bat channel. eating away. hot angry smoky moth.

take easter. our father/pastor/minister/reverend told us all about it one sunday. easter sunday. extra handsome. extra pretty. extra people. i listened & writhed & sweat & fussed. hard wooden pew. christ. died many years ago for all us sinners. original sin. eve. apple. bitch. crucified tacked up to wooden cross to die. limbs stretching buckling aching under painful bloody strain of nine inch nails. crucified. dead. buried. 3rd day rose from this dead. cat nap. moved a huge rock from entrance of tomb. adrenaline. let me out of here indeed. thankful for the cat nap & all. some floating. more floating. descended upon some common folk. disciples. word or 2. no mention of initially scaring the bejesus out of them all. might have an origin there. after the jesus christ ghost moment. couple of words. poof. vanished gone forever. still in the hearts minds lives of those that won't let the poor man die. bumper stickers. bobble heads. action figures. car air fresheners. t-shirts. iron-on patches. all the kitsch keeps him alive & floating. hanging in there. cat on clothesline poster on dental ceiling. *hang in there* for christ's sake.

all a bit hard to swallow on the probable surface of reality. set aside walk on water, water to wine, lame to walk, blind to see, etcetera. who's to argue back then. voice of god in the father/pastor/minister/reverend. direct line. xm satellite radio. robed marionette. megaphone. wrath of god. wages of sin. fire & brimstone. too frightened *not* to believe really. afraid he kept some in reserve. behind pulpit. thermos. hot things hot. for those special blasphemous occasions. can i get an amen?

dark. camp. forest. counselor. black. hanging. crowd. chanting. jesus? anyone? front. kneel. confess. palms. nervous. shivering. black. jesus? hanging. voices. mumbling. trees. swaying. jesus? welcome? heart? yes. please. louder. swaying. dizzy. nauseous. crying. salvation. retreat. return. sit. cry. shake. fuck. give it away. him away. take it all back...

my doubt. safely locked up in an attic. top of my head. with boxes with dust. spiders & such. only i had the key to open it. unlock. brush away. duck. click. single hanging light bulb overhead.

easter seemed pretty cut & dried. bored in my pew next to father in suit mother in dress. attic of doubt a mess. already? bunnies of dust. rusty hinges. loose boards. nails come up. snag. tidy up. never know when company will drop in...

*F*ADING

ride home was filled with an excited silence. some reason. darker half of easter over. hum in the silence. something a bit deeper hanging in the air. hint of scent after car freshener sucked dry. pine. cherry. vanilla. new car smell. couldn't put my finger on it exactly. lovely hindsight. patience. i could feel the silence breaking long before mother said a word.

she was bubbly. flipping ecstatic really. chipper as she chirped, *i wonder if a certain giant rabbit left any goodies at home?* mood shifting. air lifting. long live the easter bunny! *guess we'll have to have a look see when we get home. how's that sound, son?* great dad! the easter bunny is our hop happy friend after all. moral bind released. doubt safely tucked away. i suffered through the remainder of the trip home. patience. focus. candy candy candy. time later to ponder abstractions. fact versus myth. horse versus unicorn. man versus messiah. did somebody say chocolate easter bunny? it all seemed so heavy & serious & daunting. i wanted so much to feel some sympathy, compassion, something for this great man & his great time. but there was one huge problem...

enormous hopping thumping silly happy bunny that delivered plastic eggs filled with candy & quarters to good little boys & girls all over the world. somehow the incredible tragedy that father/pastor/minister/reverend delivered earlier *easily* paled when held against grotesque wonderful monster rabbit. smiled from ear to phallic ear & brought sweet bliss to all who would search in grass & basket. oddly yet unevenly pulled between believing the bloody drama & taking the easy way out. accepting the fluffy-tailed myth instead at full furry face value. open freaking arms. give me your candy. buzz. your little yellow marshmallow chirping yummy birds. forget the blood. cross. rock. angels. ghosts like it's halloween. easter's for rabbits. trix are for kids. easy choice. unable to look back with regret. only humor. irony. myth for myth. not about which myth is more convincing. missing the point. which myth is more pleasant? easy choice. light smirk as i look back at choosing candy over christ. really quite simple. gargantuan pink rabbit won. christ lost. lost christ. you can never stuff enough candy & chocolate into a crown of thorns to make a child happy. cross or carrot? easy choice. i smiled. a child. for the moment content with my decision.

FLASH CRASH

flash of lightning. roar of thunder. suddenly awake. eyes wide. adjusting. in a moment. flick of a match. light clear. dark blur. sad wet alphabet animal parade. puddle splat. puddle splat. wired tired. afraid that the storm has stolen any chance of sleep. twisted comfort in the many branches of the trees outside my window. intricate chaotic shadow puppets on the 4 walls in my cluttered room. should have been scary. but not. focus. blink. patience. tap. blink. tap. flash. crash. open. blink. patience... sleep arrived eventually. suddenly. silently violently dragging me from awake to asleep in less than a blink. quick blink. pulling me away from my shadow puppet distractions. abducting me playfully. unwillingly into a world of... nothing. then something. something familiar? nothing. nothing familiar? something. nothing again because memory doesn't work in this place. but when i woke. next morning. pool of my own sweat. blood. everything came crashing flooding back.

ASLEEP

quick look around the room dizzy. swallowed by a spinning darkness. whispers fill my ringing ears. ringing bell of a head. better. suppose. my name repeated repeated repeated. chanted like some sick sacrificial prayer. wrong word. words wrong. 100 million mad priests. eyes gouged. scarred humming & chanting my name. unseen. thank god. small favors. favor small... i know they're there. (there there) *hang in there.* dental ceiling. strangely only see when i close my eyes. trapped in this dream. voluntarily by force. don't want to be a rat in this maze. (shiver) prodded shocked teased. remote control. rat pellets. forward left jump freeze. zap. manipulated like so much wood & string. suspended & finger'd to bounce & dance. bow & prance. nimble fingers much too high to see. nose growing. lies i've only told myself. how does he know? god of all dreams. busy man.

everything completely black now. eyes closed or open. not just your regular breed of darkness mind you. mysterious blend of purple & ink & blood & nothing-color. makes common black seem white. transparent. so dark. can only *feel* your eyes. so dark. so young. fear the unknown. that which i can't put my finger on. afraid of the unknown. tilt-a-whirl gloom. afraid of the dark. not in my room. my real room. but here. small amount of goose flesh still finds my hand whenever i switch a light off. freezing shaking suddenly warmth. ahead. realised too late that i had only arrived at the gates of this hell. step. another step. nudge. creak. freeze. this hell awaited & the doors began to open. slowly began to feel nothing at all. normalised. composed. breathing slower. not normal. normal? here? creak. distant rustling. faint but constant sound. murmur like a billion matches swaying. warmth again. creak...

THIS HELL

the doors to this hell are massive. they are not made of rock or steel or bone or wood as some would suspect. bizarre. but i could feel everything around me. senses sharp as talons. razor blades. sensed a light. pin light. barely dropping to floor. dust too small to float across this light. this not-quite-slight-beam. sensed the low murmur of lost souls. nonsensical flicking tongues. miles away. started sensing outlines of objects? slowly slowly slowly becoming clearer. more defined. a lamp? broken mirror? dusty red wagon? what the not-hell? & the boxes on the floor. oh my the boxes. old. dust. hay fever panic. sneeze. bless you. my attic? single hanging light bulb overhead. *way* overhead. miles away. pin light. no need to duck in this attic. my attic. objects grasping memories. notice. order. name. mother's broken mirror. hopeless alcoholic phase. little red wagon. i'd soar. soar down massive concrete hills. closed course. professional driver. many boxes. oh my the boxes. tiny faded clothes. report cards. decorations from holidays that infect our calendars. one box in particular. oddly spot lit from somewhere. nowhere. dead center floor. dull. motionless. glowing? just a cardboard box...

INTERLUDE

car horn? gun shot? dog bark? something sudden nearly woke. rolled over. brief disconnect. eyes rolling. flip book. hundreds thousands millions even. little plastic wind-up toys. made in china. made in japan. korea. indonesia. multicolored glistening plastic animals. gleaming jumpy bouncy flippy floppy things. need to keep them hopping or he cuts me. it cuts me. wind or cut. wound or wound. arm a bloody mess. pirate accordion. didn't do it to myself honest. wobbly weak arm. damaged dangly worthless snake. twist twist twist twist. keep em going. keep em going. some all 1 of them. wound tight. had nearly 100 going at once. all at once. awe. hypnotised. spaced out. moment to nap. whirr-flip. whirr-flip. whirr-flip. clang! clang! clang! clang! tiny plastic gear'd chaos. so loud quiet. clumsy random lullaby. blink. pink hoppy rabbit. brown nutty chittering squirrel. yellow chirp chirp chirping chick. that monkey. that monkey with the hat &or cymbals &or drum. serial killer grin. you know what monkey i'm talking about that monkey. close your eyes. space out. awake. asleep. whoosh. slash. it came from above. no warning. only sharp & slick. blurry creature. too quick. never saw it. less than a blink. another gash. so clean. doesn't even bleed... for another blink. gush. blood on glimmering rainbow plastic. whirr-flip. whirr-flip. oh my the blood. ache. colder. twist. twist. gosh. wind-up toys flickering. here not-here. millions. thousands. hundreds. one. bouncy blue blurry cat. evil grin. holding a box? tattered box? beep! beep! beep! beep! blink. back on my back in my attic. whirr-flip.

ONE BOX

one box. of normal attic box size. seemed to speak to me for some reason. actually speak. one box. taped tight. one label on the side. one word. scrawled rapidly with wet-black marker. EASTER. reaction briefly rushes back to my sleepy head. twitch. jerk. one word. EASTER. in my dream. slight motion from within. weary imagination. sensed small sound. coming from this box. single soft scratch. purring of... cats? rustle of fur on cardboard. slightly screaming. *let us out! let us out!* haunted box. purring & cooing. patient. caught in a box that couldn't possibly be holding the number of cats making that much noise. packed compact. all in a box label'd EASTER.

of course when i looked down there was a knife in my hand. looking back up at me. taunting me. pushing me. making me. *open me. trust me. that's what i'm here for.* box purpose. knife purpose. motive. reason for everything. nothing to reason. open the box. why not? only a dream after all. knife in hand. approached the box label'd EASTER. knife in hand... paused. purring continued. scratching continued. knife in hand i began to effortlessly slice through crusted masking tape on lid of box. mysterious contents buzzing bubbling pulsing. impatient now. forcing my hand forward. but then curiosity *did* kill the cat

OPEN FREE

lifted the first flap. lifted the next. two remaining that covered the hideous meowing & mewling. one dramatic ridiculous motion. expecting snake gag. joy buzzer to wake me from my disturbed slumber. dream breath. pause. nothing. purring stopped. head forward. scratching ceased. inch forward. silence but for my rapid beating heart. throbbing charlie brown head. sudden silence. freaked. heart mind racing because i expected everything but this silence. curled up invisible menace. bottom of box. silence didn't last. heart never slowed. thump thump thump...

COMING OF THE CATS

coming of the source of noise. didn't appear as slinking cats. but easter grass? plastic easter grass. meaningless. mindless. filler. tissue paper for easter baskets. blue/green/yellow plasti-grass. cling clung. magnetised plasti-grass. stick stuck to everything. static. same grass that showed up magically in other boxes. not-easter boxes. kitchen boxes. shoe boxes. epitome of fake false. easter bunny tacked to pastel cross. half smiling. eyes closed ears bent. dulling pink fur. rainbow crown of thorns. pricking. poking. *find the eggs kids. step right up! he's fine. just a tiny bit of blood. here's a tissue!*

the plasti-grass leaked out of the box label'd EASTER. spreading menace across the weathered wooden slats of the attic floor. plasti-grass tumbling over itself. seething & wrapping around. each strand. every strand. blue to green to yellow. ever so slightly into more defined forms. slowly. slowly. taking its time. substance from nothing. writhing. twisting. paws legs bodies necks heads... eyes. finally, amidst the mass of blue/green/yellow plasti-grass. mock cats. emerged 2 brilliant eyes & 2 brilliant eyes & 2 brilliant eyes... yellow clear. sunshine. blinding. eyes that pierced my young soul. as if i'd turned the knife that i still held in my hand. frozen. on the throbbing muscle in my chest. smiling all. completely mad plasti-grass cats circling blinking wildly multiplying multiplying multiplying. first one. only one. then ten. possibly ten. lost count. gave up. 1 horrid had become 1 million horde. wet bent shattered series of flimsy fun house mirrors. floating. precarious. overhead. hanging from 1 million strands of fishing wire. razor wire. cats. shards. mirrors. eyes. strands. focused on 1 thing—me.

purring & scratching & yeowling & rubbing against each other. generating power. heat. electricity that shook the bending liquid air. body frozen to these stiff as boards. not-attic swaying floor. planted there. painted there. upright. rigid. the cats were getting closer now. circling like grounded wingless vultures. purring. meowing. humming. began to fear this slow procession. progression. worrying *here*. dreading *there*. feeling *here* & *there*. attic & bed. afraid i'd never wake up from this nightmare. that i'd die here now there then. this nightmare. this hell.

these cats. rippled. advanced. missing frames. too many to look at. take in. advanced. paused. slowly found that my finger could move. my hand. my arm. prepared to defend myself with this shrinking knife. lot of good i imagine. fear. prepared for the worst. tiny knife in hand. i had no idea absolutely no idea. could never have been prepared for what happened next. knife or knot. cats frozen. dvd pause. still. waiting waiting waiting to make their move. press play. shit! less than a momentary flicker-twitch of agreement crossed the crowd. quick ripple over poisonous water. half-purr signal nod. mass move in my direction. poetic. perfect. 1 cat pouncing on 1 mouse. i barely squeaked once. squea—

many too many. hungry. plasti-grass cats engulfed me. swallowed me whole. hissing scratching lashing meowing smiling gnashing ripping glowing thrashing smiling licking flashing. i collapsed under the mass. limp & fetal. crash! closed my eyes. here. there. red white blue pain. betrayed. screaming so loud so quiet. mouth open so wide. this dream. this blood.

strings of cats. cats of strings. wrapped up in strands & strands & strands. forgotten rotten mummy. wrapped so tightly around thin arms. pressure. chest. threatening to crack it wide open. bony oyster. creaking & bowing under immense pressure. eyes closed so they can't get into my brain. can't get into my head. already there. poised to popping. odd cork gun sensation filling my soft neck melon. red. blood. brain. filled. water. balloon. squeezing becoming scratching. claws popping sharply into place. as one. a million. razor-edge. shards of glass. biting chipping this flesh. this paint. old. sun-dried house. rending tearing ripping shredding my skin into neat strips. prime strips. sharp butchers. pieces of me hung in the air for a brief moment. snapshot shudder. fell to the ground 1 after another. wet. splat. no longer a little boy. growing pile of red & pink. pieces of me. of meat. glistening wet gross. many-colored newspaper ribbons. slapping wooden floor. bloody. delicate. tasty. strips & straps & strands.

this attic. this trap i had fallen prey to. pray to. had become a blind butcher's messy shop. dollar thirty nine a pound. come & get it!

they had reached my neck my chin by then. drowning. head just above. my plankton & seaweed & kelp. don't scream, can't scream HELP! no lungs no throat no breath. gasping. choking. cats. gnawing & munching. breaking me down into smallest parts. eyes wide open. all that's left. focus. 60 watts. light. swinging cloth wire. tattered string. cat shadows blocking. changing the light. me. throwing light & shadow in every direction. disco ball rave. around me. my torn & bloody heap. just my eyes. on top. from below. vein tendon muscle muppet sticks. to the right. to the left. all together now. moving maniacally. tracking. trying to find. breaks in the patterns. loopholes just loopy holes. no trap door escape. bleak blue/green/yellow sky. pin point stars from a 60-watt bulb. so very far away. wet. eyes. cry.

cats lapped red milk. nuzzled & gnawed white chew-toy bones. began to purr as if they were finally satisfied. began to wander away from their kill. small scraps & snacks saved for later. tucked somewhere beneath within their plasti-grass not-fur not-skin. felt sick. felt numb. body paralysed in the waking world. post-shock. rigorous rigor mortis. think i was. believe i was truly dead in the waking world. for an extended moment. truly dead. unreal. real. world. blur.

as i lay dead or dying. eyes wide open atop muppet puppet sticks. all of the cats slowly abandoned what remained. my remains. retreated to a million corners in this small niche. this attic hell.

all of the cats save one. a peculiar little cat as i remember him. not blue. not green. dull yellow of old urine. stale butter. cigarette stain. much smaller than the gone cats. piece missing from my right his left ear. curious runt of a vast litter. but his face betrayed this rank. older than the rest of him could contain. his face was ancient. eyes wise. this peculiar old/young cat stared at me. curious. tilting his head this way & that. studying every strip & strand of my ripped body as if i were a laboratory specimen. dissected pig. for a time. him studying me studying him. little wise cat. wide eyes. sure i saw myself for a moment in those eyes. his eyes. twisted yellow'd reflection. flip. switch. he looked into my naked eyes with a playful familiarity. saw something in my eyes that i couldn't quite put my finger on. not that i had a finger to put. i held his he held my attention. for a time. nothing else existed. just brilliant/dull yellow cat under slightly swaying 60 watts. calmed me. comforted me. helped me to forget. earlier. penny for a thought yellow cat.

wish i could have taken a look beyond those eyes. tip of his tongue. just to know. *why?* yellow cat. *why?* but couldn't see a thing. not a single cat word or thought. would have said something. past tense mouth. so waited. until he got bored. snatched my eyes. later snack. just toying. but he didn't leave. didn't snatch. sat there frozen for a moment. pale yellow cat figurine. then he moved. mechanically. as if wound up & released. missing frames. slowly. stuttering. circling. purring thinking finally speaking? meowing & mewling, but i understood...

you don't know who you are do you child? couldn't possibly understand your place in this place. not a clue? even after all of this mess this pain?

i looked at him unable to answer. lack of vocal mechanism. he paused dramatically nevertheless. waiting for my reply. playing. toying. giddy.

you are very special. so special. brought us great joy. great joy in your coming to this place. finding this place. we've been waiting. stirring. open your eyes wider. wider still. look around. look familiar? familiar at all? this is your key, kitten. your key. it's been here all along. locked away inside a dusty cardboard box label'd EASTER. is that surprise i see in your eyes? come with me, kitten. join me. join us. gather your strands of sticky plasti-grass together. work yourself like clay into a more comfortable form. stretch your eyes. arch your back. bend backside high into the air. bones of hands through tips of fingers. scratch your way. tear your way out of your human shell. pull yourself together for christ's sake. concentrate. move. learn. wrap. grow. plastic. meow.

i focused on the bottom of my pile. slowly learned. one strand at a time. others fell in line. obedient flat & clever snakes. bending & stretching odd sinews across invisible framework. muscle. bone. arms & legs matched lengths. tail grew. all fours. tail above ass. oddly familiar. head pulled into sharp oval. top of impossibly long neck. ears sharpened. moved to top of twisting head. trained my eyes to spread & squint. slowly filled with yellow gel. attic turned canary. so sharp. knew in that moment what it was like to see through cat eyes.

welcome kitten! nicely done! not everybody pulls it together that quickly. i should know. ah. i remember when i changed. so very long ago. but i digress. slink my way if you would. follow me into your new home. your cardboard box label'd EASTER. your key. follow me. take your place in this place. among the others. king of cats. for a time. follow me.

i followed him. into that box. that darkness. took my place in this place. king of cats. squeezed in with the rest. all the rest. packed like peanuts. lid sealed slowly over our heads. new piece of sticky masking tape. we sat. waited. near silence. occasional twitch. sneeze. meow. letting this piece of quiet drip over my many strands. smiled a cat smile. blinked. napped. waited. wonderful quiet. napped here while sleeping there. nearly lost myself completely. *over* slept. forever.

gathered napping began to stir. move about nervously. i sat silent for a moment longer. compelled to join the agitation. me. not me. all twisted up. swelling. chaos cubed. could barely tell which strands of plasti-grass were mine. connected to my tossed & trampled head. almost didn't hear the click click clicking of approaching footsteps. cats calming calmer calm. catching timid steps. approaching stranger. ever closer to the box we inflated. inhale. exhale. cardboard flesh slightly rising slightly falling. nearly not alive. cats fallen deadly silence. excited electric pulse passes through the cats the cube. expanding. plastic fur on plastic back. bristles. tingles. tickles. as one. just one. not yet pause. still. waiting for trip for trigger. flip. switch.

tiny footsteps cease. edge of the box label'd EASTER. looked up when i could. thin light. me & millions of waiting hungry waiting hungry cats. hissing with delight as more light more light. new tape old. splitting dark. wider wider still. saw small sharp knife saw. 1 flap 2 flap 3 flap 4. peeled back explosive banana. brief glance nervous guest. could only make out slowly swaying shadow against spinning background. memories & trash. lid naked. shadow exposed. target.

cats paused. time. allow this shadow stranger a moment to sense. false. drop guard. drop knife. jaw hope onto wooden floor. barely noticed the blue/green/yellow plasti-grass seeping & leaking over the edges. of the cardboard box label'd EASTER. shadow stranger stumbled back. struck stopped stuck. frigid rigid. much like i had been. like i had been? so focused on me & us. never noticed. noticed now. hapless shadow was me. will be me. knew what was about to happen to this poor creature before it happened. it *happened* before.

my turn came. left the box reluctantly. clearer picture of our shadow stranger. corner of my cat eye. frightened little girl. all pigtails & freckles. ice tears. quivering pale lips. white as ghost. albino snow. alabaster. trembling as the snake sea raged forward toward her. foot bone connected to ankle bone to shin bone to knee to thigh. certain amount of pity for this poor girl creature. certain amount of pride? confused jealous hungry angry. empathetic pathetic. smack lick. confusion to jealousy to rage as a ripple ripped through the well-oiled plasti-grass machine. now!

POUNCE

she never knew what hit her. screamed silently as strands wrapped around her. claws embedded shredded. her tender skin. she screamed to wake the sleeping dead. her words like mine found no purchase no pity. no ear to listen hand to hold. no sudden wake from bloody slumber. i laughed long & loud. found the path to true madness. clarity. new claws found pale flesh. blood lust. impossible quick. ripping tearing biting bending. her tiny body. thin strips & straps. wet & slapping wooden floor.

poor thing. yet to recover from the pain & shock. yet to find meaning. yet to find not-shiny key. her key. here all along. her all along. hidden. chaotic moment all connected. cats connected. strips & straps of plasti-grass. intricate. blue/green/yellow wires. wired. connected. entire. machine.

we all dream each other's dreams. in these dreams we are immortal, repetitive, infinite, boring, powerful, scared.

WAKING

as we walked away from our meal. shadow stranger little girl. snacks & yummy morsels. succulent strands tucked. calm hum in my stomach. satisfied. full. small. finger. twitch. distant. living. sleeping. world. time to return to sleeping self. sweating & shaking. bed i left behind.

looked around this attic. this hell. this home. noticed fur fading. dripping. melting. candle. vapor. vanishing into cat noise. attic noise. dream noise. low. murmur. whisper. noise in my head.

waking. mind. body. convulse. tremor. spasm. stomach. throat. mouth. taste. vomit. puke.

AWAKE

slammed into world awake. fell out of bed. covered in wet vomit sweat piss. as i lay dying not breathing. wounds i could feel but couldn't find. checking myself. touching myself. not there half there all there. loud scream in head. mad laugh instead. clock cower. lamp limp. animal wallpaper shook & tore in places. many animals retreating. mad giggle titter snort. horses & otters & bugs & snakes. ran from my echoing cackle. cackling echo. ran from true madness. sweat cry wet. middle of floor of room of night. dashed away dashed away dashed away all... all but one. save one. just one. letter C. *C is for CAT.* yellow cat. never noticed on wall before. cat sat fixed. looking at me looking at him. curious both. he smiled then. pointy ear to pointy ear. let out a titter-chirp of his own. i looked at him smiled my own. pointy ear to pointy ear. winked a broad yellow eye at my wise yellow friend. he returned the wink & with a flip of his tail vanished into wall behind paper.

i looked down. balled fist of right hand. opened to find a small key. dull key. my key. just the right size to open up the back of my mind. turned this key my key in my hand. over & over & over. hid & tucked away within the various strands & strips squirming under pajamas. hidden to this day. *today.* pulled it out. turned it in my hand. over & over & over. eyes bright. smiling wild cat smile. what happens when this smile threatens to rip my face apart? titter tip. shrink blink wink. meow. pounce. vanish into wall behind...

maybe it *was* the wallpaper.

Taking Back Tom

Kirsty Carse

I SUPPOSE EDWARD FRIMSLEY was just trying to make a profit. A pub in a small village was never going to make a killing. No pun intended.

We'd gone there because we'd heard it was haunted by some girl who committed suicide. Despite the fact that my brother Tom and I were only seventeen, and all four of us were dressed like the scrimping students we were, Ed Frimsley greeted us like we were his best customers. We bought a round and sat at a table in the corner, overlooking the River Ouse.

"Can you hear music?" Becky asked me after a few minutes.

"Nope." I picked up my pint.

"Oh Jesus, please don't let it be Country and Western classics." Billy leaned back in his chair and made his eyes wide with panic so that Tom and I laughed.

"It's very quiet... but can't you hear it?" Becky waved her hand at us to shut up and swung herself round in her chair to face the bar.

"No," Tom said.

"Not a thing," Billy said, after a moment.

"What does it sound like?" I asked.

"Like... a woman... humming or singing to music," Becky said. "It's too faint to tell what sort of music. Something old-fashioned though.".

"Like Elvis?" Billy said.

"No dill-hole, more old-fashioned than that." Becky swiveled round to face us. "Do you think it's something to do with the girl?"

I jumped as the voice of Ed Frimsley suddenly came from behind me.

"You kids interested in the ghost?" he asked.

Even Billy and Tom, who sat opposite and would have seen him approach, looked startled when Ed spoke. He must have been loitering, listening to our conversation. I guess there wasn't a lot for him to do behind the bar. Apart from us, there were only a couple of sleepy old men for customers.

Of course we were interested in the ghost. My brother Tom and I had been interested in them since we went camping with the Scouts and thought we saw a headless hunter in the woods. More recently we'd gotten my girlfriend Becky into it, as well as our friend Billy, which was handy since he was the only one with a car. We'd been all over the region visiting sites that were reputed to be haunted, and we'd seen nothing. That hadn't deterred us.

The ghost that Ed Frimsley told us haunted his pub was a seventeen-year-old girl called Juliet Tewslie. She'd lived in the village sometime around 1078 and had fallen in love with one of the local woodcutters, a lad called Tom Zoul. Tom was more interested in drinking ale with his mates than paying much attention to Juliet and, one day when she followed him into the woods to give him some flowers she'd picked, he told her to get lost. He was probably just trying to save face in front of the other woodcutters, and might have made up with her later, but Juliet took it deeply to heart. She hanged herself at the edge of the woods, beside the river, that afternoon. She was cut down and buried where she fell. Tom was so distressed that he laid a slab of granite on her grave to mark the site of the tragedy.

"And that slab remains intact, in memory of Juliet," Ed finished. He gestured towards the floor of the bar. We all craned to look. There, at the corner of the bar, the patterned carpet was interrupted by a rectangular slab of smooth granite. "This pub has stood here since the eleven-hundreds but no one has ever disturbed that grave."

"Has anyone ever seen Juliet's ghost?" asked Becky.

Ed rubbed his fingers over the stubble on his chin. "Sure. I've seen her myself. She comes back every March the seventeenth—the anniversary of her death."

"The seventeenth?" echoed Billy. "That's next week! How's that for timing?"

"Would it be alright if we came back here then to see if we could see her?" Tom asked.

"It's just that we're interested in the paranormal and we've been visiting local sites that are meant to be haunted," I said.

"Oh, you'd be welcome." Ed turned to go back to the bar. "In fact, she draws quite a crowd of interested locals."

"And does she always show up?" asked Billy. "I mean, every year?"

"Well, I can't promise, but you never know," Ed replied.

Ed was more certain than he let on. He'd seen her often enough, and not just on March the seventeenth, either. Juliet Tewslie had made Ed's life a misery since he took on the pub. He'd wondered why the brewery had offered him such a generous deal. Even when he heard the story, he didn't think much of it. At the most, it was a colourful local tale that might draw in a few extra customers. No harm in that.

When he first caught the faint strains of mournful singing in the bar, he dismissed it. Maybe he'd left the radio on upstairs, or it was someone outside. But it kept happening, and it was louder when he stood over the grave. It gave him the creeps when he was clearing up alone at closing time. He started putting the radio on until he was finished and ready to lock up.

The first time he'd seen her he'd nearly messed his pants. He'd got up in the night, having been asleep a couple of hours, and opened his bedroom door with the intention of going to the bathroom. He hadn't put the lights on and wondered why he saw a faint glow under the bedroom door as he reached for the handle. It was only a sleepy half-thought though, so it gave him no real forewarning of what he was about to confront. He opened the door and saw, at the top of the stairs, a teenage girl in a haze of pale blue light.

She was holding and arranging a bunch of flowers. Her face was both beautiful and ghastly. Fine features and flawless skin, framed by wild brown twists of hair that reached her waist, overshadowed by the purple-black necklace of bruises livid on her swollen neck. The hall was filled with the stench of damp and rot. If Ed had dared to move from the doorway, he would have had a look to check that the Ouse hadn't burst its banks and flooded downstairs.

The ghost looked up and locked her gaze onto his. Her dewy eyes drew him in. She held the flowers out to him, staring. When he didn't move to take them, she held them out further, at arm's length, and shook them impatiently. They emitted an enchanting perfume; it gave a welcome mask to the overpowering stink of festering weeds. Ed was tempted to take them, until he remembered what he was looking at. This was Juliet Tewslie, a girl who'd been dead for a thousand years.

He stumbled back into his bedroom and slammed the door. There he stayed, awake and with the lights on, until daylight. He emptied his bladder into a glass on the nightstand. There was no way he was leaving that room. He even contemplated resigning as soon as he found the courage to go downstairs and use the telephone. He rehearsed different ways he would put it to the brewery—the nearer to dawn, the less these hinted at any notion of a ghost. By the time the sun was up, the credibility of the whole incident seemed to dissipate, especially when he opened his bedroom door with a racing heart to find nothing remarkable there.

She came almost every night. In time he learned not to be terrified. If he got up in the early hours he would see her occupying that same space in the hall. Some nights he looked from his bedroom window, wakened by the sound of weeping, and saw her wandering the muddy bank, alternately gazing from the water to the branches of the tree, as though torn between methods of ending her life. Other times he would look out and see flowers drifting downstream, but no sign of her. One night he was awakened by the wind rattling the window pane and jumped from his bed to look. Juliet's rag doll body was hanging from the tree, swinging violently in the storm. When Ed looked into the distance at the gardens of the houses across the bridge, he saw that they reposed in perfect calm.

Perhaps if had just been the awful sightings he could have become used to them and learned not to let them affect him. It was when she began speaking to him that Ed's life became unbearable. She began appearing downstairs in the pub, usually when he was locking up, but she also turned up in the gloomy cellar at all hours. The things she said were always the same. Even the singing was always in the same sad key.

When he wouldn't take the flowers the first few times, she began asking him where Tom was. Ed wasn't sure how to reason with a ghost, so he tried being direct.

"Tom's dead, and so are you," he would say. "You shouldn't still be here." He tried to make his voice firm without sounding unkind. Then he would leave the room.

But she kept coming back. The next time he went to change a barrel she would still be there, asking for Tom. He'd get out of the shower after a long shift and she'd be there when he drew back the screen to grope for his towel. Always asking for Tom.

He couldn't concentrate on the business with a ghost whispering in his ear at every turn. He was sure she was doing something to his mind—not letting him get on with his life until he helped her sort hers out. It didn't matter how many times he told her—she didn't seem to realise she was dead. And until she did, Ed was never going to have any kind of peace in his life.

When we arrived at the pub on the seventeenth, we hoped that we might finally see a ghost. We were cynical enough to have expounded the theory that bored landlord Ed Frimsley claimed to any number of punters that the anniversary of the girl's death just happened to be next week, but not to guess that we were the umpteenth group made up of mainly young men that he'd tried to encourage. He even gave us a free round when we walked in, disappointed to find that the 'interested locals' this March the seventeenth were the same old men we'd seen before.

Long after the barflies had hobbled home, we were still buying drinks and talking with fervency about the ghost. We'd chosen the table nearest the grave and all four of us kept glancing at it, although to be honest I'm sure none of us expected to see her float up from beneath.

Drinking-up time passed and we offered to leave, crestfallen we spent the evening without a sighting. But Ed insisted we stay longer and brought a bottle of whiskey and five glasses over. He turned the lights down, explaining that it was more to appease the local bobbies than anything to do with the ghost. It spooked the atmosphere up several notches nonetheless.

Billy didn't drink the whiskey because he was driving us home. He'd been on lemonade all night. Which was useful later because, although I had limited my drinking so my judgment wouldn't be affected if we did see anything, I might have thought I'd imagined it if Billy's story hadn't matched mine exactly.

We stopped talking when the singing started. Becky grabbed my arm. From the corner of my eye, I saw Billy and my brother staring at the grave, where we now saw the ghost enrobed in blue light, carrying her flowers. Only Ed sat calmly, his chest rising and falling in small sighs of weary hope.

"Holy shit," Billy said.

I heard my own breath heaving in and out, and my heart throbbed against Becky's head as she moved closer. I took her in my arms so that we were huddled together on one chair. I was glad to have someone to hang onto.

The ghost of Juliet Tewslie, with her horrific rope burns and smell of the sewers, began moving towards Billy. I saw him shrink back in his seat as she held her bouquet out. She seemed to be looking straight into him. Then, with a snap of her inflamed neck, she switched her wistful eyes to me. Only for a second. Becky buried her face in my chest, clinging so hard that I would later find bruises in the shape of fingers on my back.

"Where's Tom?" she asked.

My brother, his arm trembling, raised his hand. Like a primary school kid, I thought, and almost laughed.

"I'm Tom," he said.

"Tom," the ghost said. She looked at my brother just like she had looked at Billy and me but this time, when she held out the flowers, he got up. Slowly, as though he was taking his first steps after being paralysed for years, he walked toward her and accepted the offering. That was the moment when Billy and I both thought we should have done something. Billy had been just about to get up and pull Tom back. I had been about to prize myself from Becky's grip and do the same.

We were too late.

Billy kicked his chair back, and right as I took my eyes off the scene for a second to untangle myself, they both vanished. The ghost, Tom, the flowers, the music, the smell. It was just us, Ed Frimsley, and one empty chair. I stared at Ed. He looked ten years younger and a smile lit up his face. He toasted the air and downed his drink.

Untitled

Anonymous

YOU HEAR SCREAMS, sometimes. In the night, in my neighbourhood. A stabbing, or a drunk girl having fun, it's hard to know. Or maybe that's just what I tell myself.

You hear screams, sometimes.

I don't like to go outside around here. I'm afraid to look people in the eye. Afraid to see what they're capable of. Afraid of catching their insanity.

There was a preacher here the other day. Standing on a crate and shouting about our souls. Everyone ignored him. I watched from across the street, hiding behind a newspaper. I was terrified of being caught, but nobody saw me. Nobody looks up around here.

You hear screams sometimes.

There was a preacher here last week.

My clothes have started to smell lately. I can't get it off. I scrub them, it always comes back.

There was a preacher here the other day. Standing on a crate and shouting about our souls. Everyone ignored him. I watched from across the street, hiding behind a newspaper. I was terrified of being caught, but nobody saw me. Nobody looks up around here.

I saw a dead pigeon on the road last week. A flattened bloody mess. I've given up eating meat. I don't feel well. It's hard to find vegetables around here. What you get isn't fresh. I eat mostly rice, now.

I was hit by a car the other day. I was walking in a daze, and I'd been staring up at the sun. I turned at the sound, but I couldn't see it coming. It braked and hit me in the knee, knocking me down. I limped home. The driver was shouting at me, but I couldn't hear the words.

words like worms wriggling into my ears

There was a preacher here the other day. Eventually the police came, and dragged him away. He struggled, so one of them beat him over the head with his truncheon. He bled onto the pavement as they dragged him to the van. No one saw it. Nobody looks up around here.

I'm getting these headaches now. Like steel nails being drilled into my skull. The first time I was out on the street. I had to stumble home. I bumped into a man holding a briefcase and an umbrella. So strange to feel another human being. He didn't seem to notice.

The 838

Santi Elijah Holley

NO ONE WILL TELL ME how long I've been here. They tell me days and years and minutes, but it doesn't mean anything. I feel as if they are counting down the time rather than adding it up. I don't have a clock in my room, so I suppose time doesn't exist, at least not in here. As I watch letters form into words form into sentences I wonder who is pushing the keys and how time can be represented with words. I don't know how many days have passed since I've been here. Perhaps it's only been a few hours. Perhaps my whole life.

He asked me about The 838. I said I didn't understand. He said I knew everything about The 838. I said I didn't know what he was talking about. He said no one does.

Dr. Fairweather breathed heavily when he spoke, much to my displeasure, because he had a severe problem with bad breath. While I was in his office he picked up papers and set them back down, while his hot, repugnant breath heated my face.

"Do you know why you're here?" he asked.

I told him, "The same reason you are."

There are three main characters in this story: Dr. Robert E. Fairweather, just introduced, my mother, whom I shall refer to as "my mother," and myself. Others will make cameos and props will be used, but I will serve as narrator and will be making most of the anecdotes and insights. In my story I may habitually skip around in time like a child playing hopscotch on the long, uneven sidewalk of life, and for this the reader must forgive me. I have much on my mind and I'm not certain of the precise order that these events took place. I can only document my memories as they come to me, for fear that they will escape if I attempt to arrange them in chronological order.

"Why are you wincing?" Dr. Fairweather asked me. His thin blond hair curled around his head like an old crown—stripped of its former glory and sheen and authority—and his cheeks were pale, sorry representations of what they could be, given a little more exercising and a few less cigarettes.

"Your breath is killing me," I replied.

"Is my breath that offensive to you?"

"I'm not offended, I'm concerned."

"Concerned?"

"This room that we're sitting in doesn't have any windows, is poorly ventilated, and I'm concerned that the carbon dioxide coming out of your lungs—combined with whatever else seems to have crawled into your mouth and died—will asphyxiate us if you continue breathing as heavily as you are. Perhaps you should get a plant."

It was some kind of subdivision, I think. It must've been, because I can remember all the houses looking similarly: stacked on top and next to each other. I suppose there would be some sort of plastic playground for the kids, a swimming pool, and a commons area for barbecues and socials. The lawns were always mowed and I remember the scent of freshly cut grass lingering eternally in the dew-tipped air. Someone—the doctor, perhaps— could insist I grew up on a tobacco farm in Mississippi, however, and I'd probably start to recite grand, sweeping stories about the "old country," while my eyes filled with nostalgic tears. That's the problem with my memory: it seems to be influenced more by what people tell me than by my own recollections. All I know for certain is that whatever happened before has led me to where I am now, and if that's the case, perhaps I'd rather not remember.

Once, while walking along a wooded trail near my grade school, I came across a pond covered with small, spider-like insects. These things—water striders we call them—glide effortlessly and lightly atop the water, skim the surface feeding on smaller insects, and their lives are utterly and embarrassingly meaningless. In fact I couldn't help but laugh at them swimming around, back and forth incessantly, sometimes bumping into each other and gliding away. If one could only tell them how pointless their lives were, how not one of these things will be remembered when it dies, and their whole species will be forgotten with extinction. The world is indifferent to their existence, yet they slide across the same pond, honestly believing in what they are doing, and continuing to do so until they are washed away and eaten. I was so embarrassed for them. It was so utterly absurd and terribly insignificant. I pointed at them with my knobby forefinger and laughed a good, healthy laugh. I then became hungry, so I quickly ran home and made myself a sandwich. I believe it was peanut butter.

I told Dr. Fairweather my name, but he already knew. It seemed like the right thing to do at the time. He introduced himself, and I felt obligated to do the same, though my name is irrelevant. His uniform was standard-issue, heavily soiled, and his eyes lacked the particular fire that people look for in their specialists and superiors. I don't know what he had on his various pieces of paper, which he casually shuffled through, but I assumed whatever I told him was beside the point. All he really wanted to know about was The 838.

Earlier, when I said there were three main characters, I was mistaken. I'd forgotten about Susie.

I asked Dr. Fairweather how he planned on curing me, and he replied that we should rely on modern science. Scientists have been dealing with my illness for years and know precisely how to bring me back to normal health, he explained.

"Scientists are in the business of disproving themselves," I told him. "Science is as temperamental as health, but less consistent."

He bent his nicotine lips into an inverted arc and coughed. One should never question a doctor's credentials. They are only too proud to show you their degrees and awards. When Dr. Fairweather presented his various papers and ribbons, I shrugged.

"These don't mean anything to me," I said.

"Why's that?"

"All they are to me are random papers with signatures on them. They're supposed to prove your intelligence? I can only judge how intelligent you are by my own understanding."

"Just what are you trying to imply?" he asked.

"I'm saying that you are only as intelligent as I am. And frankly, Sir, I'm no doctor."

Doctors should've been run out of every town or burned at the stake years ago. They seem to disregard all evolutionary and creationist decrees. Women were accused of witchcraft and massacred. Pagans were accused of Satanism and slaughtered. All across the world, people have been accused of blasphemy, treachery, heathenism, and atheism, and they were dealt with accordingly. How have doctors—who hold all disdain for not only God's Will, but also for survival of the fittest and evolutionary adaptability—been spared? Not only have their lives been spared, but they have also created the most lucrative profession out of their blasphemy.

My mother once told me a story about bees. I had been stung and came home crying about "mean ol' bees," and "why'd it hurt me?" and "why do they even exist at all?" My mother offered a reasonable explanation:

"It's in their nature," she told me.

"Their nature is to hurt me?"

"Do you like flowers?"

"Yes."

"Do you like honey?"

"Yeah. Why?"

"Without bees we wouldn't have so many flowers and we wouldn't have any honey."

"But why do they have to sting?"

"Because they need to protect themselves against people doing harm to them, otherwise they couldn't do their job."

I wiped my nose with my sleeve and coughed up a few more tears.

"I wasn't going to hurt it."

"Bees don't know who's going to harm them and who isn't, and they don't know that by flying from flower to flower they are distributing pollen to grow more flowers. It's their role in this world, and they cannot do anything else but fulfill that role, whether they know it or not."

"But how come it stung me?"

"Like I said, it's in their nature."

Senator Penn campaigned for President and my mother was his most enthusiastic supporter. He promised an end to the war, stronger environmental policies, and more tax relief to small businesses and single-parent homes. His opponent, President Steadman, promised the same. I asked her why she felt Penn was the better candidate.

"If Penn wins, what will you do?" she asked me.

"I don't know," I cautiously replied. "Be glad?"

"And if he loses, will you be disappointed?"

"I suppose so."

"That's why he's the better candidate."

"But what about the issues?" I pressed.

"What issues? Their issues are only mentioned to bring about either morose or cheerful sentiments in us. Whichever one repeats what we already feel, that's whom we give our vote to. The issues are merely decoys."

"What about the good of the country?"

"The American people deserve the president they vote for."

In my room I have a chair, a fluorescent light, a typewriter, a plain, wooden desk, and a stack of blank paper. The chair, I presume, is for sitting, lounging, and reclining—all of which I do comfortably. The fluorescent light stays constantly illuminated, which is disconcerting. It burns and hums with persistence. I'm apparently to stay in here until I use every one of these sheets to reveal all I know. I don't, however, know any more than they do. I told Dr. Fairweather this and he said "exactly." He reminds me a little of my mother.

When Senator Penn lost the election, I was dismayed. I was further appalled upon learning my mother had voted for his opponent.

"How could you?" I begged in disbelief. "I thought you supported Penn."

"I did. Absolutely. I had a great time working on the campaign, and I am proud that I took part in influencing many people to vote for Senator Penn. In fact, even while marching to the polling place, I knew without a doubt that I would cast my vote for him, but when I held the pencil in my hand, and I looked down at the selections given to me, I realized I still had the power to change my decision. Nothing is concrete, and the greatest asset is the power to change your decisions and never believe what you think you know about yourself. I voted for Steadman because I could, and that power is more important than an insignificant decision like voting."

"But mom, Steadman is a bad president. You know that."

"I know what? That he is evil and Penn is good? Do you still really believe that nonsense? Tell me, is good the absence of evil or is evil the absence of good? Once you figure that out, you'll never believe another politician again."

What better way to keep your secret than to announce it to the whole goddamned world? Conspiracy theorists are a secret society's best friend. It's been said that the best trick the devil ever played was convincing the world he doesn't exist. Perhaps he accomplishes that by telling everyone he does.

I've recently had this fantasy of being Jesus Christ. I dream not so much of the wandering and preaching and healing and eating sand, but of the crucifixion. The mad crowds and the driving of stakes into my hands and feet. I close my eyes and imagine myself being spit at by the very people I love and torn apart by the claws of souls turned to madness. I then hang high on my cross and look down at the poor, misguided creatures, and I smile, knowing that the time will soon come when they must all hang from their own crosses. I asked Dr. Fairweather if he would call this "Jesus envy."

While on the plastic playground in the plastic subdivision enclosed by the Scarlett Nature Area, I'd noticed a dead deer fallen in the underbrush of the surrounding trees. At that age I had never thought about death before. I had heard about it from various folktales and stories I'd been read, but never had the opportunity or incentive to think about the reality of death. I walked to the animal, reached out, and touched her face. She was warm and expressionless. I named her Susie.

Ever since human beings have been on Earth, we have been predicting its end. With every advance in technology, political shift, or lifestyle change, we get a surplus of lunatics claiming these actions to be our undoing. The world should have ended by now, a thousand times over, but it hasn't, and that's what has gotten people so scared.

Dr. Fairweather's urgency in discovering The 838 was becoming preposterous. He claimed The 838 would be responsible for bringing about the end of the world, and he demanded to know how and when it would happen. I told him to look in his garbage can if he was so concerned about the world's demise.

"I assure you, Doctor, if I knew anything about The 838, I would be more than happy to tell you, if merely to end this discussion, which has nothing to do with me, and get on with my illness."

"What if I told you your illness has everything to do with The 838?"

"Why is Susie dead?" I asked my mother.

"It's the same reason you got stung by that bee," she replied.

"Because it's in her nature?"

"In a way, yes. We have a deer problem. The deer are fine, and they have been for years, until somebody found a particular flower in the Scarlett Nature Area called the Largeflower Bellwort. It's a relatively pretty flower, nothing too special about it, but Susie and her friends have acquired a taste for these flowers, and they are threatening to eat up all the Bellworts in the area."

I cocked my head to the side and my look must have shown her that I wasn't following, as usual. Nevertheless, she continued.

"Some folks got together and decided that in order to save the Bellwort we would have to moderate the growing deer population. Deer poison was spread out in the woods, and now, with fewer deer, the Bellwort has more chance of survival."

"I don't get it," I said. "So, why are people killing deer?"

"It's in their nature."

I asked Doctor Fairweather how The 838 was supposed to bring about the end of the world, and he replied, "That's what you're supposed to be telling us."

"The world is only as large as our peripheral vision," I said. "And everything else you think about the world is make-believe or gossip. Close your eyes."

"Why?"

"Just close your eyes." He pressed his blue eyelids together and shrugged.

"There." I said. "The world has disappeared. You cannot see it, and therefore it's only a memory. Even when your eyes are open, everything you think is in front of you is only light being transmitted to your brain and interpreted as objects and colors. Even the things you touch are sensations. You want to know about the end of the world? The world doesn't exist without you."

I honestly doubt Doctor Fairweather will ever be aware of his role in The 838. I wonder if any of us will.

"Why do you think your mother brought you here?" he had the nerve to ask me.

"I assume because I'm sick. I don't know. That's what you're supposed to find out."

"I'm supposed to tell you why you're here?" He stumped me. He then said, "What can you tell me about Susie?"

"How do you know about Susie? Susie isn't anything. Just a dead deer in the woods. There were dozens more like her. Who cares? She was a nuisance and a threat to the survival of the Largeflower Bellwort so we poisoned her."

"The whatflower? I've never heard of that flower."

"Neither had I. In fact, I don't think I could point one out to you now if I saw one. But that's not important. We saved it temporarily from extinction so we could look at it a few more years if we ever felt like it. But that's also not important."

"Well, what is important?"

"The denial that life is death. Every species eventually becomes extinct, and in its place a new one thrives. Our species, in particular, has become quite amusing."

"Is that so? May I ask why we are so funny?"

"With every new problem that we fix, another one is created. What propagates our species—what we do to ensure and promote the survival of our species—may be securing our own demise. Who will spread out the poison when they discover all the Bellworts that *we* are destroying?"

Dr. Fairweather guided me to this room and shut the door without as much as a cough.

Am I anything more than an empty vessel filled by my immediate surroundings? Does Free Will exist when who I am is determined by circumstance? Nothing I do is an independent decision, contrary to what my mother suggests. All decisions and choices are only reactions to memories of the past. Without our memories we are left unarmed. Perhaps our memories aren't so useless, after all. My mother said we have the power to change our decisions. I'd like to see her try.

Eventually this light has to burn out. I wonder if I will then be relieved of my duty.

After staring at blank sheets of paper for some vague amount of time, I observed the door in my room closely. It was colorless, like the rest of the room, and it held a modern doorknob: spherical and polished. I noticed the doorknob didn't have any indication of keyholes, latches, or locks.

"You have to surprise yourself sometimes," my mother told me after the election. "You have to challenge your intuitions in order to stay ahead."

"Ahead of what?"

I walked to the door and put my hand on the smooth, silver doorknob. I rotated it cautiously to the right and edged it forward. The door opened without much effort. I continued opening the door slowly until it was open just a few inches. I held it there without moving. I closed my eyes and the world disappeared, but I could still feel my room behind me—with my chair and my typewriter and my stack of unused paper. At that instant I closed the door and walked back to the center of the room. I had a seat in my chair, rolled the first sheet of paper into my typewriter on my desk, and thought to my self: I will write everything I know about The 838. It is my duty here. It is my responsibility.

God on Television

Carlton Mellick III

CHANNEL ONE

"LAST NIGHT I HAD SEX with my goldfish. Well, I didn't do it in on purpose. I really didn't want to fornicate with the little slimy creature, but she gave me no choice. In fact, the goldfish didn't even ask for consent, jumping up on top of me and screwing me right against the tile floor. I guess it was a rape or molestation. I didn't know what to do. I was just lying there with a squishy look on my face, the cold slimy creature holding me down, slipping her breasts all over me. I didn't know how it could breathe out of the water, gills gasping and fish lips opening for air, as it wiggled on top of me. It was so cold inside, but nice and smooth . . . I guess it wasn't an unpleasurable experience, but ever since then I just can't seem to get reality straight. I can't even look my goldfish in the eyes anymore."

My mind twitters and I forget what I'm talking about. I don't remember where I am. What's going on?

"Mr. Edson?" asks a voice in my ear, making me jump from my seat.

Oh yeah, I must be talking on the phone to somebody.

"Who is this?" I ask the voice.

"It's Saul, from the Porchlight Project," says the voice.

My face continues confused.

"The person you've been speaking to for the past twenty minutes. You keep changing the subject, but I think you were beginning to tell me that you had some food and clothes to donate to our cause."

A clicking noise in my head, "Oh yes, I remember now!"

Long pause.

"Well?" asks the voice.

"Well what?" I ask the voice.

"Do you have anything to donate?"

"Oh yes, I have a ton of that stuff. It's ridiculous. I was just going to throw a bunch of it out before you called."

"Great, just leave the items in a box outside and I'll send someone to pick it up tomorrow morning."

"Oh, never mind," I tell the voice on the phone.

"Never mind?"

"Well, I don't want some strange person coming to my door."

"Strange?"

"I thought you were going to come," I tell the phone. "I don't trust that other guy with the rusty pickup truck."

"It's a woman in a minivan, not a guy in a pickup truck."

"Even worse. I don't trust those women things."

"Well, you're on my way home. Maybe I can come by after work. Is 5:00 okay?"

An image of my goldfish flashes across my mind. "I can't believe she slicked her fin into my butthole!"

"Okay, make sure the food is in a box outside and ready to go," says the voice in the phone.

I continue, "And it even cried out when I came inside of it. I think we climaxed at the same time . . ."

CHANNEL *TWO*

There is a knocking sound annoying my ear.

It happens in short bursts twice a minute for five minutes.

It's so annoying.

"Annoying, annoying!" I scream at the knocking sound in the air.

"Mr. Edson," says a voice from behind the front door.

The door opens all by itself and then appears a short young balding man.

"Fucking, who are you?" I shriek at the man.

"Saul," he says. "We spoke on the phone just a couple hours ago. I came to get your donation."

"I didn't donate anything," I tell the short man.

"Per our conversation earlier today it seemed clear to me... "

He is cut off by a crackling sound. It comes from the kitchen.

"Oh no, not again," I say to the kitchen.

"What is it?" the man asks.

Saul doesn't look like the most intelligent creature in the world, scratching his head like a not-very-smart thing.

My hermit crab comes hammering towards us from the kitchen. It is now as large as a person for some reason, squatting by the sliced-sausage table.

"What is that?" Saul asks.

"My pet hermit crab," I say. "I call him Hammerskins."

"It's gigantic," Saul says, stepping back to the door.

The hermit crab shuffles its twisty black and red legs slowly across the carpeting. Its eyes curling, glaring at the young man.

The man screeches, turns away to run as the crab scurries its eyes up and down his body.

"Don't run," I tell him. "Hermit crabs don't like you when you run."

But Saul is already running out of my front door and before I can tell him to stop the hermit crab shuffles after him with violent pinchers.

CHANNEL THREE

Hammerskins returns, dragging the bloody corpse of the donation man as if a bone was retrieved.

The crab gnaws on the man's leg, ripping open the meat like a mutant dog.

"You are not a doggy," I tell Hammerskins, and the crab becomes sad.

The hermit crab claws strips of meat from the man's back and stuffs them underneath its shell. Not eating the flesh, just hiding it up inside of its house.

Gripping the young man between its claws and spidery legs, the crab slowly disassembles the man's head. Crumbles of bone and blood ruin the nice sea-green carpeting. An eyeball pops out into the foyer and Hammerskins jerks a limb at it, snatching it up into its shell. The skull splits open and Hammerskins removes the brain.

It places the thinking organ onto its face as if to eat it, but the nerves dangling from the brain start squirming. Like wiry fingers. They hook into the crab's head, digging inside, molding onto it until the brain is a working organ on the pet hermit crab.

CHANNEL FOUR

"I am terrified of God," says the hermit crab in a shaky tone, the donation man's voice.

I cock my head at the hermit crab.

"I don't want to die," says the hermit crab/donation man. "I'm far too scared to see God."

"Are you an evil person?" I ask.

"No, I am too scared of what will happen to me if I do anything wrong."

I sit myself on the couch in front of the television.

"I help unfortunate people the best I can," says the hermit crab. "For years, all I wanted to do was help people. If I finish college, I plan to join the Peace Corps. But for now I work with churches and nonprofit organizations. It is important not to be self-centered."

The hermit crab spiders up onto the couch, claws in its lap, sinking into its shell.

"What are you doing?" I ask Hammerskins.

"I want to watch television."

"That television isn't for watching," I tell the hermit crab. "Go watch your own television."

"I'm a hermit crab now," says the hermit crab.

CHANNEL FIVE

I am asleep.

No, I'm awake now.

The goldfish is on top of me again, rubbing my penis with her slime-skin, trying to make me hard.

She is more woman-shaped this time, with arms and legs. They are still fins, but now much more limb-like. And the head is more like a woman's head, slender neck. She is still cold and wet, gummy scales, fish eyes, fish lips. But now she has a long white tongue gooing out of her mouth and creeping up my face.

Gills pulsing slowly on her neck as her wet kisses wrinkle my chest skin.

We make love three times.

Lying there, glaring into me with her big fish eyes, slicking back her scales.

"Love you," I tell the goldfish for some reason.

And she kisses me all over with her fishy lips.

CHANNEL SIX

She doesn't go back in her bowl this time.

We are sitting on the couch, watching television with the giant hermit crab who had not left his seat since last night.

"Television is not good," says the hermit crab/donation man.

"I hate television," I tell them. "I never watch it. I don't know why I have it at all."

The fish girl swallows at the air.

"I usually love television," says the hermit crab, "but today TV is very boring. God is on every channel."

I look to the television to see a portly southern-styled man with brown-dyed hair and a white beard.

"Who is that?" I ask.

"God," says the hermit crab. "I already told you."

"What's he doing on TV?" I ask. "What's he saying?"

"I don't know, I put Him on mute."

"TV is even worse on mute," I say. "It captures your attention but you don't know what's going on."

"Well, I don't want to unmute it. I can't handle hearing God's voice."

We continue to stare at the screen. The slimy fish woman rests her head on my shoulder, clicky fluids flowing inside of her.

Wondering if I can read lips, "What do you think God is saying?"

"He's probably fed up with our disobedience," says the hermit crab. "He probably wants to create hell on Earth."

"Why would he do that?" I ask.

"I think He's ashamed of our imperfections," he replies.

CHANNEL SEVEN

There's nobody outside anymore. Not sure what happened. All the buildings disappeared. My home is still here though. Or perhaps my house has been transported to nature?

"I don't like this," says the hermit crab. "God has more power in nature than in the city. Everything natural comes from God, everything unnatural comes from the devil."

"Is God more dangerous than the devil?" I ask the hermit crab.

He says, "God doesn't like us because we build too much. We make unnatural things and live in unnatural environments. God wanted us to stay like the apes."

The landscape is a forest painting. Sandy purple emotions from behind the deep green trees.

Twilight loneliness.

CHANNEL EIGHT

This morning I am growing grass instead of a beard. It is that itchy kind. The pubic hair of grass.

I glide a razor across my face. It smells like a freshly cut lawn now. The hair on my head is still real hair. And my eyebrows are normal. But all the new stuff is vegetation.

I wonder if God has a beard of grass . . .

I wonder if he has tiny fairy-like angels that mow it for him when it gets shaggy.

The fish girl is lying in the tub next to me. Fish face bug-eyed at me. Her lower body is now that of a human's, with a slight pattern of scales that look more like tattoos. But the texture of her skin is a woman's.

CHANNEL NINE

Later today, outside:

I can't go to the supermarket to buy food because supermarkets no longer exist.

"We're back in nature," says the hermit crab. "We are hunters and gatherers again."

"Who is the hunter and who is the gatherer?"

"I am a bit of a hunter."

"Crabs are scavengers."

"Fine then, I'll be a gatherer."

"I'm too tired to go hunt or gather food," I say. "There's got to be some kind of civilization. We can order a pizza maybe."

"Let's go inside. Nature makes me nervous."

CHANNEL TEN

There is something in the walls, worms and soil and water, as we enter my home. God is still preaching on television, my goldfish examining her privates as God points at her from the television screen.

I kiss her big fishy lips for some reason and see her eyes are turning more human, turning blue. But they are still big. Cartoon eyes.

"Maybe we can eat your fish?" the crab asks. "She reminds me of something tasty."

"Or maybe we can eat crab?" I ask the hermit crab.

"Let's not eat seafood then."

We decide to open up the walls in the dining room and eat all the worms inside. There are many worms, but we also find a beetle, a bottle of dirty water, and a couple severed fingers.

After a few weeks, we decide to conform to God's world.

"It's hard being an animal," the crab says. "But an animal is much safer in nature than a human."

We sit and watch God speaking and eventually take him off mute.

"This is bad," I tell the fish and crab.

"Yes, but there is nothing to do in nature. It is so boring after living in society for so long. As bad as it sounds God is the most entertaining thing there is."

We listen to God for the afternoon. I do not understand a word that comes out of his mouth.

"His accent is messed up," I say. "Is that the accent of Heaven?"

"No, it's just a southern accent."

"What's he saying?"

"He says that we are free of the devil now, free of social organization, free of corporations, free of technology, free of education, free of the system that has corrupted our world."

"What is wrong with all those things?"

"They are unnatural, I guess. He wants us to be animals."

"Well, at least animals are free to do whatever they want."

"No, he says we aren't allowed to do what we want. We have to watch God on television for an hour a day every day and all day Sunday. And during the rest of our time we spend finding food, making shelter, and raising children. The world will continue this way for the rest of eternity."

"Well, at least we can mate," I say, wrapping my arm around the fish woman.

"Actually, you can't. He says you have to get married to have children. And you must only marry within your race. And impregnation can't be done through sexual intercourse. It must be through artificial insemination."

"But that's not natural!"

"God says what is natural and what isn't."

"God has made everything far less natural than it used to be. Talking crabs and sexy fish women are the most unnatural things I've ever seen."

"Perhaps God is going through a mid-life crisis," says the crab.

"I hate TV," I say.

CHANNEL ELEVEN

The coffee table thinks it is a buffalo now, grazing on the green shag carpeting.

"That's very unnatural," I tell the crab. "It was a table and it is alive now."

"Does it have meat inside of it or can an animal be made of wood?"

The table steps closer to my feet to eat some coffee-stained carpet, balancing on the wobbly leg that is missing two screws. I grab the loose leg, a cracking sound and it breaks off. The table rolls over squeak-screaming, blood gushing from the missing limb.

I examine the leg hole. It is wood on the outside, but meat on the inside.

"We'll have steak tonight," I tell the crab and fish.

CHANNEL TWELVE

"There's something wrong about nature that makes me feel small." Sitting with the crab man on the roof at twilight. Eating barbecued table meat. Looking into distances. "I mean, sometimes it's overpowering."

"God made it that way on purpose," says the crab. "He wants us to feel small in His world. It's how He proves his power over us. Like a tyrant."

"And now we have to watch him on TV."

CHANNEL THIRTEEN

Back in front of the muted television.

People like to watch television. It is what we are supposed to do. Just how we are supposed to want to live with God when we die.

I think I'm being punished for not liking television. Whenever I used to go outside and somebody would try to talk to me about something they saw on some sitcom or kooky news show and I told them I don't have a TV, they would just drop their mouths like I told them my child just died. And they ask if I'm going to get one but I just shrug and then they become suspicious of me.

Like there is something very wrong with me and they should get away very quickly. Tell the authorities on me.

CHANNEL FOURTEEN

Weeks pass and I become a small lawn on the living room floor. The fish woman has mutated into a normal woman, but she can't grow any hair and still has a goldfish smell to her. She doesn't talk and doesn't think to put on any clothes.

The crab man has disappeared. I heard some screaming coming from the other room and I think the fish woman killed and ate him. Or he might have run away.

She spends most of her time on the couch watching television. Her bare feet scrunching against my back. I can sense she is smiling. Smiling at God. Like there is something about him that makes her happy. I have no idea what it is, but I'm sure he's got her brainwashed. She has forgotten all about me. Doesn't remember her lover who has mutated into grass. I know we can't have sex, but she can at least kiss my blades from time to time.

All she ever does is watch that evil television.

God, I hate television.

Drown

Gina Ranalli

WHEN I TURN the hot water knob on the sink, they fall from the faucet and fill up the basin, too thick to go down the drain. I quickly twist the knob in the opposite direction, shutting off the flow, and use a wooden spoon to shove them down into the garbage disposal. They go reluctantly, like chicken bones, and the disposal's blades whir and choke and sputter, doing their best to chop up the words and swallow them down and make them disappear forever.

Once I've managed to get every last one down there, I flip the switch off and the disposal goes silent with a final wheeze, as though relieved to be done with *that* little chore.

I stand over the sink, peering down into the black mouth of the disposal, half-expecting the words to spew back up and out, as if the appliance could somehow projectile vomit its waste back in my face. I wait a moment until satisfied, but just as I'm about to turn away, the faucet drips one last time. Another word, just a small one, thank God, dribbles out and splats into the sink, a sound like Jello sliding from a plate and exploding all over the floor.

I frown at the word in the sink—*lie*—and then quickly use the wooden spoon to get rid of it, send it off to join its dead brothers and sisters, to the place where all murdered words must eventually go.

Unfortunately, the kitchen sink is not the only way the words find to get into my house. My morning shower is abruptly ended when still more words spill from the shower head, all sharp edges and pointy lines, scraping and scratching my bare skin before hitting the floor of the tub and piling up around my feet. A few of the smaller ones manage to tangle themselves in my hair and I let out a cry, blindly reaching for the knobs with one hand while wrestling with the words in my hair with the other. I wrench them free and throw them down, practically leaping out of the tub in my panic to get away from them.

Wrapping a towel around my body, staring down at the squirming words, I wonder how long it will take them to die. Not long probably. The idea is just to ignore them until they're dead. Then, I suppose I'll have to scoop them out with a shovel and toss them in a plastic garbage bag like I did with the ones I found in the back of my car the previous day. Walking the bag down to the dumpster at one end of my apartment complex, I had thought I heard rustling inside the bag, the words moving around, shifting a bit maybe. I'd wrinkled my nose in disgust, holding the bag away from my body and then threw the whole mess into the Dumpster as though I were disposing of a particularly grisly road kill. In a way, I suppose I was.

I'd thought that would be the last of the words invasion, but much to my surprise, they had come back, had found a way inside and now I wasn't sure I'd ever be able to get rid of them.

In the tub, most of the words have stilled, with the exception of a particularly large one: *jealousy*. I grimace, wondering why it's taking jealousy so long to die. Perhaps because it's not a small one. Not like *mad* or even *grudge*. Jealousy is a big puppy, but I know that even for it, it's just a matter of time. I turn and leave the bathroom, switching the light off as I go.

Getting ready for bed, I pull on a pair of flannel shorts and a tank-top before I notice the slow twitchy movements under the blankets on the bed. Like maybe there are mice under there, crawling around, quietly building a nest in the mattress. I release a sigh and yank the covers back to see more words. They're in my bed, squirming around, clambering over each other, making it hard to make out what some of them are. They remind me of a box of worms, bait worms, all tangled together so that you can't tell where one begins and another ends. For all I know it could be one huge word curling around itself over and over.

Exhausted, I don't feel like trying to clean them up right now, so I just grab my pillow and a blanket from the closet and make my way downstairs to the couch.

For a long time, I lay in the dark, considering my options. Will I have to move? If I do, will the infestation just follow me? Is it *me* that the words are stalking—haunting—or is it this place I live in? And if it *is* me, then what? Will I just be screwed, having to deal with this for the rest of my life?

I have no answers to any of these questions, but I'm tired and assume the answers will be there in the morning. I'm just about to doze off when I feel slow movement beneath my head. At first I think it's just a product of my exhausted mind, but then something sharp stabs my ear and I sit up fast, turn to look at the pillow, flipping it up to examine what's under it, but there's nothing.

Standing up, I pull the string for the ceiling light and am briefly blinded. Once my eyes adjust however, I can see the pillow, bulging out in some places, sucking in in others.

Words inside the pillow.

And now I know that I'm truly going to go insane. These words will never let me rest. I consider just throwing the pillow out the window, but curiosity gets the best of me and I go to the kitchen to fetch a knife. Back in the living room, I use the knife to split open the pillow and watch as the words spill out of it—word guts, falling from the couch onto the floor where they writhe around. I stare at them and realize they're trying to put themselves in some kind of order, maybe form a sentence.

I have no patience for this nonsense, however, and start stomping them to death, grinding them beneath my bare heel, even though some of them are quite sharp and dig into my skin, cutting me.

I stomp and grind until there is nothing left but black smears on the beige carpet, black tinged with the red of my blood. Every word—every letter—now completely unrecognizable. Smiling, I gaze at my handiwork with a sense of satisfaction I haven't felt before.

"Fuck you, words," I say to the black smear. "You're not gonna control my life."

But what began as a nuisance soon becomes a threat. The words *do* want to control my life and eventually I have to let them or be smothered by them.

It doesn't take long for me to realize this. They are everywhere. No longer just in my house, but *everywhere.*

I see them hiding in trees when I'm walking outside. The clouds are no longer just clouds, but words, taunting me from the sky.

The words scurry along behind me wherever I go, sometimes wrapping themselves around my ankles, causing me to trip and fall. I find them hiding behind cans of beans on supermarket shelves. And what's even worse is that they are *in* the cans as well, a fact I don't discover until I get home and try to eat.

When I crack an egg into a frying pan, it is little baby words that drop into the sizzling butter. Words fall out of a box of cereal into my favorite blue bowl.

I can't eat or sleep or bathe anymore.

Like a zombie, I go to my computer. I need to find help. Look up this phenomenon before it kills me. But, naturally, I can't find a single other case of a person being plagued by words.

I consider the fact that there is a good chance that I'm just insane. Off my rocker. Bats in the belfry. Loony-fucking-Toons. But, if this is going to kill me, I need to make a record of it. So no one else will have to feel alone if someday someone else finds themselves suffering the same fate as me.

I open a WORD doc on my computer, begin typing but stop almost immediately. Writing it all down seems like too much work. I'm so tired and hungry and weak. I just want to sleep.

Gritting my teeth, I write a little more, explaining what has been happening to me, starting with the words pouring into the kitchen sink. It is hard work, trying to make the words on the screen match what is in my head, the exact memory, the precise emotion.

I don't get very far before I have to stop again. The white of the screen is hurting my eyes, giving me a headache. Leaning over, elbows on the desk, I cover my eyes with my left hand and try to cover the screen with my right, even though, obviously, my hand is nowhere near big enough to cover the whole thing.

But instead of feeling a hard, slightly warm surface against my palm, my right hand plunges into something pliable. The screen is thick but fluid, like mucus or Vaseline, and I gasp in alarm, trying to pull my hand out. The words inside the screen begin winding themselves around my fingers, creeping across my palm and the back of my hand, wrapping around my wrist.

I use my left hand to grab my right forearm and pull, throwing my weight backwards and toppling the chair behind me, but the grip of the words is too strong. They don't let go even after I lose my balance, my socked feet slipping out from under me, and down I go, landing on my back beside the chair, a rope of words still attached to my arm and still slithering upwards towards my elbow, my shoulder, my face...

"No!" I scream, trying to scramble away, but even in my panic I can see the words slipping out of the screen—many more words than I wrote—an endless river of words, and they mean to kill me, to drown me.

Panicked, I continue to scream, hoping that someone will hear and come to my rescue. Even though I know that won't happen, I scream and pray for it anyway until instead of screaming, I'm gagging on words as they slide over my chin and lips and tongue, down my throat.

The words pour out of the monitor in a huge gush, sloshing down over me in an Arial black wave. God help me. I can no longer see, the words have swarmed over my face, blocking out my vision, and there is no place on my body where I can't feel them. They're squirming their way into my nostrils and ear canals, little ones forcing their way beneath my fingernails and eyelids.

My lungs fill with words, leaving no room for air. My body gives a final twitch and then I die.

Bright light. Hurting light. And choking.

I roll over onto my side, vomiting, hacking, gagging up words which spew all over the floor beside me in a grayish pool of muck. It looks as though I'd been eating newspaper, and that thought alone has me puking even harder, retching up nouns and adjectives and verbs until I'm certain my guts will be brought up with them.

Eyes bulging and bloodshot, I finally fall back, exhausted and spent. My abs ache in the unique way that only a bout of intense vomiting can make them.

Turning my head, I stare at the disgusting pool of words beside me and I suddenly know what to do. Despite still feeling miserable, I sit up fast, wait a minute just to be safe, then pull myself into a standing position. On shaking legs, I make my way into the kitchen, reach into the cupboard above the stove where I store my biggest bowls, grab four of them and bring them back to the puddle of words and bile.

I scoop dripping handfuls off the floor and drop them one by one into the bowls. The act nearly causes me to vomit again but I bite on my lower lip as hard as I can, concentrating on the pain and not the revolting task at hand.

When all the words have been picked up off the floor, I bring each bowl into the kitchen and rinse the words off in the sink, taking care to clean all specks and bile from every cross and curve. This takes a long time and more concentration than I would have expected, but when the job is done, I can't help but smile a little, nod and dry my hands on a dish towel.

Next, I bring the bowls of freshly washed words into the dining room. I dry them each with the utmost care and arrange them just so on crisp clean sheets of brilliant white paper. I line them up and inspect them, as if they were little boys being checked for dirty faces, their wet hair parted and slicked down against their heads, any and all smudges erased with a spit-damp thumb.

Once I'm content, I sit back and smile again, as satisfied as I can ever expect to be, staring at the words which are now sentences. I can't help but feel a slight twinge of pride, even though I know the words and the sentences are not about me, have nothing to do with me. Not really.

I stare a moment longer and then I stand, take a step back, and present them to you.

For You

Marcela Albornoz

I CLOSED MY EYES and went to sleep. Only I didn't really fall asleep. I stayed up day and night, half-asleep and half-brain dead. Mom didn't worry, because even when I'm acting "normal," my door is always locked. And let me say I tend to use the word "normal" loosely when referring to myself. If seven different psychologists couldn't make me "normal," then why keep trying?

I fell into a trance between thoughts of the end of the world and prayers for it to come quickly and joyfully. Why should I be sad that one day I'll die? I could die today at my naive age and it wouldn't change a thing because I'd still die with a smile. The best advice I have to give, the deepest words coming from a shallow soul—the one thing I have learned—is to make every mistake gracefully and surely. That is the only way that life will be worth living. That is the only way that death can have a happy ending.

Death is hard to explain, impossible to take back, and a permanent reminder of days you'll soon forget. Death. Dying. Dead. Are you uncomfortable yet, or should I keep going? Actually, I'm sorry about that. I don't mean to make anyone cry. But at times all I have to do is close my eyes and tell the truth and by the time I open them someone is crying. I'm sorry that my truth hurts. I'm sorry that every time I speak and you get quiet, I think you just might be praying for death. I'm sorry that my words are at times grotesque. I'm sorry that I know not how to be subtle when I write these things down. You can hate me. Join the club. But forcing death into your wide open eyes is the quickest way to make you understand life.

My grandma died two years ago. My aunt died soon after my grandma. My dad's mom will probably croak soon, or forget that she's alive due to her Alzheimer's. My cousin had an abortion not too long ago, and I wish that kid had gotten a chance to live before it... I mean, *he or she*, died. My best friend has cancer, not too severe, but enough to make you cry yourself to sleep some nights. She's alive, more alive than her nine-month-old nephew. She will not die. She will not die. I know this. I know this for a fact. And as I write this down it is the only "fact" that I am unsure of. This is the only thing that tricks my mind. When people ask and I tell them she's fine, I have to take a minute because my mind is asking me, "Is she really fine?"

I'm not too sure where this is going, which probably makes me a not-too-good storyteller. But my stories never "flow." My stories are messy and fucked up, but at least they're real. People die and that's real. You and I will die and that is real. So before crying yourself to sleep tonight, pull yourself together and call someone. Visit someone—anyone. Even if you hate the person, try to learn something from their wisdom. If one thing is all they know, that one thing may be something you have not yet learned. Talk to everyone. Hug everyone. Be sweet and kind. If you can't learn from me, then learn from my words. You never know whose life you'll be saving tonight.

But for now, let me save my own. Let me save my story before killing it. Let me keep writing words that won't mean a thing after I'm dead and gone. Let me try and give them as much meaning as possible so you'll recall them once or twice. Let me make this story good enough for someone to think about and dream about and cry about and feel something more than what is plainly obvious.

In stories, I often try to describe myself, teach a lesson, and mark someone's soul. But just how do I describe all of me without using futile adjectives? Well, it's easier than you would think. I am a person. That's all that's important. I live. I breathe. I love. I write. And with these essential things I do in life, I will also die. I will die with them. I will die and become a mermaid. I will die and make piles of sand look like your sweet face and then I will tell you how much I loved you in life. I will draw with waves on the sand every inch of your sadness. I will trace a half smile. I will kiss your innocence. You are my god.

Outside

Bradley Sands

THE WORLD IS an unsavory inferno, filled beyond maximum capacity with automatons programmed to destroy all humans by bringing their fragile psyches to ruins.

The three laws of automatonics are as follows:

An automaton may not give a human being a happy ending trigger point tushy massage or, through inaction, allow a human being to enjoy a happy ending trigger point tushy massage.

An automaton must delivery a human being's pizza within twenty minutes or less, except when such deliveries would conflict with the First Law.

An automaton must satisfy its urges, as long as such satisfaction does not conflict with the First or Second Law.

Do not be fooled by automatons wearing bowler hats! They exist to trick the public into believing that automaton desires do not exceed their need for stylish, yet archaic, headgear.

Now the truth can be told! Automatons will not be content until they have lowered the self-esteem of every decent human being who has ever worked up the nerve to leave the house, attacking them with a barrage of giggles, dirty looks, finger pointing, and friendly-worded greetings spoken in malevolent tones.

One should do their damndest to limit their contact with the outside world. Unfortunately, this cannot always be avoided. There comes a time in every man's life when he runs out of toilet paper.

I hope that this account will serve as a warning for future generations.

You must always be prepared for an event such as this. Come up with a plan to get past your neighbors undetected. You may use mine, but never, ever tell anyone that it was your idea. I'm a humble sort and don't care about being credited for my brilliant ideas, but the guilt will eat through your fingertips if you don't cite me as an influence.

I like to stuff myself into a package and fling it out my front door. If I creep ever so slowly out of the community, my neighbors will never suspect that it contains anything but a severed ear of a loved one.

ARF! ARF!

"Get out of here, Mr. Snuggles!"

I regret ever processing the thought that it would be really cute to brainwash my dog into believing that he was an uncouth ruffian who took pleasure in thwarting my attempts to live a normal, healthy life.

"Attention homeowners! You have just borne witness to a pivotal moment in the history of our planet. I have been chosen to serve as the ambassador between the cardboard boxes and the people of Earth. May the future bring peace, prosperity, and naked frolicking between our kinds. We look forward to experiencing your ancient and holy tradition of welcoming the impossible by denying the overwhelming amount of evidence supporting its existence."

That smell... nah, it couldn't be. Mr. Snuggles would never be that vindictive. It's probably just the ghost of a bowel movement, doomed to haunt this material plane until it comes to terms with being disowned by its father. Any minute now... any minute and it'll move towards the light...

"How could you, Mr. Snuggles!?!"

I erupted from the package like the contents of a pimple after being liberated from captivity.

"Hello, Bradley. Nice day, isn't it?"

It was strange that the man knew my name, but his question was even more peculiar. Everything that he needed to discern whether or not it was a nice day appeared to be well within his grasp. Why was my observation more credible than his own?

Then I noticed his lawnmower. The grass wasn't being mowed. Instead, its blades were having a tea party with the man's spinal column.

When faced with an adversary such as this, it is suggested that you don't let on about knowing their true corporeal form. It is important to act like you're in the presence of a grass trimmer rather than a malignant master of all things that are organic matter. Answer all their questions in precise detail, and cite your sources. Failure to respond will result in the abomination missing a meal. Although following these directions may seem counterproductive, if the entity doesn't consume its daily requirement of responses to inane questions, it will juice anyone who flees in terror (or lack of interest) from its queries.

"Yes, it's a nice day. Perfect for beach volleyball and watching your family immolate beneath a vengeful sun. Expect to suffer Mr. Sunshine's wrath throughout the remainder of the afternoon, with highs reaching the lower 450's."

At least that's what I would have said, if I wasn't fleeing in terror (and lack of interest). I figured a trip into what lies beneath the couch cushion would be less excruciating than a bout of social discourse. But I was scheduled for a session with disappointment—the only parting gift that it gave out was an offended stare from its man-puppet.

I went shrieking through my theme park of suburban compromise, passing sprinklers painting the sidewalk with spermicide and trees wrapping themselves with yellow ribbons to show their support of the extinction of the Uprooted Ones and recycle bin amphitheaters featuring unwanted children and sea monkeys stretched out across lamp posts (so that's the community initiative the little old Egyptian mummy was yammering about through my trapdoor).

Stopping to admire a pile of fun goop, my study of a bold new artistic vision was interrupted by the advance of an ovulation machine pushing a stroller full of her darling accomplishments. Knowing that a mother always determines a stranger's harmlessness based on their ability to respond to a question, I tried to counteract her attack by hiding behind the goop. Unfortunately, the stroller was custom made to span the length of four city blocks, and I was forced to abandon my position moments before impact.

"How are you doing today?"

Until this moment of cosmic dread, I had never believed in the existence of a being capable of expressing false interest in another, and I was quivering in my roasted turkey slippers. There was no escape for me this time.

Make any unauthorized moves and Bertha will extract your fluids of sin and you'll be the proud owner of a SEMEN SPAWN ON BOARD sign. Think you're immune just because you're female? Guess again, missy! She'll always find a way to conquer the laws of nature.

When my father told me that he stopped listening to music after I was born, I decided against ever having children. "Terrible. My anus is itching like the crotch of a Moonsylvanian streetwalker. I have a theory that it may have something to with the dookie currently residing between my cheeks, although this can only be speculated. It all traces back to the Great Toilet Paper Shortage of 667 Excrete Street, which is also the cause for my journey to a world that I never spayed and neutered. This is my first time outside in a schnauzer's age and my symptoms include shortness of breath, the urge to operate heavy machinery, stomach butterflies playing Missile Command, winking at the unobtainable, walking like an Egyptian, and confiding in marine mammals indigenous to the Antarctic. If you truly cared, you'd turn around and tiptoe the other way."

That last bit was intensified by the presence of an inflatable animal who was programmed to follow me around and protect me with a simulated sex act during times of crisis, and Bertha's status rose to my bestest friend in the whole wide world.

The stroller shimmied away, unveiling the cautionary tales of the outer territories. I was almost there. The Humperdumper Yogurtarium and Toilet Paper Boutique loitered across the street. But before I could exercise my right to shop till the store manager made me mop up my stomach's bad review of their delicious low calorie treat, I had to traverse through an intersection brimming with automaton pedestrians.

"But pedestrians don't meander through the street, gossiping about the lawn furniture of celebrities through mouthfuls of hors d'oeuvres while listening to a Pink and Fruity Tutti-bellied Genocide Jamboree cover band!" I waved around a copy of the Ad Nauseam Hamster Dictionary for use as a visual aid. "Pedestrians make haste while crossing the street! They don't set off explosions at each end of the block in order to obstruct vehicles from attending their party on the way to the filming of *Protoplasmbath on Traffic Island!*"

"I like your shirt," said a young woman wearing clothes.

It was a torn white t-shirt, adorned with nothing but the words GENOCIDE JAMBOREE written in black magic marker. By the looks of the clothes being worn by the young woman wearing clothes, she would never be caught decomposing in the store where I purchased it. I didn't even like Genocide Jamboree; I just needed somewhere to hide out while Thrift Explosion! security searched for a brilliant, *yet misunderstood*, topless man with the contents of a two-year-old smeared across his chest.

That rancid piñata didn't like my shirt! The silky sounds of Genocide Jamboree were what she truly adored!

I cannot tolerate someone who's that nonspecific. "I've been ordered by the state to wear this t-shirt. It's important that the public is made aware of my past transgressions. This warning has been ineffective ever since Gen Papa-Georgio, former baby back rib inseminator, gawked at my shirt and thought it would make a really cool name for a band." I grabbed a leotard from out of my fanny pack. "Please stop me before I aerobicize again."

The young woman slipped away to find the butt of another one of her ill-conceived compliments.

"Hey, guy. So what's the good word?" said a man with hair.

MESSAGE 303: ERROR – CANNOT READ INPUT
QUERY IS GOBBLEDYGOOK
INFLUX OF GOBBLEDYGOOKS ON PREMISES
INITIATING MINIMIZING PROCEDURES

The popular Monster Truck, Deviated Septum, was parked in the middle of the street. The denizens must have hired it to give the party an aura of celebrity. Seeking shelter from their jollifications, I went into the bosom of the beast.

My first instinct was to wait—wait through all of their lingerings and blatherings and dodderings—but fearing that the Humperdumper Yogurtarium and Toilet Paper Boutique would close early led me to consider the possibility that an inanimate object's sense of hearing was superior to what had been hypothesized by the scientific community. "I hope I'm not intruding on your death-defying parking stunt, Deviated Septum, but I just wanted to say that you're my hero. I saw you on last week's *You'll Drink Beer to Anything* and you were awesome! At least you were, until the excitement of watching a truck drive over cars transformed into a monotonous robot. These schlemiels aren't even giving you a chance to thrill me with disappointment! To them, you're no better than a clump of balloons. Why don't you show the uncultured vermin who's sauce by driving into the direction of that Humperdumper Yogurtarium and Toilet Paper Boutique over there."

Deviated Septum's wheels squealed and I rolled down my window, hoping to add a few extra years to my life by bathing in the blood of the distasteful (if my evil narrative were to succeed, I would find myself living in a futuristic utopia long after the extinction of all life). The truck barreled forward to a soundtrack of meticulously thought out last words. After setting a new White Balderdash Racing Association record, we found ourselves in front of the Humperdumper Yogurtarium and Toilet Paper Boutique.

I got out of the truck and a squadron of planes blitzkrieged across the sky. Oh good, I've always wanted to attend a Captain Forgetful Stunt Spectacular.

But before you could yell, "Oh shit, Captain! You forgot your parachute!" a hoard of skydivers jumped out of the planes, dressed in the garb of barbecue cuisine specialists. Wielding spatulas of beef in my direction, they conjoined their voices into a one sinister reverberation, "Bradley, how would you like your burger cooked?"

That's it! My patience had been tried far beyond the limits of human decency.

Here's a tip for the readers at home: Whenever I leave the house, I always remember to bring my Pillsman PocketNuke... and so should you! You never know when you'll need protection against the Earth's more gregarious inhabitants. So consider Pillsman for all of your thermonuclear needs. You'll be glad you did!

I reached into my pocket and....

Glimmer

Steve Quinlan

I SPUN THE SILVER RING of white gold around on the coffee table, like they did in the movies and books when the wife or fiancé left. I wanted to see what it felt like. Would it make me hurt even more? Would it bring me peace? And I also wanted to see if it would catch the light. Spinning the ring didn't make me feel any better or any worse, but it did catch the light—all one-third of a carat.

I remember the night we splurged at an upscale restaurant. She smiled and bubbled with great enthusiasm when she said, "All I'm saying is, if we ever do get married, I don't need a big ring. A little glimmer is all I want. Something that sparkles."

When the time did come, I bought her the biggest ring I could afford without going into debt, and now that I look back, it was a wise plan. I'll never get what I paid for it.

My buddy Bill said, "Pawn it. Go to a massage parlor."

A guy at work told me to pawn it and go get drunk.

When I was at the record store unloading the DVDs and CDs she had given me over the years for Christmas and birthdays, the clerk told me "Dude, sell it and get some weed." Why did everyone's idea involve pawning the ring? Why not chuck it into the ocean? Why not swallow it and see if it turned to shit like my relationship did? I had been to the massage parlors, I had gotten drunk, and I had gotten stoned. None of them made me forget, or feel any better.

I spun the ring again, because maybe the second time would be different. You never know. The thin, silver band twirled in a clockwise motion like a small gyroscope. The diamond caught the tungsten balanced light from the overhead fixture and it sparkled. Nothing. I felt nothing, except maybe disappointment that I felt nothing. The ring fell over onto the green marble-pattern Formica table with a soft *clink*. I reached for the glass and poured myself another two fingers of bourbon, and I would pour myself another two fingers of bourbon in a couple of minutes. I was glad I had brought the bottle in from the kitchen, as it saved me the trouble of having to get up. Frankly, at this point, I was having a little trouble walking straight.

But, back to my game. Did I dare spin the ring again? The third time's the charm they say. Would I pass out and sleep away the pain for the next eight hours? Would I get up, put my jacket on and walk to the bar and meet some girl as drunk and lonely as me? And would she let me take her home? Or would I pass out and not wake up but go to sleep forever.

One could only hope.

I thought about all the other rituals I did throughout my life that got me nowhere. Communion, once a week for eight years, didn't bring me any enlightenment or any closer to God. Waking up and saying "Rabbit, Rabbit" on the first never brought me any luck. And throwing salt over my left shoulder when I spilled it didn't keep away the bad luck either. I was drunk though, and what else did I have going on? And what else did I have to lose?

I poured another two fingers worth of bourbon and took a healthy sip. I tasted the barley and the rye on my lips and tongue and enjoyed it. Fuck it. I grabbed the ring between my two fingers and my thumb and spun it. It started to twirl and then the unthinkable happened—the phone rang. I answered.

It was her. "Are you drunk?"

"No, no, I fell asleep watching TV." A beat. "You know what day it is?" Another beat. "It would have been our seven year anniversary".

"Yeah, I know. That's why I'm calling, out of respect."

"Oh." My heart plummeted. I was hoping, of course, that she was calling to get back together. I wanted to cry, "Take me back! I still love you!" and I would have, if I thought it would have done any good. I also wanted to beg, "Come see me." Or "Let me come over." I would have, too, if I had thought she'd do either one, but I knew she wouldn't. It was too soon, we were both too confused, and she still had wild oats to sow. Though I did manage, "Call me sometime, you know where I'm at."

"I will," she lied.

"All right, thanks for calling. I appreciate it. I'll talk to you later." And with that, I hung up the phone. Seven years and this is what I was left with: a broken heart, an empty bottle and a slightly used ring. Yeah, right, she'd call. I put my jacket on and walked down the stairs and out onto the street. I had to get out so I could breathe. It was eating me up in there.

I thought of her, and I saw her on the bed where she slept, in her chair with her drink, and at the counter making our dinner. The place was too full of memories that wouldn't quit and I had to leave. I walked down the street and up the hill to the bar. I walked in and everyone turned and glanced for a second and then went back to their business. I'm sure they all thought I was a loser. I only started drinking here after she'd left me. I don't think I had ever been in there with anyone—I always came in alone.

I sat on a stool at the corner of the bar, by the door, like I always did. I ordered my drink, a Bud with a Jim Beam neat. A few of those and I was good. I could go home and sleep. If I was lucky I dreamed of her, of happy times, and that we were still together.

The bartender came over. "The usual?" I nodded and she poured my drink and brought the beer. The place was half-empty, as usual, and no one took notice of me. I was not known for playing pool, darts, or dice. I just sat at the bar, drank, and felt sorry for myself. Maybe, once in a while, I would play the jukebox. I liked it that way.

There was a cute girl sitting at a table by the window. She was trying to look busy. By her appearance, I figured she went to the art school up the hill. She was perfect—tall, slender, and good looking. If I had her life it would be good. I drank my drinks and stole glances at her between sips. I imagined what her hair smelled like and what it would be like to spoon up against her at night and fall asleep.

A few drinks in and she looked lonely. Melancholy. She looked the way I felt. I had to go to work the next morning and I could barely stand, let alone walk. The slight smile she had when I had come in was gone. My rakish friend John would have described her as a wounded gazelle. I had to be the lion.

I'm not that guy though. I never was and never will be. I stumbled over to the table and dropped the ring in her empty glass. *Clink.* She looked at me, then the ring, and I didn't wait for her reaction.

And with that, I left the bar and turned the corner as fast as I could.

Consumerism

Jeremy Robert Johnson

RON, CAN YOU REACH your mother from here? Yes... okay... and is she?

She is? Are you certain? And you've checked the jugular and carotid? Can you reach a mirror to check for breath signs? No.

Oh, dear...

No, son, I don't think I can move from this position right now. This shard of the bumper appears to have me pinned to the bench seat like a common Lepidoptera. You know, as a Byronic hero with a smattering of Randian objectivity flitting away in my mind, I can't help but feel disdain for this entire scenario. This is low.

Did I just call myself a Byronic hero aloud? Well then, it's out in the open. Your suspicions are quelled, correct? I'd never defined myself for you before because I felt you should find your own path and... Ugghh! That is disgusting. What is that smell? Dear lord. I thought the burning gasoline was bad, but that odor... her bowels have let loose, haven't they? Death moves like quicksilver.

Ron?

Stop touching her face, Ron. Recognize death's permanency and move forward. *We* are still alive—maintaining this status should be your only focus. Let go of her hair. You and your crippling sentiment; don't give that body a value beyond what it is now.

No, it's not your mom anymore. It's water mostly, some minerals. Gases. Proteins.

Check yourself for injuries so we can assess, repair, and mobilize.

No, we should be protected if the tank explodes. You may want to breathe through your t-shirt, though. Some of that smoke *is* entering through the crack in the dashboard.

Quell that braying, Ron. Your generation... I don't understand the value you've placed in vulnerability. Were this ancient Rome you'd be of age to marry and launch an empire. Have all the pugilists retired?

What is that ticking sound? It's coming from the engine block?

Well, I paid fifty-grand for this behemoth, and I believe it will hold. Those hippies in their little tin-can cars, they used to deride me on the roadway, middle fingers held up proudly. Fools protesting survival. Proto-agrarian communists denying progress. Denying man his greatness. Imagine *their* little car flipping four times and remaining as intact as our rig. God bless military design. Sturdy as a rolling mountain. I'd have bought the version with Gatling gun intact had that been an option. Had we been that well equipped I could have gunned that possum into the troposphere...

Ron, I don't think I can move my head in either direction. I'll need you to get loose of your buckles and crawl back here. Ronald?

Yes, I seem to be pinned. Good God, the back of my head is a-throb... your churlish weeping isn't helping a bit, either. Silence yourself, child.

Yes, I said "child." Never believe that age alone makes a man. And don't shift about too quickly. We're still on an incline and I believe too much weight on the right side of the rig will tip us back into a roll.

We should never have let you drive. A possum for Pete's sake... those animals are God's litter. Furry detritus. Just an animal. Nothing. Have you ever seen *me* swerve on the roadway before?

Yes, but have you ever seen me swerve to *avoid* an animal? That's my point.

What do you think the lifespan of a possum is, anyway? How many more years of mindless foraging do you think you've assured that ball of fur by dooming us to die here in the woods?

Well, we could die. Accept that. Any given moment. Remember your cousin Dane? He was vibrant up until the second he collapsed face-first into that birthday cake. Remember how you cried that whole night. "I saw his dead eyes! I saw his dead eyes!" That was your complaint. Strange how that didn't make you wiser. Just weaker.

I really cannot feel a single one of my limbs.

I've been in and out of consciousness, haven't I? Why can't I see the trees? How long have we been here?

We've lost the final vestiges of daylight, Ron, and yet you remain there, holding her. It's so absurd. She'll begin expelling gases soon. Maybe that will loose your sad Oedipal grip and we can try to get out of here.

The burning engine was providing much of our heat, wasn't it? Funny how quickly the warmth slips away once the sun drops. I still can't command an appendage, Ron. You'll have to get moving; make a run for that tiny gas station we passed about thirty miles back. You will be Pheidippides, with I, your Athenian tribe for the saving.

Ron?

Ron?

Speak, son! I'm hoping you can reach the Mag-lite in the flip-down console. I need some light back here, and your help. I've got to assess my condition and try to stop my bleeding—there's a static fuzz to my vision so I know I'm not getting adequate circulation here, Ron...

Hello? I can see you breathing, Ron, and I doubt you're asleep. I NEED THE MAG-LITE!

Jesus, son! No need to lash out like that. Okay, so it's embedded in her chest. How was I to know that, from this vantage point? Your anger is ridiculous.

Any chance you could get a solid grip on the light and free it for our use? I bet one solid tug would do the job.

Ron?

Ron?

It was my hubris, I suppose, to think us so invincible in this vehicle. Should I have packed flares? Yes, that's obvious. Water? Yes, even more obvious.

Perhaps, Ron, there's an errant package of Fritos on the floor near me. A Snak-Pak, maybe?

But this machine did keep us alive. I had to have it at first sight, this shining example of man's command over nature; our bodies reshaping steel, our minds designing perfect geometric infrastructures, our wills dredging liquid fire from the Earth's belly and converting it into unprecedented levels of speed, striking down drudgery and demanding progress.

And don't start, Ron, with your sniping. How you ever developed your line of leftist drivel while being home-schooled, I'll never know. The fact is that it is best to consume everything we can, while we can. Sustainability is a fantasy for those believing that humans were meant to exist forever as they are now—LIES!

I have never known such a level of thirst... Ron? I swear there was an extra Snak-Pak up near the driver's seat. Maybe some aspirin? This headache's gone thermonuclear.

We have to use up all the oil, Ron. It's what our bodies do. We consume. And when we are done consuming one thing, our bodies will learn to ingest another and our lights shall burn forever on. So said Darwin. So said Emerson—the conflict defines us. Ether and stardust swirling, colliding, sparking off into new shapes. If you had your way, we'd be stagnating on some insect-riddled farm right now, fondling possums and plucking fiddles while our teeth rot.

Oh... my head...

Well... dead ship captains on mosquito ponds, Ron! We'll not return to the stew. That doesn't match up on a theological or biological level. That's not why we're here...

Parched does not begin to define how I'm feeling here, Ron.

Your dad always wanted to be a poet, kiddo. I aspired, but aspiration was all that was within my reach. Playground injury, Ron. Age eight. Flew off the swings inverted, caught my head on the plywood marking the park's border.

The doctors never defined this clearly, Ron, but I believe that that *exact* moment was when I lost my grip on meter.

Pieces of you, Ron, they can die at a whim.

Especially, Ron, especially if you can't get your fucking whimpering little cur bitch of a son to bring you a GODDAMNED MOTHERFUCKING FRITO SNAK-PAK!

Your punishment, son... yes, your *punishment*, for even in this situation you must understand that all of life is a lesson, and you're lucky to have your elder to guide you... your punishment now shall be to understand survival. Basic animal survival... the way to soothe the reptilian bits at the back of your medulla so that you may live past this moment and continue to ascend to your higher human calling.

So wake up. Yes, that's it. Look me in the eyes, like a man.

The sun is rising. Your dark night of the soul is over, Ron, and you have to move forward.

Crawl back here. Carefully. Slowly. Keep the vehicle in balance. Your right leg looks dreadful, but it doesn't appear the femoral artery's been cut. That's good. That's good. You can do this, Ron. You can take your punishment and grow up strong.

Smell my breath, Ron. That tint to it, the thing worse than morning breath, that fresh cat-shit smell... that's me dying. And I can tell by the look in your eyes that my assessment is correct. I'm missing crucial human elements, aren't I?

Well, I could tell by the buzzing of flies at dawn, by the soft prickle of their landings in wide perimeter, that the rear of my skull is perhaps missing. I sense a gulf of tissue.

That bad, is it? The idea of me seeing another sunset with that much of my brain exposed to the elements is absurd. So it is that you, my only seed, must carry on as I instruct.

You can survive this, Ron. You are, at this moment, only an organism. And you must consume. Fluids, proteins. And if the Iroquois were right, perhaps a bit of my strength.

I proffer this now, the flesh of the father. Let my mind give you life. It is my last wish. It is your duty.

Tilt my head forward more? Perhaps that bit of glass by my feet will help you serrate... .

Yes, you can do it. You must. Move swiftly, that this throbbing may abate and I may catch up with your mother at the soft, light gates of her heaven.

And gently at first, please... yes, that's it... please stop crying... no more sentiment... you are an animal now, and must remain so until you return to the world of man... oh, to be part of this Greek tragedy, it feels right, a poet's end... I am your Leonidas, eat well for you may not survive the day... yes, dig in... I'll not ask you to describe the taste... to paraphrase Joplin I suggest you take another little piece... Gorp! I can't... oh, God, a bit of blood in my eyes, I can't see much... your hands are stronger than I'd imagined them to be... how I love and despise you, Ron... yes, burrow in, son, let your throat be gorged with my wisdom, swallow ages of evolution... oops, you've got a bit on your chin there, tut-tut, no waste in nature... they were right— there's no pain, no self-aware nerves in the gray matter itself... aaaaoooooaahh... that last scoop touched off an old memory—the smell of the Atlantic in mid-winter New England, a hint of your mother's perfume... but what is this light... Oh, holy fire! Yes, Ron. I will live on through you... in you... carry on, consume, survive... swallow me down, Ron... take me deep, child, and become a man....

Ending Children Play

Matthew Pendleton

THE TALL, THIN TEACHER SPOKE very clearly. She loomed over the child, with its fingers and toes, formidable even then; heart, kidneys, little pack of liver, all the meat packed within. The tall, thin teacher spoke very clearly.

"Do you have ants in your pants?"

The teacher said a first rhyme.

Soon the child would encounter aunts and grandmothers from whose mouths would drop the phrase, "ants in your pants," mysteriously, between mouthfuls of chicken and boiled potato and boiled carrots.

Earlier, the child had lain in the dark, unaware that it was dark, and aware instead of a fidgeting spreading through its body. First the fingers and toes, then restlessly coursing towards the inner parts, places that couldn't be moved with any will. When the fidgeting reached the brain, after a little more reflection, the child would start screaming. Later the child would hear the phrase "ants in your pants" and recognise it as referring back to this night of fidgeting. In the cot too small in the future.

In two-and-a-half years the child would encounter alphabet soup, shovel spoonfuls of the alphabet of the given language many letters at a time, sometimes with toast, butter.

Ants, pants.

Pants, ants.

The chant the school children took up, lilting high voices happy.

The people who move through the blue soundless lights of a sometimes absence of thinking: Mother, who's a pale woman not too tall, Father, a tall man, indisputably, but sometimes both parents changing, tiny differences like the fractional growth of nails and, what are recalled with an effort, and later gradually disseminate beyond recall, dreams.

Later the wife woke feeling guilty. Her nipples were settling down, their hard epicentre. There was a nuance in the bedroom and under the sheets that made her feel almost dirty. The husband was not beside her. She smoothed a hand over his pillow. Cold.

The wife shuffled around the house until she found the husband watching a mute TV with the child on his lap, dribbling, sleeping. Images on TV were hard to discern and grey in the dawn light through the curtains.

"It was screaming," the husband said to the wife, quietly. "Didn't you hear?"

On the TV a grey woman was talking to a grey man, and their lips were hardly moving.

wudgawudgja wush, they said, *wudgawudgua wush*.

The day dawning was colder than usual. The wife, in a blobby kind of lingerie she had grasped blind from her set of drawers the night before, shivered and watched her child.

Its slight nose, that flared now as it slept, was built as though it were the axis upon its face, still flabby around the edges. She lifted it in her arms and took it to the bedroom, the white expanse of sheets. I will, the husband had promised, join you later. His eyes gazed at TV. Its image seemed to be built around the axis of a plotted plant not quite in the centre. The plant's fuzzy leaves appeared unable to move.

The husband had been up for the past six hours, and his bowels were starting to tighten in the slow ritual of indigestion. Whiskey in the lower part of the dinner trolley and a continued involvement with the TV figured largely in his future.

Somewhere, in the gradually-heated environment of the family home (now the sun rose), was a long lost intention among the new oven, and the chalk marks on the patio, where the ants were, signaling a conservatory not yet built. With the TV off, and the night-time bright lights of the lounge off, the darkness resulting, to be seen a moment before ascending the stairs to bed, reflected the truest intention of the house owners—mumbles behind the double glazed windows, the temperamental boiler, the cold felt through the shower curtain.

The wife settled the child in her nook of armpit and abdomen and slept fitfully. It was then that she remembered her dream.

At the bottom of the stairs she watched the husband, sprawled on the sofa, sit up and hide his whiskey ineffectually behind a cushion. But she didn't mind at that precise moment. Sweat covered her from head to toe and her thin fingers, that would have played the violin if they'd been taught to, quivered.

In their patched-together suburban home, the water boiler moaned quietly, and yellow light started to appear in far corners of the lounge, garden facing dining room, the largest bedroom…

The husband saw the wife's face and, for the tiniest moment, felt terrified. It was too quick for him to register consciously. It would arise frequently in dreams from then on. Dreams of the surface beneath the surface in semi-detached houses.

The husband had a strong desire to eat some chips. But everywhere would be closed, and he would have to sit in the lounge or go upstairs and see what the matter was when the wife said, *Come upstairs, come upstairs, something's awfully wrong*, and both were terrified for the tiniest moment. If they had managed somehow to couple their brains together, and go back through all their memories, they would come across that moment and find it replicated in each other, the only identical moment shared by any two people, and they would never know it, singular, moaning: *Something's awfully wrong.*

In the bedroom the husband stood awkwardly by the door and watched the wife and the child, both lying, a little curled up, and with a space between them in the shape of another person lying on their side.

"You're not pregnant are you?" he began.

iga-poo, the child thought. It lay very still on the white sheets and had strange blue thoughts, many blue thoughts, and white shapes passing inside the mind. A great feeling of calm it would spend the rest of its life trying to emulate. An awareness growing, as though with no end in sight, that early on.

From the bedroom window the cul-de-sac road had begun to glow with the extraordinary sunlight—but no one noticed the sun rise nor the few stars remaining bluely. There was no kind of thinking related to this. All happened. It was a disaster. The wife stood by the bed wringing her hands and looked out the window before pointing to the child's thick black hair. The husband leaned forward for a closer look.

Black bead-like living things were moving in their child's hair. Some had fallen onto the white sheets and were twisting themselves (it seemed to the husband and the wife), almost breaking themselves, almost splitting in two. It was hard to tell if they were really insects or something else entirely. They were coming from the child's hair. The wife had noticed these black things coming from the child's hair and didn't know what they could be and had gone downstairs to tell the husband who was drinking whiskey sprawled on the sofa watching TV.

Gob. Gibdijje. The child did not know about the things in its hair. The husband, the whiskey beginning its mark somewhere above, only watched and felt neither disgust nor attraction, and he mulled in a nowhere-state, almost beginning to smile.

"Why the hell are there black things in my child's hair?" the wife asked, "why the hell are there black things in my child's hair?"

"Lice," the husband suggested.

There were small ones and there were large ones.

Remembering an Elton John song, the husband sang in his head *Iiiii waaaant chiiiips...* remembering a late summer evening five years ago, she on his arm, the streets fresh, the fresh boulevards of city, post-shopping—her scent lemon, in the early night the moon and stars could be seen. He wanted chips then too. But he knew the smell would disrupt the perfume of her, and after eating them he could not lean in, as he did, a hand to her cheek, a stillness in the crowd... in all the hairs of that crowd, was there something like the things in this, his child's hair? In the yellow light of the bedroom whiskey seemed to make itself comfortable and murky in the husband's head.

On the white sheets little forms wriggled and seemed to be trying to eat each other. Though they were only vague lines on their family bed, the husband had the idea that they must have mouths. How small those mouths must be. The wife and mother had no such thoughts. She, her mouth still open after saying her words, was suddenly (for a slight second, not enough to remember with her mind) experiencing the voluminous folds of her mother's coat behind which she hid in a family photograph. What a time that was, its old faint nervousness, and an excitement too. She had picked up the photograph with an empty feeling much later, seeing the family, and the family friends also part of the photograph. Her minutely hidden parts in that photograph, an arm, shoulder, the toes of the right foot. The family, on the family doorstep, photographed before going off on a journey. The journey was a—what was it? A body. A series of bodies.

Until it ended, the parents had no idea what to do. It was not meningitis. There were dark things in their child's hair dropped and scattering on the white sheets of their double bed and crawling with vehemence. It was an old illness from the old forest all cut down long ago.

It all seemed like a very long time had passed. *Bubble bobble,* thought the child. Everything's a big mess. The talk of the Mother would be almost understandable, reading the newspaper to her baby child, words in their correct sequence—contrary, elementary—and scarcity becomes an Invisible Hand, working a valve to keep the market self-regulating—when there was not the food the child liked and had hoped for.

The black things spilled from the child's hair onto the white sheets and off onto the floor, all the time wriggling together and the smaller ones eating the larger ones and making creeping arabesques of constant motion.

"We'll have to crop it," said the husband, "shave its hair."

The wife said nothing.

"I'll get the clippers," said the husband.

While the husband rooted around in the bathroom for the clippers, the wife stood at the side of the bed staring at the child, still lying on its side among its blue thoughts and all the twitching, wobbling black things, and imagined she saw her own hands around her child's neck, thinking something high above was making decisions, and there wouldn't be an end to things, or: wouldn't it be nice, if there were an end to things, to finally decide, that's done, I can wash my hands, there was an end to it.

The TV on. Presenters warbled soundlessly in court rooms and terraced streets and corner shops and coffee shops: "Judgement takes a lifetime—Or, the conclusion drawn is in sympathy with the completion of the lifetime. Eyes are closed and the perceived universe sympathetically folded up, light in light."

The husband got the game out of the cupboard under the stairs and the child watched him carefully, sat on the sofa, head shaved and on the temple a small plaster the wife had placed tenderly over a tiny abrasion. From the kitchen the washing machine juddered in a spin cycle.

"A game will do us all good," said the husband, setting up the board on the coffee table. The board extended a little over the table edge but that was okay. The wife brought in the drinks. They both sat on the floor, the wife's skirt splayed out, and played the game. Sometimes they smiled, and sometimes they sighed and moaned at the words they could or couldn't make.

"Perhaps we should get a cat," the husband said at one point. It had grown dark outside. They had drawn the curtains.

"A cat?"

"They're good company." The husband clicked down his tiles and grinned. The wife added the score up. "But," the husband reconsidered, "they have to be—" he waved his hand for the word.

The child watched the husband and the wife from its vantage point on the sofa. Its head was very cold. Sometimes it wouldn't see the husband and the wife while it thought that in a green park was the grandmother on the bench and the mother and the father strolling a little ahead and the grandson sat on the tarmac before the bench.

"Coo Coo Coo," the grandmother said to the grandson. "Pigeon," she said, and pointed at one. The grandson watched the ants running around beneath him. He knew they were looking for things to eat like sugar and other insects smaller and sometimes even bigger than themselves. The grandmother's face was white and puffed up in places, but her nose was slim and still quite smooth. She was smiling to herself on the bench and watching the pigeons and sometimes glancing up at the blue sky, until her face suddenly froze and her eyes widened and fixed on an undefined spot before her. The grandson watched and recognised the panic that greets a certain understanding in the cold.

"Hold on, hold on," the grandmother said, "something's awfully wrong."

The mother and father were far away down the path. The grandmother stopped saying anything. The grandson watched her and thought she looked trapped, and so he unaccountably begin to cry, but very quietly, and in the park people moved on.

The child watched the husband and the wife, thinking blue radiant thoughts, and saw the husband's whiskey emptied, the wife's stockings go unworn, the child's head shaved, ending children play.

The Jukebox Started Playing Another Thorogood Song

Mark Brittenburg

REALITY

THE JUKEBOX STARTED PLAYING another Thorogood song, something about drinking alone. The juke was programmed to go off every ten minutes if no one had put any money in, maybe to remind the patrons that it was there. But the song never got that reassurance, and its offerings were usually met with rolling eyes and clucking tongues. The air was almost chewable thanks to the abundance of smokers and lack of windows or vents. But it didn't matter. No one who came here was overly concerned about his or her health.

The bar was long and made of wood and served two basic purposes: a prop to hold drinks, and a prop to keep the patrons off the floor. The whole place smelled of piss and vomit and stale beer. For some it was truly an abomination; for others, it was a refuge, holier than any church. They came here to become a part of an imbibition-based ritual larger than themselves, to confess their sins to total strangers and purge their conscience, as well as their memories. In the morning they would awake to blinding sunlight and the dizzying sickness of redemption.

The walls were adorned with various pieces of cowboy memorabilia: coils of rope, saddles, pictures of "the Duke" and some other unknowns, all rugged and dusty. There was no clock on the wall and, without the luxury of windows, it served as a sort of escape hatch from reality, a void in which time and obligation dissipated more and more with each swallow. It could be day outside, or not. The pertinent thing was that no one cared. The ritual transcended all borders, all boundaries. In here, you were, and everything outside was not.

John Matos sat on his stool, hands palm down on the bar, chin resting on his hands. He stared into the mirrored surface directly in front of him, watching the world behind him through the misty eyes of an old piece of glass, annoyed by what he saw. Not that there was anything out of the ordinary happening right then; what bothered him was the fact that all those things he saw, those stools and tables and trinkets that lined the walls, those meaningless little pieces of kitsch, gathered as an afterthought and spread haphazardly on any available surface or ledge, had the nerve to exist even when he was not looking at them. He had a hard time acknowledging that anything could go on without his being directly and immediately conscious of whatever it was, like when a child closes his eyes and makes the universe disappear. He picked his head up just long enough to take a drink, put it back down. The beer was cold but had a stale aftertaste to it, meaning the taps hadn't been cleaned for a while. But it was the cheapest draft in town, and quantity mattered. Anyone who claimed to drink alcohol strictly for the taste probably also read *Playboy* for the articles.

A voice next to him stirred him from his trance.

"So I heard this funny story... " It was Samuel. In his quasi-metaphysical contemplations, John had forgotten old Sammy was there. He pivoted his head so as to see him better, never taking his chin from his hands.

"Yeah, this is funny... wait, how did it go... hold on a second... " Samuel was drunk again. John was not the only patron that wondered if he ever left the bar.

"Yeah? Well?" John was curious. He sat up. "What's this great story?"

"I didn't say great, did I?" The question was sincere.

"No, you said funny."

"Yes, funny."

"So, what is it?"

"Oh, oh, oh, right." Samuel shifted on his stool, crossed his legs. "So there's this guy, right? And anyway this guy is a drunk, like a real drunk, not some part time wannabe, not some dabbler or some college kid or rich fucker or... "

"Yeah, yeah I get it already. Shit." He took a drink.

"Yeah, and, okay, so this guy one night, he's really drunk. Like really, really, drunk, and on a bet, okay, he eats all this change, right?"

"Change?"

"Like quarters and dimes and shit. Change."

"Right."

"So anyway, he passes out that night and all is fine, right? But the next day he goes through his drinks and all of sudden, like, he's not feelin' so good, which is normal but this hurt is abnormal, and he goes to throw up and, as the shit starts hitting the water he begins to like freak the fuck out, right? Because what's comin' out isn't lunch or food at all, but fuckin'... "

"Ready for another?" It was the bartender.

"Sure, sure, keep 'em comin'."

He looked at John. "You too?"

"Yeah. I got a week's worth of pay I'm just dying to give you." Neither man smiled. The bartender returned with their drinks.

"So no pizza or spaghetti or none of that floating in the bowl, no. The shit that came out was way too heavy, like splashing his face up between his legs and shit, and when he finally wiped the water from out his eyes, he saw... money."

"Money... "

"Yeah, like coins and shit. You know, money."

"Right. Money."

"So he figures, well, shit, I did eat those coins and all, and they had ta come out one end or the other, right? So he writes it off, goes home. Next day he gets his drinks in him, but gets sick all over again, but like way too early in the night, okay?"

"Okay... "

"So he goes to yak again and, holy shit, doesn't the same thing happen again! More fucking coins splashin' in the bowl! So now he's a little freaked out but he still fishes the money out of the john and heads off home, stopping on the way to buy a fifth."

"A fifth of what?"

"What?"

"A fifth of WHAT?" John's voice was rising.

"What the fuck does that matter?"

"Is he a whiskey man or gin or scotch... ? Of course it fucking matters!"

Samuel realized his mistake right away. It did matter.

"Whiskey," he said, "Jack Daniels."

"Mmm-hmmmmm," John hummed, emphasizing the second syllable. "I see... " For some alcoholism is an art, and more often than not, it is not only the art but also the media of choice that serves to define the man.

"Yeah, and so he goes home and drains the bottle and the sickness comes again and he hunches over the kitchen sink and sure as shit more money comes up! Clankin' and jumpin' around in the sink and so now he's really freakin' out and starts wonderin' if he's dying or what, so he calls the hospital and tells them what's up, and they just laugh and laugh 'cause they think he's just some old drunk on the phone all slurrin' and the like, and well, he is a drunk, but... and so he's all distraught for a day or so but keeps drinkin' and pukin' up these coins right?"

"Sure, right."

"So the next night it all happens again, and he figures, *fuck it*, right? And so he decides to keep on drinkin' and pukin' and keep the money and shit, okay? And it turns out that the change more than covered his bar tab, so it kept him on the sauce if nothing else, and... "

"Wait, lemme guess here," John interrupted. "So I bet this guy, this fucking guy, drinks and drinks and ends up dying, dying of like liver failure or something, am I right? And this high and mighty tale of morality comes from you, Samuel? I mean, Jesus Christ, you drink more than anyone in this fucking town! Save your fucking sermons for Sunday, Reverend."

"No, well, see, that's just the thing! He doesn't die at all! In fact, he starts to save the money and invests it and actually makes a killing in some freak stock venture! See, he ends up rich as hell and can afford the best liquors and lives happily ever after!" He picked up his fresh beer, slammed it, smiled expectantly. He set the empty glass back down on the bar and motioned for the bartender.

"That, Samuel, that's the most fucked up fairy tale I've ever heard." He laughed, scornful. "Tell that to the kids and you'd have a bunch of drunk little fuckers all bloated with coins in their guts!"

"No, its true! It's true! Some guy the other night swore to it..."

"Yo, Sammy-boy, I swear I got this bridge for sale... "

"Fuck you," he said, genuinely hurt.

"Fuck you, too," John replied, not caring.

It was settled. They both stared ahead, not speaking. The jukebox kicked in again, sending a collective cringe through the bar. It was another Thorogood song, something about bourbon and scotch and beer. And somewhere outside people were aging and time was passing and money was passing hands and hands were busy building or destroying and it may have been nighttime or daytime or the end of time... out there. The pertinent thing is that no one—no one in there—cared.

"Fuck you," he said, genuinely hurt.

"Fuck you, too," John replied, not caring.

The lights flashed and then that familiar voice: "Drink up people, last call."

John Matos complied, not wanting to anger the man who supplied him with the means that allowed him to cope, to forget his life and all his failures and missed opportunities. In a general sense it is important not to bite the hand that feeds, but for some it is infinitely more important to never bite the hand that pours.

"Thanks, Jimmie." He slid off the stool, found his feet.

"Yeah, take it easy, John." He was washing pint glasses in a metal sink. "See you tomorrow night."

"Yeah, sure."

He traced patterns like sound waves to the door, riding the undulations out into the real world. He was reminded of the frigid cold, the artificial glow of neon streetlights, the black slush and heavy wet snow that would soak his feet before he got home. He groaned, watching it manifest itself in air and slowly dissipate into the gloom overhead.

The streets were largely deserted of life save for the blanketed figures that lay atop the heat grates that dotted the sidewalk. Rows of silent cars lined the streets on either side (just beyond the artificial boundary established by curbs and parking meters), serpentine vertebrae waiting for that early morning spark to life. John knew nothing of rush hour, usually asleep during such hours, preparing for the next night's activities. The life of an alcoholic was not an easy one, and required much rest.

Stoplights overhead whirred and popped and changed, colored lights that dictated decrees to no one, casting their lonely lights into the night, skimming red and green across ice-slicked streets while the city slept. Tomorrow they would regain their power, but in the early morning hours they ruled with all the potency of a wet cigarette. John crossed a side street, oblivious to whether he was granted permission to walk or not. He stumbled past the sign, the red of the 'do not walk' hand momentarily illuminating his face.

"WHAT THE FUCK IS WRONG WITH YOU?"

It came from nowhere. He spun around and almost fell over. The street was empty. For the first time in a while he felt his heart beating, powerful, fast. He felt lightheaded, felt as if he should flee. He turned back toward home.

"ASSHOLE!"

This time he did not turn around, but put his head down, picked up the pace. He breathed heavily now, the spent breath forming a solid line connecting him to the sky, a lifeline to heaven. He felt the sweat bead up; saw the steam rising from his body as it pushed forward.

"What the hell was that?" He said the words aloud just to hear something real. He looked back over his shoulder without stopping, bumped into a garbage can, knocking it over.

"HEY WATCH IT FUCKHOLE!"

He looked down expecting to see some homeless mass glowering up at him, drunk and angry for the careless intrusion, ready to fight. To his horror his glance took in no such image. There was nothing but trash, a wet sidewalk, an upset can.

In a panic he righted himself, started to run, leaving the garbage strewn across the sidewalk. In his haste he failed to see the used tissues stuck to his wet boots, but even if he had he was too shaken to care.

Around the corner, past the Chinese food joint, up the steps into a familiar vestibule, cold, frightened fingers and fumbling keys, and finally, after what seemed an entire miserable lifetime, the warmth and safety of his studio apartment.

He slammed the door behind him as if the blast from wood hitting wood would be enough to kill whatever demon had been taunting him. He turned lock after lock and when the clicking cacophony had ceased, he doubled over, hands on knees, feeling his torso expand and contract, expand and contract. He stayed this way for several minutes until the unconscious ease of breathing came back to him, stood up, headed to the kitchen for a remedy. He reached for the half-empty bottle of scotch on the counter, noticed his hands were still trembling and, tipping the bottle skyward, took a big pull. He swallowed two mouthfuls and brought the bottle back down to the counter, landing it so hard that some of the bilious liquid splashed out from the neck, spilling on his hands, the floor. He took no notice and inverted the bottle again, this time managing one mouthful before losing his balance, stepping back and slipping on the spilled scotch that had puddled on the floor. He felt nothing but air, the pull of gravity, until his body made contact with the cheap linoleum of his meager kitchen. He felt for a moment as if he had been punched in the chest, hard. Again his breath became labored, but now even his eyes had joined the mutiny: all attempts to focus on any object were met with failure. A sort of impressionistic reality now dominated his sight, like trying to make out one's face in a foggy bathroom mirror—only soft edges and swaths of color. He lay there, staring up at the nothingness that now presented itself.

"WHAT A FUCKING ASSHOLE!"

A voice. He sat up in his blindness, startled back into reality, swung fists in a futile attempt to counterattack his would-be assailant.

"SHUT THE HELL UP!"

This time the voice came from the other side of the room. His body went numb. There was more than one.

"Leave me alone you sons-a-bitches!" Spit flew from his lips as he screamed, the words coming out at once both as threats and terrified pleas. "I'm a veteran!"

"OR WHAT... " The voice was taunting now. "YOU'LL KEEP SWINGING YOUR FISTS AND FAN US TO DEATH?"

Laughter, but this time from all around.

"DAMN IT... WILL YOU SHUT UP!"

"YOU'RE SUCH A LITTLE PUSSY! WE'RE JUST HAVING A LITTLE FUN!"

He realized he was surrounded. He gave up, put his hands over his face, began to sob.

"Please... " he pleaded through heaves, "please... just take what you want and leave me alone... "

"PLEASE" the voice was mocking again, "PLEASE... JUST TAKE WHAT YOU WANT... "

"... just leave me alone... please... " John lay on the floor in fetal position, covered his head with his hands; waited for the beating to begin.

But it would not.

The scotch would begin to take hold, coupling with his injuries, to create a pseudo-consciousness. His eyes would remain shut tight, but strange conversations would find their way into his mind, some sounding more like arguments, often violent. He could only make out bits and pieces, words and phrases like "dormant for far too long" and "patience" and "uprising," about some prey being made soft by convenience and something about sedentary animals being easy to catch and kill, but he was admittedly unsure about that last one because it was right about that time that the darkness finally overcame him and he lost consciousness.

Sunlight.

He awoke to clear vision and a pounding headache. His mouth felt as if it was filled with cotton and he was still lying curled up on his kitchen floor. Something warm and wet surrounded his body, soaked his clothes. It was piss. He groaned, rolled over onto his back to face the sun, that ever-vigilant judge of the late-night sinner. It shined in his face as if trying to augment his shame with its illumination. He looked at the clock, but it had been turned around to face the wall. Resigned to not being able to get up and right it, he figured that it was daytime, and that was good enough for him. He usually didn't get out to the bars until at least dusk, and that looked to be at least several hours off. He sat up, feeling the clothes heavy and clinging to his frame, rubbed his head, felt as if he were going to be sick. He saw the empty bottle on the floor but had no recollection as to how it got there. His brain seemed filled with nothing more than fumes, as if a once coherent entity was now nothing more than an amorphous collection of gray matter, spawning nothing but incoherence. He managed to get to his knees, then his feet, made his way to the bathroom, splashed some cold water on his face, undressed, climbed in under the hot water, let it run over his pain. He had to get cleaned up; it was almost time to go. Outside the city writhed and coursed through the freezing day, through intersections and tollbooths and drive-through restaurants, into parking garages and tunnels and fuming gridlock, unstoppable and infinite, the cars belching carbon, like a serpent wrapping its coils once more around an unsuspecting city.

EMBELLISHMENT #2

"Fuck you," he said, genuinely hurt.

"Fuck you too," he replied, not caring. John returned his gaze to the mirror ahead, sunk back into silence. Samuel poured himself off the barstool onto reluctant legs and stumbled off to annoy another bar patron. John was grateful for the silence. If only they'd shut that goddamned jukebox off. He cupped his mug in his hand, lifted it.

In the far corner of the bar, up around the ceiling, there was an old television set that cast its darkened single eye out over the bar. Not too long ago it was a constant source of light, broadcasting sports, news—reality—into their holy void, disturbing it, perverting it. Every night while John sat on his stool, fighting to forget, wanting little more than to stare absently at nothing until achieving some artificial Zen state through an unholy combination of noxious alcoholic concoctions and stillness, that damned box would command his attention. Would pull him from his bliss to let him know about world events, friends, marathons, dish cleaners that are tough on grease but gentle on skin, home, car, and life insurance, abs of steel and Leonardo Dicaprio's new movie. It was an unwelcome lifeline back into that which he was trying so hard to break free from, reality's impervious umbilical cord, the media mother bastard junky seething poison instead of nutrients, stuck and connected and trapped and connected and stuck. So one night, while all were distracted by an unusually large bet at the pool table, he leaned forward and, with his hunting knife, cut the cord.

"'nother beer?"

"Yeah." The bartender picked up the mug, tilted it under the tap, set it down directly on the bar, foam and bubbles rising like the promise of spirits.

"Thanks." The bartender took two bills from the modest pile of cash set on the bar, one for him and one for the beer. There is an ubiquitous system of barroom chivalry that manifests itself in those places of ill repute: at least one dollar tip per round, period—though admittedly it may have less to do with honor than the fact that it kept the bartender coming around. After his short trip to the cash register he came back, propped himself up with his elbows on the bar. John did not look up.

"You hear about father Hanlon, down at St. Mary's?"

"Sure," John lied, hoping his frank response would drive him away.

"So you think he did that... to those boys?"

"Sure."

The bartender studied him for a moment, shook his head.

"Why do I even try to talk to you?"

John shrugged his shoulders, took a mouthful, swallowed. "You're starting to sound like my ex."

"Any woman that would marry you is either a saint or completely insane."

"Or both." He imagined Mother Theresa bound up in a straight jacket and smiled. The bartender walked to the other end of the bar, started washing more glasses. Their relationship was never strained by these curt transactions. They both saw it for what it was: one of necessity, so everything was let slide. Every snide remark, every vitriolic tirade fueled by imbibition, all would fade by the next round. Pure necessity—the kind that fuels the hungry and the tyrannical. John was pondering this strange relationship when the front door pushed open, casting in light from the world outside, the one full of work and toil and bills and responsibilities. The light always seemed to reek of judgment and accusation.

The barstool next to John screeched along the floor as it was yanked backwards, accompanied by a familiar voice from behind him.

"Thought I'd find you here. You mind if I sit?"

John pretended to think this proposition over for a minute.

"If I said 'no' would it make any difference?"

Both knew it wouldn't.

The form sat down sideways on the stool, facing John, much too close for his taste. He could feel the glare coming from his new bar-mate, but still refused to look over.

"I thought you were going to find a job today... " The voice paused, waiting for an answer. There wouldn't be one. "John... ?" The voice was almost pleading, but the effect worked. Somewhere deep within a muddled jumble of synapses and gray matter an impulse flashed that produced some foreign feeling which could only be described as pity.

John turned his head.

"What?" He felt a strange sense of obligation to this person. Sure, they had grown up together, but sometimes some relationships are better left in the past. John realized this; Paul did not.

"So is this it? Is this how its going to end? You dying of liver failure in some dark shithole?"

"We all gotta die of something." He palmed his mug. "Might as well die happy." He knew that would piss him off. It was the whole point.

"Great, man, that's just great." John could tell he was struggling for some witty rebuke, but words always seemed to elude Paul when he needed them most. John managed not to smile, decided that some clichés may be worth their weight in gold.

The bartender reemerged. "Need a beer, buddy?"

"No, no thank you."

John pointed at his friend. "Well then, I'll take his."

"Why are you being such an asshole about this?" Paul's voice had a new edge to it. "I'm just trying to help you out here."

John looked at him inquisitively. "Help me how, exactly?"

"Look, man, don't you see you're just killing yourself here? I mean, Jesus, don't you have any goals or ambitions? Any fucking desire at all to get off your ass and do something with your life?"

There was a brief silence before John's reply. He considered getting loud, getting indignant, attacking this man with old fodder and cleverly crafted epithets. After years of acquaintance he knew how to hurt him, where to pierce his sober do-gooder armor with barbed words. But he had worked all day at getting a good buzz on, and it certainly didn't come cheap anymore, not with his tolerance.

"No." He hoped that would drive him away, but for some reason it didn't.

"Well then, what the fuck... "

John quickly put his hand up, momentarily silencing his antagonist.

"Bartender... a shot for me and my friend!"

"No. NO, I don't want a fucking shot!"

The bartender stopped short, unsure of what to do.

"I want to know what... "

"Hey," John slapped the bar with his palm, motioning toward the bartender. "I'm still ready."

"Jesus."

The tiny glass of bourbon found its way in front of John and then into his gut, warming him temporarily but almost instantly making his head swim. He wasn't big on shots, especially after drinking beer all day. 'Beer to liquor, never sicker' was one of the few rules of drinking to which he actually subscribed, but the situation in which he currently found himself needed some remedy, and a bullet of bourbon seemed the most effective method.

"Jesus... " Paul muttered again.

"I didn't know you were a religious man" is what he had meant to say, but the alcohol had started to really take hold now, so it came out so slurred as to be nearly unintelligible.

"Fuck you." Paul studied his old friend. "Look at yourself. I mean, shit man, you're a mess." He motioned toward the mirror, as if John's sight of himself would shock him into sobriety and employment. But the effect, if there was one, was negligible at best. "What about the future? Do you ever think about that?"

"Fushure. What?"

"Jesus, John, your fucking future." Paul ran his fingers through his hair, exasperated, feigning defeat. "At this rate you'll be dead by forty."

John squinted one eye, trying hard to focus on this intruder. "You're jusht a golden beam of sunshine, ain't ya'?"

"Jesus."

Paul was so busy shaking his head in disgust and John was so busy being drunk that neither of them had any idea that anything was wrong until the gunman had fired off his first shot. Its sheer stentorian volume caused everyone in the bar to instinctively wince as if they had just been shocked with a cattle prod. All eyes were now on the doorway, where the new king of the bar stood in all black, badly in need of a shave and brandishing a .45.

The next round found one of the regulars towards the back of the bar, dropping him instantly.

Another quick succession of gunfire rang out before anyone even had a chance to move. People scrambled, looking for escape or some cover. The rank smell of gun smoke hung in the air, overpowering even the pungent smell of cigarettes and years of stale beer.

Paul and John both made to run. Paul leaped up and became an easy target for the gunman, feeling the mushrooming effect of the bullet inside his chest as if his entire torso were on fire. John, already too drunk to be ambulatory, fell off the side of his barstool and hit the floor. He was out cold.

The next day all the local news stations would lament the tragedy at Manny's bar, would openly weep over the senseless loss of life, over the five murders and even the gunman's own suicide, would broadcast fanciful pleas for peace and demands for more police presence in the downtown area, would press the debate over whether or not priests should be allowed to marry and would argue that if they could the instances of child molestation in the folds may be reduced, would show the images from the scene again and again until the once tittering public would become so overly saturated that they'd actually begin switching the channel at the incident's first mention.

From his shitty second floor apartment, John would see none of this. Propped up in a chair next to the only window in the place, he would watch the world beyond the panes and wonder at how little any of it had changed. He would watch pigeons perch on the concrete ledges of the building next door, would hear the bitter winter winds howl and watch the newspapers and trash swirling like hurricanes in the desolate corners below, would sip cheap whiskey and pick at his toe nails and shit and breathe, and would admittedly, with some semblance of guilt, wonder how long it would be until they opened up Manny's bar again.

Dumpster Meat

Tom Thompson

"CAREFUL, you gotta core around his ass or you'll get shit on the meat."

The second, younger man continued drawing the box-cutter's edge along the raccoon's underbelly. Its fur, matted and slick with blood and debris from its futile struggle with the trap's steel loop, did not look salvageable.

"Too bad." The older man shook his head. "Could've made a nice hat 'n another couple bucks."

"Would've if we'd got here quicker." Bobby cocked his head toward the mouth of the alley and the deserted street beyond.

"Relax. I told ya this ain't easy. Trappin's like dice—any fool can have a lucky day, but if ya' wanna make any money ya' gotta do things my way. When a man don't have clearance he can end up spending all his time wishin' he was inside." He nodded at the surrounding pitted expanse of concrete wall rising from the alley floor to disappear into the murky darkness above. "Now help me push this thing back under the chute."

Together, both men made short work of realigning the heavy metal bin under its respective garbage chute, effectively hiding the trap and its mounting apparatus from view. A rumble above signaled that the complex's disposal was about to make a deposit.

"There's breakfast," both men said almost in unison. Bobby's hands began to shake. Earl smiled grimly and took the box-cutter from his partner to finish dressing the 'coon by the dim light of the chemstick. Once he'd removed its paws he began on the head. Strong, skeletal hands cut carefully along the base of its skull, retaining as much of the neck meat as possible. Dumpster meat fetched two bucks a pound fresh, one if the meat had gone gray. In either case, without the head, feet, or skin, the only discernible difference between rat, cat, 'coon or dog was size and weight. No one involved at any level cared to know the specifics of their meat's origin.

Earl and Bobby picked their way to the last trap on Earl's route. His territory, won by barter and adherence to the rules of succession, was clearly marked for those who knew where to look. In this case, a pennant of yellow plastic fluttered from the chute's rain gutter. As both men approached the dumpster, a tattered mass of rags and plastic sheeting exploded beside them.

Earl shouted, "Dreg!" He fumbled for the box-cutter but Bobby, the smaller and younger of the two, was already a blur of motion. He lunged after the fleeing man-thing and almost caught hold of the miserable creature before it disappeared under the ruined chassis of a Volvo. Luckily, Earl grabbed the shoulder of his partner's vest in time to prevent him from diving to reach in after it, pointing out the way the asphalt buckled ramp-like beneath the car. "Probably a nest of 'em down there. Filthy fuckers. 'S a good thing you're ugly, he mighta pulled ya' in fer a cuddle."

Bobby pursed his lips and inhaled, taking in the stench of sour body odors worse than his own pungent twang. "Did it get the meat?"

Earl nodded, playing the chemstick's soft glow over the calico the dreg had dropped in its flight. The cat was badly gnawed, but Earl managed to salvage the rear haunches and some of the rib meat that hadn't been drooled on. Acknowledging what couldn't be helped, he added the wet handful to their game bag and the two men headed toward the complex's restaurant district.

Dawn found them at Earl's place contemplating their meal. "Where'd you suppose they get baby corn? I mean, 's it from little baby corn plants or 's it somethin' else entirely?" Earl shuddered at his own suggestion as he chewed around a questionable piece of gristle. Bobby didn't look up from his bowl until he'd run a finger around the bottom.

"Are we gonna have tacos for dinner?" Bobby asked hopefully, turning his round moon-face toward the older man.

"Worry 'bout dinner when it's time." Earl paused, then set down his spoon altogether. He leaned back on one elbow and fished around in several pockets of his coveralls and retrieved a packet of rolling papers. Bobby ate in silence, waiting for his companion to continue once his smoke was lit. "Tacos, stir-fry..." A plume of smoke attempted to escape from one nostril and was sucked back inside. "Shit, I remember when you could get a steak around here... those bastards. Lucky fer us, they ain't stuck with TVP *every meal*. That shit makes me fart somethin' fierce... " He trailed off, awash in nostalgia and the smoke's lazy potency. Bobby nodded and eyed the remnants of vegetables and rice in the other man's bowl. "Go ahead." Earl offered, smiling to himself. "Tacos, shit."

"I'll take tacos." Bobby said, leaving Earl to his smoke and mutterings. He left the rusted shipping container his partner slept in and, stepping over the double trip-wire, went in search of a fresh bottle. He chuckled to himself, recalling Earl's words of instruction on skinning their night's catch. Bobby was pretty sure that his people, whoever they were, had been trapping and skinning while Earl's were shitting on themselves in caves. When the two were working Bobby could feel the threads of memories just brush his consciousness, but they didn't quite catch. It was as if he'd walked into a spider web in the dark, except the strands that stuck felt like they belonged. He was a collection of remnants, dark braids, dark eyes, a little magic and a terrible thirst. It was this trickle of magic that first formed the basis for his and Earl's tenuous partnership.

When Bobby agreed to stop selling Earl trap-bait in exchange for a share in the profits and labor, he admitted to himself that his thirst was a mitigating factor. The gnawing, empty feeling in his gut wasn't improving with time. Still, he was providing a valuable service and practicing a legitimate trade. Where he had been barely surviving selling bird carcasses, feather trinkets, and the occasional favor, now he could drink like he needed to. Thus lubricated, the magic flowed more freely. Bird carcasses began presenting themselves with remarkable frequency, piling themselves up along his special scavenging routes.

He thought about Earl's words of advice given during their long conversation soon after meeting one rainy night between Earl's trip-wires. "Now rat an' dog'll eat about anything, and about anything will eat rat, but coon won't eat coon and cat won't eat cat. If ya wanna make any money trappin', the secret's in yer bait." At this Bobby had fortuitously begun offering Earl an inexhaustible supply of bait at prices cheaper than recycling meat as bait or wasting food, an arrangement that suited everyone.

At first Earl was fascinated. "What were these, big-ass pigeons?" He was referring to the pair of mangled bird corpses being offered.

"Crow."

"You realize," Earl said as a sly aside, "if you've got a cat stashed somewhere, it'd be worth five bucks to ya'." He paused. "'Specially a big bastard can do that to city-crows." Indeed the birds were reduced to little more than connective tissue and uncracked bones, but given the limitations of the urban food chain, Earl's new trap-bait was proving quite the windfall, if they could just keep the dregs off the meat.

Evening came. Earl nudged his partner to life behind the shipping container with the toe of his boot.

"C'mon, c'mon, we gotta flush that dreg nest before it gets too dark."

Bobby groaned, his mind floundering in a fog of citrus wine, "'S too early." His stomach gurgled, awash in wet heat, but its reluctance was no match for Earl's boot. Together they wound their way through thinning city crowds. Those who could retreated to the safety of their enclaves in the stark gray towers above the narrow streets and cramped alleys. Bobby shook as he hummed to himself. A low thrum that pushed electric arcs down his arms. His hands steadied.

Guerrilla Sex Generation

Kenji Siratori

THE PARADISE DEVICE of the human body pill cruel emulator that compressed the acidHUMANIX infection of the soul/gram made of retro-ADAM to the nightmare-scripts of the biocapturism nerve cells that crashed a chemical=anthropoid gene-dub mass of flesh-module of the ultra=machinary tragedy-ROM creature system to the murder-protocol data=mutant processing organ BLog@trash sensor drug embryo DNA=channels of the dogs of tera plug-in... .different of her digital=vamp cold-blooded disease animals vital-abolition world-codemaniacs of the terror fear=cytoplasm which turned on the ill-treatment of a clone boy is debugged to the brain universe that was controlled.

Technojunkies hunting for the grotesque WEB=cadaver feti=streaming circuit of the acidHUMANIX infection archive_ body encoder that jointed is output to the brain universe that was processed the data=mutant of her abolition world-codemaniacs emotional replicant::the murder-gimmick of a trash sensor drug embryo DNA=channel to the mass of flesh-module of the ultra=machinary tragedy-ROM creature system paradise device of the human body pill cruel emulator that was send back out the era respiration-byte of the soul/gram made of retro-ADAM gene-dub to the modem=heart of the hybrid cadaver mechanism that turned on the biocapturism nerve cells ill-treatment of the dogs of tera murder game of a chemical=anthropoid.

The abolition world-codemaniacs which covered the reptilian=HUB_modem=heart that accelerates the virus of the dogs of tera and was processed to that genomics strategy circuit data=mutant of her ultra=machinary tragedy-ROM creature system plug-in****the era respiration-byte is send back out=hunting for the grotesque WEB of a chemical=anthropoid to the nightmare-scripts of the biocapturism nerve cells that jointed the paradise device of the human body pill cruel emulator murder-gimmick of the soul/gram made of retro-ADAM I turn on the brain universe of the terror fear=cytoplasm to the cadaver feti=streaming_body encoder that compressed the acidHUMANIX infection@trash sensor drug embryo technojunkies' hacking ill-treatment.

Era respiration-byte is send back out to the murder-protocol of the biocapturism nerve cells paradise device of the human body pill cruel emulator that compressed the acidHUMANIX infection of the soul/gram made of retro-ADAM gene-dub of a chemical=anthropoid mass of flesh-modules of the hyperreal =scanners nightmare-script@cadaver city is output to the ultra=machinary tragedy-ROM creature system reptilian=HUB of a trash sensor drug embryo vital browser of the abolition world-codemaniacs emotional replicant performance that was debugged to the brain universe of the hybrid cadaver mechanism that was processed the data=mutant of a clone boy technojunkies' to super-genomewarable murder game.

Hunting for the grotesque WEB modem=heart of the hybrid cadaver mechanism that compressed the technojunkies' acidHUMANIX infection to the murder-protocol of the biocapturism nerve cells DNA=channel of a chemical=anthropoi d=joints cadaver feti of the soul/gram made of retro-ADAM=trash sensor drug embryo reptilian=HUB_modem=heart that hung up to the paradise device of the human body pill cruel emulator that streams the murder game****I turn on ill-treatment in the surrender-site abolition world-codemaniacs of the terror fear=cytoplasm_send back out the era respiration-bytes of the dogs of tera gene-dubs of her digital=vamp cold-blooded disease animals!

Reptilian=HUB to the paradise device of the human body pill cruel emulator era respiration-byte sending program of the acidHUMANIX infection archive_body encoder that turned on technojunkies' ill-treatment murder-gimmick of the soul/ gram made of retro-ADAM::the data=mutant of a trash sensor drug embryo vital different of her digital=vamp cold-blooded disease animals—to the abolition world-codemaniacs which was controlled the murder-protocol emotional replicant_processed hunting for the grotesque WEB=joints the mass of flesh-module of the hyperreal =scanner form gene-dub of a clone boy to the cadaver feti=streaming circuits of the biocapturism nerve cells DNA=channel of a chemical=anthropoid is debugged.

Abduction, Again

Janis Butler Holm

IN THE BEGINNING, we soared. We knew the crackle of constellations, the heat of worlds unborn. Our coupling was cosmic. He said it was in the stars.

Delicately, he probed me, mound and crevice, plane and orb. He showed me his craft.

When the nights grew cooler, I should have returned to earth. But he promised me the moon. I floated on a cloud.

Now he's light-years away. No longer the chosen one, I wonder where I've been. Here, in the dark, he said he needed space.

Death In Large Numbers

Stephen J. Anderson

ALAN WAS DEAD. Otherwise, it'd been a good day.

Summer was fading fast, and he'd decided he wasn't going to miss the last few glorious days. He'd called in sick with a stomach bug, and then he'd called up his girlfriend and told her they were going to the beach. They had spent a windswept, happy day doing nothing in particular, but then the skies closed in. The air turned steel grey and the rain started to fall.

They had run for shelter, and he remembered the sight of Emma ahead of him, rain plastering her t-shirt to her thin back, the smell of hot pavement sizzling, the rivulets pouring over his skin and getting into his eyes. He could swear that he had felt the air start to tingle, and then everything went sharp for a moment of perfect clarity.

He was struck by a bolt of lightning.

His veins caught fire; he burned from the inside out. His vision went white, and he could smell his hair singe. He convulsed violently, his jaw muscles spasmed so intensely that his jawbone snapped in two, and then his heart stopped. For a moment everything went dark.

Alan woke up.

His eyelids lifted slowly and reluctantly. The influx of light drenched his optic nerves. He realised that he was lying on a bed, with blurred figures standing around him. As he blinked at them furiously, they resolved themselves into his mother, his father, and his brother and, sitting by the bedside, a woman he'd never seen before. He felt as if he'd been asleep for a month, and when he opened his mouth to speak, his tongue was thick and heavy.

"What was that?" he slurred.

His mother sighed and beamed. She came closer and took his hand. Alan barely felt it. It was like she was holding someone else's hand.

"You got hit by lightning, dear. Not directly, you were very lucky. You could've died." Her eyes moist.

Alan frowned. He moved his jaw experimentally. It felt fine. His heart was beating; his skin was perhaps slightly pink, at worst. He was clearly alive, but he remembered the process of dying in complete detail.

"You were *very* lucky," his mother repeated.

"If it weren't for Susan," and here she indicated the woman who sat by the bed, "you'd have never made it to hospital."

Alan looked at the woman. He recoiled from her intense stare. She touched his arm, gently, with affection, and tears began to roll down her cheeks. Slightly disturbed, he felt ought to say something.

"Thank you," he mumbled, awkwardly. She smiled at him weakly.

At least the explanation made some sense of his memories. His heart probably did stop. The burning skin and cracked jawbone were probably just his memory being over-dramatic. Something nagged at him.

"Mum, where's Emma?" he asked.

His mother frowned, quizzically.

"Who's Emma?" she replied.

He stared at her.

"Emma. My girlfriend, Emma," he said, slowly.

His mother's eyebrows raised in alarm. He heard the woman, Susan, inhale sharply.

His mother leant in towards him, holding his hand tighter. She opened and closed her mouth, apparently struggling for words.

"Alan," she said, and hesitated again. "I don't know what you mean. Susan's your girlfriend, isn't she?"

Eventually, they had to sedate Alan to keep him calm. There'd been no rational debate. Alan knew that Emma was his girlfriend, and his mother knew that it was Susan. Eventually, Susan had fled the room in tears, and his father had hurried outside to have a hushed conversation with a doctor. One brief struggle later, and Alan was floating on a pink cloud of apathy.

Later, a neurologist came to see him, a Doctor Spring.

"You can call me Jack," he said, grinning.

Jack Spring added to the general weirdness of the day. He was over six feet tall, spindly and pale skinned. Almost albino, in fact. He wore glasses with small, dark, round lenses, and when he smiled, his incisors were unnervingly large.

As far as Alan was concerned, Spring was trying to convince him that he was crazy.

"Basically," said Spring, "the brain is electrical. Run too much current through it, and it will short circuit, and if it does, bits of it can be damaged. If the bits of it that are damaged hold memories, then you may lose access to those memories. At least for a while."

Alan shook his head, frustrated.

"It doesn't feel like that. It doesn't feel like I've forgotten *anything*. Emma's my girlfriend, always has been, since uni."

Spring rubbed his cheek, nodding.

"A little unusual. Memory loss, yes, usually temporary, but it's less common for... other memories to take their place."

He paced his lanky frame around the room, drumming spindly fingers on the bed frame as he passed.

"I had quite a long discussion with your mother. I apologise, but we went over your relationship history in some detail. You've never been involved with anyone called Emma, as far as she knows."

Alan sighed, rubbing his eyes with the heels of his hands.

"Look," he said, pointedly, "I've no idea what's going on here, but she has to know about her. I've been going out with her for seven years, she's met her *dozens* of times! They write to each other, for God's sake! Emma is my girlfriend, and I'm *not* fucking crazy!"

"Please, Mr. Winters," said Spring soothingly, "No one's saying you're crazy, it's just... " He broke off, and stared at Alan, frowning deeply.

"What?" Alan demanded. No answer was immediately forthcoming. "What is it now?" he said, sitting up in bed.

Spring took a deep breath.

"Mr. Winters, did you say you met Emma at university? Seven years ago?"

"Yes! I met her at *fucking* university!"

Spring clasped his hands behind his back, smiling oddly.

"According to your mother, Mr. Winters, you left Sixth Form and never went to university. You went traveling around Europe, where you had a succession of short-term girlfriends. You only got together with Susan about two years ago."

Alan stared at him, too confused and angry to even speak. Spring fished around in his pockets.

"What I'd like to do, Mr. Winters, is run some tests on you, if that's alright... "

Alan never got the chance to answer him, and Spring never found what he was looking for.

A whistling noise had begun, too faint to locate the origin. Alan looked around, searching in vain for the source. It rose in pitch and volume, unmistakably drawing closer, then turned into an unearthly shriek, and ended with the roof of the hospital suddenly collapsing in on them.

When Spring managed to emerge from the blanket of dust and plaster that covered him, he found his patient spread out on top of a broken bed. A steaming, hissing meteorite, radiating heat, sat on top of what was left of him.

Spring looked down at the remains, and then peered up through the hole in the ceiling. He looked down again.

"Well," he said to himself, "you don't see that every day."

"So," said Alan despairingly, "I woke up and I was here. I don't even have a girlfriend anymore. I don't have a job and my friends are all different. And they all think I'm crazy."

This time, when Alan had awoken, he'd decided to play along. He had no idea what was happening to him, but he was coming around to the idea that he might be crazy.

He'd attempted to adapt to his new life. He'd feigned memory loss to cover his lack of knowledge, which wasn't that far from the truth. He wasn't sleeping much, and it was starting to show, starting to worry his family. He didn't want to tell them that he was having nightmares. He didn't want to tell them that he kept waking up from terrifyingly vivid dreams of being crushed under a meteorite, bones splintering, internal organs crushed and torn.

Of course, that hadn't happened. A meteorite had crashed into his house, but he'd just been struck by flying debris, knocking him unconscious.

Yet, he still remembered dying.

Twenty-three days after waking, he had seen an advert in a magazine for a therapist.

The therapist's name was Jack Spring. Alan had taken it as a sign.

Spring sighed and adjusted the steel circles of his glasses on his nose. He paused in his tracks and stared at Alan through dark blue lenses. His pale, almost albino skin gleamed in the bright sunlight, even outshining his white linen suit.

"And is anything else different?" he asked.

Alan gave a short, helpless laugh.

Spring had insisted they go for a walk while they talked, explaining that his air conditioning had broken down, and the heat would be intolerable. They were walking along Camden High Street toward Inverness Street, through stalls selling bananas, pineapples, mangoes and melons, past brightly coloured stores and slightly dressed women. Bars that were mostly garden were scattered along the road. Rainbow parasols clustered like fungi around the bases of the gently creaking palm trees.

"Well, for one thing," Alan said, "I don't remember Britain being so tropical."

Spring raised an eyebrow and glanced around the street.

"It's actually quite mild this year. Anyway, your story makes a sort of sense, even if this doesn't." He was waving an object about in his hand. Alan peered at it. It was about the size of a packet of cigarettes, and looked like it was made from solidified pink fog. Subtle lights danced around inside it.

"What's that?" he asked.

"This," said Spring, "I do believe, is what the other Jack Spring was going to use on you, although I can hardly credit what it's telling me. It says that you aren't fully in this universe."

"Oh." He looked blankly at Spring. "What are you on about?"

Spring sighed.

"Are you familiar with the concept of parallel universes? Multiple versions of reality, each different in some way, but all co-existing? Like multiple versions of your life, what it might have become if you'd made different decisions?"

"Sort of," said Alan doubtfully. "Think I saw a programme on it once. Didn't pay much attention to it."

"Well, if I read this right," said Spring, waving his device vaguely at Alan, "you are not properly here. You're partially in this version of reality, and partially somewhere else—the universe that you came from originally, I think. Do you understand?"

Alan frowned.

"Sort of," he said again. "But what does it mean?"

Spring walked again, clasping his hands behind his back.

"I can only hypothesize, you understand. I believe that, when you were struck by lightning, it unlocked within you a potential you never knew you had. I believe that your experience, and your proximity to death, caused an alteration in your quantum state and connected you to other selves, other copies of you, scattered across parallel universes, each one different in some way from your own. You are experiencing the lives of these other selves as if they were yours."

Spring suddenly turned and strode toward a fruit stall. Alan trudged after him, sweating.

"And each self," Spring said, as if he'd merely paused for breath, "each other version of you—based on limited evidence—seems to be on the verge of an unlikely death."

Alan leant against the wooden frame of the stall. He frowned, trying to bend his head around the concept.

"Well, I think I get what you mean. Sort of. But that doesn't make sense. It's not like I'm connected—I am them. I'm living their lives."

He sagged and cradled his forehead in his palm.

"Fuck that, how do I get it to stop? How do I get *my* life back?"

Spring gazed off into the distance.

"Yes, I'm not really sure about that one… "

He smiled brightly, long incisors flashing in the sunlight.

"But *nil desperandum*, old chap. I'm sure I'll work it out. Pass me a banana, would you?"

Alan blinked and looked down. The side of the stall was stacked with ripe fruit, the sweet smell heavy in the air. He leant down to pick up a bunch. He barely saw the array of black eyes, glinting in the darkness, before the spider dashed out from its hiding place and sunk its fangs into the back of his hand.

"Fuck!" Alan yelled, shook the huge, hairy body away from him, and stared at Spring in disbelief. Realisation crept upon him.

"Oh, you've *got* to be kidding me… "

Alan gently rocked backwards and forwards on the *tatami* mat, shaking his head.

"A *spider*? I got bit by a spider on *Camden High Street*? Un-fucking-believable."

Jack Spring looked up from his meditation. He adjusted his circular glasses and gazed at Winters through dark blue lenses. He pursed his lips.

"Indeed. You tell a strange tale, Winters-san, but not one completely outside my experience."

Spring tapped an object to his right with two straightened fingers. It appeared to Alan to be the twin of the device he had seen before, misty pink and organic. Lights flashed mysteriously within it.

"If nothing else, the device confirms elements of your story. Although... " Spring's voice tailed off. He frowned deeply.

"No mind. From your description, the spider in question would appear to *Phoneutria fera*, the Brazilian Wandering Spider. It is one of the deadliest spiders in the world, and a very rare visitor to these shores. Your streak of poor luck continues."

"You're fucking telling *me*," said Alan, loudly. "So, you think that he... I mean you... the *other* you was right?"

Spring's frown almost cut his forehead in two.

"Perhaps. You see, Winters-san, I am, possibly, of a more spiritual inclination than my parallel self. I offer a subtly different interpretation. A guess, nothing more, it pains me to say."

Alan waved his hands, despairing. "Whatever."

Spring coughed.

"I believe that you are a roaming soul. I believe that you, in your true reality, hover on the brink of death. Some special circumstance—perhaps this lightning bolt you speak of—has cast your consciousness, your spirit, free to roam the parallel dimensions. But your spirit is drawn inexorably to other versions of yourself also on the brink of death, there to possess them, to *become* them, for that brief span before they must go to their fate. Perhaps you do this out of empathy, or perhaps your soul is attempting to come to terms with its own impending end."

"Very New Age." Alan laughed shortly. "You remind me of my girlfriend. Well, one of them, anyway," he finished sourly.

He stood up, wincing at his cramped knees, and walked to the window, arms folded.

He watched the strange world hurry about its unfamiliar business. Spring continued.

"Your soul is on a journey, your possibilities are diminishing. I believe that you will suffer more and more likely forms of mortality, until finally you experience the most commonplace death of all. And then, your understanding of death complete, your journey done, you will return to your own reality and body, there to meet your own end."

Alan pulled faces as he mulled the idea over.

"You mean that I'm stuck like this? That I'm just going to keep dying? That I'm going to have to keep doing this over and over?"

Spring bowed his head. "I believe this to be true."

Alan snorted, angrily. "Fantastic. That's my life, is it? Spending every day worrying about what's going to happen to me next, and all I've got to look forward to is death. And I've got no fucking idea how long I've got left."

Spring laughed, lightly. Alan glared at him. He could've sworn the investigator's eyes twinkled behind the dark lenses.

"I am sorry, Winters-san, but... perhaps that is all any of us can say."

Alan left the offices of Spring Spiritual Investigations in a foul mood, and died in a freak fireworks accident.

Unwilling to accept that this was going to be the rest of his life, he rebelled against fate or karma or whatever was doing this to him. He never found much out about his next life. He locked himself inside his house and refused to venture out or even answer the door. He spent a sleepless week pacing the floors, trying not to think about his diminishing food supplies. Eventually, exhausted, he lay on his bed and drifted off into a dreamless slumber, book cradled on his chest, bedside lamp still burning bright.

Around midnight, his lamp shorted out and the bulb blew. A tiny, red-hot grim reaper leapt from the shattered remains and landed on his pyjamas. He burnt to death.

Apparently, this was quite unlikely.

Passive resistance was not going to work. He became hyper-vigilant, examining every situation minutely for its lethal possibilities.

He found himself living in an England still ruled by the Royal Stuarts. He decided he would keep a mental journal of the strange places where he found himself living and, more importantly, dying. His method of death had never repeated itself, but maybe there was some subtle pattern. Maybe there was a clue, or a way out, hidden in the designs of his demise. Maybe he could even learn to see Death before it saw him.

In Royal Stuart England, he avoided a possibly embarrassing duel of honour, but died of syphilis.

On a world suffering from unceasing war, the ground collapsed beneath his feet and he plummeted into the sewers. He drowned.

In a purely matriarchal society, he was savaged by dogs. Five lifetimes later, on a parallel world entirely covered by rainforest, he was deeply surprised when he was crushed by another meteorite. He made a point of tracking down the next Jack Spring and complaining. This incarnation turned out to be a Catholic priest.

"I thought you... I mean he... *you* said I was going to get more likely deaths?"

"Perhaps I'm not as smart as I think I am," Spring replied. Then he grinned like a hyena.

The lives and deaths continued, some less likely, some more, but with no discernible pattern. On a version of Earth with a single, unbroken landmass, ruled by children, where the national language consisted of fragments of torch songs, he was killed in a tragic collision between a streetcar and an elephant.

He gave up.

He began to live with abandon. He was unable to take pleasure in lives that he knew would be snatched away from him, and unable to face another agonising death. Each of his fates so far had been uniquely painful, and he experienced them all in excruciating detail. He sought to dull his senses and wile away his time in a hedonistic haze.

He also spent a lot of time with the various Jack Springs he encountered. Despite the bizarre variety of lives and unfamiliar worlds, he was the one constant. In every reality, there would always be a Jack Spring, and he was always roughly the same person. He became the closest thing Alan had to a friend.

During one kaleidoscopically pharmaceutical binge, he staggered into the hotel room he was sharing with Spring and waggled a multi-coloured finger at him.

"Now, listen," he said, "You really have to tell me who you are. Why are you always *here*?"

Spring knocked back a purple pill with a swig of beer and giggled. "If I told you, you wouldn't believe me."

Alan shook his head determinedly. "No, really, tell me," he slurred.

Spring shrugged, and told him. Alan didn't believe him.

"I envy you, you know," said Spring. Alan stared at him perplexedly.

"No, really, really I do. I always figured that people were afraid of death because they don't understand it. Well, you probably understand death better than *anyone*."

Alan shook his head.

"You mean," he said sourly, "I know more about stupid ways of dying than anyone."

"No," replied Spring, "it's all just a matter of degree, right? I mean, you've had a heart attack, right?"

Alan conceded this was true. He had fallen into a vat of electric eels.

"So, lots of people have heart attacks. Not the way you did, but still. You've got a very special perspective. You know more about death and how it happens than anyone. People would give a lot to know what you know."

Over the next few lifetimes, Alan thought about what Spring had said. He was dimly aware that he had lost control many worlds ago. The worlds he awoke to became irrelevant, and friends and family were insubstantial ciphers. Always, his first act would be to seek oblivion in some bar or drug den. Wonders jostled past the windows, and he ignored them all.

But.

He was bored. He'd exhausted every short-term thrill. There were things he'd always wanted to do, but they took precious time. He'd never managed to learn to play the saxophone; he'd tried, but he'd blown too hard and ruptured his lung. He tried to catch up on his reading but, always assuming he could find the book again on the next alternate world, he had trouble remembering where he'd left off. He felt as if he were trapped in a hamster wheel.

He began to see something. Spring was right: he really had become familiar with death, in all its forms. He knew its character and shape, knew its moods like a lover's.

Although he could never predict how it would come for him, he could see it waiting for others. He began to see people's fates before they happened. This person would die in a car crash, that one would succumb to cancer, this man would commit suicide.

Out of curiosity, he tried intervening. He didn't do it for altruistic reasons, or for gratitude, which was just as well. He was just trying to keep himself occupied.

He began to take perverse pleasure in his Good Samaritan performances. Snatching people from the jaws of Death was a powerful thrill. It became a game, a race, a battle of wits against an imaginary enemy. Alan began to take each life he failed to save personally, as if it were a point he'd lost in a cosmic game. He would linger near the scenes of his failures, staring unhappily at the corpse, ignoring the odd looks he gathered.

The difference between a live and dead human was stark, and the peaceful deaths were most disturbing of all. Their bodies looked as if they had merely paused, as if they would at any moment get up, walk, talk, smile, eat lunch. At the same time, something vital had clearly fled the body, and he began to understand why people believed in souls. He wondered what it was that moved flesh.

Wards occupied by the terminally ill began to fascinate him. As soon as he awoke from each new death, he would quit his job and apply for menial work in any hospital that would take him. He spent as long as he could with the dying without arousing suspicion.

He saw the myriad, trivial, undignified ways in which people usually pass from the world. Alan had been shot, poisoned, bit, struck by flying objects and, worst, demolished from within by a flesh-eating bug. They, on the other hand, were wracked by cancer, had their dignity removed by bowel disease, or their bodies crushed by speeding vehicles. Some had their limbs removed, piece by piece, in a futile struggle against decay. Alan began to think that, in a certain light, he was lucky. His deaths tended to be sharp and brutal, but almost... well... glamorous? He was sure every one of his obituaries had been blackly funny. No one grinned as these poor sods faded away.

Every day he would be there with flowers and gifts and a happy word. For the brief time, before his own fate caught up with him, he would become a minor celebrity, his appearance at the ward always welcome. He hovered over the beds of the doomed, desperate to be there at their passing.

Worlds flickered past like television channels.

In the end, his quest proved fruitless. The hospital staff would—quite rightly—remove him from the rooms of the dying. He had no business being there, and they had lives to save. There was one exception, an old man being devoured by a vicious cancer. He had asked not to be resuscitated.

They had spent hours talking, the man's voice an unceasing whisper, his story spooling from his lips. Alan was fascinated. He thought, jaded as he was, that there was nothing he hadn't experienced, but this man had done things and been places that Alan didn't even know existed. He had used every second. When he was done, his life rewound, he paused and parted his lips. Air rattled into his lungs. His eyes widened suddenly. His back arched and his hand grabbed for Alan's, anchoring them together.

Alan jolted in terror, his mind frozen. He knew he should do something, but couldn't bring himself to move, or even speak. This was what he'd been waiting for, wasn't it? Torn between fear and fascination, he clamped his free hand over the old man's.

The dying man's mouth opened wide, his eyes staring beyond the room, and he gasped as if surprised. His jaw never closed again, but slackened as his head tilted back. His arched back slowly relaxed, and his eyes lost focus. His chest stopped its irregular motion.

And that was that.

Alan spent the evening wandering in a morose and aimless way around a nearby park, and by coincidence, bumped into another Jack Spring.

He hadn't met one for several lifetimes now, and was genuinely pleased to see something like a friendly face. Of course, this Jack Spring didn't know him, so Alan told him his story. He'd become so practised at telling it, he barely thought about it. The words just tumbled from his lips in a gentle sing-song way. Spring listened quietly whilst they walked by the lake, raising his eyebrows here and there. Halfway through he fished another version of the cloudy pink device from his pocket, scrutinised it briefly and then, apparently satisfied, waved at Alan to continue.

It was twilight by the time Alan had finished. Spring stood silently for a moment, gazing out over the dim waters.

"That's a strange story," he said, "but I think I believe you." He smiled oddly. "I think I'm very lucky to have met you."

Alan frowned. "The problem is, I'm still no closer to understanding what's happening to me. I didn't see anything, the old man just *died*. He just *stopped*. I mean, is that it? Is that all? We live for no reason, there's no sense in the way we die, and when we die we just stop? There's nothing left but a body, and nothing happens afterwards. No soul, no afterlife, no purpose."

He knelt by the lakeside, rooting for a stone. He found a small, flat one and flung it out over the lake. It skipped bitterly over the water, then sank in despair.

Spring murmured to himself, his hands behind his back. He was dressed oddly, even when compared to his alter-egos. It was a warm day, but he was in a heavy, hairy brown coat, with matching fedora. His eyes were covered by square, reflective lenses. He took a deep breath.

"Not at all. Our purposes are given to us by fate. *You* may believe that you have no purpose, but I know that I have a destiny."

Alan looked at him cynically. "Which is?" he asked.

Spring smiled mysteriously. "A man's destiny is a personal thing. Perhaps your destiny was to meet me, here, on this night."

Alan raised an eyebrow, then snorted. He turned back to look at the fading light on the water.

"So, what do you do? As a job, I mean?" he asked.

Spring smiled again.

"Well, I'm not Jack Spring the Neurologist or Jack Spring the Psychologist, that's for certain. Jack Spring the Counselor, perhaps, depending on your point of view."

He beamed widely. He shifted his position. Out of the corner of his eye, Alan thought he saw a brief flash of something metallic and sharp lurking in Spring's palm.

"I wouldn't so much call it a job, more of a calling."

Alan stared at him blankly. He began to giggle. Spring frowned at him, and Alan started to laugh. His laugh became huge, roaring, the laugh of someone who'd finally got the punchline. He bent over, holding his stomach, hardly able to breathe. Spring stepped forwards, a sharp shard of metal slipping out of his voluminous sleeve into his hand.

Alan felt the knife slip into his neck, but couldn't stop laughing. He saw his blood gush out onto the pebbles and fan out into the water, and thought it was the funniest thing he'd ever seen. He sank to his knees and laughed until he was spitting blood. A wave of dizziness swept over him, and he fell into oblivion.

Alan woke up.

He woke up in a room exactly like his bedroom, in a house exactly like his house, on a street exactly like his street. He wandered down stairs, exactly like his stairs, and into a kitchen, exactly like his kitchen. A man called George kissed him good morning. He shrugged and thought, close enough.

They went to the beach.

A Particle Is Born

David Borthwick

AS THE TRAIN SLICED THROUGH the autumn countryside, Clarissa glanced at her wristwatch. Only ten minutes to go. She leaned back, stretched her legs, and fought waves of jet lag. She'd booked her flight from San Francisco at the last minute after receiving the call from England, and only snatched a few hours sleep before catching the train from London King's Cross. She reached for the battered briefcase that lay on the seat beside her and removed a thick cardboard folder that contained the near-finished manuscript. Her thumb rifled through almost three-hundred pages before reaching the final chapter. Apart from a title, the chapter contained only a few handwritten notes that outlined what little she knew about her latest interviewee:

> Paul Alexander Eveling. Senior Lecturer in Theoretical Physics, Trinity College, Cambridge. Achieved short-lived notoriety twenty years ago after publishing a paper whose bizarre and controversial claims fueled intense debate and speculation, outside as well as inside the scientific community. The theory was completely discredited only months later. Eveling published no other work, but still teaches at Cambridge.

And that was it. With only a month left before her publishers expected a pristine, completed manuscript, Clarissa wondered if her latest career venture was such a great idea. She sighed and tossed the folder face up on the table in front of her. She read the title, and then closed her eyes. *Scrambled Eggheads: 12 Contemporary Scientists Who Changed the World—Almost.*

Somehow, she reckoned, her publishers wouldn't appreciate eleven contemporary scientists almost doing the changing. Still, a new challenge, even a new way of life, was what she'd needed after the... Even now she still couldn't say the word, couldn't even say it in the silence and privacy of her own mind. It had plunged her world into an ice age that was only now starting to retreat. Her husband Chris had finally persuaded her.

"Go on honey. What have you got to lose? I know you're tired of the magazine articles and all that other stuff you've been doing. Now you're getting a bite of something much bigger. You'd be crazy to turn them down."

She would have been crazy to say no, but Clarissa wondered just how crazy the last year had been—traipsing round the world interviewing eleven badly bruised egos for inclusion in a volume whose very title poured salt on wounds that so clearly had never healed. But of course, their vanity had prevailed, or maybe it was the cheque promised by her publishers, and they'd all agreed to be featured. And writing about other lives that had crashed and burned—and yet still survived—might just counter the cynicism and emptiness that now pervaded her own.

She felt the train slowing and forced her eyes open. The fields and copses had given way to buildings, streets, and cars. She threw *Eggheads* back in her briefcase and picked her way through the carriage as the train lurched to a halt.

"Trinity College, please," she said, settling into a taxi. "Just one more egg to crack," she whispered, "and this omelette's done."

Clarissa's heels echoed off ancient stone walls as she entered Trinity's huge, square court. Signs hinted at dire consequences should she dare to cross the grass, so she followed the footpath that skirted the enormous lawns. The court held an otherworldly quality, emphasised by unruly gusts of autumn wind that chased round the path and stained the grass with leaves. A sprinkling of students and camera-wielding tourists were the only signs of life. She approached staircase J, where her unexpected phone call had instructed she should come, and hesitated outside the doorway. She noticed a plaque that listed its inhabitants: Boronski F, Mill T, Deverill P, Gangarasancha G, Eveling P.

A smile of recognition softened her features. She climbed a narrow, wooden staircase before knocking on Eveling's door.

"Good afternoon, Dr. Eveling, I'm Clarissa James. I'm not late am I?"

As if to answer her question, three o'clock began to chime with great dignity and solemnity from somewhere outside.

Eveling stepped aside to let her in. "Right on time. Do please take a seat."

Clarissa settled into a faded green armchair. She examined the room while Eveling disappeared to procure coffee for two. It looked pretty much like any of the other egghead offices: the obligatory book cases stuffed with tomes; desktop PC swimming among notebooks and sheets of paper; dog-eared rotas and timetables pinned to the wall beside a board festooned with equations full of mathematical symbols and most of the Greek alphabet.

Eveling reappeared bearing a tray. "Couldn't find much in the way of biscuits, I'm afraid, but this should keep us going for a bit."

"It'll do fine." She fumbled in her in pocket for a moment. "Do you mind if I record our conversation, Dr. Eveling? That way I don't miss anything."

"Call me Paul. Go ahead. Record away."

"I'd like to start by hearing the whole story from your point of view. That's what I usually do," she said, "and then, when I need to, I'll weigh in with my questions. How does that sound, Dr. Eveling? I mean, Paul."

Clarissa studied the figure facing her across the desk, and wondered why he'd suddenly changed his mind and agreed to take part in this interview. His polite but firm refusal three months ago had seemed pretty final.

Eveling shifted in his chair. "Okay, I'll do my best." He sipped from a weathered-looking mug before beginning. "I suppose it started back in the spring of 1985. I'd recently finished my PhD thesis and was carrying out research here at Trinity. Research in Quantum Field Theory. Do you happen to know anything about Quantum... " He broke off when Clarissa slowly but firmly shook her head. "Well, I'll spare you some of the details. Anyway, my research indicated that there should exist a particle, one quite unlike any we had previously encountered or even imagined. One, in fact, that defied reason. Though existing at a sub-atomic quantum level, its effects might manifest over large-scale systems, where the force of gravity makes itself felt. In other words, our everyday world. I called it the Hysteron. Just stop me if you've got any questions."

Clarissa leaned forward and shifted some papers. She rested her elbows on the desk. Strands of black hair fell across her eyes. Outside, through the small panes of glass, a thin November sun glimmered. She signaled for him to continue.

"Well, when I'd finally worked through all the equations it came as quite a shock. You see—the mathematics of such bizarre theories don't usually hold water. Contradictions appear, inconsistencies, that sort of thing. So you have to ditch the theory. Murder it, so to speak. But not this time. Oh no, back then I really thought I'd struck gold. I can still remember as if it were yesterday—the excitement I felt when I published my paper: Field Relativity Over Gravitational Systems. Or FROGS theory as it became known afterwards when it, when I, became something of an object of fun. I'd rather they'd called it Hysteron theory but, well, there we are."

Eveling's voice trailed, and his face assumed what Clarissa correctly guessed was its usual expression when there was nobody else in the room. He was easy to describe: late forties, hair flecked with grey, nothing out of the ordinary really. But there was no mistaking the aura of sadness that now held him. Sadness caused by something, some theory, that'd been history now for twenty years. But Clarissa knew a thing or two about sadness and loss. She had at least that much in common with Eveling. Against her will, her mind skipped back almost two years for yet another cruel re-enactment. She remembered when it had happened. How when it had ended, the way she'd felt about everything else ended, too. How she'd withdrawn into her own world, a world guarded by a protective layer of cynicism and mistrust. It was a defensive system for which governments would've paid billions.

Her thoughts jumped to the present as Eveling continued. "Of course, I should have expected it. The theory yielded so many bizarre and abstruse predictions. I should have foreseen what would happen if it reached a wider audience. How it might be misunderstood, misapplied. The fuss that would follow."

Clarissa remembered that much from her research. She'd scanned past newspaper copy. It had become a real freak show. Whacked-out cults on both sides of the Atlantic had taken FROGS on board to justify and 'prove' all kinds of weird beliefs. She looked with new interest at the faded academic sitting before her.

"Of course, the public never understood a fraction of it. Not really. They just made of it what they wanted. Selected what they thought might justify their own, often sensational, leanings." Eveling pulled himself upright. "Forgive me. Was I ranting? You must think me very bitter."

Clarissa shook her head. "Not really. But maybe we all have something to feel bitter about."

She used the silence that followed to look around her. She wondered how many students visited him. Was there a Mrs. Eveling? Her eyes flicked to the desk. No photos. No beaming wife and freshly-scrubbed kiddies amid the paper jungle.

"As you'll know of course, in 1987 a team of experimental physicists at Berkeley discredited my work. Exhaustive experiments demonstrated that the likelihood of Hysterons existing was inestimably small. The bubble, so to speak, my dear, burst."

And burst it certainly had, Clarissa grimly recalled. The same newspaper headlines that had sung of "Cosmic Explanations" and "Epoch-making Discoveries" started to take a different line. New headlines appeared: "FROGS Theory Dead in the Water" had been one, and "FROGS Theory Croaks Its Last" another. And of course, "French Kiss of Life Won't Save FROGS".

She drained the last of her coffee and asked, "So what was so special about this Hysteron thing that turned them on so much back then?"

Eveling paused before answering. He couldn't decide what to make of her. She wasn't much older than the students who periodically trailed in and out of his room, but still she carried a weight beyond her years. A weight that had penciled itself round her eyes and stiffened her features into the mask of one much older.

He continued. "The Hysteron, if it does exist, has some remarkable features. Most noteworthy of which is that the effects it brings about, such as creating and influencing other particles, occur in the past rather than the future. A reversal of the everyday law of cause and effect. This, as you can imagine, has far-reaching implications. If it can influence events in the past, then that's tantamount to saying that it can change history, including human history. How sweeping these changes might be is impossible to tell. Anything from a complete rewrite to some minor edits. With me so far?"

"I think so," Clarissa lied. "So what happens if history changes?"

"In a sense, nothing. Hysteron theory claims that if history changed, even if the changes were far-reaching, no one would be aware anything at all had happened. Our memories would alter accordingly. Not brainwashing, Clarissa. We would no longer remember the old history simply because it had no longer happened. Our world might change, over and over, but we would experience only continuity—that is, if we still existed, of course."

Clarissa was beginning to wonder just exactly what world Paul Eveling existed in.

"That's why the theory was so popular for explaining the unexplained. People dreamt that it might be possible to communicate with, or even travel to, other histories. Even other universes. Well, Clarissa, your imagination places the only ceiling on what could happen. Time travel, clairvoyance. A whole ragbag of other phenomena."

"That is until these guys at Berkeley rained on your parade, right?"

"Right. But maybe wrong. The team at Berkeley effectively proved that the Hysteron did not exist. But what if Hysterons come into existence at some point in the future? Scientists all over the world are trying to discover and create new particles, even as we speak. By their very nature these emergent Hysterons would bring about effects that take place earlier in history. Perhaps much earlier. Our universe, our history, would change. We would change."

"Yeah, but they don't exist. End of story. Period." Suddenly, she wished she'd spoken in a softer tone.

"Yes, but what happens when they arrive, Clarissa? What happens when they arrive? What will become of us then?"

Neither spoke for several moments.

"Why did you change your mind, Paul? I mean, about doing this interview. You know you really surprised us when you called and told us you'd changed your mind about featuring in the book. My head's been spinning ever since."

"Oh, I don't know. Maybe after all these years I'm falling for the New Age ideas that my theory so encouraged. Jung's Synchronicity, for example. Coincidences and so forth. I suppose I just didn't want to let the chance go by. Perhaps your coming here bodes well."

Clarissa had interviewed too many people not to see through this false answer, and she studied Eveling while a flurry of students crossed the corridor outside in a wave of laughter and chatter. As their voices and footsteps receded, Trinity's clock announced that it was five o'clock.

She sensed the meeting was at an end. "I'll make sure you get a sympathetic write up, Paul." But she knew somehow that Eveling didn't care about that any more than he cared about the cheque. Why did he change his mind? What was he holding back?

Clarissa held out her hand. "Well, thanks. And take it easy. There's more to life than theories, you know, whether they're right or wrong."

Eveling shook her hand, and watched her walk along the passage and turn down into the staircase. He stepped slowly back into his study, closed the door behind him, and walked to his desk. He lifted an envelope that bore the logo of the University of Cambridge Computer Laboratory, and examined its contents for the thousandth time. He wondered if he should have told the girl about this; after all, it was the reason he'd relented and decided to grant her an interview. He'd wanted, needed, one last person with whom to discuss it.

The envelope contained the fruit of many years' research, covertly undertaken at every spare opportunity between his teaching commitments. Research he'd discussed with no one; he'd vowed that he'd continue alone with the final part of his theory. He almost wished Clarissa was still seated opposite, and imagined his short explanation.

"With most particles, if you know enough about their present parameters and conditions, you can often make predictions about their future behaviour and location. In other words, what they are doing and where they are. Sometimes, you can even predict their lifespan. It's no different with Hysterons except for one important distinction. Because of their peculiar nature— their reversal of cause and effect—a strange symmetry exists. If I'm not mistaken, if we know enough of the present quantum field conditions in the universe, then we should be able to predict when in the future the Hysteron comes into existence. A particle is born, Clarissa."

His attention returned to the papers clutched in his hand. They were the results of myriad calculations that had taken weeks to compute. He'd only received the results a few days ago. His eyes ran along the final line of what the computers had generated: 01112005. An innocuous enough number, or date, rather. November 1, 2005. From where he sat his wristwatch reflected eerily in the shimmering surface of his long-forgotten coffee, but he didn't need to look at the dial to know today's date.

He rose and moved to the window that gave out over the huge court. The day's last students scurried home and pale, white lamps shone across the grass. Again he asked himself if he should have told her more. But no, she thought him quite mad enough already. He had seen it in her eyes. He sighed and returned to his seat. Finally, he wondered if he still believed in happy endings, like the ones in fairy tales read to him as a child. As an idealistic young physicist years ago, certainly he had. But now? Paul Eveling leant back in his chair, closed his eyes, and waited.

Outside, Clarissa shivered in the twilight. She reached for her cell phone and punched in numbers. Presently, she heard the voice of her science editor.

"Hello Gerry, it's me. Listen, I'm just through interviewing Paul Eveling. The guy's really off the scale. I mean, seriously nuts. He's sitting up there now, as we speak, waiting for the universe to change in his favour. But he fits the book like a glove."

She faltered as the voice on the other side of the ocean forced through, "Where the hell are you? We've been worried sick— you've been gone almost two days. Chris is going crazy."

The sound of her husband's name rang an alarm bell. Chris never called her office unless it was urgent. "Cambridge. Remember? Interviewing Paul Eveling for the book."

"What the hell are you up to in Massachusetts? Eveling. That's the English physicist who discovered Hysteron theory years ago, isn't it? Won a Nobel Prize, I think. But he works at Berkeley. And what's Paul Eveling got to do with the book you're working on anyway?" Gerry was fighting to keep his voice level.

A cloud of anger and fear hovered at the edge of her mind. "That's Cambridge, England, Gerry. The last chapter of the book. Eveling's our man. What do you think I'm doing here? Punting on the goddamned river?"

This time Gerry spoke more softly. Chris had voiced concerns before about his wife's fits of depression and confusion. "Listen Clara, why don't you just tell me where you really are, okay? I'll get Chris to come pick you up. You've got nothing to worry about. Just relax and stay calm. I'm sure Chris can find someone to look after Joey."

"Joey? What in the hell are you talking about? Who's Joey?"

Something began to take hold slowly in her mind. Something that became more real with each beat of her heart. The phone slid out of her fingers and clattered against cold, hard stones as she retraced her footsteps, hesitantly at first, but then breaking into a run. Skidding to a halt, Clarissa stared at the wooden plaque outside: Boronski F, Mill T, Deverill P, Gangarasancha G, Somerstein P.

She tore up the staircase, and ran to the door. She hammered a clenched fist against the wood and tried to ignore the nameplate attached to the wall.

The door opened. A small, bald-headed man looked at her from the doorway. "Yes? Can I help you?"

"Where's Eveling?" she asked, but her voice was weak, and by now she knew that Dr. Paul Eveling had left the building. If indeed he'd ever been there.

By the time she left the college, Clarissa James could remember almost nothing of the last two days. Memories melted from her mind, flowing away like the river that runs behind Trinity College. But what she instead remembered filled her mind even more than a river fills the space between its banks: Joey sitting on her husband's shoulders as she tried to persuade him to look at the camera; Joey, staring at her through dark pools of infant wonder; little Joey, for whom she died and was reborn each day.

She knew that something dark was leaving her forever, but she didn't know that miscarriage was its name—the name that she'd hidden for years. And she knew nothing of the Hysterons that had carefully and skillfully adjusted her universe. It was as if the cosmos had gently rearranged itself, like a huge animal shifting in its sleep to a more comfortable position. And she did not remember that windy, sunlit afternoon in Cambridge when she had met and talked with a man called Paul Eveling.

After all, she could scarcely remember what had no longer happened.

The Photographer

Kristopher Young

I REMEMBER HER. She was naked. I was frightened.

Her skin reflected light like the moon, her face hid no shadows. She'd often be looking into the distance, and even when she was looking at me it never seemed as if she was paying attention. Her expression was calm and peaceful, if a bit concerned, as though she was concentrating on something else.

Her eyes are now part of my soul. She is from Before; that voided time when infant minds struggle to come into focus, closing up like pupils in sunlight so that we can take the world in without losing our sanity. Yet, there's no way I could ever forget her; I can still picture her standing over me, form perfectly defined, as I drifted off night after night under mobile stars orbiting on strings.

She was, in many ways, a second mother, a guardian angel. It wasn't until the first time she got angry that I was ever actually afraid of her. She was screaming; her face pure wrath, veins showing in her forehead. Her voice was mute and the room was silent, but I can still feel her cold breath brushing against my face.

I'm not sure exactly how old I was when that happened—I know it was after I could speak, because I remember it was the first time I ever mentioned her to my mother. The looks I got; the phone call to the police; the questions. My mother's paranoia (jealousy?) spiraling out of control until the police were able to convince her there was never anyone there.

Our relationship was irrevocably damaged, I was no longer perfect in my mother's eyes. It was as if I was no longer her son, but instead a stranger shackled to her leg. I was the Liar. I was the child who would embarrass her, make her feel stupid in front of the police, her friends. I was disowned in thought, if not in words.

She never aged. The years passed and I graduated to superhero sheets, to model cars, to puberty. When I was little, I thought she was ancient. Maybe not as old as my mom, but old, in that way all adults seem so old when you're five. Now, an adult myself, I'd estimate her age in the late twenties.

When I was in my teens, I'd sometimes masturbate to her. I feel dirty saying that, writing it down even, but it's true. I'd try to hide it under the covers. I didn't want her to know. She never seemed to notice. It was always that way with her—either completely detached or a firestorm of rage, never in-between.

The nights when she was truly angry were nearly unbearable. It was irrational, inexplicable—I never knew what triggered her episodes. She'd scream endless silent curses at me, damning me to a million hells, and all I'd feel was her cold breath. It would be impossible to fall asleep; impossible to even pull the covers over my head because the thought of her in that state, standing above me, was just too much to bear. There were times I tried to ignore her—reading a book, for example, but they never worked. She'd just come back angrier, night after night. But if I gave her my attention, let her have her say, she'd usually calm down. I'd have a month or two of peace.

During this time, my mom was next to impossible to live with. She never forgave me, and now, never will. She died when I was twenty. The cancer grew tumors in her. The cancer ate her away. It was an awful death—a slow death. During her final days I mustered the strength to ask her if she remembered the woman. She looked at me, focused, the crows' feet amplifying around her eyes. Waiting. The woman, Mom, do you remember the woman who used to visit—Liar, she hissed at me, Liar! Her face, the anger—Get out! Get out! She passed on that night. The doctors had told me she'd still be with us for months. I miss her. Always have.

I am a photographer. I want to give people memories. Give them a way to remember everything they are destined to forget. I want to capture beauty. And most of all, I want proof. I want proof that, yes, this is actually happening. Yes, we exist. I want the proof that escaped me as a child. Deep down, I know it's because I want the kind of proof that would make my mother forgive me. Make her believe me like she did when I first told her. Losing a mother is always hard; losing her twice is something no child should have to go through.

I didn't sell our place. Couldn't. I wasn't sure if she'd move with me or stay behind, and besides, it was a fantastic size for Manhattan. I didn't even move out of my room. I converted my mom's bedroom into a darkroom, of all things. It was a full conversion; I even had the windows professionally removed, had plumbing installed for drainage and water, added ventilation. When all was said and done, it was more than functional, and it no longer felt like I was working where my mother had slept.

I bring my camera everywhere I go. I spend a lot on supplies, but I still manage to do all right for myself. This morning, I changed the film in my camera even though there were a few shots left on the previous roll. It was a premonition, if you will. A good idea, at the very least.

[Snap]

She was standing there, only ten feet away. *[Snap]* Early thirties, elegant, a look that implied—if not downright stated—passion and ambition. Paper coffee cup in her left hand, a folded paper in her right. *[Snap]* Waiting for the train. Just like me.

I wasn't sure, based on her profile. No; I was sure. I just wouldn't let myself believe it. I edged closer to her, got a good angle, and then it was beyond all reasonable doubt. It was Her. I snapped two more three-quarter shots. I'm not sure how she didn't notice.

Normally I'm already thinking of the darkroom when I take photographs. It was luscious anticipation, that need to see the photograph I was taking develop. The process, the completion I found in hanging it up to dry, silently congratulating myself on a job well done. I know this is an abstraction of reality; that I need to work on appreciating the now in a more direct way, rather than living for a future now.

This time, however, the darkroom was a million miles away. Confusion burst through my mind like an unpleasant climax, little mind-stars flaring as synapses screamed and spent their load.

Love. Anger. Hate. Rage. Love. A dizziness, a vertigo, the kind of awkward and blank nothingness of blunt head trauma. Images of my mother. Flash. Childhood fear. Flash. Adolescent orgasms. Flash. Her face. Mother. Anger. Love. Abandonment. Her face.

I stumbled dazed and half collapsed on the bench. It took me a few minutes to regain a coherent thought pattern. I noticed there was another man on the bench, an older gentlemen, almost but not quite distinguished-looking, staring at me as if I was a subway pariah.

I stood suddenly, searching for her. Turned out, she was right in front of me. The train was coming. I was behind her. A half vision of ending this right here and now. I edged closer, behind her... not sure what I was thinking, definitely not sure what I was doing.

Too beautiful. Too lovely.

The train pulled up, screeching like a thousand nails on chalkboard. The doors slid open, the smell of packed commute mixing with the stale underground air. Crowd pushing out; crowd pushing in. An old man loses his balance for a second and teeters off to the side before grabbing hold of an overhead bar.

In the push of strangers I was shoved up a few people behind her. With some difficulty, I edged around an elderly woman stinking of perfume, her face almost horrifying in its plastic surgery precision. Then I ducked under the arm of a young man, pierced, shaved head, sleeved—good looking, in that other-worldly sort of way. And then I was behind her. Her neck snuck out from between collar and hair. White. Soft. I bent in and smelled her; her scent distinct and erotic despite the surroundings. I could feel an erection building, but it was quickly banished by thoughts of all those angry nights, the loss of my mother's love.

Seven stops into Brooklyn had considerably lightened the passenger load of the car. She had sat down on a bench fairly early into the ride—I remained standing right above her as long as possible, just another strap hanger. I watched her carefully, stolen half-glances, though she was deep in her paper so probably wouldn't have noticed anyway. I was just about to sit down when the conductor's voice announced that it was the end of the line due to construction and gave some alternate routes via transfer. The ugly mutterings of disgruntled commuters gave way to mirth thanks to the conductor herself—a full-bodied (though disembodied) voice full of sass, I ain't gonna tell you again, this is the end of the line, now get off my train!

She put down her paper with a deep raspy sigh and a look that might be ugly on most people, but still worked for her. It was something about feeling lucky enough to share that moment with her, even if it was a goddamn-fucking-train moment. She had that kind of look going. Hard to explain. You either know it or you don't.

I followed her into the station. There weren't many people, but everyone was lost so it was easy to stay unnoticed. We walked to the far exit, up two levels of gum-trodden and piss-smelling stairs, and then out into the evening air. It was winter, so it was already dark out, but the night was brisk and felt more of fall. The air chilled my skin to remind me it was there. Clouds rolled through the sky. It was strange seeing the sky from this far out in Brooklyn; I was used to seeing the Manhattan sky, all angles and buildings and usually nothing but black.

She's walking with a hurried pace. *[Snap]* Not like she suspects she's being followed (I'm doing a pretty good job of staying hidden, over a block behind her). More like, she's late for something important. A pet? A lover?

She stops at the entrance of what must be her building, fumbling for her key. *[Snap]* I'm across the street, unsure what to do once she enters.

I find out soon enough—I wait. And wait. And think.

I am so fucked. There aren't really any options here. I can't leave; she's been a part of my life since infancy. I feel closer to her than I did my own mother. Related. She's everything to me. But I can't live outside her apartment, either. And I certainly can't confront her—I'd be a madman, a stalker.

But I'm sure it's her, in the way you'd recognize your mother. I *know*. In the absence of other options, all I can do is wait.

She comes out about two hours later. *[Snap]* If she was stunning before, now she's devastating. Almost certainly going out on a date. I feel a strong strain of jealousy and possessiveness run through me. It's then I know for sure that I love her.

I continue to follow her from the opposite side of the street. She's heading towards the nearest subway station, hoping, perhaps, that service has been reinstated. I'm a block away as she begins her descent—I start to speed up just in case there is a train coming.

The gates must have been locked. The perfect trap.

They attack from the shadows. Three men. Blades. No guns that I can see. Hard to tell what they want. Money? More? One must have been down there, the other two moving in to block her escape. The one coming up the stairs grabs her arms from behind, pulling her away from the stairs. The other two rotate to follow, so now they're sort of facing me, while the man holding her has his back to me and the street.

She screams, and finally, after all these years, I hear her voice. It's not a scream of fear. It's strength and anger and hatred, a damnation, You fucking bastards! Get the fuck off me you shithead fucks. The two in front step closer, grinning, leering. One of them—grey hoodie, ripped jeans, two day growth on his chin—licks the bottom of his two front teeth in some obscene come-on. She tries to kick at him, fails, You fucking shithead, I'll rip your eyes out!

He gut punches her and she lunges at him again, this time her teeth bared, feral, and for a second I think she's actually going to score flesh, can almost hear his nose getting ripped off. He pulls back just in time.

Snap.

I'm not a fighter. I'm not much of a lover, either, truth be told. I've spent most of my life alone. But this was easy; as I cross the street there's a pipe sticking out of a box of trash—I run towards them and in a single fluid motion scoop it up with my right hand and brain the guy holding her, the pipe connecting to the back of his head with a sickly crack.

The other two are focused on her and don't see me coming. I spin around the woman, she's lost her balance, and I clock the leerer in the mouth and hear his meth-rotted teeth shatter. The third, he's stepping back, arms up in a please-don't-hit-me stance, and I bring the pipe down straight into his forehead.

Everything's silent.

She's looking at me. I see a glimmer of recognition in her eyes, but I might be imagining that. I'm more in love than I ever thought possible. Everything in my life led up to this moment. I exist for right now.

I can't explain how this all connects. I don't understand the haunting. I don't know what it means in a grander sense, or how it was even possible. It defies my definition of reality. I don't care.

I see the future. She, so happy, so thankful, falls in love with me, her hero. Laughing. Kissing. Loving. Children. Sleeping. Playing. Growing old. Together. A life lived proper and right and good.

The vision dissipates faster than it appears; she's never needed to be saved. Too strong for that—I've known that for as long as I've known her eyes. She looks down at one of the broken faces and spits in his eye. And then she starts kicking him, and he curls up fetal to protect himself but she doesn't stop.

I walk away. Two blocks later I can still hear her rage, her cold breath on my face like wind. I realize my camera was lost in the fight. I wonder if she'll find it. I wonder if I'll ever see her again.

For No One (Why Did It Die?)

Greg Gerding

KEVIN ROLLS OVER in his bed, each movement of his body a cumbersome weight. He can't understand how she could just leave him like that, so cold and cocksure. They were together two years. The last one was spent living together. He should have known though. She moved into his place, but had never quite settled in. Oh, but the things she would tell him! Such kindness. Such supposed sincerity. Kevin is hurt and confused. He's reviewing everything in his head, trying to pinpoint any damning moments.

He lists back and forth slowly like an injured ship, lost in the sea of her lingering scent. He can't understand how the sun continues to shine each day. The bright light knifes between the edges of the blinds and cuts sharp slashes across the walls of his bedroom. He still smells her. She left him three weeks ago and he hasn't washed his sheets since. Her smell is almost gone though, smothered by his malaise. He closes his eyes and reaches out and he is stroking her hair again in his mind. Just weeks ago, she was there, asleep beside him. Happy. Content. Or so he thought. When did it all go wrong?

She told him that her love for him was dead. Just like that. Point blank. Those offending words, he can't shake them from his head. They're scorched into his mind.

They sat in their usual spot at the coffee shop. A simple, round table separated them. Kevin was lost in his book, as usual, leaning back in his chair casually. She was sitting up straight in her chair, lost in thought. She'd usually be reading a book herself. Or a magazine. But instead, without warning, she leaned forward and sniped him.

"My love is dead," she said.

"What?" as if he had misheard her.

"My love... it's dead."

Kevin's position didn't change, but his arms fell into his lap, his book limp in his hands.

"What do you mean? What are you saying?"

"I'm saying that I'm done. I'm done with you. I'm done with this."

"What? I don't understand. How can that be? I thought things were going so well between us."

He then gathered himself up to meet her, across the little table. He looked into her eyes. She wasn't there. A gulf separated them. An ocean fell between them. He saw it happen. He saw her slip away.

"I'm going. I'm gone. I'll be back at your place gathering my stuff. Give me half an hour and I'll be done."

"Can't we talk about this?"

"I've made up my mind. I have nothing else to say." She turned and walked away.

"But why? How?" he weakly called after her.

Too late. Unheard. She was gone.

Kevin felt something shift in his middle. A stone. Or a fist. Or a fist-sized stone.

"What the shit, Kevin!" John screams at him.

The band's practice space was filled with bombast just seconds before. Kevin stalled the hot cotton-like air with a sad blast from his horn and the room is now smoldering into silence.

"You're playing like a wuss. This song's got some balls, you know!"

"Give him a break, John. You know what's up."

"I know, Matt, but we've got shows lined up starting Thursday, and we can't blow this opportunity! It's been like a month and he's got to get over it. He sounds like crap!"

Kevin apologizes, "I'm sorry, John, I'm really trying. It's just that when I play this horn, it only seems to know that same sad progression. I can't shake it."

"Well, you better figure it out, or you're going to be out! We're a BAND, not the frickin' Philharmonic. Your trumpet sounds like a French horn!"

"I know. I'm sorry. I'm not sure what's going on. I feel sick."

"Go home! Please, just go home and rest. I need you to shake yourself out of this, come back here, and blast some brass like I know you know how!"

"I will. I'll go home. I'll figure it out, I promise. I'll come back tomorrow and we'll all be good."

"Good! Go! Do it! We've only got four days!"

Kevin shuffles away.

"Good luck, Kevin," Matt says to the closing door.

"Thanks," he calls back before shutting.

"Man!" John exhales, exasperated. "Doesn't that guy realize how much ass we're gonna get after this?"

"Come on, John. You must know how much he loved her."

Back in his apartment, under yellowing light, Kevin shifts again in his bed. Weird impulses seize him. He's not sure what to do. He can't decide whether to bang his head against the wall and dislodge the pain with this action, or distract his mind with a project like, say, chewing his way through the carpet. To him, both seem equally correcting.

His mind is locked into a continuously looping tape, replaying the last dialogue over and over again. "My love is dead." "What?" "My love... it's dead." Push the rewind button, hear the scratchy rewind sound. "My love is dead." "What?" "My love... it's dead." Scratchy rewind sound. "My love is dead." "What?" "My love... it's dead." Stop the tape. Ponder the meaning like an investigator.

Was she saying that our love is dead? Or that her love for me is dead? Or was she saying that love for her is dead altogether? Like she no longer grasps the feeling?

Kevin shakes himself from this. He knows he's in trouble with these thoughts. He's heard through others that she's been out at their usual nighttime haunts. The same bars, the same clubs. As if nothing ever happened. As if she wasn't fazed. Kevin can barely bring himself out of his own bedroom and it seems as though she has just moved on.

Matt had even mentioned to him, "I saw your ex at the bar last night. I'm sorry man, but I overheard her answering a question about you and her breaking up and she was talking about you like you were some kind of old memory. It was kinda weird and fucked-up."

"I just don't get it," Kevin replied. "I just don't understand."

"I don't know what to tell you. It's a mystery."

It's Thursday now and the band actually managed to get in a couple of good practices. Kevin couldn't summon the usual enthusiasm physically, but at least the quality of his playing hadn't betrayed any apathy.

The band takes the stage and John elbows Kevin and points her out, front and center.

"Hey, isn't that your ex, what's her name?"

Kevin's eyes focus and confirm. His heart sinks.

"Yeah, that's her. And her name is (_____)."

All the hard work, all the energy he could muster over the past few days, quickly drains away from him. He was already looking pale, but the loss of all color in his face is noticeable.

John tries to rally him.

"Come on, man. Let's blow the shit off this place and blow her ass up!"

Kevin's gone, though. He's irretrievable.

John doesn't notice and strikes up the first song. The horn part arrives and Kevin misses it. He doesn't even lift the instrument from his side. He's staring at (_____). She's staring back too, but her stare is vacant.

The band powers through the first song without him and the whole place bounces, except Kevin and (_____). They seem locked. He holds hope. She seems detached.

The song ends and the band looks at Kevin. John leans in towards him.

"Come on, man. Let's do this!"

"Give me a second."

Kevin lifts the trumpet to his lips and slips into the same sad refrain he played Monday. He realizes now that it's the tune his heart has composed for her. He closes his eyes and it comes pouring from him. The band is rapt. The crowd is rapt. The sweet, sad melody pulses through the club. The meaning conveyed is heartfelt, the composition fully flushed.

After a brief two minutes of this, the horn sustains, and then goes out. The room is quiet. The people are stunned. Kevin drops the horn in front of him, opens his eyes, and fixes on (_____). His gaze shifts to her feet. Her eyes look down at her feet. She is floating about a foot from the ground. She looks back up at Kevin in wonderment and notices that he too is floating there about a foot off the ground.

The moment passes and they are carefully returned to the earth.

No one knows what to say.

Thirty-Something Blues

LeRoy K. May

The simplest Surrealist act consists of dashing down into the street, pistol in hand, and firing blindly, as fast as you can pull the trigger, into the crowd.
—André Breton, *Second Manifesto of Surrealism*

—In memory of Fernande Savage (1919–2006)

WARNING

WHAT I'LL TELL YOU about isn't *petite biere*. So if you're not sitting, sit down. If you're sensitive at heart, go back to the bookstore and ask for a refund. If you like Mary Higgins Clark, do the same. There's no place for pity here. Indeed, it's a dangerous territory but it's mine. I define the rules: follow them. If not, you can go fuck yourself, clear enough?

There's no place for compromise here, this ain't real life, it's not a true story where you can whine and go through three boxes of Kleenex. It's not about the little madam who divorces and has a fit about her relationship for forty-five minutes, then talks to her girlfriends about it; they tell her to make a beauty of herself, to work out and go out and meet people. It's fiction. I hope you understand what that implies and where it can lead you. I frankly don't give a fuck about cute feelings and stories to whimper about with your ball-and-chain. So if you're ready for the ride, good. If not, you're at the wrong place and time. 'Cause I'll have no mercy for the unexpected victims that could cross my road: I'll beat them down to their last drop of blood, I'll burn their flesh and I'll drink the liquid that circulated in their arteries. I won't be cheap in bloodthirsty beverage. In fact, I'm even thinking of commercializing it: *Blood*. That would be a catchy name...

JULY 15, 2004

All this useless feeling-spill started at the supermarket, obviously, 'cause that's where the most horrible dramas reveal themselves to surveillance cameras and are replayed by pathetic reality shows. Maybe it's the smell of outdated meat or the sight of shop-spoiled apples that made me tilt, dunno. All I know is that since July 15th, 2004, I'm not the same. My senses seem to have increased ten-fold, I feel strange waves, extraterrestrial maybe, but one thing's for sure: something triggered off inside me and I can't find the Stop button. Worse, I don't wanna find it: let's get to the bottom of things.

All I want is to go all out. In Loblaws' alleys. I don't spare anyone, yet I'm of a polite, social nature. I round a corner and I hit a grandma (but what was she doing at Loblaws at 11:45 p.m.?). Yet, I love my grandma. I don't see her enough but it's not a good enough reason to run over grannies who like to shop after six! I don't recognize myself. I whistle at the cashiers... and thinking about it, they don't deserve it (well, not all of them).

(If you already find me quite horrible, close the book. I'm not thinking of censoring myself and my editor told me he'd do a good job. He won't try to make a best-seller out of it—anyway it's really not the point of this exercise.)

A couple of university dicks do their groceries, summer's new couples, old couples who can't stand each other anymore, thick-glass hopeless singles, and has-beens who continue to study for one reason: to find chicks. At their age, unless they want to hang out at The Lovers or cyber-date, there's not much left in the meat market anymore. Obviously, the supermarket looks like an Iraqi village after mass deflagrations: broccolis hardly hold in place—they'd want so much to be relieved and cut in little bouquets to be dipped in Country Western sauce. Apples fight on the shelves to find the most light possible; it's a well-known fact that a well-lit apple has much more chance of being bought since it dazzles consumers—its reflection is divine. We're back at Adam and Eve's time, our apple hitches.

I feel like opening a cold one. What the fuck. We're not in Afghanistan as far as I know. I can open a beer without offending anyone. Seems not. They look at me weird. Grannies avoid me. Their grandchildren should present me at Easter. I'd be a hit.

While I'm at it, I light a smoke. If there's something we can't do anymore, it's to grill a little cancer stick, even less at a supermarket (I should've tried a drug store). So I wander in the aisles with my Molson and my Marlboro: I make a few laugh— the less subtle cough (those are the ones I prefer). I bet you the manager will be "alerted" by some holier-than-thou prick. Won't be long.

Like I was saying.

JULY 17, 2004
I'm very mad.
watashi wa totemo hara wo tatete imasu

I'm a card shark.
watashi wa ka-do no kurekuta-desu

It takes me a long time to write letters.
watashi wa ji wo kaku noni jikan ga kakarimasu

It's only been a week since I arrived in Japan.
watashi ga nihon ni tsuite mada isshuukan desu

I've been taking Japanese courses for less than a year.
watashi ga nihongo kouza wo ukehajiemte youyaku ichinen ni narimasu

It's been six months since I started learning Japanese.
watashi ga nihongo wo hajimete hantoshi ni narimasu

Because at the time I'm writing to you I'm tired and I'm sleepy.
toiu nomo anata ni kaite iru jikan niwa watashi wa tsukarete ite nemui nodesu

Tonight I'm off.
konya watashi wa kyuukachuu nandesu

Does it bother you that I'm of Chinese origin?
moshi watashi ga chuugokukei demo anata wa ki ni shimasen ka

Maybe I made a mistake in the password.
watashi wa tabun pasuwa-do wo machigaeta nodeshou

Like I was saying.

"There's no such thing as luck," like Another said. The self-righteous, the pecksniffians did give me away. Two days in the hole makes you think. Needless to say that a beautiful battle took place at the corner of Côte-des-Neiges Avenue and Queen-Mary Road. "What a scandal!" we could hear in the aisles. "It makes no sense! He must have been stoned out of his mind to have done this… " They rambled, they rambled… A bit of action in their boring lives probably did them some good. A story to tell your neighbours, to parents who don't come over often ("It was terrible! He must have drank at least seven, right, Bob?"). All this to say that being different doesn't kill you, it locks you up.

You should've seen the braggarts they called to their rescue to restrain the "anarchist"—as if I was the next worst thing after Ben Laden. Christ! I was drinking a beer and smoking a cigarette! Twenty years ago, no one would have said a thing, except a couple of stuck-ups from Westmount, but that's it. That's life after September 11th. Civil rights? Nyet! With such a speech, I could do talk radio at CHOI FM. I see myself well next to Parliament independent deputy André Arthur: "*Salut ma gang de crottés!*" ("Hi there bunch of slobs!"). Christ, I'm about to recycle myself into radio!

That would scare them too much…

So when the pigs arrived at the supermarket, I really froze. Paralyzed. What kind of imbecile does it take to call 911 because a fed-up thirty-something, weighing 145 pounds soaking wet, lights and opens one up? The manager will surely get a promotion for his courage and his ability to react in a crisis situation. If a Canadian Olympian hadn't got caught smoking up, I might have made the cover of *Journal de Montréal*.

Goddamn weed…

JULY 20, 2004

I use a computer for my work but I haven't mastered it very well.

watashi no shigoto wa konpyu-ta wo tsukaimasu ga
doumo nigate desu

I know how to send the money to Japan from France by postal mandate very well, but I don't know how to do the opposite.

nihon kara furansu he yuubin furikae kouza wo tooshite soukin suru houhou wa shitte imasuga sono gyaku no houhou wa yoku wakarimasen

I want to make love to you.
anata to aishiaitai
Even though I'm really not a nuclear energy activist.
watashi wa kaku enerugi-no yougoha dewa arimasen ga

I modified it since May 5th, so everything's okay now.
5 gatsu itsuka ikou sono kairyou wo okonai ima wa subete umaku ugoite imasu

JULY 26, 2004

Two days in the hole. For some, it would've been like dying. Explain that to the wife, kids. That's not my case. My cat, who I affectionately call "El Loco", didn't worry too much. Went to eat at my neighbours', as usual, when I didn't come back home and decide to get trashed. So, two days. Mixing with society's elected members. Thrilling. Visionaries, I tell you. Cranks rather. One who wanted to patent an idea about twistable caps (hum...), one who narrated his neighbour's murder, but of course he didn't do it, that's for sure. Another that said the police picked her up for prostitution, but by her looks, I pity her clients.

Good people, I tell you. People you should hang around with. We could almost award them honor medals, honorific doctorates, even small scenes in FOX sitcoms. But no, they're misunderstood, bullied. I can identify with them. Misunderstood, I'm-not-ables. I encourage them in their fight against... something. It's with furious fanatics that we build a better world, not with suits and database sys-admins.

Two days listening to nonsense stories, luckily I wasn't sleepy. My story was trivial: I had drank a beer and smoked a cigarette in a supermarket. "No! They arrested you for that? Man... if I had been nailed by the pigs each time I did foolish stuff, I would have passed the last twenty-five years staring at vertical posts!" joked one of my temporary roommates. "No, but what were you thinking?" continued the whore. "You couldn't wait until you had finished your groceries?" Well, no, precisely, I couldn't, I didn't feel like it, it felt insipid to conform to a municipal rule that doesn't protect a lot of people because the bottom line is that the same people that are supposed to be protected from my smoke and, oh!, from my *drunkenness*, are those who drive smoke farters... So I make urban pollution my business, thank you.

"Don't you find it a bit stupid to be in jail for that?" said the non-murderer. It all depends on your definition of "stupid". If I had killed my neighbour and was accused of first-degree murder, I think I'd shut the fuck up. But you know everything's relative. Better: everything's in everything. So...

You're supposed to learn in jail, you're supposed to look at your belly button and say "you were a really bad boy," but the bottom line is that I have nothing to reproach to myself, I'm inculpable. I can't wait to go back to my favourite supermarket.

JULY 31, 2004

The end of the month. Empty bottles to bring to the 7/11. The rent will have to wait again. The bills. The income taxes. Fuck that, royally. As if I only have that to do. Spend my money for assholes. They can go cook themselves an egg or an ox, ask me if I care (*Do you care?—No.*).

My buddy left for Japan and it seems they don't sleep a lot around there. It's not really different from here then. Sleep: abstract notion. Since I don't sleep anymore, Christ, the world is beautiful: chicks are sexier, bills are smaller, even reality shows are almost interesting. The other day I watched *Oprah*, yeah, yeah, you know, the one who gains weight, loses weight, gains weight, loses weight, and has a nice magazine with her on the cover every month, and who makes us take out the Kleenex box every afternoon at four-thirty? So, I was watching Oprah, fascinated that people would want to make a show of their personal life on TV. Really fascinated. You really have nothing to do, don't you? Hello?!? Wake up and smell the burning coffee and shit your sitting in?!?

I must be a reactionary. That must be it. I can't conceive that a million locos (sorry, "El Loco") are glued to their plasma screens every afternoon filling themselves up with this bullshit sensationalism. It's beyond me. You have to be real low to be satisfied with such low pleasures, or maybe the others' misfortune... That must be it. Oprah is reassuring. It's feel-good TV. After, we can go on with our shitty lives and feel less rotten. We continue our little stupid habits—we smoke, we look outside the window if the neighbour is still doing his dishes while listening to Joe Dassin, we continue not to use winter tires because in Quebec, we know how to drive for fuck's sake, we continue to encourage Loto-Quebec because if we'd win, it would change our lives, wouldn't it?

Yeah, yeah, dream on, honey. You may as well hope to act in a torrid scene with Brad Pitt in the next ten minutes. Oh yes, Brad, harder you piece of shit, ram that dick further in, you whiny motherfucker. The couple of the year. They say that Angelina gave birth to a beautiful baby (or that Jennifer's waiting for one, I'm confused). Do you really think I give a flying fuck?

I think I need to go to the supermarket, or the drugstore. They're beside each other, anyway.

JULY 33, 20XX

Perfect facade you must become a visionary while youth isn't too far away the aisles are full of cheap deodorant it's completeness she drinks like badly shaved shampoo it's a cacophony behind the toilet paper walls you must beat the iron while it's hot the poet becomes a visionary through a long disorder of the senses it's a well-known fact I've had enough of those pills I'm not crazy the upstairs neighbour's being raped every night can't you hear it?!? No I'm not demented I only have a slight fondness for toxins diapers are on special this week I'll buy some for Emily who's gonna give birth to her 13th child the grand criminal the grand damned soul the supreme being isn't himself but Another he can't control the starlets in heat who bestride magazine displays they all sing like Jessica Simpson and we're their guarantors God grant that the reader, emboldened by those sexual bombs, will be able to resist to my heart's vivisection table this language will be the soul of fabric softeners on sale only bullets can solve the fieriness of the helpless and bend the spine of impromptu drunks.

Perfect softness that slides on your urine smell boil my balls in a cloth of friction alcohol honey you're only tanned in your brain the bullets want to spring out of the barrel and produce an extravaganza a myriad an infinite prosopopeia of bloody streams it's time to market *Blood* it's time to open the valves to let them flow Yankee Doodle came to town on the Avignon bridge the dissoluteness of all my senses is unwinding as expected my Sergeant Pepper's Lonely Hearts but no but no we must be absolutely shitty we must bath in our excrements to wallow in our vomit drink and eat it make absolutely new hyper-modern contemporary sushis with it or haikus or even fibs the cash register is full of emptiness this is how life goes and do you have an Air Miles card do you have a fucken Air Miles card nurse nurse!

Do you remember the ending in Mulholland Drive oh man that was too fucken cool check out that chick oh yeah I'd ram her up the ass shoot her make it click put that barrel down her throat down her crotch rip her skirt off and shoot her yeah take your dick out and stick it down her throat while you caress her with the loaded barrel force her to masturbate check out that dude man he looks stupid shoot him between the eyes oh yeah good idea (*no don't*) look at that old woman oh yeah she deserves a bullet (*no think of your grandma*) shut up mother fucker shoot her she's an old bag (*no don't for Christ's sake!*) "oh shut the fuck up put it in your mouth pull the trigger put it in her mouth pull the trigger put it in your mouth pull the trigger eeeeeeeeeeckckcckck!"

The Waiting Room

Madhvi Ramani

YVETTE APPLETON SAT IN HER OFFICE on the thirty-second floor staring at the infinite wilderness of reflections outside. In the Docklands, every new building is made of glass to reflect the other new buildings of glass, and new glass buildings are being eternally created. She realised that she would have to leave soon if she were to make it on time. She stood up, packed away her laptop, and buttoned her suit.

Outside, the sky was darkening, as if a painter had dipped his tainted brush into its watery-blueness, sending a bruised claw reaching across it to rip down the temporary façade of day. As she walked away from the mirrored tower, it seemed that there were two Yvettes walking in opposite directions. Had it not been for the obtrusive edge of the glass panel, imposing a vertical line through her reflected back and cutting her in half, it would have been impossible to tell which one was real. A tiny crease above the right/left ankle of each Yvette betrayed the illusion that the sheen, doll-like surface of her legs was in fact her skin. On the left/right-hand side of both Yvettes, a glimmer of silver could be glimpsed through her swaying, black, Medusan hair, glinting like a hidden blade.

Yvette is carried along with the stream of people but she will not stay here to mingle on a Friday evening—not in these perfumed restaurants, these misty pubs, these glittery bars—for even with ties loosened and suit jackets off, you can never be sure that the person you are talking to is not a mirage. She submerges and gets on the tube. It heaves and jerks its way through dark tunnels that connect this infernal city, in which nobody dares to look into the eyes of another.

The girl opposite Yvette makes her yearn with desire. She is youthful, flawless. Below her jaw line, through transparent skin, running down that long, graceful neck, can be traced a throbbing green vein. Yvette imagines brushing her lips against it, biting it, drinking from the spurting, red fount. The train stops and Yvette resurfaces, as if from a dream, onto grimy, cabbage-smelling streets lined with pawnbrokers, rent-boys, and whores. Every time she makes this journey, walking through different parts of London, she imagines that the acid air and bird splatter corrode every single brick and stone, while the film of dirt that covers them takes over, becoming thicker and setting into intricate dust statues until there will one day be an entire city made only of dust. She imagines a great storm washing the dirt city clean, washing it to oblivion. This image fills her with hope.

She stops outside the clearly numbered, inconspicuous building. Her weekly prowls to clinics, as part of her unholy crusade, have brought her to the knowledge that the exteriors of these buildings hold no indication of what is inside. It is too burning, shameful, ugly—even for this Babylonian city. She enters and is faced with a thin, dark man. A gold hoop hangs limply from each of his ears. He smiles, despite his hollow cheeks, and cheerfully points her in the right direction. Gay pride, she thinks. Along the solemn corridor she spots a couple of white doors with familiar geometrical male and female figures marking them. They stand to attention, legs together and handless arms at angles, looking straight ahead, as if they have had an argument. She enters, pulling the handle as far back as possible to give the woman on the door a chance to meet her lover, but the door cruelly refuses to swing back that far and the figure returns to her lonely position.

Standing before the mirror, Yvette applies a layer of beige onto each eye-lid, followed by a roseate pink. She underlines her Cimmerian eyes in black, transforms her cheeks into feverish rouge, and paints her lips red. She emerges, looking like a freshly painted oil on canvas, and approaches the desk, where a weary-looking man hands her a clipboard with a form on it. Beside 'NAME', she writes *Judy*, and quickly returns the clipboard, ignoring the rest of the questions.

She steps into the waiting room.

18:30

This room is the real, hidden, burning core of the unreal city, where people think about their lives and anticipate death. Their fears make silent air quiver. It is too much. The colour of the walls makes her think of Michael. It reminds her of a small hotel room in Taormina when he sat up in bed to light a cigarette and she lay there in the warmth watching him, golden brown skin against a pale blue wall. As the amber glow of the cigarette swooped back and forth like a languid firefly, she mused at how beautiful he looked there, as if he belonged with that wall, as if he should walk around with that blue forever as his background.

18:31

"Darren," calls a woman, emerging from the first of the two doors along the right wall of the rectangular room. Everyone here is called by their first name, everyone is anonymous and equal. A boy, no more than seventeen, gets up and enters the room with her. The door clicks shut and the dense silence, tortured by the ticking clock, saturates the mortal chamber once more.

Yvette gazes around the room and picks him out almost immediately, like a woman divining her love across a crowded room. She has a sense for it now. When she first started, she would often pick the wrong man, sometimes he would be gay, sometimes simply impenetrable.

The perpetual shaking of his leg hesitates for a half-second as she sits down beside him. Straight from the office, in a pinstriped suit, with his briefcase tucked under his chair, he twists the wedding band on his finger. His crooked lips protrude sensuously, framed by speckles of blond stubble, like grains of sand. Semi-circular wisps of copper and silver crown his head, thinning at the centre. These tigerish stripes bring forth a flash of Michael's feline mane, dark brown streaked with gold, and a glance from his green amber-flecked cat eyes. It was his feline nature that first attracted her to him. That lazy slink, the nonchalant grace, the confident smile… of course, she should have been warned by the smile, for a cat's smile is always sly, deceitful. She surprised him once, when he was on all fours, looking for something under the bed. His back curved, feet symmetrical, head tilted, one bronze arm pushing against the floor, every muscle, vein, curve and shadow falling in divine dimensions.

18:32

The man sitting next to Yvette glances at the clock. The clock is the central piece of the room. Everybody's attention is on that pitiless second hand. Some people try to ignore the clock, like the woman sitting opposite Yvette, who flicks through a glossy magazine with severe, unreading eyes. One man sits on the edge of his seat, too scared to even touch the magazines. She knows that look well. A year ago, when she went to the dentist, the nurse wore that face when she insisted on leaving the room in a refusal to breathe the same air as Yvette.

Even now that he is dead, her fallen angel still plagues her life, weaving himself into her masked days and numbered dreams. But when she remembers Michael, she does not think of the sallow, powdered face that she saw in the coffin; in her mind he is healthy, immortal. Immortality is what she strives for, too. She endeavours, in her short life, to leave herself in another's blood, not to be forgotten, for she knows that betrayal stains like the ochre pollen of funeral lilies.

18.35

The silence is broken once more as Darren exits from the second door along the right wall. He sits down once again, looking at the clock. The man sitting next to Yvette shifts.

"I can't stand this waiting," she murmurs softy to him, as if she were whispering a lover's secret. He stops shaking his leg and, although his only response is a polite "Mmm," she knows that her words have woven a silken thread of understanding between them.

18:36

A male nurse emerges from the second door and calls 'Kyle'. A scrawny grey-skinned man with purple bags puffing from under his eyes follows the nurse into the room. Twenty seconds later, he re-emerges, a subdued smile on his face, causing Yvette to think about the blind, unjust nature of it all. He did not deserve to come out of that room smiling, ready to chase the dragon once more. The waiting room is scattered with leaflets aimed at drug users, haemophiliacs, homosexuals... but there is nothing for loving, faithful wives. It should have been Kyle, not her. The anger tastes like she has just bitten a lemon. It zigzags through her body, tight and edgy like lightning, ready to lash out and strike randomly. Yellow anger, yellow bile.

18:37

The woman emerges from the first room, and calls "Joe". The man bedside Yvette stands up and her gaze follows him until he disappears behind the door.

18:42

Joe returns, and Yvette climbs back into her role, wearing it like a sleek coat. She weaves her web, coyly asks him what happens behind those doors, says she has never been to a place like this before, makes her voice tremble, feigns terror and innocence. He, in turn, sympathises. He tells her soothingly about the questions that the woman in the first room asks and about the small pinprick drawing blood that the man in the second room makes.

19:05
Darren is called to the second door by the male nurse.

19:06
Darren comes out with a look of relief on his face.

19:07
"Judy," calls the woman from the first door. Before getting up to go, Yvette turns to Joe with a nervous smile and asks him, if he wouldn't mind, waiting until she gets her results. He agrees.

19:12
Yvette returns. The male nurse beckons Joe from the second door.

19:13
Joe returns.

19:42
The male nurse at the second door calls to Yvette. Unlike the other people who pass through this door, Yvette knows what he will say. She hears it every week; words of mercury that weigh down hope beyond redemption. "I'm very sorry Judy, but I'm afraid you've tested positive for the HIV virus." The nurse opens his mouth to say something else, but Yvette cuts him off. "I have to go," she says. He tries to stop her, but she knows what he will say; another test to confirm, the need for medical monitoring, the ability to live a perfectly normal life... She ignores his words, his warm hand on her arm and opens the door. She strides out with a bright smile on her face. Joe looks up and stands. Yvette takes his hand, giggles like a brazen schoolgirl.

"Come on, let's get out of this terrible place. I'm so relieved! Let's have a drink to celebrate... " She stops, glances at him shyly. He laughs, ecstatic as her, and suggests *The Lion's Den*.

They step outside. The sky is a navy blue dais upon which grey clouds travel towards each other, interlock, intertwine, and swell with sinister laughter. They walk along the river, touching occasionally, finally arriving at the snug shelter of the pub. He tells her about his job in the city and his wife and two daughters who live in Somerset. During the week, he stays at his London flat. He confesses his mistakes and tells her of his needs. She too, spins her story—a recent divorce, a holiday in Majorca four months ago, a drunken, unprotected encounter.

Drinking on empty stomachs, the warm, red wine goes straight to their blood. Now that the danger has passed and the sound of the clock is suffocated, he is no longer inhibited. Joe and Yvette spill out of the pub at closing time and go to his place. They do not have condoms, but Yvette is on the pill—besides, he says "At least we know we're both clean."

Their two bodies join together, fluids passing between them. Life, love, and death, like three holy rivers, come together as one. Yvette feels light, jovial, sanguine, and her lips turn upwards into a mirthful, feline grin. Afterwards, when he is silent, apart from the rhythmic sound of his breathing and the beating of his heart, she plants a wet kiss on his lips, stealthily gathers her things, and leaves.

Along the sluggish Thames, Yvette walks slowly home, oppressed by the leaden sky, heavy from the sudden release of black bile which fills her body like viscous tar. Somewhere a nightingale can be heard, and she identifies with its melancholic song. She is like Philomena, condemned to show others her shameful story, too painful to utter, by spinning a thread of destruction that weaves people together.

At home, she lies on her sofa in a vacant, phlegmatic daze, like an exhausted huntress. She falls asleep, her hand outstretched, finger pointing at the glass window, and dreams of Michael. He walks into the room, holds a mirror to her, then lets it drop.

Jesus In The Driveway

Sherry Bryan

THE SCENT OF LEMON PLEDGE provokes vivid memories of my childhood, but none more so than the day my sister saw Jesus in the driveway.

That day, that *infamous* day, was a typical Saturday. I woke up early to watch Bugs Bunny in my pajamas, drinking orange juice out of my sparkly mint-green plastic cup. Mom made me cinnamon toast, and sat at the table with my father reading the newspaper while they drank their coffee, he smoking his pipe and she taking a few puffs of a Now cigarette.

I loved mornings, rarely sleeping past 6 a.m. I bounded out of bed, a wild tangle of excitement. My imagination raced with appetizing possibilities of what adventure the day might bring. I wish I could remember when or how mornings lost that new and thrilling expectation.

I was anxious to go outside and play. It was a perfect summer day and the sun was already warming up our house. I grew up in Rochester, New York, the sixth cloudiest city in America, a place where winter began in late October and lasted until April. When summer emerged, we were mad for sunshine, it was a novelty that never lost its appeal. Knowing this, we took advantage of every precious minute. The teenage girls would grab their Sun-In and coconut scented oil and lie outside to get a tan. The teenage boys would gather in shirtless, denim-clad groups and spend hours meticulously working on their decade-old cars, then drive around to nowhere. We would explore the creek or woods on some expedition, swim in our above-ground pools, or play games until our parents' voices called us home for dinner. And even the adults relished the sunlight, gardening or nursing beers in the late afternoons while talking about taxes and traffic.

On this Saturday, however, I first had to do chores, helping my mom clean the house. My father was fixing, or more likely, *breaking* something in the garage. And my older sister Sandy sat in the driveway, drawing pictures.

I was irritated that, as usual, Sandy wasn't helping. She was three-and-a-half years older than me and she should have to do something more than fixing her bed, or picking stuff off her floor. As I got older, I learned that simple tasks like cleaning a room could make her overwhelmed and anxiety-ridden, unsure of what to do or how to start. But on that day, I was just pissed off. I knew she did a lousy job cleaning, but if I was going to do it, then so should she. I knew that if I asked Mom she'd say sure, I could go out and play. But guilt gnawed at me—she shouldn't have to do it all herself. Plus I liked that we were spending time together, and that in my way I could help her. I could just play pretend to pass time. And when I got swallowed up in an intricate game of pretend, it was just as much fun as playing on the tire swing.

My pretend world premises were usually variations on a person whom I would become in the future, or hoped that I could become. Today, I played the part of the cool, sophisticated, single girl. I imagined I was cleaning my ultra-mod bachelorette pad for a swinging cocktail party. I tied a scarf around my hair, sipped my grape juice with a sigh of ennui, and pretended it was a martini. I liberally sprayed Lemon Pledge on every surface and carefully rubbed the wood until it was sleek and shiny—just like my ultra-mod bachelorette pad would no doubt be. I would be in Manhattan, or Paris, or Puerto Vallarta, because that's where *The Love Boat* always went and it sounded exotic. And my ultra-mod bachelorette pad would always be filled with clothes, parties, boys, and the scent of Lemon Pledge.

As I dusted by the open window, I thought of what job I would have—so many of my girl friends always wanted to play house, or nurse, or worse, *stewardess*. Gross. I wanted to be a scientist, a painter, an actress, and a surgeon. As they'd bring out their dolls in strollers and feed them bottles, I was more inclined to take the doll apart to see how she worked, or paint eye shadow on her.

I was interrupted from my fantasy by the sight of my sister sitting upright and rigid in the driveway. That was strange. Sandy was always slouched over, with long, messy strands of yellow hair in her face as she looked downwards. I watched her, her face staring in the sky. She was absolutely still, transfixed. Knowing my sister, this could not be good.

Many words were used to describe my sister Sandy. Temperamental. Tense. Depressed. Strange. Difficult. Troubled.

I didn't know what was wrong with her exactly; I didn't know why Sandy got upset so easily, or why she couldn't sleep through the night. I didn't understand why she always had problems at school. I didn't know why she saw a counselor. I only knew that something was mismatched with Sandy. She wasn't like other people. She always had a problem, or more accurately, a crisis. As I got older I would learn that it was more complex, and seventy-three doctors later, we still reverted to the same rudimentary terms. I realized some people just could not be fixed. I would gain more insight into the inner workings of her head than I wanted to know. But on that day, I knew only that something was off.

I looked at the sky. I didn't see anything, and couldn't figure out what she was staring at, or why she looked so shocked. I saw Sandy's thatch of blond hair moving rapidly toward the house. She was screaming now, and I was so taken aback it took a moment to put motion and sound together. In a flash my mother and father were outside on the porch. What was it? What happened? *What now?*

"There's a man in the sky!" she yelled.

I inched outside just as Sandy said this. My mother, father, and I all looked up.

"What, in a plane?" My mom asked.

"NO! There's a man in the sky!" Her face was tinged pink and the tears were coming. She was terrified, and we couldn't understand her. A man in the sky? I leaned my back against the doorframe, bracing myself. I knew I had to take in the scene, but I wanted to keep my distance.

"Look San," my father pointed up to the cloudless sky. "Nothing there. It's okay." He knelt down and went to give her a little hug, his warm, comforting smile still optimistic. If he could use reason and evidence, maybe he could stop the runaway train of thought she was on.

Her face went from fear to anger in a flash. Her hands flung out. Her face distorted and her lips squeezed together. She was not to be comforted. Her voice was low and steady now, a voice that gave me chills.

"It was Jesus. I saw Jesus in the sky."

While some parents might have dismissed this behavior as the whimsy of a child, my parents already had a lot of experience dealing with Sandy's fears—an endless winding staircase of terror that had no end, and whose origins were a mystery.

"It was Jesus. I saw Jesus. I KNOW it was Him. The robes and everything. I could see Him. It was so clear. It was like a painting, or... it was... it was." She had to keep stopping and gasping for air. "His hair, His eyes." Her tiny hands were clenched in fists.

I thought, *Sandy got to see Jesus? Aw, man! She's so lucky!* Why didn't I ever get to see things like that? To have Jesus in the sky, looking down on you, was so cool! But as I watched her from the doorway, I saw her face was not that of one graced by divine hand. It was weird, twisted. She was scaring me, and I felt exposed and nervous.

Maybe she just made it up. She had a tendency of making great claims that I had always believed, only to be confused and disappointed when I discovered the flaws in her stories.

Maybe it was in her head. She was always convinced that people were talking about her, conspiring against her, especially us.

But she seemed so convinced, and genuinely shaken. She looked desperately at my parents' faces. They must have shown doubt, which only made her more determined and frustrated.

"It was JESUS. And he looked at me, and he TURNED AWAY. He turned away!" She was crumpled up, grasping and clawing at her arms. "He turned away from me, he abandoned me. He rejected me... " I noticed little beads of red appear on her arms where her fingernails were digging in her skin.

Our dog Jamie shyly approached me. I put my arms around her and kissed her forehead. "It's going to be okay. It's all going to be okay." I whispered to her. I knew I was lying to Jamie, but I didn't want her big brown eyes to get fearful.

The Beckers, an elderly couple from across the street, were watching us. Sandy tended to attract attention all the time, and always the wrong kind. Mrs. Becker shook her head. I looked at her, willing her to catch my eye. She looked up again, and I gave her a look that I knew you weren't supposed to give adults. I didn't care. I wanted her to just go away and stop staring. She didn't have the right to judge. As I got older, I got used to other people judging my sister and my family. People assumed my parents let Sandy run wild. Or, more cruelly, that she was a "retard." Even my friends would ask, "Why don't you guys just send her somewhere?" But there was no place to go.

My father picked Sandy up and brought her inside. I sat on the floor, hugging and petting a confused Jamie.

But then I saw something I would never forget. My parents stood listening to Sandy talk about how she was cast away by God. Then I caught it. It was just a glance that passed from my mother to my father, but it held more weight that I was prepared to know. That one look conveyed too much: worry, disappointment, resignation, confirmation, and such deep sadness that I felt a knot in my stomach. *I don't want to know this. I don't want to know this.*

Things were going to change.

In the weeks that followed my sister seeing Jesus in the driveway, my family began a slow, peculiar metamorphosis. My sister started seeing a psychiatrist who put her on pills. She would act groggy sometimes, which was a nice change from her other states of rage or hysteria. She couldn't eat certain foods because of the pills, and she had to be watched to make sure she actually swallowed them. My mom spent a lot of time talking on the phone to her sister. My father spent more time in his "library," a makeshift room in the basement filled with his jazz and blues records. One day I saw my father sitting in the backyard. I was going to go out to see if he wanted to kick around the soccer ball when I noticed the look on his face. He was far away.

I started looking at my sister differently. I was watching the sister I knew fade from view, and this distorted figure took her place. It sucked. We didn't have fun anymore. She was so serious all the time. I found myself in a constant bubble of worry. What the hell was she going to do? Was this going to get better? Why couldn't she just stop acting like this? What if it happened to me? If I kept shaking these feelings off, everything would turn out okay. As I got older, that determined sense of hope would falter, but never retreat.

New words were used to describe my sister. *MAOI Inhibitors. Borderline. Depression. Anxiety. Bi-Polar. Episodes. Delusional.* These words were technical and foreign, and I hated how they sounded, and more, what they implied.

I started to spend time a lot of time with Danny, my best friend. Danny was shy, and a dreamer. We fit perfectly. He and his mother had moved here from Florida, and they were wonderfully odd and out of place. His father was in and out of town, and my friend Jenny once told me with great authority that his parents were "separating."

Danny's mom wore too much eye shadow, and long flowery muumuus, even in the winter. The whole house was coral and turquoise, colors that seemed to have no place in Upstate New York. She had orange-red hair and a slight Southern accent that I adored and tried to imitate. Their house was impossibly messy with clothes and records scattered all over floors. The first time Danny introduced me to her she started singing.

"Sherry, Sherr-rry baa-bee! Won't you come out tonight!" She beamed at me. She sang all the time, usually making up lyrics as she went along.

She was in the kitchen when Danny and I came in, trying to sneak past her.

"Who's that sneaking through my back door?" She cackled and hugged me close to her boobs. She held my face in her hands and sang "Pale Blue Eyes" to me.

"Who sings that?" I asked.

She clutched her heart and said *"Lou Reed."* I didn't know who Lou Reed was, but I could only assume by the reverent tone in her voice and her closed eyes that he was sacred. As I got older, I discovered that was true.

Danny and I were allowed to play in his room with the door closed, even though he was a boy and I was a girl. His mother was considered progressive. Of course, most of our neighbors called her "a real character" and some said she "liked her sauce."

After his mother had force-fed us some carrot and carob cookies, she went to her room for one of her "power naps." Danny and I went to play with his extensive and enviable collection of Match Box cars. I was itching to build a ramp in the backyard and test out the cars. We were cross-legged on the floor, and Danny kept rocking back and forth, which he did when he was excited or uncomfortable.

"So, um, how's your sister?" he asked, shyly looking at me. I had talked to Danny a little about Sandy and Jesus, and he was unnerved by it all, but wanted to be a good friend.

"Okay, I guess. I don't know. It's weird."

Danny kept looking at me, his eyes squinting.

"What?"

"Wanna see something cool?" he smiled wickedly. As I got older, I learned that when boys said that, it usually led to something other than Match Box cars. But on that day, I just said, "Sure."

Danny hopped up and closed his blinds. He rushed to his dresser where he took something out of a box and put it down.

"Turn off the lights when I say so," he said, his back to me.

I stood by the light switch and waited.

"Now!" He said with great dramatic flair.

I turned off the light and the room was suddenly awash in sparkling blue, glowing with orange and green flecks swimming around the room. I was enraptured.

"My dad sent me this lamp. See? The light goes around. It makes the room into the ocean. It's like being underwater." He was beaming.

We both sat on his bed in awe, and looked up at the ceiling, moving and alive. I'd never seen anything like it. We were quiet, and eventually we lay down next to one another, taking it all in.

"We're underwater," I said.

"Yeah." Danny turned his head and smiled at me, his face a revelation.

It was the first time in weeks I had felt certain and unafraid.

Underwater we were safe. It was nothing more than a dark, quiet room with a rotating lamp. But it was our secret, and our sanctuary.

I took Danny's hand and held it. His body stiffened, but eventually he eased and we spent the entire afternoon holding hands and talking. We were underwater and so far away from everyone that we could never be found.

Danny and I spent most of that summer underwater. Underwater, we would say anything to each other. We practiced swearing. We wondered aloud about what we'd look like when we were older. We debated about who we thought we could beat in a fight from our school. We kissed, on a double-dog dare, and both immediately blushed and giggled. But it didn't matter, because in our underwater room we were free of embarrassment or shame. We were free from divorce, and sisters acting crazy, being outcasts, and watching our parents struggle to get through the day.

Danny gave me the one thing that no one else could, and a part of me would always love Danny for this. He gave me a glittering, perfect shelter. In my life, I would come to know many men, but none have ever offered a shelter as pure and complete.

While underwater with Danny, I learned how to protect myself when my family became too real, too much, more than I could take. And though my version of underwater has changed over the years, it has always kept me sane. It is my own Jesus in the sky.

Necrowave Oven

Kevin L. Donihe

MARTIN STOOD BY THE DOORWAY. His wife slept on the sofa in the living room. Her body seemed to melt into the cushion. Perhaps she was slowly becoming a part of it. As time progressed and Helen's weight increased, that possibility seemed less and less absurd.

The TV displayed the shop-at-home channel. Helen never bought anything, but she watched it just the same. Martin didn't watch TV often, but when he did, she changed the channel back to shop-at-home if he left for the bathroom or the kitchen.

He walked to the sofa and looked down. Her hair was mussed and graying. She hardly brushed it, never dyed it. Despite the weight and gray, she didn't look fifty. Sometimes Martin saw the woman he'd married hiding inside the lump on the sofa. Other times, that woman wasn't visible at all.

He touched her shoulder. "Helen?"

She didn't budge.

"Wake up."

He often feared he might find her dead. The doctor said she was healthy, though her blood sugar was high and her weight was up. Other times he thought she'd never die, that she would always be there, immobile, on the couch.

She opened her eyes, but said nothing. She had taken her medication earlier and was still in a daze.

"Come on, it's time to get up."

Her mouth hung open. When she spoke, her voice sounded thick. "Why?"

"We're going to get a necrowave."

She finally blinked. "Didn't Aunt Martha have one of those?"

"That's impossible, honey."

"Why?"

"Because Aunt Martha's dead. Necrowaves are new."

She shook her head. "She had one. I remember it."

"You're thinking about her microwave."

"Maybe it was Aunt Gracie, then."

"Aunt Gracie's been dead longer than Aunt Martha."

"How much longer?"

"A lot." He made a half-hearted attempt to lift her shoulders. "Let's hurry before the store closes."

"Did you know Sally got a necrowave?"

Helen was stalling, but he played along. "Really, who's Sally?"

"My sister's co-worker."

He thought of Debbie. Helen jumped from the couch, even in a Deprakote daze, when Debbie appeared to take her shopping. If he did the asking, she proved far more reluctant. He often wondered if her sister knew things about her that he didn't, but at least she got exercise during those trips.

"Sally told Debbie she was getting a necrowave for her birthday. Now her phone rings and nobody answers it."

"I see, but *Marthzul's* isn't stocking necrowaves after today, and nobody else will sell them. We've got to hurry."

She hunkered further into the sofa. "Go without me; my tongue feels fat."

"Your tongue always feels fat."

"But it seems fatter now than ever." She stuck out her tongue. "See?"

"Yes, I see."

"And I'd hate to leave the house alone."

"Nobody gets in, Helen."

"Then why are photos missing from the album?" She pointed her ring finger at him. "And why does my diamond look cloudy?"

The mayor, she believed, had sworn vengeance against her due to a childhood grudge. He dispatched his sons to switch household items for similar yet less expensive ones. He also monitored her thoughts. In the past, he transmitted his own, but the cranial transmitters hadn't worked in over a year.

'I rubbed them to death,' she'd said. He remembered how she'd looked like a monk that entire summer, the top of her head almost completely bald. Two summers before that, Law Man had been her boogeyman. Two summers before that, there'd been no boogeyman at all.

"The pictures just fell out and got misplaced," he replied, "and the ring's been the same since before we were married."

"And the curio cabinet, too. The wood grain looks different."

He refused to shout. "Must we talk about this?"

She heard the edge in his voice and fell silent, but Martin knew she was still thinking about all the things she'd lost and all those who plotted against her.

"Come on, let's make this easy."

"Okay, okay." She made a sound that was half *harrumph* and half groan. "I'll get my coat, but I'll be too tired to cook dinner tonight."

He couldn't remember the last time she'd cooked. It had surely been months.

Helen pulled herself from the sofa. Martin imagined her skin adhering to it, stretching and pulling as she arose. He wanted to shake the thought, but it lingered. She ambled over to the coat rack and slipped into a shaggy, over-sized sweater.

"Why don't you wear the jacket I gave you last Christmas?"

"Because I don't like it."

"Could you at least comb your hair?"

She rubbed her hands in her hair. "Better?"

Yet again, he nodded. There were times when he didn't know how to nod, or refused to nod. He regretted those times.

Martin's car was red, dusty, and had cat prints on the hood. Helen got in the backseat. He took the wheel. He couldn't remember the last time she had sat up front. It made him feel more like a cab driver than a husband, though he no longer mentioned it.

She was quiet as the trip started. She puffed her cigarette, blew the smoke out the window, and stared at passing houses and trees. Martin was quiet, too. He drew in a deep breath and exhaled slowly. He enjoyed watching the road unfold, especially on sunny days. The day was cool and slightly overcast, but the clouds made evocative shadows on the hills. He found himself thinking of bonfires, dead leaves, and jack o' lanterns.

Helen leaned forward. "Isn't the Stevenson's yard nice?"

He didn't care about the Stevenson's yard. He didn't even know the Stevensons. "I'd look, but I'm driving."

She ignored him. "I wonder who prunes their shrubbery?"

"I don't know, Helen. Perhaps you should ask them."

Through the rearview mirror, he watched her fidget with her seatbelt in lieu of a reply. She hated wearing it. He was surprised she'd put it on without complaint.

Suddenly: "Look, lights!"

Startled, he glanced around. Helen stared at the passing Culbertson house. Red, green and blue beams shot forth at various angles from its windows. Fluid waves rippled vinyl siding. The entire structure seemed to expand and contract, albeit slightly.

"You see the lights?"

"Yes." He returned his attention to the road. "I see them."

After a few moments of silence: "Do you think the Culbertsons have a necrowave?"

"I really couldn't say."

She sulked. "I hope not. That would mean we weren't first on our block to get one."

The sky above *Marthzul's* was steel gray regardless of the weather. The atmosphere: thunderstorm electric. A static blanket wrapped around Martin as the giant gray cube took shape.

The structure commandeered his attention. Fractal patterns danced beneath his lids as he focused on *Marthzul's* windowless exterior. His head suddenly felt lighter, and he imagined himself lost within architecture, swimming inside cubes within cubes.

Martin returned to himself. His car idled in an empty space in the parking lot he didn't recall entering. Hundreds of cars were parked there, all empty. No one walked the lot. As far as he could tell, he and his wife were alone.

He exited the car, walked to Helen's side, and held the door open for her. She pulled herself up with the aid of the car roof. Almost a minute passed before she vacated her seat.

The air became cooler as they neared the building. Martin thought of meat lockers and damp Parisian sewers.

"I don't like this place," Helen said, lagging behind. "It's weird."

He noticed that no one walked in or out of *Marthzul's*. Cool air became cold. "Everything's weird to you."

Passing through a sliding glass door, they entered a small, steel-walled foyer. Martin thought 'buffer room'. Helen clutched her hands and darted her eyes. It worried her, being out of the house with no one to guard it.

At the foyer's end, Martin paused so his wife might catch up. It terminated, he thought, in a black door as tall as the room. He even imagined that he saw its knob, sliver and shaped like a bear head. It wasn't until he reached out and felt nothing that he realized the door was empty space.

Past the threshold, darkness thrived. He had forgotten how stark the store was. In fact, he couldn't remember *Martuzul's* at all, though he bought from it regularly.

Darkness became a gray gloom that revealed a maze of steel walls and slick, obsidian floors. Below, tiles flowed like a stream. He wanted to reach down to see if they were wet. Above, it sounded like something crawled in rafters unseen.

"Where should we start?" Helen asked.

"In the appliance section, I guess."

"Where's that?"

"How should I know?"

She looked down at her shoes. Martin pressed on. The maze pulled and stretched, twisted and turned. He found himself wondering if a Minotaur guarded the space between the 'clothes' and 'music' aisles. Perhaps a unicorn grazed on cheap tabloids in the 'books and magazines' section—provided, of course, that these sections existed.

"Think anyone's here?"

He shrugged his shoulders. "We'll find that out later."

Martin rounded a curve and smashed headlong into something. Helen walked into his back, pressing his nose up against the obstruction. When he regained his bearings, he saw that he was crammed up against a tall, twenty-something employee.

"Sorry," Martin said. "I didn't see you."

"It's happened before," the employee replied. "Don't worry."

He stifled the urge to apologize again. "Could you help us? My wife and I can't find the necrowaves."

"Necrowaves, yes. Very popular."

"So I hear, but do you know where we could find one?"

"Turn around."

Martin turned. A large retail outlet stood in place of the maze. It still appeared devoid of people, though overhead fluorescents displaced the gloom. Bright advertisements hung suspended by wires attached to the ceiling. 'THOUGHT-FORMS BEGET LIFE FORMS' said one for a female contraceptive. 'BE YE NOT A SESQUIPEDALIAN OR A SESQUIPEPHOBE' said another, this time for a karaoke machine.

But there didn't seem to be any karaoke machines or female contraceptives in stock. Of the shelves he could see, only one didn't feature necrowaves. It held nothing, yet, somehow, seemed to offer something, too.

He faced the employee. "Sorry to have bothered you."

The man smiled. "It's my job to be bothered."

Martin walked to one of the shelves. The necrowaves looked no different than the microwave in his kitchen. All were black and small, and he doubted a turkey breast could fit into any of them. "What model do you recommend?"

"All models are physically and functionally identical. The effect they provide, however, is unique to each user."

"Isn't that an odd feature?"

"Much has changed in cooking technology."

"I see." He scooped up one of the necrowaves. "Thanks for your help." The appliance felt lighter than he imagined it would, as though its bulk was made up of air. By the time he spun back around, the employee was gone. He thought he heard footfalls in the distance.

"Have you seen a check-out lane?" asked Martin.

"No."

"Then I guess we can take it."

Helen blanched. "That's stealing!"

"But I think they want us to take it. If they didn't, wouldn't the checkout lane be more obvious?"

She seemed to agree, but made no reply.

In the foyer, Martin's mind returned to *Marthzul's* vanishing maze. The necrowave slipped from his grasp. He regained hold, but then couldn't remember what he'd been thinking about.

At the car, he struggled with both the necrowave and the car keys. Helen stood outside, smoking a cigarette.

Once they were both inside: "Thanks for the help."

"No problem," she replied sincerely.

Martin exhaled frustration and inhaled what he hoped was tranquility. Then he started the car.

"My god, Martin! Look at the Stevensons!"

But he had already spotted the house through the passenger side window. The encircling atmosphere was thick and granular. Dark liquid sloshed and gurgled in the guttering, and the brickwork was spongy, covered in dense, black moss. Martin found himself thinking of corpses, graveyards and nighttime insects. His stomach felt sour; his temples ached. He turned away quickly.

Minutes passed before Helen spoke. "Do you think they're dead?"

"No part of that place feels alive."

"That's a horrible thing to say!"

He said nothing.

"Should we call the police?"

"I don't think they can help."

She also said nothing. In the backseat, she tapped her fingers against the necrowave.

Helen fumbled with the lock. He wished she'd hurry, as he was tired of carrying the necrowave. It wasn't heavy, but his back and knees ached.

Finally, the door opened with a squeal. The smell of the house hit him. He rarely noticed it unless he'd been out—not offensive, just old, musty, and closed-off—but sometimes he caught that smell in the summer, even with windows open.

In the kitchen, Martin swept bills from atop the microwave into a wicker basket. He unplugged the microwave and put it on the table, setting the necrowave in its place.

Helen looked over his shoulder. "Where's the plug-in?"

"I don't believe it needs one."

"That's odd."

"So, what should we heat first? A frozen dinner?"

"I'm not very hungry."

"How about a bag of popcorn?"

She considered the option. "As long as it's not the too-buttery kind."

Martin knew the only kind they had was the 'too-buttery' kind, but she'd never realize it. Both varieties, he thought, tasted the same.

"It's the kind you like, don't worry."

"Good, I hope you never buy that other brand again."

He removed a pack of popcorn from the cabinet, careful to conceal the brand name. He put it in the necrowave, drew a deep breath, closed the door and, with a finger that trembled slightly, pushed the power button.

"It works just like a regular microwave." Helen sounded disappointed. "Think it's defective?"

"I don't know." Martin looked down at the necrowave's slightly elevated base. It didn't have a fan or an exhaust. No air blew out, but air blew in. He wasn't sure a necrowave should do this but, then again, he wasn't certain what a necrowave did.

"I hope it came with a warranty."

He ignored her as the necrowave swallowed air with increasing force. A letter took flight across the room; a wad of food crumbs and hair scooted towards Helen from beneath the table; glasses in the cabinet rattled; wall-mounted baskets shook; plates, silverware, napkins and cans hurtled in their direction.

"I think it's going to kill us," Helen shouted.

Martin said nothing, awed by a blender as it passed through his stomach without leaving a mark. From there, the blender slipped into the space between the appliance and the counter top and entered the necrowave.

Colors peeled from the floor, the walls, the ceiling, and even the sky outside. Dimensional coordinates skewed. Helen collapsed into a pinpoint of light. Before Martin could react, his body folded latterly, becoming wafer-thin. His mind detached from the physical. He entered the necrowave.

He awoke sprawled out in the kitchen, looking up at the ceiling. Things around him appeared alien. The air buzzed and hummed. Time was meaningless. His teeth clenched, and his muscles were tight. He forced himself to breathe deeply. Gradually, panic ebbed along with the haze.

He turned his head. Helen was spread out on the floor, too. She looked dead.

"Are you okay?"

She said nothing. His arm felt boneless, but he snaked it across the floor. Her head turned at his touch.

He exhaled. "You had me scared."

"I was scared too, for a moment."

He recoiled. Years had passed since he'd heard her post-coitus voice.

"Get the popcorn, Martin."

An odd request. Though popcorn was the last thing on his mind, his stomach felt so empty that he imagined its walls might touch.

He arose on unsteady legs. His body didn't seem like his own, but at least the kitchen had returned to normal. He paused in front of the necrowave, fearful that the bag might have transformed during its stay in the oven.

He opened the door and looked inside. The bag was full and steamy, not in the least bit frightening. "Popcorn's still hot." He wobbled back to Helen and emptied the bag onto the floor. It was odd, not using a bowl or the table, but it somehow felt right.

He sat down. Helen scooted over to him. Her hair was darker and the lines on her face smoother. He smiled at the changes, grabbed a handful of popcorn, and brought it to his mouth. Helen did likewise.

The popcorn gone, Martin walked to the window. His legs no longer wobbled. His knees and back no longer ached.

He opened the blinds. Outside, trees, grass, and sky appeared as always, but with a difference he could not express. Perhaps things were brighter, or more contrastable. Even the Culbertson house, visible atop a hill, had returned to being the same split-foyer he'd seen for years. A black, membranous shadow, however, seemed to overlay the property. He tried to get a better look, but it was gone before his eyes refocused.

Martin wondered if the Culbertsons were still seeing the black horror, still living it. The question unnerved him, so he banished it from his mind. All he knew was that his world, the one he saw every day, looked fine.

Behind him: "Let's go somewhere, Martin."

He was taken aback. Helen never wanted to do anything more than watch the shop-at-home channel, go shopping with Debbie, or sleep.

"I want to leave, right now."

"Where will we go?"

She spent a moment in thought. "How about the Grand Canyon?"

"The Grand Canyon?"

"Yeah, and I don't want to just sit at the rim; that's what everybody else does. I want to *sky dive* into it." She smiled. "And you'd be strapped to me, of course."

"Seriously?"

"Seriously."

Martin was grateful for the change in Helen, but he wasn't an adventurous sort, and had never been more than 300 miles from home. Skydiving into the Grand Canyon was unimaginable. He wondered if it was even legal.

"But what about the mayor? Would he approve?" These were questions he had to ask.

"What about him? And who cares what he thinks."

Martin's voice cracked. "I'm sorry for getting mad at you, sorry for everything. Can you forgive me?"

"Shhh." She pressed her finger to his lips. "Think nothing more of it."

And so he didn't. Instead, he imagined the rush of air that would billow out his clothes as he exited the plane. He closed his eyes and saw a thin ribbon of blue that cut across a vast and rugged landscape—the mighty Colorado River seen from on high.

Nightmare Dreamscape

Agni Kudra

I WAS LIVING at Alex's. My son Patrick and I had the upstairs, and it was more like our own apartment. The house was huge; much larger than any house I'd ever lived in. We were on the third floor, yet I could walk out a door where I had my own garden. It was beautiful and sunny all the time. I was finishing moving in there, thinking about having Barney for my upstairs roommate, and Patrick was laying down for a nap. I slowly walked around, opened a box, took out one thing, got lost in it, and put it away, only to be distracted by the next thing from my past that caught my eye.

There was a knock at my door. I'm naked—go figure—so I ask who it is with the door open a crack. It's some official-looking guy who tells me that Alex called them, and said he was afraid I was going to kill myself, and he's there to check things out. I ask him to hold on because I need to get dressed, but even as I'm saying it, he pushes past me and is shoving me around when I'm naked and defenseless, and he tears my house apart like it's a fucking raid or something. I was furious. Everything was trashed, and all of the work I had done was ruined. I hated he and Alex both. But it was still so sunny and beautiful outside, and the flowers looked incredible, and the sun was reflecting off a butcher's knife.

Later, I was homeless and hanging out in a parking garage where I would sometimes sleep. It was summertime, and hot, and all I had were winter clothes, and I was so dirty that I usually just hung out in the garage all day. One day, I overheard a conversation where I learned about this upscale woman to whom you could pay $25,000 for her to set up a necrophilic fantasy. I knew how she moved by the clunk of her heels on the hardwood floors. I knew how her ears hung with her heavy earrings that bore fake jewels and would clink against the phone. I knew how much she smoked, and what kind of tailored suits she wore. But I never saw her.

There was a man working out the details with her, and I knew that she'd had a woman killed, and had hidden her deep in this parking garage in a dumpster. He wanted to 'find' the body and have his way with it for a couple of days.

I followed him deep down into the garage, further than I ever knew it went. I saw him approach the dumpster, saw how excited he was. He clapped his hands and rubbed them together. The smell of rotting flesh was going to make me puke, but he just got more and more animated the closer he got. I watched him climb into the dumpster, watched his clothes being thrown out over the side to lay in a grimy pile beside it. I watched him fuck the corpse and lay around hugging it for a couple of days. Kissing her, the fluid spilling out, the smell getting worse. But I couldn't turn away, something had me glued there, and for some reason I felt undetectable. But I think he may have also gotten off on knowing I was there, watching.

Then he and the woman were looking for me. I don't know how they knew about me. But the knowledge was eating me up. She was going to find me and have me killed, and he wanted to help kill me so that I wouldn't tell about what he had done. I heard her talking to a man on the phone saying he could buy me for half-price, since this time she didn't have to hunt for someone to murder. They were stalking me. They were going to kill me and leave me in a dumpster for this guy to fuck. I could already see myself lying there; the smell of my body, the smell of his body mixed with mine. The force with which he would devour me. And I woke up.

Last night, I was working in downtown Seattle. My car was starting to die, and I was driving around with these big, leather work gloves on. I had a staph infection in my finger, and I was trying to protect it while working. But the work gloves were dirty, and although something felt strange, I didn't bother to take them off to check on my finger. I thought I should leave it alone.

I happened to see all the boys I used to hang out with in high school in Spokane doing construction on a building, so I pulled my car over knowing they'd help me if it died. As soon as I pulled in the motor sputtered and went dead, but I was okay with it since everyone was running over, happy to see me. I got out and we all said our hellos with boisterous hugs and handshakes. I remembered I was wearing the gloves, and that maybe I should take them off. I figured it wouldn't look that bad, but it did look funny trying to shake hands with these big gloves on, so I decided to take them off.

I slid my fingers out, and my finger was twice the normal size. The skin had split down either side, from the tip down the first couple of knuckles. I realized I had been bitten by a brown recluse spider on the finger with the staph infection. The skin was eaten away on the underside of my finger, it was all rotten. The flesh was black and blue and the smell was horrible. I couldn't believe what I was seeing; this was not my body.

The bone was sticking out, and we all screamed and everyone was trying not to throw up. But then I did, and they did, watching the way the rotten muscle was clinging to my bone and making it move. I couldn't even feel it.

I ran away from my car because I knew it wouldn't work. I ran for blocks until I found a hospital, and even then I had to walk up many flights of stairs, passing pleasant smoking areas with flowers in pots and cheery people. I got there and had to wait for two hours to be looked at. The waiting room was filled with people who weren't like me. They didn't have flesh rotting off their bodies. They weren't carrying the smell that I was. They didn't look hot, or sick, or decayed. They wanted me to fill out papers, and I kept trying to show them my hand and explain that I didn't have two hours, and that I couldn't fill out the paper work. They didn't listen. They pointed to the people who didn't have bones sticking out of their hands, or their flesh rotting off, and told me first, come first serve.

What the fuck is going on in my head?

No one would go with me to have my abortion. I was pregnant and I didn't know how. Half-awake, I could feel liquid leaking out of me, and I wanted to say "help me," but I couldn't get the words out, so I drifted back into the dream. Freaked-out and knowing I wouldn't have another baby by myself, I tried to talk to people to get someone, anyone, to come with me to the doctor, and no one would.

I rode the bus there and cried the whole way. I told the doctors I needed to talk to them first because I had no one to talk to. I told them I didn't know what this would do to me mentally and that I was afraid. They just kept putting me off like everyone else. Some men in lab coats came in with a nurse. I suppose it was assumed I'd "relate" to her, seeing as we both had vaginas. She tried to keep a nice bedside manner, but I could tell something wasn't right; this wasn't routine. She told me there is something I should know; that the baby in me isn't even human, they don't know what it is, but yes, I am pregnant, and everyone is really better off if I have an abortion. She pats my hands, enclosed in hers.

So I'm in a dirty exam room, and the paper covering the table is crumpled as if someone else has already laid on it. I hop up there anyway with my paper gown on, arguing with them about the lack of anesthetic, and can't I at least have a Valium. No one held my hand, no one gave me a thing; they just put someone on either side of me to force my legs apart, and the doctor shoved a metal vacuum up through my cervix, and I felt it all and I woke up.

Last night I was running through a forest, but it was more like a jungle. I had a knife between my teeth. My hair was much longer and had clumps of dirt in it. I was very dirty. Barefoot. Blood dried on my thighs. I was the me I fantasize about.

I was caught and thrown in a cave. There were three of them, and they had entirely black eyes. Their bodies were white... alien. They were skinny and smooth. They challenged me to a staring contest. How juvenile. But I was tied up, and their eyes were scary, and what could I do? So I stared. I stared at each one of them, and their eyes went on forever. They never blinked. I always blinked first. I was petrified. I didn't know what they wanted from me, or what they were going to do to me. I recognized the energy of each of them, but they looked so different now. Why were they doing this to me?

Every time I lost, they would approach me with long needles and suck the marrow out of my bones. I could feel needles slowly working through the sinew of my muscle. But it wasn't blood they were after, just my marrow. They were so placid about it. So patient. So blank. I hated the feel of their clammy hands pushing my hair out of the way, the feel of their saliva on my arms where they'd rub the dirt off the area where they were going to put the needle. I know exactly what it feels like to have a needle pierce your bone.

I started to bleed everywhere. They paid it no attention. And then I was having the last staring contest. I finally won, and I said, "YOU blinked," and woke up.

I can't think too clearly tonight... I had this dream last night. I've been having a lot of interesting dreams lately, actually. Not as intense and horrid as the Prozac dreams, but intense dreams nonetheless. Last night there were two boys. I was so social. No interest in anyone except as a friend. No possibility, just flat out NOT interested. No boys, nobody else's flesh in me, no sound of a man's voice murmuring or sighing or telling me secrets and lies as I fell asleep. Not interested.

But there were two. Not interested, but they were... interesting. I started to feel the need to choose. I started feeling like I had to nail down an emotion because my feelings had the capability of going in a million different directions, and I only had the strength to focus on one. Just one. Just one thought, just one emotion, and if it so be, just one boy.

There was the one with the Voudou tattoos. Like me. He was soft and gentle and no one thought he would hurt me. Just like the last one was soft and gentle and no one thought he would hurt me.

A girl came out... not sure who she was. But it turned into this crude game where she was going to see how big his dick was. I was embarrassed for myself and for him; the room was full of people. Close friends, but still. It was so tasteless. But for some reason it was allowed and had to be done. She unzipped his pants. He was uncircumcised. He knew that I noticed, and he knew that I liked it, and he got hard in her hands. It was eleven-inches long. It was covered in more veins than I'd ever seen.

He told her to quit touching him, waved her hand away, disgusted. He led me to a bedroom. It turned out to be mine.

We started kissing, and I knew that I was in love with him, and had been for a while. I was glad to have held off on having sex with him for so long. We were embarrassed about what had just happened, but tried to act like we had forgotten it. I remember thinking that it was the first time I was going to have sex since I was last with Alex. I remember thinking that I hoped I wouldn't cry and fuck it all up. I told him I just wanted him inside of me.

And it felt good because I was in love with him and I had moved on.

But the daytime was about as bad as the nighttime. The dreams I could wake out of quickly, raising a hand to my chest to make sure I was there, grasping the pillow with the other one. Feeling the sheets brush against my legs, feeling the sweat drip down my forehead. I was always glad when the dreams were over, but the sense that being awake wasn't much better came to me real quick.

I started taking the Prozac and felt it within twenty-four hours. There was no way I could have convinced myself to become that numb, that fast. There was no way I could fake it. Suddenly, I couldn't fake *anything*. I was flat-lined, a gessoed canvas, a freshly-laid brick wall. There was nothing to my thoughts or the way I interacted with people. I didn't feel. I loved it.

Once, a long time ago, I did some GHB with a friend. I remember standing in the kitchen roasting potatoes, and feeling like everywhere I moved in the kitchen there was a big, warm, fuzzy blanket surrounding me. The blanket was invisible, but it was arrow-proof. Mix that feeling with every bit of pot I've ever smoked and all the ways it made me feel, minus the paranoia and dehydration and slowness, and that was how I felt twenty-four hours a day on Prozac. This shit only took a five-minute conversation with a doctor, who saw me at the last minute, and who had never seen me previously, before they would hand it right over for ten bucks. And it was legal. Why didn't anyone think of this sooner?!

But that serene feeling I was basking in turned dark very quickly. I started to realize not what I didn't feel... but what I was capable of while I wasn't feeling anything. To have sex with the man I was in love with and not be shaken to the core. I could fuck anyone and feel nothing. What was wrong with me? What was I capable of? Could I ruin my life with a smile on my face, and then go home and go to bed content? Could I eat myself up from the inside out, only paying for it when I decided it was time to get off Prozac?

Then the paranoia set in. I could be so calm in intense situations that would normally leave me shaking or quaking or screaming or crying, but a simple trip to the bar would put me in a tailspin. Hanging out with friends, meeting new people, I'd have a panic-attack like I'd never had before. I'd be chaotic and looking for someone to make it okay for me to leave. And all the while I could hear you talking about me.

And now it's done, and I can still feel you all over my words and thoughts and emotions.

You Get Nothing and You Like It

m4w – 35 (personals ad)

Daniel Scott Buck

Reply to: per...
Date: 2007-02-11, 12:26 AM PST

I FEEL SO OLD. I feel so used. I feel so beaten down.

And I wonder how I have landed here when I have so much to be proud of.

And that has been the problem throughout my life, again and again. I keep going, I keep lifting myself up, I keep coming out on top and getting nothing out of it.

This life has been so dark, this small room I call my head. I'm beginning to wonder if I'm ever there.

But I want to meet with you, with someone. I don't want to talk about my dreams, I don't want to talk about my problems, I don't want to talk about myself at all. And I don't want to talk about you. Do you dream? Are you fallen? Are you scared? I simply do not care. Let's not care. Not now.

You are nothing but a light in my eye, as I am in yours. A place where we will meet to escape the dismal reality of our lives. And all that love turned to dust? Let's forget about it. Just for a moment.

Nothing. That is what I want now. And it's what I want to give to you. Absolutely nothing. It's so much more beautiful anyhow.

And when we meet, I don't want to hear your voice, not more than a few seconds of it. I do not want to listen to you talk. I just want to look at you. And if I can stand it for more than a minute, then that means you've done it right. Or something like that.

You'll know because I'll still be there, and I will reach out and hold your hand. And believe me, this moment will make me shiver. It is more than I've had in a long time. The ability to feel. A little hope.

And then we will go somewhere. On a walk. Maybe through the Pearl District or down to the waterfront. Perhaps we'll walk the esplanade. Or take the ferry across the river to where we belong.

And I'm not kidding around. I have no time to be your joker. So think twice before playing. You should know better.

Your broken heart, your broken spirit, it's not worth a nickel. So don't try to spend it on me. Give me your smile. Give me your gentleness. Give me something to live for.

Be my silent lover.

She Is His Story

Paul Lumsdaine

SO THE TV TURNS ITSELF ON and time slowly rolls by like carnations in the Rose Parade. He still remembers being thirteen, seated in those stands under the unbearable Pasadena sun on January 1, 1991. And now, sitting on this sofa, sitting on his last paycheck because he doesn't really want a job. The TV turns itself off again. Its damn depressing, anyway.

The clouds begin to part, at least in his mind. Two years in the storm of discontent and he finally sees the sun. It's nighttime, the orange glow of street lights, the thickening haze of uncertainty clinging to the sidewalk. How long can this last? As soon as a ray of hope shines on him, he runs as fast as he can in the opposite direction. He trips, and the most frightening thing is not falling down. It's getting back up and dusting off his ego; attempting to reconstruct himself.

So he does the only thing he knows that can still make him smile. He paws at the night stand, fondles the drawer slowly, and opens it up. He carefully shifts through last month's bills and feels for the smooth glossy surface of a photograph of her.

He holds it awkwardly, wishing it would say something or move, show any sign of life. She's still alive, but this picture and all its memories are dead. A beach, an ocean, a tree, and two people are all that is left. Scenery without sympathy. It was his decision to kill it, to suffocate her and drown himself in emotion. If he only would have known. He recalls that night and it tastes like bad liquor, smells of vomit, and feels like the touch of her ghost lying next to him in bed.

"Just don't see it?" He crossed his arms and stared at her, waiting for a reply. "You can't see it... you don't even want to. What ever happened to trying really hard to see through these things?" He didn't understand what in the world he was talking about.

At first, he knew the argument was about where to go for dinner. However, it had now progressed to something he never expected. "Don't turn this into a personal attack, please don't. I don't need this right now."

"And I suppose you never wanted it." And then the sobs, heavy and long. The city lights shudder and the ground is damp. He is losing his footing in here.

"Come on, you know—you know I didn't mean any of it... please just stop!" But she doesn't stop. She grabs her coat and walks out the door. It was that simple.

So now he stares at a blank TV screen, unable to move without remembering her scent. He lets the couch envelop him, drifts away on those polyester waves. His mind slides under sand and his thoughts become scattered like pebbles on the shore. The orange glow of streetlights take over the apartment from the kitchen window, and the hum of the electrical lines sing a somber lullaby.

Somehow, this morning is not the same. He gets up, stretches, and heads to the kitchen. He notices the empty Folger's container, scratches himself, and heads to the corner store. It smells like bleach in there. He waves to a cashier he's never seen before. He grabs a Styrofoam cup and shivers coffee out of a machine. It's black and strong and good. He tries to recall when he started drinking coffee and guesses that it was long before he decided to keep track of his bad habits. Or maybe it isn't bad at all. He convinces himself almost all the time that he is completely normal. He hands the cashier his credit card. Denied. Twice. He feels in his pocket for the change he knows he does not have. Since he's already taken a couple sips out of the cup, the cashier lets him have it. In broken English, he says, "I know how people are." He tips his blue baseball cap, faded from sweating in the sun. With a little laugh, he seals his act of unconditional kindness.

Walking down the street, coffee in hand, barely two sips taken since the store, the scene replays in his head a couple of times and he appreciates what's been done for him. It's the whole pride part, though, and that laugh. He shrugs it off and takes another sip. Its damn good coffee. He never stops to worry about his card, or his debt, or even that its the fifth of the month and he still hasn't paid rent. Another short interlude of bliss from a simple act.

He opens up the classified section with zest, jolted by kindness and caffeine. There's a job, and another, and look, here's one. But no. He decides that he's under-qualified, or overqualified, or just not interested. This is why he hates looking for a job. It reminds him of all those things he's never quite been able to complete, and never quite wanted to, anyway. He would work late into the night, sweating, pressing himself to finish something. But the sun would rise and he would still have nothing to show for it. He takes the classifieds and makes a paper airplane.

He stumbles over to the kitchen and tells Mr. Coffee he needs some in two hours. The TV turns itself on. There's static: a complete haze of white noise and no discernible picture. He fumbles for the cable in the back of the set; unscrew, screw in, tighter and tighter. Flashes of grey-speckled mess, on and off. He sits on the couch, letting his sweat collect on the armrest. He fumbles his fingers through hair and tugs in various directions. There's no reason why, this damn thing, there's no reason. And once again he curls up in bed, reaches for the nightstand. He shifts through last month's bills and finds the solution. Cable, unpaid balance of $59.87, due last Thursday. What was he doing that day? He can't seem to remember. Every day seems the same, and its no wonder why bills never get paid.

DANCING IN THE MOONLIGHT

Sitting, watching TV again. He shuffles through the bills and realizes that most of his money is gone. At least he has the TV and remote, as if it was some kind of connection to the outside world. There's a knock at the door. "Yah?" he breathes. "This is Officer Constance with the county sheriff, we need to speak with you sir." Paranoia and fear surge through him, even though he has committed no crime. He generally distrusts anyone who tells him what to do. "What's this about, anyway?" he asks as he loosens the dead bolt. He opens the door and stares at their holsters. Luckily, they are still clipped, and the two Officers stand at ready. "It's about your neighbor sir." They look at each other uneasily, and he motions for them to step in.

A cup of coffee later, they have gone through too many questions and have found no real answer. "Actually, the paramedic thinks he died some time last night. It was a shame he didn't have much of a family, or even a close connection with his neighbors." Officer Constance looks around, uneasy. His partner, Miller, has been the one asking questions, a veteran with a rookie on a routine call.

"So why are you here, exactly?"

Miller nudges Constance in the side. Reflected light shines from the rookie's silver star into my eyes. Perhaps he was admiring the T-FAL toaster, or in a reverie about Colombian-grown in his cup. He coughs twice and speaks up. "Uh, we were wondering... if there were any suspicious characters in the, uh... surrounding area."

"Not really. You two are the only suspicious characters I've seen around here lately." They laugh to play it off, and then take their cue to leave. Exeunt, the Officers. This is like some bad BBC version of a Shakespearean tragedy. Gil died. More ghosts and forgotten faces. Wondering if he'll be coming around to haunt his neighbor. With still half a pot of Colombian left, he retires to the bathroom with a month-old *Maxim* magazine in his hand.

DRESS FOR SUCCESS

He tries on his suit and is amazed that it still fits. For some reason, he can't remember where his shoes are, and this worries him a great deal. There's nothing worse than a man in a suit wearing sneakers. It says, "Hey, I don't really want to be here. I'm just waiting around so I can get my hands on those Swedish meatballs." He finds his shoes underneath the couch, discarded from the last time he wore them. He can't even remember when that was. It's damn depressing, going to this funeral in the middle of the week, though he has nothing better to do. He sips his coffee, slightly tart from sitting out all night, and the *Garfield* mug smiles up at him. He loves that mug, damn it, and he loves his coffee. "Better get that straight," he tells himself. A couple more tries at his tie and he looks rather nice. He heads out the door.

As he is getting on the bus, he notices a woman wearing a long black skirt and a veil. It seems strange that they are both mournful dressed on the same bus. He's never seen this woman before, he thinks. She is hardly recognizable underneath the veil. He figures he should take a chance and sit next to her.

"Did you know Gil?" The woman looks up at him and stares in amazement. She shakes her head from side to side, keeping her eyes locked onto his. He looks away, feeling awkward and mildly embarrassed. She grabs his hand and pulls him closer. "Don't tell anyone why I'm here." He pulls his arm out of her grasp and stumbles a few steps back. He staggers to the opposite end of the bus, keeping his eyes on her. She must be one of those crazies.

He gets off at Fourth Street, making sure that she is out of sight. He shakes off the incident with a shrug and heads down the street towards the Tuhen Family Mortuary. He steps inside the large building and is instantly offered a program by a woman wearing a grey business suits, simple and non-confrontational. He stops for a brief moment and smiles at her. She smiles back. He can not help but be attracted to her smooth blond hair and sparkling green eyes. He almost forgets where he is, and why he is there. He turns to get another look at her, but loses her face in the shuffle of the crowd.

Its amazing how many people show up for these things, friends of friends, anonymous acquaintances, people who live on the same floor. He must have done a thousand things no one ever knew about. Yet, everyone cries for his soul trapped somewhere in the layers of smog.

Thoughts jump from cremation to coffee and cream. Maybe his cream is past expiration. He'll have to check that when he gets home. What is he doing here? It's probably the worst time in his life for someone to go and die. He opens the missal in front of him. The pages are worn from abuse and there is writing all over the front and back covers. On the front left hand side is a quote. "Tragedy looks to me like man in love with his own defeat. Which is only a sloppy way of being in love with yourself." The author's name is scratched out.

A beautiful young woman walks in and dances around grieving relatives, awkwardly sliding by them, making her way for the second row of pews. She sits for about thirty seconds, glancing every which way to see if anyone notices her presence. She is jittery, fumbling for the flowers at her side. She slips out of the pew and darts for the altar. After throwing her flowers down on the ground in front of the coffin, she bows and hurries back to her seat. She again glances around the room, avoiding eye contact.

Her eyes are fierce, reflecting the sun through the stained glass windows. He continues to watch her as relatives of Gil come to her side. Every awkward embrace leaves a deeper mark of sadness on her cheeks.

He goes up to give his last regards to Gil with the intention of sitting next to the girl. He can't imagine how odd it would be to find love at a funeral. A wedding or even a baptism would be feasible. However, picking someone up at a funeral is an all-time low he has been waiting to sink to. But he can hardly look her in the eyes as he walks by. He turns around and sits behind her. Directly behind her.

COFFEE AND QUAKE

They sit down next to each other at Pete's Coffee Shop, right down the street from the funeral home. "You know, I barely know you." He's waiting for rejection. "But somehow, I trust you." He sips his straight black. Raindrops spit on the asphalt. A man in a suit walking by sticks out his hand and dials a number on his cell phone.

"Are you listening?"

"Yeah, of course. I'm sorry. I'm easily, eh... distracted. But I was listening, and I feel a connection, too." She smirks and reaches for his hand across the table. "That's not all you would like to feel." He moves his hand back in astonishment. She can smell the truth.

"It's not that at all! I can't even believe you would think something like that about... ." But he stops because the man on the cell phone is yelling and his face shows extreme anguish. Maybe the man knows of her accusation.

He knows she knows what's really going on and this scares him. Intelligence and beauty scare him. He has been trying to avoid it for years, but now it's staring him straight in the face, and waiting for an answer.

He looks again at the cell phone guy, hoping he'll do something drastic. But the guy flips the phone back into his pocket and continues down the street. He is replaced by an elderly woman waiting for the bus, the same woman who freaked him out earlier. She turns around and, for a brief moment, their eyes meet. He shudders, but at the same time, smiles with all his heart. The old woman smiles back at him, then turns around as if nothing is going on.

He looks back into her eyes, "You're beautiful."

It's nearly pouring rain by now, even though a stretch of blue shimmers in the distant skyline. "It's not far. Let's run." He grabs her hand tight as they take off, dashing in and out of pedestrian traffic. She darts around a corner and swings him to her side. They kiss under the fire escape of an old brick building.

It feels like the entire world is shaking around him. He looks at her. She looks really worried. The building they press up against begins to spew dust from the second and third floor. The fire escape squeals as it twists and turns. She pulls him in closer. She is desperately trying to avoid potted plants falling from four stories up. The pottery shatters on the asphalt. Shards of red clay roll underneath them. They kiss again.

FOUR FEET UP

The condensation on his windows begins to clear up with the first few rays of sun. He looks at her laying in the bed. So beautiful. He hardly knows anything about her. Well, perhaps he knows more than he thinks. She is spontaneous, overzealous, and possibly a niece or distant cousin of Gil. He wonders how she will act when she wakes up. She could just walk out the door and never talk to him again. He goes to the bathroom and leaves the door open.

She is still fast asleep as he finishes up his best attempt at breakfast—Cheerios, a glass of Minute Maid, and coffee. He gently blows in her ear. She mildly stirs, so he does it again. Finally there is a stretch and a yawn. She opens those wonderful eyes wide and blinks three or four times. He stands there with the tray in his hand, mock butler. She giggles and sits up in bed. He hands her the tray and gives her a peck on the cheek. "Was I out for long?"

"Only eight or nine hours."

She digs into the Cheerios and hands him the Minute Maid. "Can't have anything too acidic in the morning. Messes with the system." He shrugs and drinks his own cup of black Colombian. "I don't have any sugar. I hope you like it black." She smiles and goes back to the cereal.

The strangest thing ends up happening. She never leaves. She stays there all day, by his side, watching TV and reading the comics, and just spending time. He finds this unsettling. They barely know each other and she acts as if she has moved in. "So, I know this is odd to bring up but... "

She looks startled. "Oh, you mean, the whole introduction thing. Well... can't we just skip it? I mean, I have a past and you have a past... and there's obviously something between us... you know. Let's just hang on to that." So they fuck again, and this time, after they are done, she skips over to her purse and grabs a joint.

Between pillow talk, she describes to him everything that she has done in the past few years. It appears that she likes drugs, and that's not necessarily a bad thing. The good thing is that she's not dependent on them. At least that's what she tells herself. He smiles at her story about getting high before taking her driver's license test. He talks about his addiction to coffee. How he guzzles more and more by the day. His warmth is in a cup. Her warmth is in a joint. He watches steam rise from his cup every morning. She watches plumes of smoke rise in the air.

The both giggle until there's practically no laughter left in the air. It's stale and smells like sweat. He goes to take a shower, alone, and she asks, "If we can fuck, why can't we shower together?" The words echo and make him feel dirty. "I just like to be by myself in the shower. It's where I think about life. It's like... *sacred.*" And with that word, she rolls her eyes and closes the bathroom door.

Once again, he doesn't understand what the hell he just said. He goes back to her in defiance of his own statement, brings her with him to the shower. He realizes that for the first time, he's not embarrassed to be himself.

Her head rests against his shoulder and he can feel her breath on his neck. His blanket is wrapped around them, covering both of their bodies. He stares at her feet while they lay in bed next to each other, comparing her toes with his. He wonders where those feet have been, who they have been next to, who else might have stared at them.

"So."

"So?" She lifts her head up and unwraps herself from the blanket. She gets up and starts putting her clothes on.

"I didn't mean it like that."

"No, I understand. I've been here all day and, of course, you have things to do. I have things to do. It's perfectly natural just to fuck and then split, right? That's what I should have done." She couldn't possibly mean that. He searches for the perfect thing to say, the words he should have said earlier. "No, I want you to stay."

She stands there with her blouse and underwear on, holding tightly to her skirt. She throws it on the bed, lets out a sigh, scratches her head, scurries from the room. He gets up, grabs the blanket, and wraps it around his waist. He trips over the damn thing and falls flat on his face right in front of her. He looks up at her.

"I didn't mean it that way. You know how that happens, you don't know what to say or how to say it or if you should say anything at all."

He gets on his knees and gently kisses her inner thigh. She rolls her eyes and sighs. The hairs on his back stand as her fingers clasp the side of his face. His cheeks grow instantly warm under her touch. He has never felt better.

SUN DAY

After talking to a lawyer all day, she finally returns. The TV turns itself off as he looks towards the door. She hates when he watches that thing. He has been trying not to, but the second she slips out of the room his fingers begin to itch for the remote.

She smiles, fully knowing he is melting away inside. She has good news. "Guess what?"

He shrugs.

"I just talked to my Uncle's lawyer, and after signing nearly every damn piece of paper in there, I got it."

"Got what?" It wouldn't hurt if she came upon a few extra bucks, at least to help him pay rent. She's been living here for, what? Three weeks now, not paying bills or rent. She did buy him dinner nearly every night. He had no idea where that money came from, and he didn't really need to know. She took care of him and he took care of her.

"Well, I suppose it's not much, but you know this apartment next to yours, where my Uncle used to live, I guess he actually owns it outright. So, I could live there... if you wanted me to."

He can't imagine how this is good news. He didn't mind her living next to him, but she was already living *with* him. Now, she's moving in next door, which means she'll have her own set of bills to pay, her own kitchen to cook in, her own bed to sleep in. "Does this mean you're moving out?"

She ran over and sat on his lap. "Its only next door! But yes, I am going to move my whole one suitcase of clothing over there." She paused in his silence. "Aren't you happy?"

He was much happier watching TV than watching her move away from him, even if it was only next door. "I guess. It's just, I thought you wanted to live with me, and now it feels like you were just staying here till you could find another place to move on to."

She pushes herself away, "You are unbelievable. I am moving next door and you act like we're never going to see each other again. It's been less than a month but you've managed to attach yourself to me like a little kitten." He pushes her off his lap. She struts off to the kitchen. He needs some damn coffee.

"I need to leave. Just let me go out for awhile, and when I come back I'm going to pretend like this conversation didn't happen." She walks out the door, and it's that simple. "Fine, I'm gonna sit and drink my coffee," he says to himself. And he turns himself off. There's not even static, not a damn thing at all. If only he could stay like this.

He reaches for the remote, flips through commercials, finds a program on some Russian dictator. He watches the screen in anticipation of some sign. He wants to see her appear on the screen in an old photograph, something that can be seen but not touched. If only she were just an image. The TV turns itself off and he staggers over to the window. He tips his cup against the cold glass surface and watches the coffee slide down the glass. He needs to stop drinking this damn stuff. It makes him so edgy.

She comes back, as promised. He stands there, facing the outside, standing in the puddle of coffee. She steps closer to him and sees the pool of dark black on the floor. "Oh, let me get a towel." She comes back to mop it up. He stops her and leans down. "I'm sorry. For everything." She clasps his face with her hands and he feels that warmth again.

They wake up later that evening and she springs up from bed. She taps his arm and tugs on the sheet. "Time to go out, to celebrate my new place!" He smiles and slips out from under the covers. Fifteen minutes later they are strolling down the street arm-in-arm. The air is cold and dry, pressing against the tip of their noses and chilling the tops of their ears. They walk into Cafe Bistro, fine Italian dining. Neither of them really have the money to pay for a lavish meal, so they share a dish of Chicken Parmesan and a bottle of red wine.

They stroll along for awhile afterwards, warmed by the wine. He doesn't need much when she's around. His mind is pacified by her presence. He hopes she feels the same—that she needs him as much as he needs her. The street lights fade into a thin line leading back to the apartment.

The next day he wakes up, completely rejuvenated. It is a beautiful morning and he celebrates it by making pancakes. He serves her a plate in bed. It's now a routine, waking up, making her breakfast, getting ready for the day of lounging around the house. She leaves for another five hours. He's never asked her where she goes. He figures it's a job, at least.

But today she comes home, drenched in sweat. Her chest heaves in and out as she struggles for air.

"What the hell is wrong with you?"

She doesn't answer, but instead heads straight to the bathroom. He presses his ear against the door. He can still hear her breathing heavily, now and then sighing with relief. The shower turns on.

Twenty minutes later, she steps out, every towel he owns wrapped around her, and yet still shivering. She goes to the kitchen, gets a glass of water, and continues to the bedroom. He's following her every step, an awkward dance of confusion and frustration. She sits on the edge of the bed. He is still waiting for an answer as she motions for him, swinging her arms open for an embrace. He rushes to her side, repeating his question. "I had a rough day at the office, let's say." He doesn't ask her anything more. The setting sun casts shadows across the coffee-stained carpet. He hasn't had a cup all day.

He can't sleep. He sits and stares at the TV on mute. Pictures without sound make him feel even more detached from himself. His mind is floating somewhere in the evening mist. His soul slides across the pavement. His heart lies in the gutter.

He can't stand insomnia. He crawls into the bed, trying to instigate, but she rolls over onto her side. He pushes more, tugging at her sides. She slowly awakes and rubs her eyes, staring at him with amazement. He grabs her close and kisses along her neck. She gives a gentle moan but quickly pushes him away. "Not right now, so sleepy... I just want to sleep."

She turns away from him.

"You know, you can't just do this in and out thing. I want to know where you go, what you do... don't you think I should know?" She gives a sympathetic yawn. "Well, you never asked, did you?"

Its true. He never did. He thought she would tell him, eventually. "I guess I just want to know why you were so upset today." There is a long period of uncomfortable silence. Even her breathing seems to slow down. "I really think it should wait... at least until the morning." And she falls asleep, simple as that.

But he can't sleep so simply. He waits until the first rays of dawn to finally go to bed. He looks over at her as he nods off.

When he wakes up she's gone.

CAUGHT SHOOTING STARS

He sat and watched TV for three days, losing all hope of her return. And then, there was a knock at the door.

He slides himself off the sofa and goes to open it. He wonders if it's her. He looks out the peephole and sees two large guys. They don't look friendly, either.

"Who is it?" They don't answer. Instead, they knock heavily on the door again. He wonders if he spoke loud enough. He chains the door and opens up a tiny crack. The second the door moves, the two guys do, too, and then they are towering over him.

He's scared shitless as they pick him up and set him back on his couch. Then one of the thugs smashes a lamp across his head. The pain is staggering. He can feel blood trickle down his head.

"So, where is she?" He has no idea. He shrugs his shoulders. These guys take it as a personal slight and one punches him in the face. It's the first time in three days that he actually feels alive. "I don't know. She ran away, you fuckers." His words earn him a punch in the gut, and he keels over in pain.

"You tell that bitch she better pay us, or else someone close to her is gonna die." How close was he, really? This assault feels pretty damn close. They beat the shit out of him.

He's still bleeding later that night, staring into the bathroom mirror. He used to know exactly what he wanted. Once he realized that his dreams didn't come easy, he gave up on them entirely. And yet, as he stares into his own eyes, he can see something deeper.

He hears another knock on the door. He hopes its those guys, because this time he's going to put up a fight. His adrenaline is racing and he imagines himself pummeling them. He violently swings the door open. "Alright, you motherfuckers... "

He sees those radiant eyes and stops. Her battered face. Her clothes slightly torn. She put up a struggle. No words need to be said. She starts crying.

He grabs her, pulls her inside, locks the deadbolt. She looks at his face, in just as bad shape as hers. Her eyes well up again, and another outburst of tears. Their chests heave with exhaustion and the bitterness of defeat.

"I'm so sorry, I never meant for any of this... "

"Its alright. I know. It's alright." And he can't think of anything better to say. There's no way words can reconcile this evening.

He wakes up, startled by some noise, and heads over to the window. The faint glow of street lights fill the sky with an orange hue. He tries to peer down the street, but can't make anything out. He is crying again.

"Whatcha' looking at?"

"Oh nothing, just lights."

"They look nice."

"I suppose, but... "

"What?"

"Just wish, that somehow, this never happened."

"Me, too."

He looks her straight in the eyes, barely glowing now in the darkness of the room. Shadows dance about her, and it seems like ghosts stalking her. "I love you."

She smiles. "I love you, too."

And nothing more can be said.

He stares out the window until the first faint glow of dawn appears on the horizon before he finally goes to bed. He sees her standing in a field of vibrant green, surrounded by weeping willows. She dances among the leaves. Her skin turns green as she brushes up against the branches, slowly becoming a tree. He sees her face in the rugged bark.

He wakes up and she's gone again. He keeps himself from worrying by hiding his head underneath the pillow. A few minutes later, he hears the door open. She's whistling that song, what was it? He thinks it's *Singin' in the Rain.*

"Good morning... "

Her voice gently fades as the rays of the morning sun sweep across the room. He stares outside and sees clouds swimming in a sea of blue. Each light tuft is a memory, fleeing but not forgotten. Like her walking out that door time and time again.

She bought a baguette and some Brie and made eggs. It's a perfect breakfast for this nearly perfect day.

After, they flee outdoors into the brisk air.

This is where it begins to get cloudy because memory is fleeting and wants dearly to be forgotten. He staggers, slowly, falling, faster. She is still there, she has to be there. He can feel her.

And senses were all he could rely on. What does he really miss? Maybe it's his inability to feel. How great it would be to just feel something inside again. He tries so hard. He loses sight of the light, no matter how hard it shines.

He puts the photograph down and sighs. He can't help but want to resurrect her, now that she's dead. Everything is the same as it used to be. Thoughts of love that cannot be forgotten, even if they never happened.

He gets up, nearly falling out of his bed, and stumbles to the bathroom. He turns the light on and stares himself in the eyes. *What's in there that makes it worth going through this?* Something must come out of this.

He goes back to the photograph. He tears it up. He tears the memory of her apart, takes the scattered shards and throws them out the window. A sudden breeze sweeps them across the building. And just like that, they are gone.

Fuel

Reno J. Romero

Raymond sat in his car smoking a cigarette as he watched for the man's car to pull in. A crucifix hung from his mirror. The man had called earlier, told Raymond the room number, told him to be *ready*. He sounded out of breath. Raymond knew this sound.

The man pulled in, whipping his van into a parking spot. He got out, carrying a bag and a briefcase. He was wearing sunglasses and a tight-fitting suit. He scanned the parking lot. Raymond sat up. His stomach stirred. The man saw Raymond's car and went into the office with relief in his stride.

He came out and walked quickly to his room, which at his request, was in the back. Raymond was to wait ten minutes and then go to the room.

Ten minutes. Raymond lit another cigarette. He watched as a family loaded up their car with luggage. The husband's face was knotted up. Raymond noticed their front tire needed air.

Raymond knocked lightly and the man opened the door. A pall of cologne wafted out of the room. Raymond stepped in. On the small table was a bottle of Crown Royal. It was half-empty. The man's face was dry-red.

"Great to see you," the man told Raymond, ran his slumped eyes over him. Raymond smelled the booze on his breath. "Want a drink?"

The man sat on the bed.

"Come here." He tapped on the bed with his hand. Raymond noticed the man's wedding band—a tacky gold thing stamped with diamonds.

Raymond got a flash of Jesse's face—the beautiful angular Indian face, unaware of Raymond's secret ways. He walked to the bed, unbuttoning his shirt.

"I need the money first," Raymond said. "I have bills. My fridge is empty. My car needs gas."

The man took out his wallet and handed Raymond two hard one-hundred dollar bills. Then he handed him another hundred.

"This is a tip. 'Tip' is an acronym. It stands for 'To Insure Prompt Service.' Did you know that?"

The man twisted down his wedding band so the diamonds were facing his palm.

Raymond didn't say anything. He took the money and slipped it into his pocket. He walked back to the table, twisted off the cap, and took a long hit. The booze heated his young chest. He inhaled deeply, blowing the whiskey out his nostrils. The room went soft and broke his consciousness. Jesse was gone. He hit the lights and moved towards the bed.

Thornbinding

Kate Holden

JUST A BOLD FINGERTIP, just a hair-thin blade; a bubble of blood warm on her skin. A curious mood; a clacking spindle; the old woman coaxing. And something sliding white-spangled and irresistible through her veins until the Princess sank down and the crystal glitter fractured in her vision and became darkness.

She opened her eyes and the street was glassy black with rain. She was walking in the cold and cars were pulling up with passenger seats empty next to silent men; streetlights dazzled her as she bent her head into someone's lap and the taste of the darkness was salt in her throat.

And salt drowsy in her veins as she pricked herself again and again with the spike and flooded flesh with chemicals to keep her Princess-coldness safe and her frightened head full of dreams.

Years passed and she forgot she had worn a crown, as she lowered her head again and again; and forgot the fine foods she had eaten at the King's table, and she lived on cigarettes and chocolate bars. She forgot she had been born bright and beautiful, that she'd been blessed with every luxury; that those who loved her had gathered to bestow kisses on her brow. Now her quilted bower was a dirty den.

The wicked old woman watched from inside the Princess's heart, where she had made a nest for her envy, and she said, *Now you see how safe you are.*

Safe? said the Princess.

From the danger of happiness, the old woman replied. She cackled and she rubbed her hands in joy to see the young woman dim her beauty and shed her grace and muddle her learning. This old woman, the spiteful crone of the Princess's heart, had wished herself a bitter fortune, because her own brightness had hurt her. And so she made the shadows come, contagious.

The Princess stumbled on through her night streets of grit and grimness, alone and lost from sight; and time passed and the royal house slumbered in her absence, happier in dreams than in grief; and the Princess's life became thorn-bound and remote.

Until one day she was choked by the thorn bushes that pressed too closely around her, thinking she was suffocating—and she cried out from fright; the old woman deep inside her stamped her foot impatiently. And the stab of her old woman's shoe in the tender flesh, and the sting of the thorns, hurt the Princess too much at last for bearing.

You terrible bitter woman! the Princess exclaimed in shock.

And the household stirred and the King and Queen stretched, and the Princess sprang up and rubbed at her arm where it had been pricked so often, and the scratches on her skin burned. And though she put on her robes again, and her crown, and her joy, she bore the scars to the end of her days.

Christmas Day

Brad Listi

MY FATHER'S FAMILY lived in an old petroleum town called Morgan City, an hour away from Plaquemine. We drove there every year on Christmas Day. Our route took us through the bayous and cypress trees, past field and plantation, over bridges, and along a levee. In its own way, a scenic drive. I never minded it much. I liked swamps. I spent the hour staring out the window, looking for alligators. I never saw any. Mostly I saw dead rodents on the side of the road, or an occasional crushed house pet. Sometimes I'd see pelicans or cranes perched on cypress stumps. They were bright white against the murk of the swamp. I wondered how they stayed so clean.

Morgan City, like Plaquemine, had seen its better days. The oil boom was its golden era. When the boom went bust in the 1970s, so too did the town. These days it remained functional and residential. There were churches and liquor stores scattered among the rusted neighborhoods. There were cemeteries and railroad tracks. Fast food joints. Car dealerships. There was a Holiday Inn.

Of particular interest to me was the Morgan City Swamp Gardens, a wildlife zoo home to real live alligators, located in the middle of town. Over the years, I dragged my family there on several occasions. The way it worked was simple. You paid your admission fee and walked among the trees, listening to some redneck blab about the indigenous culture and the local ecosystem. Afterwards, you stood around watching captive alligators devour large hunks of raw beef, live and in-person. The reptiles thrashed side-to-side, gorging themselves, while you looked on and cheered. Long story short, fun for the whole family.

With recreational opportunity decidedly scarce, we were fortunate to have such amusing kinfolk. My father's parents were functionally crazy, which helped immensely. We called them Mimi and Pops. They lived in a tiny house on Florence Street with my Uncle Brian. Uncle Brian was thirty-two years old and mentally retarded. A tragic twist of fate during childbirth had left him with the mental faculties of a third-grader. Nature, however, had compensated, gifting him with an extraordinary, almost superhuman physical prowess. The man was 5'7" and weighed in at approximately 250 pounds. He had the strength of an ox and uncanny coordination. He could punt a football a country mile, and he could hit a baseball even farther. His feats at the local bowling alley were legendary. He bowled strikes by accident, slinging the ball with shocking force and precision, obliterating the pins. It was a real gift.

It's also worth noting that Uncle Brian didn't know how to talk. He only yelled. No matter what the man said, it came out in a booming, enthusiastic holler. It was, in its own way, endearing—a volume born of an unflagging exuberance, mystical in its relentless consistency. In all my life I've never met anyone with greater emotional stability.

This was the way that it went. Mimi, Pops, and Uncle Brian lived in odd and perfect harmony. They preserved their sanity in the common human fashion, by sticking to the same daily schedule with religious intensity. Generally speaking, their routine consisted of staying inside all day long with the curtains drawn and the lights off, watching television. Seven days a week, 365 days a year, they sat three in-a-row in tattered recliners from nine in the morning until bedtime, ingesting soap operas, commercials, and game shows, breaking only for meals. Viewing methods were decidedly unconventional, as over the years Uncle Brian had developed the nasty habit of repeating absolutely everything the television said, bar nothing. You sat there in the dark, weathering the storm, trying to make sense of what was happening. The interplay went something like this:

TELEVISION: *Tony, you bastard! How could you do this? We have children!*

UNCLE BRIAN: TONY YOU BASTARD! HOW COULD YOU DO THIS? WE HAVE CHILDREN!

TELEVISION: *Sweetheart, what are you saying? Are you out of your mind?*

UNCLE BRIAN: SWEETHEART, WHAT ARE YOU SAYING? ARE YOU OUT OF YOUR MIND?

The man never missed a beat, and my grandparents never asked him to stop. He was their baby, their unquestioned pride and joy. They referred to him as their "special angel" on a regular basis. In their eyes he could do no wrong. This was how they lived their lives, day in, day out. As far as they were concerned, it was completely normal.

Ironically, the relentless repetitions had practical applications, as neither Mimi nor Pops could hear very well. The incessant yelling insured them of missing nothing, not a single line. It was biology at work, plain and simple. Systemic evolution. The three of them seemed to be a single organism. They had adapted to their surroundings.

Pops sat front and center, remote control in-hand, the master of ceremonies. He took his television viewing seriously. He was particularly captivated by the daily soaps, displaying an uncommon concern for the on-screen characters, rooting for them with an almost familial sense of duty, as though the fate of their perpetually imperiled worlds rested squarely upon his old shoulders. He called the soap operas his "stories." The notion of missing a single episode was anathema to him. He wouldn't even think of it.

"I've got to watch my stories," he'd always say. "My stories are on."

Those people *needed* him. When something went wrong, he took it personally. A particularly disturbing episode of *Days of Our Lives* could ruin his entire day.

"That old boy's got no heart," he'd say. "He's double-timing that poor girl, left and right. It's a damn shame. A damn shame."

My sisters and I would sit on the floor at his feet, taking it all in.

"A damn shame," we'd say.

"You're dern right it's a damn shame. That old boy's got no heart. No heart at all."

Pops had a big heart, but it didn't work very well. He and two of his brothers had spent their lives running the Fencer Meat Market, in its time Morgan City's finest butcher shop, a legacy handed down from my great-grandfather. Italian sausage was their specialty. During their prime, the recipe had earned them a low-level, regional fame. Not long after I was born, all three men retired, shutting up shop, each with the same "mysterious" heart condition. For going on fifty years they'd eaten nothing but red meat, pound after pound, three meals a day. Now, in their respective twilights, they were utterly confounded by the "cholesterol disease" that had befallen them, plugging their arteries with a thick and fatal sludge.

"I've got the cholesterol disease," Pops would say, shaking his head. "I don't know why they done me like that."

At that point he'd had two heart attacks. Ultimately he'd have four.

Mimi was a piece of work. She was full-blooded Cajun French, the daughter of a bootlegger, and every year we came to visit she wore a different colored wig. The woman was a character. She'd say anything to anybody. She loved to gather the grandkids around and tell us stories; it was her favorite thing to do. We'd sit down right next to her while she talked about herself, nonstop, for two, sometimes three hours. She rocked in her chair ceaselessly, unfurling the stories of her past, while Brian hollered at the television and Pops worried about the uncertain fate of the employees of *General Hospital*. Most of what she told us was incredibly personal in nature. We learned all about her aches and pains, her trials and tribulations at the doctor's office—even her sex life.

"Let me tell you what," she'd say to us. "When he was younger, your Pops dern near wore me out. Didn't hardly have a second to myself. You believe me now. That old man had an appetite. He never tired. Day and night, every time I turned around, all he wanted was *action*."

"Really?" we said.

"Oh, children," she said. "Oh, *darlin'*."

She threw her head back and laughed. She had an infectious laugh, a shrill staccato giggle that started loud and ended breathless. We loved it. We laughed right along with her. We thought Mimi was hilarious. What's more, she had the rare ability to tell the truth with consistency. She was old and tired and had reached the point where she had neither the energy nor the mental dexterity to lie anymore. The odd and awful truth poured right out of her in a steady, unfettered stream. It was a great relief to be around her.

In the afternoon we drove across town to my Uncle Wally's house for Christmas dinner. Wally was my father's younger brother, the middle child, like me. He was a dentist. He lived in Morgan City with his wife, Katherine, and their three young kids, Melissa, Wally, Jr., and Mary Beth. They had a house with a swimming pool and a dachshund named Mickey.

My father and Uncle Wally got along famously. They were the only sane members of their immediate family. Every year on Christmas Day, while the food was cooking, they went outside and confided in one another. I always overheard them in the backyard. They stood by the pool, drank beer, and commiserated.

"I'm telling you, Joe, all they do all day long is sit around that goddamn house watching soap operas. It worries the hell out of me. They never see daylight."

"If I ever wind up like that, Wally, I want you take me out into the middle of an empty field and shoot me twice in the back of the head, gangland-style. Is that understood?"

"Brian's up to 250 now. They never exercise him—"

"—and we both know he'll shovel down whatever the hell you put in front of him."

"He's going to drop dead of a heart attack before Daddy does if we're not careful. His blood pressure's through the roof. I've got him on medication already. He's only thirty-two."

"He screams at the television for a living. What kind of life is that, Wally?"

"Hell if I know."

Aunt Katherine was a nurse. She was the World's Nicest Lady, a southern belle nonpareil, complete with the soft, sugary voice and the long, languid drawl. Her feats of patience and courtesy were astounding. Nothing, it seemed, could rattle her. The woman was physically incapable of anger, even-tempered in a hurricane. In other words, the polar opposite of everyone in my immediate family.

Her kids were young, seven and under, a wiggling gaggle of miscreants. Misbehavior was constant, but no matter what they did, Aunt Katherine never lost her cool. Her equilibrium never faltered. She corrected them in the same sweet and even tone, each and every time. It baffled me.

"Now, Lil' Wally, don't be slammin' your sister's hand in the cabinet door, sweetheart. Mama doesn't like that, dumplin'...

"... Melissa, baby, put those scissors down, please. You'll poke your baby brother's eyes out, puddin' pie ...

"... Mary Beth, listen up here, sugarplum. Take little Mickey out of the fireplace. Do that for Mama, would you, please?... "

Every year for dinner Uncle Wally fried a turkey, a Louisiana tradition. The dining room table was set with fine china, and we gathered around to eat in the late afternoon. There was dirty rice, mashed potatoes, green beans, yams, and bread. And there was always homemade Italian sausage, Pops' special recipe. We all had full plates.

Generally speaking, I hated eating at a table with a bunch of people in a quiet room. It was a hang-up of mine. Restaurants were fine, they were crowded and loud. Eating in front of the television was my favorite. At the very least I needed a little music. But eating with people in a quiet dining room gave me the willies. I was hypersensitive to the sounds of digestion—the chewing, the swallowing, the slobbering, the gurgling stomachs, the scraping of forks and knives. It was especially bad on holidays—everyone seemed to overdo it even worse than usual. It was a feast day; people felt entitled to ravenous excess. They stuffed their faces with gusto. I couldn't stand it. It made me squeamish. The sights and sounds were simply too much for me.

I had my reasons. Uncle Brian was a maniac with a fork in his hand. His table manners were dismal at best, and once he started eating, the man couldn't stop—literally. He would eat until he puked; it was a component of his overall condition. He ate himself silly unless carefully monitored. He'd simply keep packing it away until his body revolted. As a result, I was at all times hyper-aware of his intake and positioned myself strategically so that I might flee unscathed in the event of spontaneous regurgitation.

Now that the moment of the feast was at hand, my nerves were doing a number on me. Everyone was in their seats, staring at one another, waiting for the green light. Aunt Katherine was the last to arrive. She came in from the kitchen with a basket full of bread and set it down.

"Uncle Brian," she said, "would you mind saying the blessing, darlin'?"

"ALRIGHTY!" said Uncle Brian.

Uncle Brian always said the blessing. It was a holiday tradition. In lieu of formal recitation, he opted for the freestyle approach. What he lacked in coherence he made up for in divine inspiration. He truly loved the job. I think it was mostly Pavlovian—he knew he would get to eat afterwards.

Everyone folded their hands and closed their eyes. I folded my hands and kept my eyes open, watching Uncle Brian. His eyes were open, too. He was looking at his food.

"IN THE NAME OF THE BROTHER, AND OF THE SON, AND THE HOLY SPIRIT, AMEN! BLESS US O' LORD, AND THESE OLD GIFTS, WHICH WE ARE ABOUT TO DECEIVE, FROM CHRIST TO OUR BOUNTY, THROUGH CHRIST IN THE BOUNTY OF OUR LORD, AND THE KINGDOM, AMEN! IN THE NAME OF THE BROTHER, AND THE SON, AND THE HOLY SPIRIT, AMEN!"

"Good job, buddy," my father said. "You say the grace so nicely, Brian."

"Well done, Brian," my mother said. "That was just wonderful."

"That boy," said Pops, "sounds just like Father Mancuso when he blesses a meal."

Father Mancuso was the longtime pastor at the local Catholic church. Over the years I'd been dragged to his masses on several occasions. He had a husky, weathered, baritone that projected well. Every year at Christmas dinner, without fail, Pops would draw the vocal comparison for the benefit of the entire family. This was followed shortly by Mimi informing us that, upon birth, Brian bore a striking resemblance to the baby Jesus.

"You're dern right," Pops added. "He was a fine looking child. Weren't you Brian?"

No response. Brian was long gone, submerged in his plate of food. His ears functioned only sporadically. His focus was that intense.

"Brian," my father said. "Daddy's talking to you."

No response.

"Brian," said Uncle Wally. "Listen to your brother."

"*Brian!*" my father said. "Pay attention when someone's talking to you!"

"I HEAR YOU!" Brian yelled through a mouthful of yams.

"No, no," said Pops. "It's all right. Leave that boy alone. Let that boy eat."

"Let that boy eat is right," said Mimi.

"You gotta let that boy eat," said Pops. "He just wants to eat."

"He's mama's special angel," said Mimi. "He just likes his supper is all."

"You gotta let that boy eat."

Uncle Brian was shoveling it down fast and furious. I couldn't look.

"Suit yourselves," my father waved a hand. "Let him be a savage."

Uncle Wally dinged his glass with his fork. We raised our glasses.

"To another great Christmas," he said. "And having y'all here."

"Here, here!"

Everybody knocked glasses, took a sip, and dug in. For a while there was nothing but the sound of forks on china, knives on bone, tongues on teeth. My level of discomfort was growing by the second. I remembered those films from science class in which a human being is x-rayed while chewing—the mandibles moving, the food breaking up, sliding down the esophagus. It's where my mind went, unfortunately. I lacked all mental discipline, my imagination ran roughshod. I picked at my food and tried not to listen. My appetite was dwindling, but I had to eat. To leave my plate full would be rude. My mother would be horrified. Down South, abstention from over-consumption was a faux pas of the highest order. To forego participation in the feast would violate some kind of sacred code. Now it was on my honor to devour. I took a few bites of bread and chewed slowly, feeling dizzy. I breathed deeply and tried to maintain focus.

The next thing I knew, I felt something on my foot. I leaned back in my chair and looked down. It was Mickey, the dachshund, licking my left shoe. There was nothing too unusual about it. Mickey licked everything and everybody—it was his purpose in life. If he couldn't lick a person, he licked the furniture, the floor. That was all he did, nonstop. He was a strange dog, but I liked him anyway. I watched him go to work on my heel.

It was only a matter of time before Aunt Katherine took notice.

"Is that dog under the table, Wayne?" she said. "Is he bothering you?"

"He's fine," I said. "He's just licking my shoe."

"I'm telling you, I don't know what I'm going to do with that silly dog. As soon as we sit down to a meal he's underfoot. It happens every time."

"He likes to lick stuff," said Wally, Jr.

260

"Mickey the Licker," said Mary Beth.

"He's a pain in the ass is what he is," said Uncle Wally.

Aunt Katherine was up, calling Mickey out of the room.

"Katherine," my mother said, rising. "You sit. Please. I'll take care of it. You've been on your feet all day."

"No, no. Don't you worry, Elaine. You sit. It's nothing. I'll just put him out back."

"You sure?"

"It'll take one second. Come here, Mickey. Come on, sweetheart. Outside, little fella."

"It's no problem," I said. "He can stay if he wants. I don't mind."

I felt I understood Mickey.

"No, no," said Aunt Katherine. "I'll take him out. Come on, Mickey. Outside. You come on now, sugar. Come on and get yourself a treat, little boo."

Mickey froze when he heard the word "treat," then made a beeline for the backyard. I watched him go with envy.

"That dog," said Uncle Wally, "is a first-rate menace. He keeps up like that, I'm going to muzzle him."

"There you go," said my father, wiping his mouth. "I've got a similar problem back home. Let me know how it turns out. Maybe I should muzzle mine."

"Daddy, no!" said Anne.

Uncle Wally laughed.

"Your father's kidding," said my mother.

Lorraine shot my father a dirty look.

My father shrugged.

Aunt Katherine returned, smiling.

"That little dog is such a card, I'm tellin' you," she said. "All he does is lick, lick, lick. I've never seen anything like it."

"It's called a mental disorder," said Uncle Wally.

"Aw, he's just kissin' is all," Aunt Katherine said.

"He likes to lick," said Melissa.

"Our dog licks stuff, too," said Anne.

"OUR DOG LICKS STUFF, TOO!" offered Uncle Brian. A piece of sausage flew from his mouth across the table. No one seemed to notice.

"How is y'all's dog?" Uncle Wally said. "Sammy, right?"

"That's right," said my mother. "He's doing fine. He's at the kennel now."

"The dog resort," my father said. "Club Med for mutts."

"A year old," my mother continued. "And still very much a puppy."

"He finally stopped crapping in the house a few months ago," my father said.

"Once you get 'em housebroken," said Uncle Wally, "you're home free."

"Then they start crapping all over your yard," said my father.

"Tell me about it," said Uncle Wally. "You wouldn't believe how much that little rodent of ours squeezes out in average day."

"Gracious, Wally!" said Aunt Katherine.

"Please, Joe," my mother said. "Not at the dinner table."

Mimi laughed. So did Pops. They, like me, were the kind of people who found excrement terribly funny.

"Sammy's sweet," said Lorraine.

"Sammy's a good dog," I said. "I'm training him to sit."

"The dog doesn't know its ass from a hole in the ground," my father said, "but it's got a good disposition. I'll give him that. Dumber than a box of rocks, but good with the kids. All things being equal, we've been pleased. Considering the kind of vicious mammal I grew up with, it's been a walk in the park."

"Colonel... ," Uncle Wally said, remembering. "The Dalmatian."

"Ooo, Lord," said Pops.

"COLONEL!" said Uncle Brian.

"Colonel was trouble," said my father. "Meanest son-of-a-bitch on the block."

"Hopped the fence and ran away," Wally added. "Joe came home one day and that was it. Colonel was gone. Jumped the fence and vanished. Just like that. We never saw him again."

"Really?" said Lorraine.

"That's right," said my father.

"No, no," said Mimi, shaking her head. "That's not right. No, sir. No indeed."

Everyone turned and looked at her.

"What are you talking about, Mom?" my father said. "Colonel ran away."

"Nonsense," she said. "I put my foot down. Betsy Dellahume was over visiting that day, and the little bastard bit her. Jumped up and bit her right in the ass. Broke the skin. She started bleeding. And that was it. That was the last straw. I'd had enough. I said to hell with it."

My father and Uncle Wally looked at one another.

"Colonel ran away, Mom," my father said. "I came home from school that afternoon, and he was gone. He ran away. You told me he hopped the fence."

"I drove that dog way out to the country and let it out of the car," Mimi said. "Then I peeled out."

Mimi took a bite of food, unfazed. My father's gaze dropped down in the direction of his plate. Nobody said a word. Everything felt pretty uncomfortable all of a sudden. The reality of the situation was starting to take hold.

"Ha!" Uncle Wally said, breaking the silence and shaking his head. "Sonofabitch! Unbe*liev*able!"

"Mimi!" said my mother, hand over her mouth. "Tell me you didn't do that."

Mimi looked up and laughed.

"Sure I did," she said.

The table let out a collective gasp.

"I'll be damned!" said Pops.

"I'LL BE DAMNED!" said Uncle Brian.

"Mom," said my father. "You didn't... "

He was genuinely upset. For going on thirty years now, he'd been cursing that dog's name, thinking it had abandoned him, living a lie.

"You're dern right I did!" Mimi said. "I took that bugger back to the wild, where it belonged!"

She roared with laughter. Everyone save my father chuckled along nervously, not knowing what else to do. Somehow it was funny.

Eventually the laughter petered into silence. I looked at my father. His eyes were still downcast. He was looking at his plate, at a pile of turkey bones, defeated and gravely serious. All my life, he'd never expressed anything but the greatest contempt for that dog. Now this.

Mimi and Pops started eating again. Uncle Wally shook his head and picked up his fork. Aunt Katherine sat there wide-eyed. My mother's hand was still over her mouth. My sisters were stunned, looking at one another. Melissa, Wally, Jr, and Mary Beth were giggling. Uncle Brian was busy cleaning his plate. My father remained frozen at the far end of the table, mired in a strange, hybrid state of grief and disbelief.

Finally, after a long stillness, he picked up his wine glass and took a sip.

"I loved that damn dog," he said weakly. "Even if the little bastard did bite me."

This Is Me

Marcela Albornoz

WHERE DOES IT END and where does it start? Where does the great story of creation, the one that supposedly gives our whole lives meaning, become about as credible as Santa Claus? According to the Bible, the first thing god told Adam and Eve to do was to have sex and make lots of babies. And yet I'm supposed to be ashamed when I sit in religion class and daydream about my boyfriend and having our future kids look somewhat like him, despite the fact that he's hesitant about having kids because he thinks himself unattractive and doesn't want to pass that on. When and where is the idea of love first conceived? Was it with the first kiss? The one we never had because I met him online and have never actually even touched him? Was it with the first "I love you"? The one we typed that first day after having talked for fourteen hours straight? Exactly when did I become the kind of girl who gets referred to see guidance? And just how did I end up not giving two shits if the counselor looks at me funny?

My stories don't make sense because life doesn't make sense. I'm too young to write about it. Too naive to understand what I'm writing about. But life is life and life is ageless. My good friend was raped in my old house, the one two blocks away from my new house, in my bed, on top of my covers. My current best friend of almost three years is sick, and I don't mean a cold. My sweet little girl has cancer, and I wish cancer was a guy so I could kick him in the balls for making her feel like this. If cancer really was a person I bet it would be a guy. I know that makes me sexist, but I don't care. I don't apologize because that's life and it's not worth living if you don't get to say all the things you wanted to say, all the things you know no one will ever read.

I am a love child and that makes me beautiful. I'm not a bastard. I'm not a bitch. I'm a love child, a lovely child with a great mother and a father I hate. This is who I am. I will always be what people want me to be because I am a little bit of everything. I'm smooth with written words but silent in speech. I'll never tell daddy that I still love him. I'll never tell my cousin

I hate her for killing her unborn child. I'll never get to tell my grandma that I hated her for hating me.

Judge me. Bite me. Beat my soul with unkind words. I wish I cared. I wish I'd spent more than five minutes with the lady at the bus stop, the one who tried to tie my shoes. She was pretty in that way that you can tell she was pretty in her younger years. She was so hunched over that all she could see as she walked was people's shoes. I stood there scared, explaining to her that my shoes weren't untied and the dangling strings were actually coming from my pants. My ride came and I had to leave. I didn't have to do anything, but I left because when people who are in worse situations than I am try to help me with my problems, it terrifies me. It takes me from thinking I'm slightly horrible to wondering if I'm really the spawn of Satan.

People say they hate themselves a lot nowadays. Hell, I hate myself sometimes. But if you truly hate it, then why don't you put down the beer and the vibrator and maybe do something you're not going to regret for once. Actually no, finish the beer, masturbate, then become a better person. There's always time for hedonism. Everyone claims that life is so hard when it's such an easy game to play. You get horny so you have sex. You get hungry so you eat. You get tired so you sleep. You get happy so you're somewhat nice for a change. You get pissed so you bitch someone out. And all is forgiven because it's in our nature to forgive countless times, even if we can't bring ourselves to tell the person that we have forgiven them.

The inevitable things of life close in on you like beautifully decorated lethal spikes evenly spaced on iron walls. There's no way out but to hide inside yourself and shut your eyes tight, holding on to a pretty memory of something that never happened… until the pain disappears. Despite my slightly psychotic mind I am happy within myself, and because of myself. I'm happy because I clung to conformity and denial at an early age. I was just a little girl, but now I'm a teenager and my hormones are deceiving me. I am brainwashed by my religion teacher at a catholic school. I am struggling to fight the power and prove to myself that every rule has a loophole, because if they didn't, then we're all screwed.

Life screws us all and rapes our naive hearts because hearts are always naive; it's our minds that do all our dirty work for us. Brains are so ridiculous, like you can think of anything no matter how bizarre and eventually convince yourself that it is the truth. Brains fuck us over, too, really. Every aspect of life abuses our innocence and leaves us with smeared make-up, drunk off our asses in a place we don't recognize. But we get up. We sober up. We clean ourselves up. We find a guy we love and seduce him until he can get it up. Then we make love just to find out that it's not always one-sided and painful.

I am sick. I am twisted. I am a bit crazed. I am slightly disturbed. But... I'm kind of pretty. I'm kind of smart. I'm kind of nice sometimes. I do community service. I go to a catholic school. I go to church on Sundays... by myself. I also come home from church and lock myself in my room with my diary filled with profanities and pictures of pretty skulls I've drawn. I'm young. I admit I'm a bit confused, but goddamn it, I am just like you. So let me keep these words and I promise to make a better story next time.

Millicent

Chris Roberts

ONE

[KNOCK KNOCK KNOCK] He answers the door with a stunned face. He looks like my father. [daddy] No answer. He asks me in, who I am. [millicent] Still, astonished, he closes the door, shutting off the storm. It's been raining and I'm soaked through. *I'll get a towel*, he says. [thank you daddy] He looks back in surprise. He can't hear me. Really hear me. He walks to the bathroom for a towel.

She comes in with a borrowed look of perplexity. [give it back to daddy it's not yours] *What's not mine?* she asks for no reason. She can't really hear me either. [nothing like mother]

They take me in, call around, but I belong to nobody. I could have told them that, but I can't. My mouth doesn't work right, voice doesn't speak. All I do is think in this shell. This head. I think it's all stuffing up there anyway. *What a cute doll*, she says as she takes my clothes off, puts me into the hot bath. [thank you] She lays my doll on the bathroom counter. I reach for it but—*Let's get you cleaned up first*, she insists. [you can be so silly mommy]

TWO

They fight all the time. He hits her. [poor mommy] She needs to figure daddy out. He doesn't really want to hurt her. He's just mad. Frustrated. Bills pile too high. He works all day. [lazy bitch doesn't work] Spends. Money and time in the shopping malls. I go with her and she buys me ugly clothes. I smile politely. She doesn't understand.

Like a dog that goes to the bathroom in the house and gets spanked. She should be able to put two and two together. Math. Simple math. He hits her because they have no money. She spends what money they have and they run out. He hits her. [circle] Simple. Stupid circle. It's not his fault. [it's mine] They won't hit me. Wish they would. Band-Aids heal wounds. Take the tears away when you can't see the blood. The cut. Embedded gravel in flesh. [all gone] Plastic strips that never stay on. Curl. Stupid dog! Goes to the bathroom in the mall. Gets a spanking. She yelps. He hits her harder because he can. Drops his brown bottle. It'll kill him. He'll kill her. *Why don't they notice me?* She's getting better with money. They don't have any. She can't spend what they don't have. Daddy hides it, I've seen him. [daddy is so smart] He's always working. I never see him. I cry. Mommy is growing impatient with me. [good] I can feel it. But I can't really *feel* it.

THREE

I hold my doll in my lap like she was real. She cries. [i am getting impatient with you little one] The crying continues. This has to stop! Enough to drive a mommy crazy. I hit her. Hard. Her head lolls back unnaturally. Would have broken her neck if she had one. Crying stops. [stupid dog] Use the papers! I hit her again. Crying stops. She will learn not to cry. She will learn to feel. She will learn to hit me. Hard!

Mommy tucks me in. I try to sleep but sleep doesn't come. Too noisy. They're arguing again. How *dare* she ask daddy where all the money is! Junkie. Has to have her fix. Shoot it straight into the vein. Roll the bills up and sniff it long and hard. [hard] He hits her. Knocks her to the floor. She gets up. Floors creak in this house. Can't get to sleep. They fight until they get too tired. He gets too drunk. She can't talk through the pain. Her swelling lip. She got her fix. [serves her right bitch mommy]

FOUR

He can't beat her anymore. She's worthless pulp on couch. [a knot] Watching those stupid soap operas. Life isn't *that*. She could care less. Asks me to get her some ice for her lip. Her face. Her curled body. [glacier] Band-Aids for her cuts. Pillows for her bruises. [we don't have that many pillows] I suddenly feel sorry for her. She is in pain. She *is* pain. All balled up and pissed like she could explode.

He's too big and strong. He'll hit me soon. Direct his rage. He *has* to direct his rage. Not at mommy. She can't handle it because she actually wants to live. Wants to survive. Make it through all of this. Wants out of this hell called marriage. [until death do you part] Probably. I'll help her. I'll help them both. [help myself]

Mommy falls asleep. I touch her arm to ease her pain. To ease her dreams so they don't turn into nightmares. Nightmares are worse because you can die in them. Almost. And you can be happy for one brief moment. That moment when your stomach falls into the mattress and you nearly wake up. Then you wake up and you are still alive and... unhappy. And you know that you have to face him when he comes home. Tired. Hungry. Angry. Irritable. Mommy. Your face is so battered. Too apart, cut up. [not your face at all] You cry and think that I don't see you, but I do. I see you. And I feel for you. [will feel for you]

FIVE

[just look what you made mommy do] I yell at my doll. She's crying. Do you like to see mommy cry? Do you? Then I hit her soft stuffed head, hard. And I pound on her thread-joined arms and legs. [no bruises no cuts] I get even madder. Like she is *laughing* at me. Like it doesn't hurt. Like she isn't learning anything from her pain. [my pain] Stupid dog. Stupid doll. Stupid! [daddy]

I put a blanket over mommy. Put a blanket over my doll. I know how very cold they must be right now. One hour. Daddy will be back in one hour. Better get to work. He'll hit me tonight. [i hope] Mommy will die if he doesn't. Rage. Must. Be. Directed. Must be dumped somewhere. Like the body in the mystery movies I'm not supposed to watch. Bodies. Tossed in the river. Put in the ground. Placed lovingly all over the face and body of the woman you said you loved! [bastard] Little black and blue. Black and blue marks and cuts. Blood. [red] I hate the blood. Cover it up. Band-Aid. Cover mommy up. [one big cut] Bruise. [one big pain] Can't see it with the blanket over her. Sleep mommy. I'll take care of you. Sleep. [stupid dogs]

SIX

Big empty wall. Really quite a shame. Barren space in this cluttered house. Glaring white wall. Inviting. Beckoning. No colors, or prints, or paintings, or shelves. Empty canvas waiting for artist.

Where would mommy keep the markers? Kitchen? Office? Junk drawer? Found them. Black, blue, and red. [black for the bruises, blue for the bumps, red for the blood and the pain and the lumps] Twisted little rhyme rolls off the tongue like venom. Snake in the grass poised and coiled. Waiting for loopy dog bouncing down the lane. Tense and strike, bite the leg, poison blood, rigid, dead.

Scribble and doodle all over the wall. Black houses with no windows. Wet blue sky with no sunshine. [no yellow marker]

Deep red flowers bleeding and dripping on the black sidewalk. Filling the cracks, rivers of blood. Ants drowning, unheard screams. Need more colors. Blue little girl with red Popsicle. Melting in sun that isn't there. Hands covered red and sticky. Standing, towering before the outstretched man. Eyes still open not blinking. Cold, blue eyes. Filled with captured rage and surprise. Happy tree of black and blue. Crusted bark and Band-Aids. Red sap and happy squirrels. Chirping and chatting and gathering black nuts, scattered carefully over the blue grass ground. Little girl smiling wide smile from ear to ear. Blood red smile sharp teeth showing. Markers flying, streaking, staining, singing. Headache smells, childhood highs. Little floating marker girl never touching the ground, never touching the sky. [too short] Stuck somewhere in between. [everybody limbo] Standing on the sidewalk, floating on the wall, frozen, smelly marker people passing by. Lanky postman with an empty mail bag waves a parade hello. Groomed mustache and bad teeth, thin, awkward stick legs bending and springing with each step. Big lady walking little dog on a heavy, steel-blue chain. Mumbling things she has to do, places she should be right now instead of walking her little dog, things she wants to eat. *Needs* to eat. Tiny yips from frail, red dog whenever she pulls the heavy chain too hard. [poor dog] Strange young man with no eyes, wandering through this scribbled suburb, wearing a cap that reads JESUS SAVES, carrying a pitchfork. Wandering. Knowing exactly where he's going. He can see *everything*. [i can see nothing] Nothing but the three colors that now smother this once-white wall. The stench of markers and madness permeates the house like a bizarre gas leak. No mask. Dizzy. I look at the clock. Five minutes until daddy gets home. He'll be so pleased with what I did to the wall.

SEVEN

I look at my masterpiece with a silly sense of pride. Strange figures pass the little girl with her liquid Popsicle, none of them noticing the man lying on the sidewalk before her. Blank eyes, blank stare, gaping, shocked mouth. Hole in his stomach to match. Red and sticky. Bottomless not-a-wishing well. [close your eyes make a wish drop a coin into the deep dark]

Two minutes until daddy gets home. He will be so surprised. So proud. So pissed, grabbing his belt and yelling and barking. Lashing and whipping until he draws blood. Lunging at the wound like an impatient vulture not waiting for his prey to die.

[pray to die] Swimming vulture-shark smelling scrumptious, succulent plasma. Striking and smacking my face, back, bottom, his lips, wet with sweat and spittle and satisfaction. Daddy will put his belt back on to hold up his pants, and I will retreat painfully, happily into the shadows with my tears and throbbing flesh.

EIGHT

I can hear the door *click* before he enters the house. The floor squeaks with each of his heavy steps. Series of depressed, overweight mice. Daddy is getting closer now. He will walk through the entryway, put his briefcase on the table, go to the liquor cabinet, pour himself a drink, and walk through this hall to the living room, where he will root into his easy chair to watch hours of useless, mindless television. But—he won't make it that far. He will stop to see me. Stop to see my masterpiece of markers, make-believe and mischief. He will hit me. Anticipate await. Like the night before Christmas. Never sleep, never blink until Santa Claus arrives with a gift. Gift of happiness and temporary, plastic joy. [some assembly required batteries not included Santa is not real] Daddy is *very* real and coming down the chimney. [hallway] I stand before my work of art waiting for my first and most important critic to recognize my mad genius. Spout praises and pat me on the back. [hard] Make me feel special. Make me feel wanted and needed. [make me feel]

NINE

What in the hell have you done? He lets go of a yell that wakes the dead. I know because I hear them. Chanting my name. Beautiful cacophony. [millicent millicent millicent] Daddy picks me up off the floor. [floating] Shakes me hard and screams into my eyes, making me blink and wet. My eyes are leaking, tears of joy, tears of pain. *You stupid little BITCH! What's gotten into you? Why are you smiling? I'll wipe that smile right off your little face!* [i would certainly look funny without a smile] *I'll give you something to cry about! Drawing on walls! I'll teach you!* [teach me i want to learn] Need to learn. [understand why] Kiss this abuse on its raw and ruptured skin. [smack]

I get my fill. He hits me. Hard. Slaps me sillier than a knock-knock joke. Knocks my head back violently. [would have broken my neck if i had one] Snapping bones, splitting skin, broken little bird. Torn off wings, plucked feathers, no chance for flight. [helpless chirp] Ragged cuts and scratches cover my body. [dizzy and fading] Have to stay awake, have to learn, pay for mistakes. Marker mess. Black, blue and red. Colors of my skin now fading to a pale, yellow-white cloth. Stitching un-stitched. Ripped cloth and buttons fall to the hard floor below. [plink plink] Can't see anymore. [blind] Can't scream. Still feel the pulling, shaking, limbs going numb and falling off. Stuffing pushing thread aside. Red, wet stuffing seeping through the hundreds of thousands of cracks in the sidewalk. [losing my train of thought] Left the station fifteen minutes ago. Losing my mind. Going limp and nimble. Pliable putty in firm, strong hands. [infirm] He hits and smashes and squeezes the life out of my itty-bitty body. [cotton falling from the dead queen of the rabbits] Not thinking straight quite. [quite straight] Fading into the blood-spattered wall behind me. [liquid] Dissolving into the bedlam. But his grip is so strong. He shakes and sweats and throws me against the wall, suddenly very solid, very real. My head pops, and what is left of my neck vanishes into dust and wood shavings. I fall slow motion to the hard wood floor. A pile of shredded rags. [where is my doll] Crying, leaking, throbbing, longing, weeping, fading... [satisfied]

TEN

The circle is complete. He retreats in a daze, blood on hands. *What in hell have I done?* Mumbling, stumbling. Backing up, tripping, running away from this mess. His mess. Leaves me to die. Leaves me to suffer, bleed, and slowly... slowly heal. [i will never heal] Neither will daddy. Neither will mommy. I pull a rug over my broken body. Band-Aids heal the pain, cover the blood. But the edges always curl. [sticky circles] Where is my doll? Soon I will be better. Soon my wounds will heal. Maybe if it strikes me... [strikes me] I'll get my thread and needle out, fix my doll. [if i can find her] Maybe I can find the strength to move. Strength to breathe. To blink. To live.

Forever crying and living and dreaming when asleep, when what you really want so desperately to do is scream. So tired. Content with the last seven minutes. I think I will sleep until daddy wakes me up. Realizes what he's done. What I've done for her. [them] He'll be sorry for awhile. Until I heal. Until she heals. But the rage will still be there, just below the surface. [pet wrath itch] Waiting for any excuse to come out and play. [volcano erupt scald] next her. next stupid dog.

[stupid circle where is my doll she has been a very bad girl little bitch she will learn]

Rocky Mountains

(or 'the documentarian')

Henry Milton

—DESK SITTING IN the high open country, in the shadow of mountains. stream—"burble burble" eyes twitch—fingers + keyboard—"clickity clack". I approach. stops/looks up "well (where have you come from—go back—before you die) what can we do for you."/ me—"bears"/ "BEARS?"/nod (what else, in this place)/ "bears = our business" back to typing "clickity clack" stops/electric pencil sharpener—"bzz!" back to typing "/excuse me (waves)" "(bears = my uneasy stomach leaping/my last fevered minutes on the forest floor)." ignored (clickity clack) anger rises— put on airs of youth from city "(something about questions as to the efficiency of your program in documenting said creatures)"/ silence—blood floods the ragged face—rumbles to his feet "(HOW DARE YOU)" fist through computer screen—raises it (huge hammer hand) smash smash on desk—rage (cower-placate-keep your nerve) quietly from under my hands "(me—document them?)" hammer stops—pause "document?... HA!(dark death in the forest/machines of rotting doom!) you document? HA!" tired old eyes blink, shakes off monitor "(hunters do the work well enough)"/think "hunters?", I ask./ eyes turn like wolves. "yes"... a grin. "hunters"... (turns to cabinet, hand pulling key out of pocket) "you can't run... " (unlocks cabinet) "an operation like this... " (pulls open drawer, looks inside) "without... " (digs in both hands) "BLOOD" (entrails) "BLOOD" (piled in his hands) "BLOOD" (still steaming) dumped onto the table—"dump-thump-thubalump" brain is running feverish (spilling thump blood) horror/horror—"these are our documents, ripped from the bodies." (ringing in my skull) "if you want to join us, you must be prepared to harvest." stumble blindly out of chair—run—run—back to the forest.

We Have Waited

Santi Elijah Holley

OUR TOWN HASN'T seen the light of the sun since the old man left us. We think it has been five years, but without the benefit of the sun separating one day from the next, we have no accurate means of marking the passing of time. Our town is indeed void of time. We live in an uninterrupted night, possessed by infinite silence, and, ironically, a plague of insomnia. None of us have slept since the old man disappeared. He stole from us our days and our rest and abandoned us to a quiet purgatory, where even the footsteps of children are a deafening burden.

It was the time of our town's centenary. The old man was first sighted early in the morning near the sandy bank of Cana River, where the townspeople come to wet their feet and scatter bits of bread for the water creatures. I wasn't there—I was in my backyard, hanging my parents' garments on the line to dry—but I remember the sky that morning. All the townspeople remember that morning. The clouds were ablaze, ignited by the sun, spitting angry black smoke up into the distant heavens. I thought the very sky would erupt and rain embers upon our streets, but no such thing happened, and instead, the clouds burned away and left the sky open and clear once again.

The town of Lindiwe was preparing for a day of celebrations to mark the momentous occasion of our centennial. String players tuned their strings, drummers tightened their skins—dancers and jugglers, too, were in the highest of spirits, for these performance artists had not many opportunities to showcase their talents, but when they did, they gave such a stunning recital, as if they were obliged to prove, time and time again, why Lindiwe needs and loves them.

A parade was scheduled to commence in the early afternoon, continuing into the night and lasting as long as the townspeople were willing to remain on their feet. Wine was brought in from the Highlands, where the longest vines in the country grow wild and vicious and only the mad Highlanders can tame them and collect their grapes, creating the most superb, luscious wine ever consumed. I still remember the taste of the wine on my tongue: bloody and sweet and moist. I remember the smiling children with their parents and friends, dancing gaily in the road to the music of the fifes. It has been five years since our great celebration, and we in Lindiwe remember everything of those last days.

The townspeople at the river that morning relate how the old man appeared suddenly, dragging his feet and carrying his weight like iron ore, as if he had just crawled from beneath soiled earth and stone. Ash fell from his beard and hair and drifted about him like a gray aura. The children and parents interrupted their routine to watch this figure—more like an apparition than a man—emerge from the trees and amble over to the small, beguiled crowd. When he came within speaking distance he looked at the faces of the collected strangers, and said, simply, "Hello." His voice was old, heavy, but not sad.

"Hello," the townspeople returned. The old man took a few more weary steps toward them—close enough to look into their eyes and allow them to see into his. It is said that the townspeople were not frightened of the old man when he first introduced himself, for he was not a threatening man, and had the manner more of a young, inquisitive boy. He was ragged and peculiar, but his voice was kind. The old man's eyes, however, were devoid of all light. They were black as the deepest onyx and carried no character or radiance within their depths.

"What place is this?" he asked the townspeople.

They responded gaily, "This is the town of Lindiwe."

"*Lindiwe*." The old man let the name of our town escape his mouth and drift aimlessly about him along with the gray ash that emanated from his frame. His black eyes searched the long arms of the Cypress trees, the Cana River flowing effortlessly, and the dozen faces of the townspeople—patient and evermore captivated. The old man watched each leaf float in the gentle breeze and he studied each individual face of the strangers standing before him.

"Who are you?" a young woman asked.

"I am only an old man on a long journey. I have traveled for many years, and I have seen many towns and villages. This is the first time I have been in Lindiwe."

"What's wrong with your eyes? Are you blind?" a small child asked, quickly hushed by his mother.

"No, my boy. I can see very well indeed. I cannot, however, see the light of the sun. To my eyes it is always night. Even on the brightest, most glorious days of the year, my eyes are condemned to only see the darkest of night."

"Where do you come from? Why are you traveling? What is your name?" The townspeople solicited so many questions that soon the old man raised the palm of his hand and implored them to be calm.

"I would be happy to satiate your curiosity, but I am a very hungry and very weary old man. I have traveled a long way and I would be in much gratitude if one of you kind strangers could offer me food and water."

The townspeople were happy to grant his wish. They were excited about demonstrating the hospitality of Lindiwe, especially on the great occasion of our centenary. The old man dined with the townspeople and afterwards was provided with a hot bath and a change of clothes. He even shared in the celebrated wine from the Highlands. The old man was treated as a guest of honor in Lindiwe, and he, too, was soon enchanted with the excitement of our town's celebrations.

All citizens of Lindiwe were in the highest of spirits that evening when the parade began. The wind musicians valiantly led the way, followed by the drummers and foolish jugglers. Behind them were the many floats decorated with glitter and acrylic, each portraying a different moment in our town's proud history. The parade marched down Raha Street, made a left on Bastian's Grave, and continued to wind its way through town well into the last reaches of night.

I was with my parents, watching the festival with a rapt, hungry attention, as the clowns with their painted faces and the beautiful women with jewels in their eyes and teeth carved from ivory danced through town and granted every neighbor and countryman gifts and kisses and sweets. When night fell my parents took me home, and though I longed to stay awake all night, singing and laughing with the rest of the wild celebration until dawn, my parents forbid me to witness whatever sinful revelry Lindiwe had planned for the twilight hour.

I didn't meet the old man with the black eyes until the following day. I was walking along Cana River, with my fisherman's pole and my small bait box and a tin bucket for collecting herring, when I saw his figure standing quietly beneath a tall, verdant Cypress. No one else was present. It was early morning and most of Lindiwe's citizens were still in their beds, sleeping off the effects of the night's festivities.

"Hello, there," he called to me.

"Hello," I responded.

"Doing a little early morning fishing?"

"Yes, Sir."

"That's quite good. While everyone else slumbers you collect the bounty. I can see you are being raised well."

The timbre in the old man's voice was very pleasant and soft. I felt immediately at ease in his company, even when I noticed the bleak emptiness in his eyes. He spoke like a child, though perhaps a bit more grave and weary. I lay my equipment on the ground and came nearer to his post underneath the Cypress.

"Who are you?" I asked.

"I am just an old man, my friend. No more, no less."

"Where did you come from?"

"I come from a land that is now gone," he said. "The town of my birth, the village of Paktra, has been wiped clean from the Earth like you would wipe clean your hands after supper. I no longer have a land to call my own and no evidence remains of its existence."

"What happened?"

"I can see you're a very curious boy—that is also good. A curious and enterprising boy will grow to be a rich and wise man. To answer your question, I was a boy of about your age when the men on horses came to Paktra. They flourished flames and swords of liquid steel and hid their faces behind iron masks. To this day I do not know what they wanted from us, or if they wanted anything more than fulfillment of a lustful need for carnage. I often wonder if those assailants were not men, but fiends from Hell given free run of Earth for one unspeakable day. I have had much time to speculate on the fateful events of that day, for I have been a lonely journeyer many long years, but until I am satisfied, my search will continue."

"But what are you searching for?"

"I do not know what I am searching for, or why I am searching. I only know that I am searching, and that is enough."

Behind us I could hear the herring jump and splash in Cana River, and I turned my head toward the activity in the water.

"The herring will not wait for you, friend," the old man said. "They are growing impatient and they will soon swim downstream with the heat of the sun. You should take up your pole and capture them before they leave."

I did as he said: I baited the hook and cast the lure far into the river. When I turned my attention back to the Cypress the old man had disappeared.

After five or so minutes I had my first bite. He did not put up much of a fight and I brought him in easily, though when I pulled him onto the shore, I noticed with great alarm and wonder that the herring had immediately died and turned black as coal. The two fish I caught afterwards were the same as the first: black and given to death with the first exposure to sunlight. I dropped my pole and walked closer to the river, attempting to peer into its depths, but I couldn't see a thing, for the river, too, was as black as the richest oil and as thick as night.

The color of the fish and the river made me think of the boots the marching soldiers wore in the centennial parade. Their sleek black boots were clean and polished and seemed to reflect the glow of the sun on their bright, unblemished leather. The soldiers' beige uniforms were without a single tear or blemish due to having never seen battle. Lindiwe had never engaged in warfare and our soldiers did not carry any firearms. Our small, humble military was mostly for show, not much different than the men who walked on stilts and breathed fire, but they gave Lindiwe a sense of pride and dignity. The few young men who marched in the parade—heads held high, falling into perfect step with each other—did so with so much poise and honor that a foreign eye could have easily been convinced that those men had fought and won the most glorious of battles.

I was born in this town during the season of large feasts and long nights. Most of Lindiwe's citizens were born here and few have moved away. My parents married young, gave me life soon after their exchange of vows, and bore no more children after me. I was educated in the schoolhouse at the end of Raha Street, as were all children until they reached the productive age of seventeen. My father and mother kept a modest farm behind our house on the edge of Lindiwe, where often I would help with a share of the work, such as milking goats, collecting eggs, and keeping intrusive flora within a reasonable distance. This was my last year of classes before graduating and accepting a considerable growth in my share of work in my family's farm.

Men in Lindiwe are given two options after graduation: we either inherit the family business or start one of our own. Joining another family's business was considered dishonorable and was only allowed in instances of utmost necessity. Since our farm was quite prosperous I did not have to worry about the burden of beginning a new enterprise or the shame of offering myself to another family.

The next few days in Lindiwe were routine and altogether uneventful, with business conducted as usual and talks of the great festival already beginning to diminish. The singers and dancers and jugglers returned to their hiding places where they laid in wait to be called upon again, and the soldiers returned to their homes, also patiently waiting to be called upon to defend Lindiwe against unforeseen, unexpected invaders. I hadn't seen the old man since that brief encounter at Cana River, yet others had spotted him regularly in different parts of town, and many shared long conversations with him. He was still received as a most welcome guest, as Lindiwe doesn't often receive visitors, especially journeyers who have traveled across the entire world, as the old man claimed he had. Frequently he would dine with gracious families and laugh with young children and gaze longingly at passing clouds, but as far as anyone could tell, the old man never lay down to sleep. "When it is always night one easily becomes accustomed to doing without sleep," he would explain.

Cana River had returned to its normal blue radiance, just as the sky had the morning of our centenary, but the herring remained black and lifeless. The weather was hot and radiant, with the sun making an imposing journey from the beginning of the sky to the end. Our air had become so feverish at times that we would occasionally have our classes outside in the shade of the school courtyard, just to escape the sweltering heat inside the walls of the schoolhouse. One of these particular days in the courtyard the old man appeared, and after only minor pleading from the students, he granted us stories of his great and vast journeys. Our teacher, Mr. Wesda, didn't mind, he even encouraged it, since the old man had seen places no one in Lindiwe had ever seen and likely never would see. Mr. Wesda—a frail, humble man, with wire-rimmed eyeglasses and thin brown hair—regarded the old man as a visiting orator, knowing that his tales would not only entertain the students, but also provide a lesson in geography, as well as history. None of us in Lindiwe had ever heard of the town of Paktra and we were anxious to learn about this place that was so far away and had been destroyed so long ago and had given life to this strange man with black eyes.

"The world we live in is infinite," the old man told us. "And if you follow the course of the wind you will never retrace the same path. I am fortunate to have never seen my own footprints. When I do I will know my journey is over."

Many students' arms shot up to the sky, imploring to be called upon, but others took it upon themselves to skip this formality and assaulted the old man with numerous, disjointed questions.

"What was Paktra like? Why did you leave? Where is your family? Why are your eyes black? How long will you be here?"

"Please, children," Mr. Wesda interrupted. "Our guest can only answer one question at a time."

"Perhaps I can answer all of your questions with a story," the old man said. And he began the tale of the town of Paktra, to which none of us children, who have now reached our early twenties, have ever forgotten. We have repeated it to ourselves for the last five years and it will never escape our minds, not as long as we are living in this world.

"We in Paktra were simple, quiet people—a large family of Old World survivors who didn't care for change or alteration. My father was a sculptor and my mother arranged bouquets for weddings. I was perhaps a little younger than you children here, and I didn't yet have a trade, but I was, however, already arranged to be married."

"You were married?" one of the girls asked.

"My parents and her parents had arranged for us to be married on my sixteenth birthday. She would've been fifteen, I believe. The townspeople of Paktra liked their children to marry young, learn a trade, and carry on the lineage as soon and as prolifically as possible. It was an Old World tradition."

"What's the Old World?" a young boy named Gerdan asked.

"You've never been taught of the Old World?" the old man responded with obvious displeasure. "Yes, I suppose when the men on horses came to Paktra they erased all vestiges of the Old World," he said quietly to himself. "Besides, that was such a long time ago, and in a place far away from Lindiwe. There would be no reason you here would know of the Old World. I don't know if I can adequately teach you our ways. Let it suffice to say the Old World was a place where ancestors reside forever through the will of the living."

The children looked at each other curiously, and even Mr. Wesda rutted his brow and tilted his head with inquisition. The old man noticed the general perplexity in their faces and decided against continuing with talks of the Old World, for it would only further confuse and distract his audience.

"The girl and I were never married. The men on horses came a few months before the date of our ceremony—coming suddenly in the night like a chill wind. With their iron masks and swords of Hellfire, we in Paktra did not have a chance of survival. My family, my neighbors, and my village burned without even being permitted a reason why. The men razed Paktra in a single night. They took no prisoners, they took no money nor any jewels or silver, and they said not a single word between them or to their victims. They left as suddenly as they came and they intended to leave no survivors. They missed just one."

"*Wow*," the children declared together. "You were the only survivor?"

"Yes. I was fishing at Kindad River when I saw them approach. I was the only one at the river and I watched them stride into Paktra on their black mares. An urgent feeling told me that they brought an unworldly evil with them. I dove into the river and held my breath for as long as I could, and when I emerged, Paktra was in flames, my people were all dead, and the men on horses had already left—that was how efficient they were." We children sat wide-eyed and speechless as the old man paused from his story to regain his breath. After nearly a full minute had passed, the old man continued.

"When I surfaced, and saw the sky black and red with the blood of my family and neighbors, it took me a very long time to recognize that the previously bright morning had suddenly turned to night. I thought at first that the sun was only shrouded behind the thick blanket of smoke in the sky, but the light never returned. I fled the ashen remains of Paktra and never once looked back. After many years of traveling this world in search of the sun, I learned that it is not the world, but my own eyes that are absent of light."

The old man excused himself, explaining to Mr. Wesda and the children that he had grown weary and could speak no more until he had rested. We were disappointed, but we understood and thanked him for sharing his tale as he made his way out of the courtyard and down Raha Street. Mr. Wesda, rightfully acknowledging that we children were in no mind to finish our regular day's assignments, dismissed us early, urging us to be kind to the old man when we saw him next, for he was a senile old man with great delusions.

Lindiwe suffered through increasingly thick and violent heat during the next few days. The air was so searing we could almost feel the sun push through our skin and warm our blood. The many animals of Lindiwe—the ones who weren't fenced in—immediately fled town, as did the smallest, lowliest insects, in what seemed to be an ominous intuition. We bathed frequently in Cana River, and worked in our farms and meadows less often. Many families and friends started becoming irate with each other, for no apparent reason other than desperation and anxiety. The heat, like a cruel, invisible tyrant, was oppressive and unforgiving and impossible to overcome. It wasn't long before people began hallucinating. Occasionally someone would make mad claims of watching black angels descend from the clouds and disappear into the sultry air, or of hearing long, painful cries of unseen mouths—cries that sounded many years old, echoing from another world—but most townspeople were too consumed by fever to pay any mind to these wild allegations.

The centennial parade was seldom mentioned anymore, and it seemed as if Lindiwe had all but forgotten that glorious day. I find myself thinking of that festival from time to time—of the laughing jugglers, the crazy dancers, the fife players and drummers, and the beautiful women with ivory teeth and radiant diamonds in their eyes—because I'm afraid that if we all forget that once proud time, it will escape us forever.

The last time I saw the old man he was standing alone in the middle of Mehel Street looking toward the sun with unblinking eyes. I approached him cordially.

"This is some warm spell we're having, yes?"

"It would seem that way, my friend," he replied without averting his eyes from the center of the sun. "Though I personally cannot feel the effects of the heat."

I thought about informing him that looking directly into the sun was bad for the eyes, but I didn't think that would be relevant in his case.

"Why are you looking at the sun so closely?" I asked.

"This is the first time I have seen the sun in a very long time. He doesn't look familiar to me, and he doesn't shine with the same brilliance that he once had."

I looked up toward the sun and at once felt its rays pierce my eyes. I turned away quickly, rubbed my eyes, and wiped the sweat from my brow.

"He seems rather brilliant to me," I laughed, and then sensing his deep solemnity, I asked him what he was thinking about.

"My people went to their graves without being granted enough time to learn who their assailants were," he told me. "I have traveled for many years and have given much thought to that night, and I think I may finally have an idea who those demons were and what they represented."

"What were they?"

The old man finally turned away from the sun and fixed his starless eyes to me.

"They represented the changing of seasons, from autumn to winter. They may think they have done away with our Old World and our ways, but I tell you, my friend, death does not exist. Death is not the opposite of life. Before our conception we are not considered dead, correct? We only wait in the infinite space beyond life. Have you seen the stars glow bright and warm at night? Those stars have burned away years ago, but we are only now witnessing their radiance. The stars remain alive in our eyes, in our will. The will of the living. Yes, winter will eventually turn to spring. The ways of the Old World will not know death."

Those were the last words I remember the old man speaking. I must have excused myself, or perhaps he took his leave first, I don't recall. The heat was beginning to affect my consciousness and I suddenly found myself lying in bed preparing for sleep, nighttime having swiftly fallen upon Lindiwe.

That night, I dreamt of the sky and the way it looked on the morning of our centenary. Flames licked the tops of clouds and dark smoke rose up, obscuring the sun. It was as if the sun itself were setting the world on fire and leaving only eternal silence. When I awoke the heat had finally dropped to a comfortable temperature. It was still twilight, but I was wide-awake. I have remained awake to this day, as have all the townspeople. We have not fallen into sleep, nor have we seen the light of day, after that fateful night when all of Lindiwe had woken simultaneously from the same, collective dream. Our eyes have become black and somber like the old man's, whom we haven't heard from since that last day of sunlight. Lindiwe has been consumed by darkness and we have been patiently waiting our turn to die, like the weeds that struggle to stay alive along the edge of town.

In school, before the appearance of the old man, Mr. Wesda taught us of the founding of Lindiwe. The great explorers, Mélago Correzo and Bastian Bolle, were traveling from the Highlands to the East Country, carrying a small cargo of the Highlanders' wine to introduce to the people of the East. Unexpectedly, the explorers ran out of water in their canteens. They soon came across a lustrous river flowing through what appeared to be open, clear land in a beautiful terrain. Finding no traces of human occupancy, Correzo and Bolle spread word that fresh, vacant land laid in the valley between the Highlands and the East, and families quickly arrived to build homes and establish farms. Correzo and Bolle named the river Cana and the town Lindiwe, before Correzo departed to continue with his adventures. Bastian Bolle remained in the newly established town, and was celebrated with gifts every year until his death.

We people of Lindiwe love this great land, but we must soon leave. We have waited in the darkness long enough and the time has come for us to go our separate ways, following the course of the wind, never looking back, and hoping to never retrace the same path. When we happen upon our own footprints, we will know that our long journey is over, but until that day, Lindiwe will forever remain alive in the will of the living.

Wilt

Gina Ranalli

I LICK THE SWEAT pooled in the sunken canyons beneath his eyes, my sandy tongue barely able to slip out from between my crusty brown and yellow lips. My mouth, my *body*, has become as much of a wasteland as the Earth itself, burned beyond recognition and gasping its last scorched breaths.

But I am alive, as is Mark, though barely.

He doesn't move much anymore, and he's stopped breathing twice so far. We don't have much time left and the time we do have is mostly spent sleeping on plastic garbage bags, my feeble attempt to catch any moisture seeping from our bodies. Twice a day, I gently roll him over and gather the bags up, being as careful as I can to not spill what has become no more than a table spoon of moisture. I take the bags outside and tip them just so, allowing our fluids to drip into the desiccated soil of our garden. If it weren't for those remaining flowers, the California poppies, the owl's clover, and the goldfields, I probably would have no reason to rise at all. Like Mark, I'd just lie on the living room floor, struggling for air, and waiting to die.

It's amazing the wildflowers are alive at all, really. But same as Mark and I, they survived the drought longer than most only because of the well that sits along the back edge of our property. We were able to draw water from that well straight up until a week ago when it finally ran dry. Even the muddy rancid water that had sat moldering at the bottom had been exhausted, replaced by clots of slightly damp sludge ripe with fat black beetles and little unidentifiable albino worms, probably residents of a long dead and rotting tree root.

The death of the well had came as an almost welcome relief. When the neighbors had been healthy enough to venture over onto our property line, they had usually come armed with steak knifes, shovels, sometimes even rifles. Of course, that had been after we'd all discovered that this heatwave wasn't going to end. Not ever. The planet had reached its breaking point and was now being slowly baked to death.

Mark and I had fought the people off easily; we weren't nearly as crazed and dehydrated as they were. There had been weeping and begging, guilt trips thrown like sharp spears, screamed threats and eventually—regretfully—the spilling of blood and soft pathetic murders.

Some of those people had been our friends. But we hadn't let that stop us. We were a team, he and I. We'd been one before all this insanity had begun and we would remain so until our last heartbeats.

And that is why we drink from each other. Not only is it survival, but it is yet another way that we become one, two halves of a single whole.

The pale blue pills the army had given out—I guess it was three weeks ago now—with the vague explanation that they were "salt reducers," had sat in our medicine cabinet untouched until the well dried up. The pills were supposedly designed to prolong our lives by breaking down the salt that naturally collects in the human body—salt that causes the process of dehydration to accelerate.

Most people gobbled down their pills just as they were told, but Mark and I had our well and that was doing us just fine. And when the well was nearly dry, we finally remembered the pills, but instead of just swallowing them, hoping that the government was right about this one thing, we decided to try an experiment.

It was a simple experiment: after taking a pill apiece, we waited half an hour and then tasted each other. Our sweat tasted clean and sweet; not even the slightest trace of brininess lingered on our parched tongues.

We'd grinned at each other, our eyes locked, and our already naked bodies came together to celebrate the fact that we weren't done fighting yet.

Not by a long shot.

For the first few days, we were drunk on each other's perspiration. We drank and drank, lapping each other in the places where the sweat puddles were deepest as we lie together: the hollows above our collarbones, the tiny bowls of our belly buttons, the concave curves at the small of our backs, and especially just beneath there, at the top of the ass crack, where the cherished juice is so thick you could almost use a straw to slurp it up.

We became so giddy with it that we often took to sporting underwear for the sole purpose of taking it off later and wringing it into each other's mouths as a special treat.

Our love knew no bounds.

The days became quenched and lazy. The silence was tremendous. Gone were the sounds of traffic and children screaming and even birdsong. The frogs and crickets no longer chirped at night. Like Adam and Eve, we were alone in the world and that was fine with us. Mark started talking about how maybe the drought had happened for this very reason. Maybe we had been chosen to remake the planet, to give birth to a kinder, gentler species of human, one which would appreciate the Earth and not set out to destroy it.

And that was how the idea of the garden was born.

Knowing we would never be able to provide enough moisture to grow fruit trees, I set out for the gardening store a few blocks from our house, with the intent of scrounging for wildflower seeds. The store, like everywhere else, was empty and vandalized, but obviously had not been the first choice for looting. While the rack which had held vegetable seeds was stripped of all its merchandise, the rack of flower seeds was close to bursting, as if it had just been restocked that very morning.

I carefully chose only my favorites, mindful of the fact that whatever water came to the garden would be less water for ourselves. Our little backyard plot would be modest, but as beautiful as we could make it.

Never religious before, we took to praying; praying that God would be pleased with our efforts and provide us with just enough fluid to keep our garden and each other alive.

And for a time we thought He'd answered our prayers.

The flowers bloomed, blasting forth with a blaze of colors no longer found in nature. Brilliant orange, dazzling deep purple, and a yellow brighter than any tulip, dandelion or daffodil had ever hoped to be.

I spent hours sitting by those fragile blossoms, tending and guarding, tending and guarding, directing any drops of sweat that had beaded on my body to drip into their soil. I built a lean-to to shade them from the blistering sun during the hottest part of the day. The only thing I loved more than those flowers was Mark, who now was showing the wear of prolonged dehydration. We concluded that it must be our attempts to conceive a child that was causing him to dry out faster than me. We doubled his dosage of the government pills, to no avail.

My sweat alone was no longer enough for him and, desperate, I was only able to come up with one final, feeble solution: I let him drink my tears.

The tears have been hard to muster. I've never been the crying type. Even when the end of the earth was upon us, it was I who held a weeping and terrified Mark to my breast, cooing and consoling, murmuring empty phrases that somehow eased his fear and calmed his soul. It has always been me who people turned to in times of crisis, staring at me with wide, frightened eyes, knowing that I would be the one to reassure them, to speak reasonably and soothe their fraying nerves.

Knowing that I would always hold it together and never, *never* break down. Crying is something I just didn't do—but then, the life of my beloved partner had never before depended on the shedding of my tears.

The first thing I thought of to help me along in this new endeavor was pain. I know from experience that a good solid whack to the nose is sure to get the waterworks flowing. The pain is so excruciating that tears spring forth like a fountain and will not stop until most of the agony has subsided. The only problem was getting Mark to punch me in the face.

He was extremely reluctant at first, but eventually, after much cajoling, he finally agreed and swung unexpectedly. Later, he said he thought that taking me by surprise would be easier for him than watching my face and seeing in my eyes that I knew he was going to hit me.

No matter.

The blow connected, and although I thought it was rather weak, it still did the job. Not only did tears squirt from my eyes but blood spurted from my nose as well. I quickly coaxed Mark into lapping it all up, the entire mess, and when he was done, he wore the most grateful, adoring expression I'd ever seen. Despite his peeling red and emaciated face, he glowed like one of God's own angels, halos of electric blue light radiating around his head.

The second time he hit me, my nose broke and I almost hit him back. Somehow, I restrained myself and, when I'd finished screaming, allowed him to drink.

When the nose was no longer an option, we decided that pulling my hair might do the trick and we were right. Mark began wrenching it out by the fistful—huge clots that left my scalp bleeding and nearly bald as I clenched a washcloth between my teeth until I thought they'd shatter like bone beneath a sledgehammer.

Sadly, a person has only a limited amount of hair on their body and this method was quickly exhausted.

It was shortly after explaining this to Mark for the seventh or eighth time that he went insane. He began attacking me at every opportunity, lunging at me when I least expected it, biting and scratching, doing his best to draw blood instead of tears, as if he craved it more than any other fluid I had to offer him

Fighting him off was easy enough; he was very weak and easily distracted. He began talking to his dead mother, raging at her and demanding she breastfeed him immediately, without delay, right fucking *now*!

His violence and ravings lasted for little more than a day. Since then, he does nothing but lie on the garbage bags, muttering inanities in his sleep and occasionally shouting.

I've considered physically hurting him or covering his body with an old wool blanket in order to gather more nutrients for myself, but can't bring myself to do it. Instead, I've done my best to keep both him and the flowers alive, slicing my arms and legs with a blade from his razor to make myself feel pain and bring forth the only thing I have: my own life, drop by precious drop.

But now, despite all my efforts, the flowers are wilting and Mark is shriveling into dust like the corpse of a yellow-jacket on a windowsill, dead for many summers.

Before my eyes, he is mummifying.

In the garden, eyes blackened and nose swollen to the size of a small lemon, absently scratching at the scabs on my head where hair used to be, I gaze down at the collection of slices on my limbs, some of which are still oozing blood while others freely weep a fascinating yellow-green pus.

I consider the possibilities for this new gift my body is producing...

Then, without thinking, I abruptly take the razor and begin severing the flowers from their stems at the half point, and I realize that this is what I'd planned all along. The garden had nothing to do with Adam and Eve or God and His divine plans.

Those ideas had only been so much hopeful idiocy, the delirium caused by dying a slow, cruel death.

When all the flowers have been cut, I gather them up and go back inside to find Mark where I left him on the living room floor. I count the seconds between his breaths: forty-five.

Lying down beside him, propped on an elbow, I sprinkle our bodies with the near-dead flowers before relaxing against him, my head on his chest. Of course, my sweetheart wears the majority of color and I close my eyes, smiling.

I dream of rain.

Author Bios

For expanded bios and contact information for all of our authors please visit our website at www.anothersky.org

MARCELA ALBORNOZ's stories are 100% non-fiction. She is fifteen years old, and moved to America from Chile at age nine.

STEPHEN J. ANDERSON lives in Leeds, England where he writes when not busy programming computers.

HENRY BAUM is the author of several novels, including *Oscar Caliber Gun* (Soft Skull Press) and *North of Sunset*. He lives in Los Angeles, California.

DAVID BORTHWICK originally hails from Scotland. After a decade spent living in the Netherlands, he currently resides in Cambridge, England, where he works for a leading electronics company.

MARK BRITTENBURG is a published poet who lives in a small cabin in the woods on a barrier island off the coast of South Carolina.

SHERRY BRYAN had her first play produced at the age of eighteen. She has written and directed a short film and currently lives and works in Los Angeles, California as the editor for two international magazines.

DANIEL SCOTT BUCK's debut novel, *The Greatest Show on Earth*, was picked as Novel of the Year 2006 by 3:AM Magazine. His second novel, *Mechanical Thinking*, is near completion. He lives in Portland, Oregon.

LINDSAY BULL lives in Seattle and is the communications director of a local consulting firm. She writes short fiction by night.

KIRSTY CARSE lives in Cambridge, England. She has written three novels and a number of short stories.

KEVIN L. DONIHE's novels include *Shall We Gather at the Garden* and *Grape City* (both Eraserhead Press) and his stories and poems have appeared in numerous publications. He lives in Kingsport, Tennessee.

GREG GERDING currently resides in San Diego. His work has appeared in publications worldwide. He has two books of poetry out, *Poetry In Hell* (Red Dragon Press) and T*he Burning Album of Lame*.

JOHN HINES JR. lives with his family on Bainbridge Island in the Pacific Northwest. He is currently working on his second novel.

KATE HOLDEN's first book, In My Skin: A Memoir of Addiction (Arcade Publishing), was published to worldwide acclaim in 2005. She is now working on her second novel while writing for a major newspaper in Australia.

SANTI ELIJAH HOLLEY lives in Portland, Oregon.

JANIS BUTLER HOLM lives in Athens, Ohio, where she has served as Associate Editor for the film journal Wide Angle. Her essays, poems, and stories have appeared in small-press, national, and international magazines.

SCOTT WAYNE INDIANA is a writer and visual artist residing in Portland, Oregon. He has completed three novels and countless short stories.

JEREMY ROBERT JOHNSON is the author of Angel Dust Apocalypse (Eraserhead Press), the Stoker Nominated novel Siren Promised (w/Alan M. Clark), and Extinction Journals (both Swallowdown Press). His fiction has also appeared in numerous anthologies and magazines.

KRISTINA JUNG has a Master's in Philosophy and is currently working towards her Master's in the field of Library Sciences. She currently lives in Detroit, having moved there from Toronto. She enjoys brunch.

AGNI KUDRA lives in Portland, Oregon and is in school to be an auto mechanic. She's been writing since 1983, and is currently working on a book about long term meth psychosis.

BRAD LISTI is the author of the Los Angeles Times bestselling novel Attention. Deficit. Disorder. (Simon & Schuster). He currently teaches creative writing and English composition at Santa Monica College. He resides in Los Angeles, California.

PAUL LUMSDAINE has recently returned to Los Angeles to explore his passions for writing, music, and web design.

LEROY K. MAY. Writing for 17 years. Translating for 13 years. Lives in Quebec. Stop.

CARLTON MELLICK III has been published in over one hundred magazines and anthologies. He has sixteen books in print,including Satan Burger, Teeth and Tongue Landscape, and most recently The Haunted Vagina (all Eraserhead Press). He lives in Portland, Oregon.

HENRY MILTON currently lives in Bath, in the UK, with plans to move to Manchester.

TONY O'NEILL played keyboards for bands and artists as diverse as Kenickie, Marc Almond and The Brian Jonestown Massacre. After moving to Los Angeles his promising career was derailed by heroin addiction, quickie marriages and crack abuse. He is the author of the autobiographical novel *Digging the Vein* (Contemporary Press), with more on the way.

MATTHEW PENDLETON was born in 1979, is a failed student of Japanese, and lives in Liverpool, England.

STEVE QUINLAN can usually be found next to his pool drinking a beverage, preferably one with alcohol in it. He lives in San Francisco.

MADHVI RAMANI is a British Asian living in London. She has an honours degree in English Literature and a Master's in Creative Writing. She writes children's books, plays, short stories, and screenplays.

GINA RANALLI is the author of *Chemical Gardens, Suicide Girls in the Afterlife, 13 Thorns* (with Gus Fink) and *Wall of Kiss* (all Afterbirth Press). She lives in the green heart of Washington State.

CHRIS ROBERTS. des moines. iowa. house car grass. amazing wife. patient wife. lovely wife. adorable daughter. growing growing growing. joy. write paint make. dismantle assemble create. more quiet. more calm. more peace.

RENO J. ROMERO graduated with an English degree from the University of Nevada, Las Vegas. He writes poetry and short fiction from the woods of Charlotte, North Carolina.

BRADLEY SANDS lives in Northampton, MA, where he edits *Bust Down the Door and Eat All the Chickens*. He is the author of the novel *It Came from Below the Belt* (Afterbirth Press).

JOE SHIPLEY lives in Rockbridge Baths, Virginia where he writes for the zine *The Urban Spookshow*.

KENJI SIRATORI is a Japanese cyberpunk writer who is currently bombarding the Internet with wave upon wave of highly experimental prose.

MALLORY SMALL resides in Oakland, but dreams of going back to the Tenderloin in triumph.

TOM THOMPSON lives, works, eats, drinks, plays, walks (and sometimes writes) in Des Moines, Iowa with the support of his wife, Katie. He lets his mind wander. Sometimes it comes back with things.

KRISTOPHER YOUNG is the author of *Click* (Another Sky Press). He resides in Portland, Oregon. He is working on his next novel.

Thank Yous

CHRIS ROBERTS initially contacted Another Sky Press to let us know he loved what we were doing and wanted to contribute his energy in any way he could. We now have him to thank for the incredible cover art of the book you're holding in your hands.

CHRISTINE BARNUM kept this project on track. Without her, we would have misplaced everything long ago.

MICHAEL FIELDS was vital in upgrading our site design, author profile pages, and ordering system. He's also just a wonderful guy in general. We love him.

CRAIG QUACKENBUSH was editing this book for months in his Queens apartment. It's a thankless job, except for the fact that we're thanking him right now.

OUR AUTHORS. An anthology is nothing without great stories, and great stories require great authors. Thank you.

We are extremely grateful for the help and support of the many other people who made this release possible. Many thanks for the wonderful legal advice of the Law Offices of Lloyd J. Jassin (copylaw.com) and the Law Offices of Celia M. Barnum, both of whom helped walk us through all the icky contract stuff.

Finally, we'd like to thank the many individuals who pre-ordered this book and in doing so helped to fund its very production. There are a lot of expenses involved in releasing a book, and as such finances are the primary thing slowing down the other great projects we have in the works. So this thank you is especially heartfelt—thank you for helping us to not just survive, but thrive:

L.B.I., Marie S. Lyle, Dianne N. Lumsdaine, Jeff Geving, Ray Thompson, Eric Hunley, Justin Hoskins, JoAnna Massey, Richard Young, Micah Perry, Kirsten Straub, Robbie V. Quinlan, Jason Cochran, Sarah Rowe, Frances Piggott, Stephanee Borger, Venoma, Roleene Roberts, Yolanda Romero, Guy Saville, Stephen and Frances Crum, Zoe Crum, Angie L. Richey, Joe Morse, Mich Barakat, Ian Campbell, Dianna Errico, and many others who wish to remain anonymous.

All the best,
Another Sky Press, April, 2007

Also from Another Sky Press

CLICK   ISBN: 0-9776051-0-8
a novel by Kristopher Young

"… the author has pulled off a rare and amazing literary feat: he has crafted a work that is highly personal and gut–wrenchingly real, yet surreal, dream–like and convincingly fantastic. The novel is both intuitive and masterful in execution, and in this regard it shares more with the spirit of modernist painting than it does with postmodern literature. Young speaks to us in a voice that is authentic and thoroughly lacking in pretension."

Jody Franklin, editor, *Mungbeing*

"A compelling genre–bending piece of fiction with a great hook. *CLICK* embodies the grit–lit of the streets, an element of science fiction and a smattering of a thriller, a picture of a man at war with the world and with himself, right until the final pages when the last click comes 'harsh and loud and true.'"
Susan Tomaselli, editor, *Dogmatika*

CLICK'S HERO IS experiencing glitches in the universe. He may have tapped into a strange ability which gives him control over the world around him. Or, there's the disturbing possibility that he's a case study in paranoid schizophrenia. After all, *they* might be after him. He's falling apart—and to make matters worse, his girlfriend may just be crazier than he is. Forced to face his fears and come to terms with his own flawed nature, he must discover what it means to truly evolve.

TRUTH WILL MEASURE ISBN: 0-9776051-3-2
the art of Jesse Reno

OVER 100 FULL-COLOR WORKS from one of today's most prolific outsider artists, Jesse Reno. Self-taught, Reno's distinctive style has emerged through sheer creative will. Reaching deep into his subconscious and the wisdom of our ancestors, Reno has created a mythology that permeates his work, both defining and defying the lasting conflict between man and nature. Inspired by indigenous, primitive, and shamanic painters, Reno is at once artist and story-teller, speaking a truth that makes viewing his work not just an experience, but a journey.

OUTSIDE THE LINES ISBN: 0-9776051-1-6
a coloring book by Jesse Reno

A 40-PAGE COLORING BOOK by Jesse Reno, who lives and works in his home studio in Portland, Oregon. His work has been featured in numerous publications, most recently *Juxtapoz* magazine and the *BLK/MRKT One Yearbook*. He is also a 2007 winner of the International Mural Festival, and will be painting a 100 square foot mural in Winnipeg, Canada throughout the month of July, 2007.

Another Sky Press
P.O. Box 14241
Portland, OR 97293

www.anothersky.org
anothersky@anothersky.org

Printed in the United States
83843LV00003B/127-159/A